制胜新托福系列

风向标
*Wind Vane*

# 制胜
# 新托福听力

Bruce Rogers（美）编著

# THE COMPLETE
## GUIDE TO THE
## TOEFL® TEST: LISTENING
## iBT Edition

# TOEFL®

外语教学与研究出版社
**FOREIGN LANGUAGE TEACHING AND RESEARCH PRESS**
北京 BEIJING

京权图字：01－2009－4022

The Complete Guide to the TOEFL Test: Listening iBT Edition
Bruce Rogers

## 图书在版编目(CIP)数据

制胜新托福听力 ＝ The Complete Guide to the TOEFL Test: Listening, iBT Edition ／（美）罗杰斯 (Rogers, B.)编著 . — 北京：外语教学与研究出版社，2009.11（2010.11 重印）
　　（制胜新托福系列）
　　ISBN 978－7－5600－9122－8

　　Ⅰ. 制…　Ⅱ. 罗…　Ⅲ. 英语—听说教学—高等教育—自学参考资料　Ⅳ. H319.9

中国版本图书馆 CIP 数据核字（2009）第 203144 号

悠游网—外语学习 一网打尽
www.2u4u.com.cn
阅读、视听、测试、交流、共享
封底刮刮卡，获积分！在线阅读、学习、交流、换礼包！

出 版 人：于春迟
责任编辑：韩晓岚
封面设计：刘　冬
出版发行：外语教学与研究出版社
社　　址：北京市西三环北路 19 号（100089）
网　　址：http://www.fltrp.com
印　　刷：中国农业出版社印刷厂
开　　本：889×1194　1/16
印　　张：18
版　　次：2009 年 11 月第 1 版　2010 年 11 月第 2 次印刷
书　　号：ISBN 978－7－5600－9122－8
定　　价：31.90 元（含 CD-ROM 光盘 1 张）
＊　　＊　　＊
购书咨询：(010)88819929　　电子邮箱：club@fltrp.com
如有印刷、装订质量问题，请与出版社联系
联系电话：(010)61207896　　电子邮箱：zhijian@fltrp.com
制售盗版必究　举报查实奖励
版权保护办公室举报电话：(010)88817519
物料号：191220001

新托福考试于2004年10月在北美发布,并于2006年秋季正式登陆中国。考试全程约3.5~4个小时,远远长于旧托福考试。在规定时间内,考生要在模拟的真实场景下依次完成读、听、说、写4个部分的测试。新托福考试除了将4个分项考试有机结合,综合考查考生的英语语言能力外,还增加了新的试题形式,包含了考查单项能力和综合能力的多种任务类型的测试,不仅对考生的听力能力提出了更高的要求,还增加了口语测试部分,这都给外语学习者带来了更大的困难。它是对考生的心理适应能力、英语语言运用能力、社会交际能力和相当程度压力下的身体承受能力等个人综合实力的巨大挑战。对熟悉旧托福考试和相应的应试技巧的中国考生来说,要顺利通过新托福考试,无疑难度加大了。

针对这种情况,外语教学与研究出版社同圣智出版集团合作,联合推出了"制胜新托福"系列,旨在帮助中国考生熟悉新托福的考试形式、应试策略和考试技巧,训练考生在真实考试情境下的应对能力,进而真正提高考生的英语语言能力。该系列图书由美国著名的英语教学和托福考试培训专家编写而成,书中所有的训练材料同时适用于自学备考和课堂教学。

## 本系列图书的主要特点:

### ● 全新的托福训练材料

◇ 详细介绍新托福考试,全面收录考试题型,提供科学系统的应试方案和解题技巧;
◇ 提供大量典型例题、专项强化训练和两套模拟试题;
◇ 口语分册对口语测试的逐步讲解和技巧分析可帮助考生顺利通过个人陈述和双向交流部分的测试;
◇ 所有练习均为模拟训练模式,让考生身临其境,提前备战。

### ● 全面、翔实的备考指导

◇ 精心设置的词汇训练不仅有助于考生记忆词汇,更有助于其改善发音;
◇ 讲授考试中的重要技能——笔记的记录方法和技巧——并提供笔记范本,能有效提高考生在听力、口语和写作测试中的应试能力;
◇ 针对考试中的语法重点和难点提供详细指导,帮助考生强化语法知识。

### ● 全方位的多媒体辅助材料

◇ 互动CD-ROM提供两套模拟试题,考生可以根据自身情况进行定时和非定时测验;
◇ 试题训练和实境测试紧密结合,图书与MP3内容形成互动。书中的口语和听力试题在光盘中均有相应内容,提供的练习时间与考试完全一致,考生能及时了解自身水平。

希望本系列图书的出版能够助中国新一代的托福考生一臂之力,顺利迈出留学生涯的第一步。

外语教学与研究出版社

# CONTENTS

# PREFACE

## TO THE STUDENT

If you are preparing for the TOEFL® (Test of English as a Foreign Language) iBT, you are not alone. About a million people all over the world take the test every year. A high score on this test is an essential step in being admitted to undergraduate or graduate programs in the United States and Canada. But preparing for this test can be a difficult, frustrating experience. Perhaps you haven't taken many standardized tests such as the TOEFL test. Perhaps you're not familiar with the format, or you're not sure how to focus your studies. Maybe you've taken the test before but were not satisfied with your scores.

And now the TOEFL iBT (iBT = Internet-Based Test) is a much more communicative test. What new skills are required? What tactics are needed for top scores? How can you best practice for this version of the test?

You need a guide. That's why this book was written—to guide people preparing for this important test so that they can earn the highest scores possible.

*The Complete Guide to the TOEFL® Test: LISTENING, iBT Edition* is the most complete, accurate, and up-to-date preparation book available. It is based on years of experience teaching preparation classes in the United States and abroad. It is simply written and clearly organized and is suitable for any intermediate to advanced English language student.

This book offers a step-by-step program designed to make you feel confident and well prepared when you sit down in front of the computer on the day of the test. It teaches you the test-taking techniques and helps you polish the language skills you need to do well on the test. And *The Guide* is an efficient way to prepare for the TOEFL iBT. By concentrating only on the points that are actually tested on the TOEFL test, it lets you make the most of your preparation time and never wastes your time.

## ABOUT THIS EDITION: WHAT'S NEW?

This edition of *The Complete Guide to the TOEFL® Test: LISTENING, iBT Edition*, like the TOEFL iBT itself, has been completely updated. It reflects the changes made in the format, the items, and the basic philosophy of the revised exam.

In the Listening Section of the test, the lectures and conversations have gotten longer and more involved. However, note taking is now permitted. There are also some new question types in Listening. The Guide to Listening offers tips and help with note taking as well as experience with answering all types of questions about the lectures.

Another new feature of the iBT test is the "authentic language" used by the speakers. On past forms of the test, the speakers sounded like actors reading from a book. On the TOEFL iBT, the speakers sound more natural, like real professors giving classroom lectures or real students discussing campus situations. The new Audio Program for this Guide reflects these changes, and the lectures and conversations have the same feel as those used on the actual test.

Another new feature of this textbook is the section containing Communicative Activities, which provides ideas for interactive activities that will further develop students' listening skills.

# ORGANIZATION OF THIS BOOK

**Getting Started**   Two sections introduce you to the book and the test:

▶ **Question and Answers about the TOEFL® iBT** This section provides you with basic information about the design of the Internet-based test and helps you understand the revised scoring system.

▶ **Ten Keys to Better Scores on the TOEFL® iBT** This section presents the "secrets" of being a good test-taker: arranging your preparation time, using the process of elimination to make the best guess on multiple-choice items, coping with test anxiety, pacing yourself during the test, and other important techniques.

The Guide to Listening consists of the following:

▶ **An introduction** which provides basic strategies for the Listening test.

▶ **A preview test** to give you a feel for each part of the test and to provide a basis for understanding the lessons.

▶ **Lessons** that break down the knowledge and skills that you need into comprehensible "bites" of information. Each of the six lessons in The Guide to Listening concentrates on one of the main types of questions asked about the conversations and lectures. There is extensive practice for listening, taking notes, and answering questions. Each lesson contains sample items from the preview tests that illustrate exactly how the point brought up in that lesson is tested on the TOEFL iBT.

▶ **A review test** that goes over the points discussed in the lessons. This test puts together the points practiced in isolation in the lessons.

▶ **A tutorial** covering important testing points that require more time to master than points brought up in the lessons. The tutorial for this section is about note taking.

▶ **Communicative activities** that are designed to encourage classroom communication.

**Two Practice Listening Tests**   Taking practice tests is one of the best ways to get ready for the TOEFL® test. You can take these tests in the book or on the accompanying CD-ROM.

**Answer Key and Audioscript**   Answers and explanations for questions and a script for the Audio Program are provided. This resource is also available online at elt.thomson.com/toefl.

# TO THE TEACHER

The TOEFL iBT puts a lot of emphasis on communicative skills, and as much as you can, you should put the same emphasis on interaction in the classroom. In the past, a lot of TOEFL test preparation involved coaching students for the Structure Section of the test, but the TOEFL iBT does not directly test grammar. No matter which of the four parts of the test you are preparing for, be sure to have students work in pairs or small groups and encourage lively give-and-take discussion.

Students who feel perfectly comfortable taking long multiple-choice tests may feel more challenged by some of the communicative tasks they are given on this test. It is recommended that in every class you do some practice for the Speaking Tasks. You might, for example, begin with two or three students giving one-minute timed, impromptu talks. These can be "integrated" tasks based on summaries of newspaper articles or news stories from television or radio, or they can be "independent" tasks based on students' own experience. Make sure everyone gets a chance to talk, and get the rest of the class involved in asking the speaker questions about the presentations.

At least once a week it is useful to work on one or more of the Communicative Activities. These are designed to get students involved in talking and working together by playing games, having discussions, or working on projects.

A good way to begin the course is by taking one of the two practice listening tests. This familiarizes students with the test and shows them what to expect when they take the actual exam.

You can work through the lessons starting at the first lesson, or you can begin with the section in which your students seemed to have the most problems on the first practice listening test.

It is certainly important to give your students exposure to computers. However, the computer skills required to take the test are relatively basic and the focus should be on applying language skills and using test-taking strategies, not developing computer proficiency.

Following are the amounts of time suggested to cover each section of *The Guide*. These times are approximate and will vary from class to class.

| | |
|---|---|
| Getting Started | 1 to 2 hours |
| Guide to Listening | 14 to 18 hours |
| Practice Listening Tests | 1 to 20 hours per test section |

What if you don't have time to cover everything in *The Guide?* Don't worry! *The Complete Guide to the TOEFL® Test: LISTENING, iBT Edition* was designed so that you can skip parts of the exercises and lessons and still improve your students' scores.

I welcome your thoughts, comments, questions, and suggestions. Please feel free to contact me via e-mail: Bruce_Rogers_CGT@mail.com.

# ABOUT THE AUTHOR

**Bruce Rogers** has taught test preparation and English as a Second/Foreign Language courses since 1979. He has taught in the United States, Indonesia, Vietnam, South Korea, and the Czech Republic. He is also the author of Thomson's *The Complete Guide to the TOEIC® Test* and *The Introductory Guide to the TOEIC® Test*. He lives in Boulder, Colorado, USA.

# ACKNOWLEDGMENTS

I would like to thank all of the English-language professionals who provided their comments and suggestions during the development of *The Complete Guide to the TOEFL® Test: LISTENING, iBT Edition* as well as earlier editions.

Thanks to the students of Front Range Community College and Cambridge Center for Adult Education who allowed me to use their writing and speaking samples and to the professors at the University of Colorado who allowed me to sit in on their lectures. Thanks to Kevin Keating, University of Arizona, for suggesting some of the Communication Activities.

Special thanks to Jody Stern, Charlotte Sturdy, Linda Grant, Chrystie Hopkins, Merrill Peterson, Jennifer Meldrum, and Anita Raducanu for their expert help and advice.

**Thomson ELT would like to thank the following reviewers for their contributions.**

**Joshua Atherton**
University of Texas
Arlington, TX

**Consuelo Fernandes Barbosa Ivo**
Centro Cultural Brasil Estados Unidos
Campinas, Brazil

**Valéria Benévolo França**
Cultura Inglesa Rio Brasilia
Botafogo, Brazil

**Dorina Garza Leonard**
Instituto Tecnológico de Monterrey
Monterrey, Mexico

**Claudia Hernandez**
Colegio Patria de Juarez
Mexico City, Mexico

**Eduardo Ipac**
Centro Cultural Brasil Estados Unidos
Campinas, Brazil

**Ruo-chiang Jao**
Merica Language Institute
Yonghe City, Taiwan, China

**Rangho Jung**
EG Language School
Seoul, South Korea

**Maria Aurora Patiño Leal**
Instituto Tecnológico de Monterrey
Monterrey, Mexico

**Dr. Carolyn Prager**
Spanish American Institute
New York, NY

**Dr. Karen Russikoff**
California State Polytechnic University
Pomona, CA

**Joan Sears**
Texas Tech University
Lubbock, TX

**Barbara Smith-Palinkas**
University of South Florida
Tampa, FL

**Kwang-Ja Son**
Moonjin Media
Seoul, South Korea

**Robert Richmond Stroupe**
Soka University
Tokyo, Japan

**Graciela Tamez**
Instituto Tecnológico de Monterrey
Monterrey, Mexico

**Grant Trew**
Nova Group
Osaka, Japan

**Gabriela Ulloa**
Instituto Tecnológico de Monterrey
Monterrey, Mexico

**Hilda Zacour**
Instituto Tecnológico de Monterrey
Monterrey, Mexico

# GETTING STARTED

# QUESTIONS AND ANSWERS ABOUT THE TOEFL® iBT

**Q: What is the TOEFL Test?**
**A:** TOEFL stands for *Test of English as a Foreign Language.* It is a test designed to measure the English-language ability of people who do not speak English as their first language and who plan to study at colleges and universities in North America.

Educational Testing Service (ETS) of Princeton, New Jersey, prepares and administers the TOEFL test. This organization produces many other standardized tests, such as the Test of English for International Communication (TOEIC), the Graduate Management Admissions Test (GMAT), and the Graduate Record Exam (GRE).

Although there are other standardized tests of English, the TOEFL test is by far the most important in North America; ETS has offered this exam since 1965. Each year, almost a million people take the TOEFL test at testing centers all over the world. About 5,000 colleges, universities, and other institutions in the United States and Canada either require students from non-English-speaking countries to supply TOEFL test scores as part of their application process or accept TOEFL test scores as evidence of a person's proficiency in English.

**Q: And what is the TOEFL iBT?**
**A:** For more than thirty years, the TOEFL test was given as a paper-and-pencil, multiple-choice test. In 1998, a computer-based version of the test became available in many parts of the world. The newest generation of the test, the TOEFL iBT (Internet-based test), was introduced during the 2005–2006 academic year.

As the name implies, the test is delivered over the Internet. Test-takers work on the tests at individual computer stations at official testing centers. The test is offered only on scheduled testing dates.

The TOEFL iBT is significantly different from the computer-based version of the test.

**Q: Different? How is the TOEFL iBT different?**
**A:** For one thing, the basic way in which the TOEFL iBT tests English is different. The new test emphasizes a test-taker's ability to *communicate* in an academic setting. For that reason, a Speaking Section has been added and the Writing Section has been expanded.

Specifically, the TOEFL iBT differs from the previous version in the following ways:

▶ There is a new Speaking Section that tests your ability to communicate orally. You record responses that are scored by raters at ETS.

▶ You are allowed to take notes during all parts of the test.

▶ There are "integrated" tasks that require you to combine your speaking and writing skills with your reading and listening skills.

▶ Grammar skills are tested indirectly, especially in the Speaking and Writing Sections. There is no separate grammar section.

▶ There are some new types of questions in Reading and Listening.

▶ The lectures and conversations that you hear on the audio portions of the test are "authentic English." In other words, the language that you hear is more natural, more like the language used in the "real world." It contains the pauses, repetitions, self-corrections, and "umms" and "uhs" that you would expect to hear in a real lecture or conversation.

▶ The test is *not* "computer adaptive" (unlike the previous computer-based version). In other words, if you answer a question correctly, the next item is not more difficult, and if you answer a question incorrectly, the next question is not easier. All test-takers see the same question during each administration of the test.

▶ There is a new scoring system.

**Q: Why did the test change?**

**A:** One reason is that, over the last thirty years, most language teachers have changed the way they teach. The emphasis is no longer on analyzing and learning individual grammar points or memorizing vocabulary. The emphasis is on communicating in the target language in a meaningful way. That's why the new version of the TOEFL test measures your ability to communicate orally and in writing.

Another reason for the changes is that university admissions officers wanted more information about incoming students. Can they read and understand materials in textbooks? Understand and take notes on lectures? Hold conversations with teachers, administrators, and other students? Write papers involving a number of sources? The new test indicates whether candidates have these skills.

**Q: Is the TOEFL iBT more difficult than previous versions?**

**A:** The Reading and Listening Sections and the Independent Writing Task have changed only a little, and you will probably not find them more difficult than similar sections in earlier versions of the test. However, the Integrated Writing Task and the Speaking Section may seem challenging because you do not have much experience with this kind of task. With the practice that you get in *The Complete Guide to the TOEFL, iBT Edition,* you should feel much more comfortable and confident when you actually take the test.

**Q: What format does TOEFL iBT follow? How long does it take to complete?**

**A:** The Internet-based test is divided into four sections: Reading, Listening, Speaking, and Writing, each with its own time limit. The four sections are always given in the same order. The first two sections, Reading and Listening, are mostly multiple-choice questions, while the Speaking Section requires you to give short oral presentations and the Writing Section requires you to write short essays.

The entire test takes from three and a half to four hours.

## TOEFL® iBT Format

**1. Reading**
   3 readings (about 600 to 700 words per reading)
   39 questions (12 to 14 per reading; mainly multiple-choice)
   **60 minutes**

---

**2. Listening**
   2 conversations
   4 lectures/discussions
   34 questions (5 per conversation, 6 per lecture; mainly multiple-choice)
   **About 50 minutes**

---

Mandatory break: **10 minutes**

---

**3. Speaking**
   2 Independent Tasks  (based on your own knowledge and experience)
   4 Integrated Tasks (based on short readings and/or lectures)
   **About 20 minutes**

---

**4. Writing**
   1 Independent Task (based on your own knowledge and experience)
   1 Integrated Task (based on a short reading and a lecture)
   **50 minutes**

---

**Total time: 3-1/2 to 4 hours**

---

The actual numbers in the chart above may vary from test to test. In the Reading Section, there may be four or five readings and from 36–70 questions. The Reading Section may vary in length from 60 to 100 minutes. In the Listening Section, there may be additional conversations or lectures and from 34–50 questions. The Listening Section may last from about 50 minutes to about 90 minutes.

**Q: How does the scoring system for the TOEFL iBT work?**
**A:** You will receive a Section Score for each of the four skill areas and a Total Score.

| | |
|---|---|
| Reading | 0 to 30 |
| Listening | 0 to 30 |
| Speaking | 0 to 30 |
| Writing | 0 to 30 |
| Total Score | 0 to 120 |

In addition to the numerical score, ETS will send a score "descriptor," a short written description of what English-language skills a typical person at your score level has or does not have.

In the following chart, you can compare total scores on the TOEFL iBT with scores that are approximately equivalent to scores on the computer-based test (TOEFL CBT) and the paper-based test (TOEFL PBT).

| Total Score | | |
|---|---|---|
| TOEFL® iBT | TOEFL® CBT | TOEFL® PBT |
| 120 | 300 | 677 |
| 115 | 280 | 650 |
| 110 | 270 | 637 |
| 105 | 260 | 620 |
| 100 | 250 | 600 |
| 95 | 240 | 587 |
| 90 | 230 | 570 |
| 85 | 223 | 563 |
| 80 | 213 | 550 |
| 75 | 203 | 537 |
| 70 | 193 | 523 |
| 65 | 183 | 513 |
| 60 | 170 | 497 |
| 55 | 157 | 480 |
| 50 | 143 | 463 |
| 45 | 133 | 450 |
| 40 | 120 | 433 |
| 35 | 107 | 417 |
| 30 | 93 | 397 |
| 25 | 80 | 377 |
| 20 | 63 | 350 |
| 15 | 50 | 327 |
| 10 | 37 | 317 |
| 5 | 20 | 310 |
| 0 | 0 | 310 |

**Q: What is a passing score on the TOEFL test?**
**A:** There isn't any. Each university—and in some cases, each school or department—has its own standards for admission, so you should check the requirements for the universities that you are interested in. (These are generally available online.) Most undergraduate programs require scores between 65 and 80, and most graduate programs ask for scores between 70 and 100. In recent years, there has been a tendency for universities to raise their minimum TOEFL test requirements. Of course, the higher your score, the better your chances of admission.

**Q: How and when will I receive my test scores?**
**A:** You can obtain your scores online about fifteen business days after you take the test. You will also receive a written notification of your scores by mail shortly after that. The admissions offices of universities that you designate can also receive your scores online or by mail.

**Q: How do I register for the TOEFL iBT?**
**A:** You can register online at http://www.toefl.org. You may also register by phone or by mail.

**Q: What computer skills do I need to take the TOEFL iBT?**
**A:** The computer skills required are very basic ones. You really only need to know how to point to items on the screen and click on your choice with a mouse, as well as how to scroll up and down through a document. For writing, you also need basic word-processing skills.

**Q: What do I do if I need help?**
**A:** There is a Help button on the task bar for each section, but this button will only give you the directions for that part of the test. It will not give you any hints to help you answer questions or solve any technical problems. Clicking on Help is basically a waste of your time.

If you have a problem with your computer or need some other kind of help, raise your hand and a test administrator will come to you.

**Q: Where is the TOEFL iBT given?**
**A:** It is administered at a network of testing centers that include universities, bi-national institutes, and ETS field offices all over the world. When you register for the test, you will be assigned the closest test center. Most test centers will offer the TOEFL iBT thirty to forty times a year, depending on the size of the center.

On a given day, ETS will give a different version of each TOEFL test in each of the twenty-four time zones of the world. This prevents a person who takes the test in one time zone from giving information about the test to people in other time zones.

**Q: Can I choose whether to take the TOEFL iBT or earlier versions of the test?**
**A:** No. Once the Internet-based test has been phased in, you will no longer have the option of taking the computer-based or the paper-based test.

**Q: How much will the Internet-based test cost?**
**A:** The TOEFL iBT will initially cost US$140.00.

**Q: What should I bring with me to the exam site?**
**A:** You should bring your passport or other ID with you. You will have to check all other personal materials before you enter the testing room.

Don't bring any reference books, such as dictionaries or textbooks, or any electronic devices, such as translators, cellular phones, or calculators. You are not permitted to smoke, eat, or drink in the test center. You do not have to bring pencils or paper. (You will get a pen and a booklet of blank paper for note taking.)

**Q: How can I get more information about the TOEFL test?**
**A:** You can contact ETS via e-mail or get updated information about the test from the ETS TOEFL iBT home page: http://www.toefl.org.

# TEN KEYS TO BETTER SCORES ON THE TOEFL® iBT

## ⊙— #1: INCREASE YOUR GENERAL KNOWLEDGE OF ENGLISH.

There are two types of knowledge that will lead to better scores on the TOEFL iBT:

▶ A knowledge of the tactics and techniques used by smart test-takers
▶ A general command of English

Following a step-by-step preparation program for the TOEFL iBT such as the one in *The Guide* will familiarize you with the test itself and with the tactics you need to raise your scores. The practice tests that are part of this program will help you polish your test-taking techniques.

But no matter how many test-taking tips you learn, you won't do well without a solid foundation of English-language study. The best way to increase your general knowledge of English is to use English as much as possible.

If you have the opportunity, taking English-language classes is an invaluable way to prepare for the test. In the past, students would sometimes say, "I can't go to English class today; I have to prepare for the TOEFL test!" This is no longer a good excuse. The TOEFL iBT tests a greater range of English-language skills, and any English class you take will help you prepare for the test. General English classes are now a form of TOEFL test preparation, and TOEFL test preparation classes will now teach more general English.

Conversation classes and presentation-skills classes will help you prepare for the Speaking Section of the test. Of course, reading classes can help you prepare for the Reading Section, listening classes for the Listening Section, and writing (composition) classes for the Writing Section. Although there is no special grammar section on the TOEFL iBT, structure (grammar) classes will be useful for both Writing and Speaking. Academic skills classes can help you with note taking, reading and writing tips, and test-taking skills.

Non-language classes taught in English (business or biology, for example) are also a useful way to improve all of your skills. The TOEFL iBT was designed, after all, to measure your ability to do well in this type of class.

You can also improve your English outside of the classroom. Reading English-language books, magazines, and newspapers can improve your reading skills and build your vocabulary. So can visits to English-language Web sites. Going to lectures and movies, watching TV, and listening to news on the radio are ways to improve your listening skills. If you are living in an English-speaking country, take advantage of this fact and talk to the people around you as much and as often as you can. If possible, join a "conversation partners" program. If you are living in a non-English-speaking country, try to find people—native or non-native speakers—that you can have conversations with.

One important job is to systematically build your vocabulary. An improved vocabulary will help you on every section of the test. You should keep a personal vocabulary list in a notebook, on index cards, or on a computer. When you come across an unfamiliar word, look it up and record the word and its definition.

## ○— #2: LEARN AS MUCH ABOUT THE TEST AS POSSIBLE.

It's important to have up-to-date information about the test. ETS has said there may be minor changes in the format of the Internet-based test in the future.

You can get a lot of information about the test from the *TOEFL® Information Bulletin* for the current testing year. You can download it from the TOEFL Web site (www.ets.org/toefl). Paper versions of the bulletin are available at many language schools or international student offices.

There is a lot of other information and practice available on the TOEFL® Web site. You can join the "TOEFL® Practice Online Community" (for free) to get the latest information about the test and to take an official practice test and get daily study tips. There is also a discussion board on which you can read messages from other people who are preparing for the test and you can post your own questions and tips.

## ○— #3: MAKE THE MOST OF YOUR PREPARATION TIME.

You need to train for the TOEFL test just as you would train for any important competitive event. Naturally, the sooner you begin training, the better, but no matter when you begin, you need to get the most out of your preparation time.

One good way to organize your preparation time is to make a time management chart. Draw up an hour-by-hour schedule of your activities. Block out those times when you are busy with classes, work, or other responsibilities. Then pencil in times for TOEFL test preparation. You'll remember more if you schedule a few hours every day or several times weekly than if you schedule all your study time for long blocks on weekends.

One good method of studying for the TOEFL test (or almost anything!) is the "30-5-5" Method:

▶ Study for thirty minutes.
▶ Take a five-minute break.
▶ When you return, spend five minutes reviewing what you studied before and previewing what you will study next.

## ○— #4: BE IN GOOD PHYSICAL CONDITION WHEN YOU TAKE THE TEST.

Of course, you should eat healthful foods and get some exercise during the time you are preparing for the test. The most important concern, however, is that you not become exhausted during your preparation time. If you aren't getting enough sleep, you need to reduce your study time or cut back on some other activity. This is especially important during the last few days before the exam.

### O— #5: GET SOME COMPUTER PRACTICE.

If possible, take at least one of the practice tests on the enclosed CD-ROM. These tests closely simulate the actual test. Also, try to take the test that is available on the ETS Web site.

The computer skills that you need for the Reading and the Listening Sections are very basic: scrolling, pointing, and clicking.

The most difficult skill is the ability to word-process (type) your two essays for the Writing Section. If you are not accustomed to working on an English-language keyboard, you should get as much typing practice as possible to improve your speed and accuracy.

You also will have to record your responses for the six Speaking Tasks by talking into a microphone. Talking into a computer microphone may be a new experience for you. Get as much practice doing this as possible.

### O— #6: BECOME FAMILIAR WITH THE FORMAT AND DIRECTIONS.

You should have a clear "map" of the TOEFL iBT in your mind and know what is coming next. You can familiarize yourself with the basic design of the test by looking over the chart in the Questions and Answers section (p. xiv) and by taking practice tests.

The directions for each part of the test will always be the same, and so will the examples. If you are familiar with the directions from using this book, you can immediately click on the Dismiss Directions button and save yourself a little time during the test.

### O— #7: ORGANIZE THE LAST FEW DAYS BEFORE THE EXAM CAREFULLY.

Don't try to "cram" (study intensively) during the last few days before you take the test. Last-minute studying probably won't help your score and will leave you tired. You need to be alert for the test. The night before the test, don't study at all. Find your passport and other documents you will need. Then go to a movie, take a long walk, or do something else to take your mind off the test. Go to sleep when you usually do.

On the day of the test, wear comfortable clothing because you will be sitting in the same position for a long time. If you are testing in the morning, have breakfast before the test. If other people from your class or study group are taking the test on the same day, you can have breakfast together and give one another some last-minute encouragement. Give yourself plenty of time to get to the testing center. If you have to rush, that will only add to your stress.

## ⟶ #8: USE TIME WISELY DURING THE TEST.

In the Reading and Listening Sections, there is no time limit on individual items. However, there are time limits for the sections (60 to 100 minutes for Reading and about 50 to 90 minutes for Listening). These time limits are fairly generous, but you still need to be careful to give yourself a chance to answer all the questions. You need to find a balance between speed and accuracy. Work steadily. Never let yourself get stuck on an item. If you are unable to decide on an answer, guess and go on.

In the Speaking and Writing Sections, there are time limits for each of the tasks. You need to practice these tasks so that you can complete your responses in the amount of time you are given.

For all four parts of the test, the most important timing tools you have are the on-screen clocks. Glance at these now and then to see how much time you have left. However, don't become obsessed with checking the clock.

## ⟶ #9: FOR MULTIPLE-CHOICE ITEMS, USE THE PROCESS OF ELIMINATION TO MAKE YOUR BEST GUESS.

Unlike some standardized exams, the TOEFL iBT doesn't have a penalty for guessing on the multiple-choice sections (Reading and Listening). In other words, incorrect answers aren't subtracted from your scores. Even if you have no idea which answer is correct, you should guess because you have a one-in-four chance of guessing correctly. However, whenever possible, try to avoid guessing blindly. It's better to make an educated guess. To do this, use the process of elimination.

The process of elimination is a simple concept. For each multiple-choice question, there is one correct answer (or two on some Listening items). There are also a number of incorrect answers, called *distracters*. They are called distracters because their purpose is to distract your attention from the correct answer. You need to try to eliminate distracters. If you can eliminate one, your chances of guessing correctly are one in three, and if you can eliminate two, your chances improve to one in two. (And if you can eliminate three, you've got the correct answer!) Often, one or even two distracters are fairly easy to eliminate.

What if you eliminate one or two choices but can't decide which of the remaining choices is correct? If you have a hunch (a feeling) that one choice is better than the others, choose it. If not, pick any remaining choice and go on.

Remember, in the Reading and Listening sections, you should *never* leave any items unanswered. *Always* guess. (The Reading Section has a Review Feature that lets you check very quickly what items you left unanswered. You should use this feature just before the end of the Reading Section.)

## ○━ #10: LEARN TO FIGHT TEST ANXIETY.

The TOEFL iBT and similar tests (such as SAT, ACT, GRE, and GMAT) are often called "high-stakes tests." This means that a lot depends on these tests. They can have a major influence on your plans for your education and career. A little nervousness is normal. If you were going to participate in a big athletic contest or give an important business presentation, you would feel the same way.

There is an idiom in English that describes this nervous feeling quite well: "butterflies in the stomach." These "butterflies" will mostly fly away once the test starts. And a little nervousness can actually help by making you more alert and focused. However, too much nervousness can slow you down and cause you to make mistakes.

If you begin to feel extremely anxious during the test, try taking a very short break—a "ten-second vacation." Close your eyes or look away from the monitor, take your hand off the mouse, and lean back in your chair. Take a few deep breaths, shake out your hands, roll your head on your neck, and relax. Then get right back to work. (Don't use this technique while you are listening to a lecture or giving a speaking response.)

A positive, confident attitude toward the exam can help you overcome anxiety. Think of the TOEFL test not as a test of your knowledge or of you as a person but as an intellectual challenge, a puzzle to be solved.

# GUIDE TO LISTENING

# ABOUT LISTENING

The Listening Section – the second section of the TOEFL® iBT – tests your understanding of spoken material and your ability to answer questions about the conversations and lectures that you hear. It contains two conversations and four lectures that take place in a university setting. (Some tests may also include an extra unscored conversation or lecture. You as the test-taker will not know which will be unscored, so it is important to do well on all of the conversations or lectures.) After each conversation or lecture, there is a set of questions asking about the information that was presented.

Skills that are tested in this section include the abilities to

▶ understand the main idea or topic of the conversation or lecture
▶ understand supporting ideas and details of the conversation or lecture
▶ draw inferences
▶ identify the speaker's purpose, method, and attitude
▶ recognize the relationship between parts of a lecture (cause and effect, comparison/contrast, chronological order, and so on)
▶ understand how the speaker's intonation affects meaning
▶ analyze and categorize information in order to complete summaries and charts

When you begin the Listening Section, you will see a computer screen with a photograph of a test-taker wearing headphones. This screen will tell you to put on your headphones.

The next screen tells you how to change the volume by clicking on the volume icon on the toolbar. Subsequently, you will see the directions screen. After you click on the Dismiss Directions button on the toolbar, the Listening Section begins immediately.

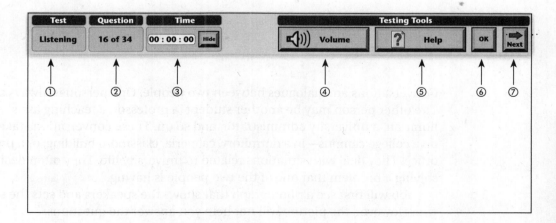

Toolbar button #1 tells you that you are taking the Listening Section. (You should already know this!) Button #2 tells you the question number that you are working on as well as the total number of questions you must answer in this section. Button #3 is a clock that keeps track of the amount of time you have to work on the Listening Section.

On the right side of the toolbar are the "Testing Tools." The volume button (#4) allows you to change the volume at any time during the test. The Help button (#5) gives you the directions for the Listening Section—however, it won't give you any real help! After you have answered a question, you need to click on the OK button (#6) to confirm your answer, and then on Next (#7) to move to the next question. You cannot go back to a previous question after you have confirmed your answer or listen to a talk a second time.

The Listening Section of the TOEFL iBT is *not* computer-adaptive. In other words, the level of difficulty will not change according to your ability to answer the previous question.

## TIMING

You have twenty minutes in which to answer the questions. This does *not* include the time you spend listening to conversations and lectures. Individual questions have no time limit. You can take as long as you want to answer a question, as long as you finish the entire section within the time limit. The entire Listening Section (including time spent listening) will probably take you about sixty minutes to complete.

**Note:** *Although the TOEFL iBT gives you an indefinite amount of time to answer individual Listening questions, the multiple-choice questions on the Audio Program (tape or CD) for* The Guide *are separated by a ten-second pause. You will have a little more time to answer matching, ordering, and complete-the-chart questions. If you prefer, you can pause the Audio Program and take a little more time to answer questions.*

## THE CONVERSATIONS

Conversations are dialogues between two people. One person is always a student. The other person may be another student, a professor, a teaching assistant, a librarian, a university administrator, and so on. These conversations take place on a college campus—in a dormitory, cafeteria, classroom building, or a professor's office. They deal with situations related to university life. They often deal with solving a problem that one of the two people is having.

You will first see a photograph that shows the speakers and sets the scene for you. However, the picture will not help you answer the questions.

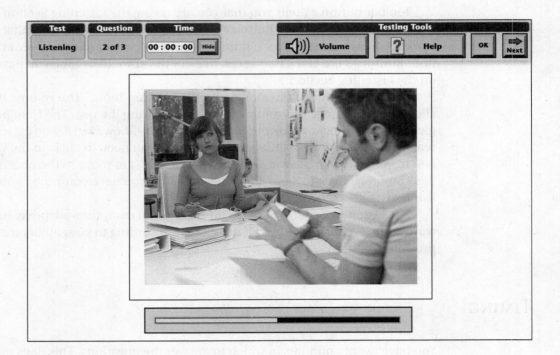

At the same time that the picture appears, you will hear the narrator say, "Listen to a conversation between _____ and _____." The photograph will remain on the screen while you listen to the conversation. Conversations last two to three minutes, and there are from twelve to twenty-five exchanges between the two speakers. Conversations are followed by a set of five questions. You will *not* see the questions until the conversation is over.

Below the photograph on your computer screen you will see a time bar that tells you approximately how much longer the conversation will last. A line in the time bar moves from left to right as the conversation progresses. The time bar on the screen shown on the previous page, for example, indicates that the conversation is about halfway over.

## THE LECTURES

Lectures take place in a classroom and are usually given by a professor. Lectures may be monologues (one speaker) or academic discussions involving the professor and one or more students. They involve a wide variety of academic subjects: anthropology, biology, history, literature, chemistry, psychology, and so on. Lectures last five to six minutes and are about 500 to 800 words long.

You will first see a screen that identifies the type of class in which the lecture is given.

**BIOLOGY**

You will then see a photograph of a professor lecturing or having a discussion with a class. The narrator will say, "Listen to a lecture in a biology class" or "Listen to a discussion in a psychology class." Again there is a time bar below the photo that tells you approximately how much longer the lecture will last.

In many of the lectures you will see a "blackboard screen" that presents specialized vocabulary from the lecture—the kinds of terms a professor might write on a board during a class. Test questions are not about the information on the blackboards, so try not to get too distracted by the words.

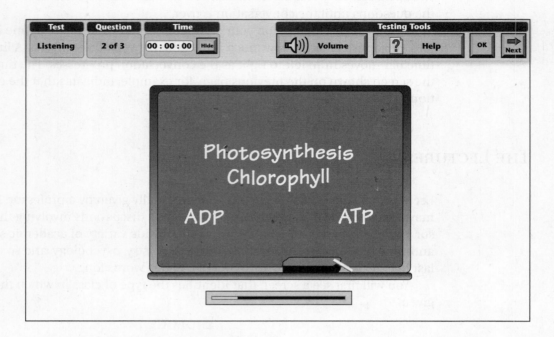

Sometimes you will also see a photograph, drawing, map, or chart related to the lecture.

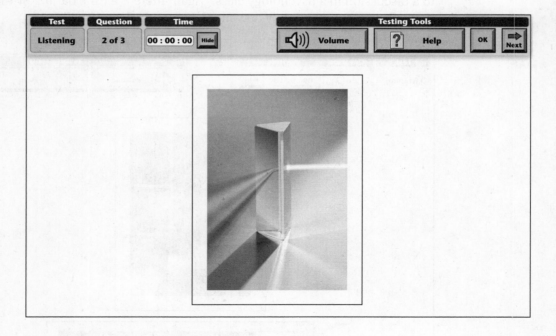

## AUTHENTIC LANGUAGE

In the Listening Section of the TOEFL iBT, conversations and lectures do not sound as if they are being read aloud by actors. The speakers sound "authentic"—like people actually having conversations or giving lectures. This authentic language may include the following features:

▶ Polite interruptions

**Professor**

Okay, let's move on to the topic of . . .

**Student**

Excuse me, Professor Wade, but could we go over that last point one more time?

▶ Mistakes and corrections

**Professor**

Unlike most drums, tympani produce a definite pitch when struck. It was in the sixteenth century that they became a common feature of the classical orchestra. Wait. No, it was in the . . . uh, 1600's, in the seventeenth century, I should have said.

▶ Hesitations and repetitions

**Student**

Professor Jackson, excuse me, let me get this straight. You said that in the Canadian parliament, that the . . . umm, Senate was the upper house but . . . uh, that the House of Commons . . . uhhh *(pause)* that the House of Commons, the lower house, actually has more power?

**Professor**

That's right. In practice, the House of Commons is the dominant branch of Parliament.

▶ Digressions

**Professor**

There are plenty of good reasons why New York City became the financial center of the country. Of course, it's not just finance. New York is a cultural center, an artistic center. I mean, if you want to see a good play, if you want to go to a good museum, then you go to New York, right?

But anyway, one reason it became a financial center is that . . .

▶ Reduced speech

**Student A**

So are you *gonna* sign up for Professor Kimble's sociology class?

**Student B**

I guess. I've *gotta* take at least one more social science class.

(*Gonna* is the reduced form of "going to." *Gotta* is the reduced form of "got to.")

▶ Sentence fragments
**Professor**
William Blake. A great poet. At least in my opinion.

Most of the speakers will have standard American accents. However, some speakers may have a regional U.S. accent (southern U.S. or New England, for example) or an accent from another English-speaking country (the U.K., Canada, Australia, India, or New Zealand, for example).

## THE QUESTIONS

The chart below shows you the kinds of questions that are typically asked about the conversations and the lectures. The chart also shows you in which lesson in *The Guide* you will find more information and practice for this type of question.

| Standard Multiple-Choice Listening Questions | | | | |
|---|---|---|---|---|
| *Type of question* | *Explanation* | *Example* | *Probable number per test* | *Lesson* |
| Main-Topic Questions | These ask you what subject the conversation or lecture is generally about. | What is the main topic of this conversation?<br><br>What is the primary topic of this lecture? | 1 or 2 | 9 |
| Main-Purpose Questions | These ask you why, in general, the speakers are having the conversation or why the lecture is being given. | Why is the man/woman talking to the professor?<br><br>What is the main point of this lecture? | 1 or 2 | 9 |
| Factual Questions | These ask you about supporting ideas or details mentioned in the conversation or lecture. | What does the speaker say about _____?<br><br>According to the professor, where does _____?<br><br>According to the lecture, why does _____? | 12 to 18 | 10 |

| Type of question | Explanation | Example | Probable number per test | Lesson |
|---|---|---|---|---|
| Negative Factual Questions | These ask which of the answer choices is *not* true, according to information given in the conversation or lecture, or what information is *not* mentioned in the passage. | According to the lecture, which of the following is NOT true?  Which of the following is NOT mentioned in the lecture? | 2 to 4 | 10 |
| Inference Questions | These ask you to draw conclusions based on information given in the conversations or lectures. | What does the man/ woman imply about _____?  What can be inferred about _____ from the lecture? | 3 to 5 | 10 |
| Purpose Questions | These ask you why a speaker mentions some point in the conversation or lecture. | Why does the professor mention _____? | 2 to 4 | 11 |
| Method Questions | These ask you to explain how the speaker explains or accomplishes something in the passage. | How does the speaker explain the concept of _____?  How does the professor introduce the idea of _____? | 1 to 2 | 11 |
| Attitude Questions | These ask you how the speaker feels or thinks about a certain issue, idea, or person. | What does the speaker say about _____?  What is the professor's opinion of _____? | 1 to 2 | 11 |

LISTENING

To answer standard multiple-choice questions, you simply click on the oval next to the answer choice that you believe is correct, or on the choice itself. This will make the oval appear dark. You then click OK, followed by Next.

## Other Types of Listening Questions

Some listening questions have special directions, as described as follows:

### Questions with Multiple Answers

Some factual and negative factual questions have two or even three (out of five) answers. You must click on two or three answers before you continue. These questions have boxes rather than ovals next to the answer choices, and when you click on each choice, the box is not completely blackened. Instead, an X appears in the box. You have to mark two (or three) choices before you can continue to the next question.

Which of the following are the most likely sites for active volcanoes?

**Choose two answers.**

☒ The Pacific Rim
☐ The Atlantic Basin
☒ The Mediterranean Belt
☐ Central Asia

According to the professor, which of the following persons became presidents of the United States?

**Choose three answers.**

☒ Thomas Jefferson
☐ Samuel Adams
☒ James Madison
☒ John Quincy Adams
☐ Benjamin Franklin

There will probably be three to five questions with multiple answers in each Listening Section.

You can find more information and practice questions in Lesson 1.

### Replay Questions

Some questions first replay a short portion of the conversation and lecture and then ask you a question about what you hear. These questions usually ask you what the speaker meant or why that speaker made a comment. Replay questions require you to go beyond the literal meaning of statements in the talk. The meaning of the expression may depend on the speaker's intonation or tone of voice. These questions are marked with a headphones icon.

You see a screen on your computer that says:

> Listen again to part of the conversation/lecture.
> Then answer the question.

**Professor**

So, I don't have to go over that again, do I?

What does the professor mean when she says this? 🎧
- ● She thinks the students understand the point.
- ○ She doesn't think this is an important point.
- ○ She doesn't have enough time to review the point now.
- ○ She thinks this point is especially difficult to explain.

There will probably be four to six replay questions in each Listening Section. For more information and practice questions, see Lesson 4.

## *Matching Questions*

Matching questions ask you to match characteristics or specific information with general categories.

Match the animal with the appropriate category:

**A. Bear**              **B. Frog**                  **C. Snake**

| Amphibian | Reptile | Mammal |
|-----------|---------|--------|
| **B. Frog** | | |

To answer this type of question, you simply click on each answer choice and then drag and drop it into the appropriate box.

There will probably be one or two matching questions per Listening Section. For more information and practice questions, see Lesson 5.

## *Ordering Questions*

Ordering questions ask you to put four (or sometimes three) events or steps into the correct order.

The professor describes the process by which a tornado forms. Put these steps of the process in the correct order.

**A. Warm air rises quickly, pulling more warm air behind it.**
**B. Masses of cool air meet warm, humid air.**
**C. In-rushing air begins to rotate, forming a funnel cloud.**
**D. A zone of thunderstorm clouds develops.**

| 1. **B. Masses of cool air meet warm, humid air.** |
|---|
| 2. |
| 3. |
| 4. |

To answer these questions, you first click on the A, B, C, or D answer choice, then on the box where you think it belongs.

There will probably be one or two ordering questions per Listening Section. For more information and practice questions, see Lesson 5.

### Complete-the-Chart Questions

Complete-the-chart questions test your ability to classify information or to determine whether or not points are made in a lecture. They ask you to complete charts that summarize all or part of a lecture.

In this lecture, the professor describes mature soil. Indicate whether each of the following is a characteristic of mature soil.

| | Yes | No |
|---|---|---|
| Contains more microscopic life than immature soil | ✓ | |
| Consists of three layers | | |
| Consists mostly of broken rock fragments | | |
| Is darker in color than immature soil | | |

To answer these questions, you first click on the A, B, C, or D answer choice, then drag and drop the letter into the box where you think it belongs.

There will probably be one or two complete-the-chart questions in each Listening Section. There is more information and practice for this type of question in Lesson 6.

## NOTE TAKING

Note taking is encouraged on the TOEFL iBT, and the notes you take can be very helpful when you are answering the questions. To help you improve your note-taking skills, the Listening Tutorial (pages 149–161) contains information and exercises to help you develop this ability. You may want to begin work on this section *before* you start working on the Listening lessons in this book.

## Tactics for Listening

- As with all sections of the test, be familiar with the directions. When the directions appear, click on the Dismiss Directions button and begin the Listening section right away.

- Take notes and use your notes when you answer the questions. Try to record as much information as possible in your notes.

- Time management is important. Remember, you have as long as you like to answer each question, but you must complete the section within the time limit. Keep your eye on the clock and on the icon that tells you which question number you are working on.

- Always answer promptly after the answer choices appear, not only to save time but also to keep the listening material fresh in your mind. Refer to your notes as necessary to help you answer the questions.

- Don't spend too much time on any one question.

- Use your "power of prediction." As you are listening to the conversation or lecture, try to guess what questions will be asked.

- If you are not sure of an answer, try to eliminate unlikely choices. If you have no idea which answer is correct, guess and then go on to the next question.

- Concentration is very important in this part of the test. Once you have answered a question, don't think about it anymore—start thinking about the next question. Focus your attention on the voices you hear and the words on the screen.

LISTENING

▶ Now start the Audio Program. 🎧

This section tests your understanding of conversations and lectures. You will hear each conversation or lecture only once. Your answers should be based on what is stated or implied in the conversations and lectures.

You are allowed to take notes as you listen, and you can use these notes to help you answer the questions.

In some questions, you will see a headphones icon: 🎧. This icon tells you that you will hear, but not read, part of the lecture again. Then you will answer a question about the part of the lecture that you heard.

Some questions have special directions that are highlighted.

During an actual test, you will not be allowed to skip questions and come back to them later, so try to answer every question that you hear on this test.

On an actual test, there are two conversations and four lectures. You have twenty minutes (not counting the time spent listening) in which to complete this section of the test.

On this Preview Test, there is one conversation and three lectures. Most questions are separated by a ten-second pause.

▶ Listen to a conversation between a student and a professor. 🎧

**Now get ready to answer the questions.**
**You may use your notes to help you.**

1 of 23    What is this conversation mainly about?

○ The student's grade in her geology class
○ The topic of a research paper that the student must write
○ A class assignment that the student did not hand in
○ The reason the student did not attend class

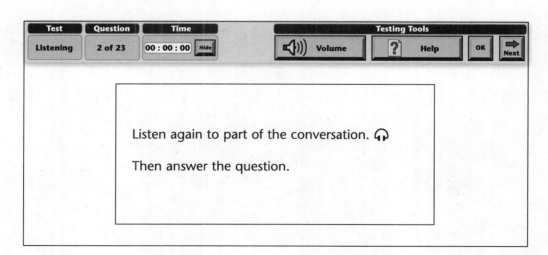

2 of 23    What can be inferred about the student?

○ She has never attended the professor's class.
○ She is not sure what course the professor teaches.
○ She is not sure that the professor knows who she is.
○ She is not certain that the professor's name is Dixon.

3 of 23    What assumption does the professor make about the student?

○ That she got up too late to attend his class yesterday
○ That she missed class because she had to go to the airport
○ That she is coming to his office to apologize for missing class
○ That she is unhappy about the research paper assignment

4 of 23    How did the student first get information about the topic she wants to write about?

○ From a magazine article
○ From the Internet
○ From the professor
○ From a television show

5 of 23    What is the professor's attitude towards the topic that the student wants to write about?

○ He does not think it is a proper topic for a research paper.
○ He thinks it might be a good topic if the student researches it carefully.
○ He believes students should not write about theories that have not been proved.
○ He thinks it is much too narrow a topic for her research paper.

▶ Now listen to a lecture in a biology class. 🎧

## BIOLOGY

Biomes
Tundra
Taiga

**Now get ready to answer the questions.
You may use your notes to help you.**

6 of 23    What does the professor say about the word *taiga?*

○ It is no longer commonly used.
○ It refers only to certain forests in Russia.
○ It was recently invented by biologists.
○ It has the same meaning as the term *boreal forest.*

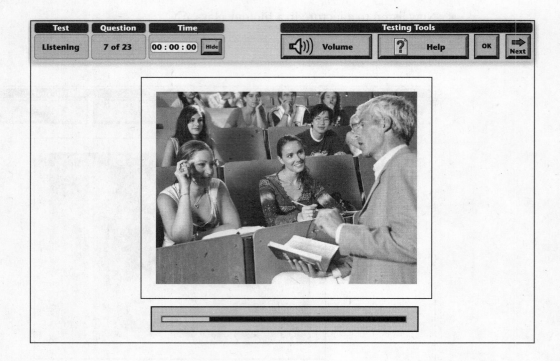

| Test | Question | Time | | Testing Tools | | | |
|------|----------|------|--|---------------|--|--|--|
| Listening | 7 of 23 | 00 : 00 : 00  Hide | | 🔊 Volume | ? Help | OK | ➡ Next |

**7 of 23** Why does the speaker say this? 🎧

○ To explain why he finds the taiga a less interesting biome than tropical rain forest

○ To emphasize that this sub-zone is far less varied than tropical rain forest

○ To explain to students why he is talking about the taiga today, not in a few days

○ To try to encourage students to find out more about different types of biomes

**8 of 23** The professor discussed three sub-zones of the taiga. Match each sub-zone with its characteristic.

Write the letter of the answer choice in the appropriate box. Use each answer only once.

| A. Open forest | B. Closed forest | C. Mixed forest |
|----------------|------------------|-----------------|
| Larger needle-leaf trees grow closer together. | Some broad-leaf trees grow here, especially near water. | Widely spaced, small needle-leaf trees grow here. |
| | | |

9 of 23    When discussing needle-leaf trees, which of these adaptations to cold weather does the professor mention?

Mark three answers.

☐ Their thick bark
☐ Their dark green color
☐ Their deep root system
☐ Their conical shape
☐ The fact that they are "evergreen"

10 of 23    What characteristic do all of the predators of the taiga have in common?

◯ They all migrate during the winter.
◯ They all have thick, warm fur.
◯ They all turn white in the winter.
◯ They all hibernate in the winter.

11 of 23    What does the professor imply about moose?

◯ They are more dangerous to humans than predators.
◯ They have almost vanished from the taiga.
◯ When fully grown, they are in little danger from predators.
◯ Because of the value of their hides, they are often hunted.

► Listen to a discussion in the first class of a business course. 🎧

## BUSINESS

Now get ready to answer the questions.
You may use your notes to help you.

12 of 23    Professor Speed mentions several stages in the history of the case method. Put these steps in the proper order.

Place the letters in the proper boxes.

A.  **Harvard University School of Business begins to use the case method.**
B.  **Columbia University Law School begins to use the case method.**
C.  **Chinese philosophers use a similar method.**
D.  **Harvard University School of Law begins to use the case method.**

1. 
2. 
3. 
4. 

13 of 23    What does Professor Speed say about *exhibits?*

○ They are the center of every case.
○ They consist of ten to twenty pages of text describing a business situation.
○ They are generally obtained from the Internet.
○ They consist of statistical information about a company.

| Test | Question | Time | | Testing Tools | | | |
|---|---|---|---|---|---|---|---|
| Listening | 14 of 23 | 00 : 00 : 00  Hide | | ◁))) Volume | ? Help | OK | ➡ Next |

14 of 23    What does the professor mean when he says this? 🎧

○ He wants to know if the class can answer his question.
○ He's not sure exactly when the case study method was first used at a business school.
○ He wants the students to express their opinions about when cases were first used.
○ He's not sure where the case study method was first used.

LISTENING

15 of 23     Why does Professor Speed mention his wife?

   ○ She uses case study in another type of class.
   ○ She also teaches in the business school.
   ○ She studied law by using the case study method.
   ○ She disagrees with the professor's opinion of cases.

16 of 23     In this lecture, the professor describes the process of the case study method. Indicate whether each of the following is a step in the process.

Put a check mark (✓) in the proper box for each phrase.

|  | Yes | No |
|---|---|---|
| Analyze the business situation and exhibits |  |  |
| Role-play |  |  |
| Run a computer simulation |  |  |
| Give a presentation and write a report |  |  |
| Visit a real business and attend a meeting |  |  |

17 of 23     Which of the following reasons does the professor give for using the case study method?

Choose two answers.

   ☐ It builds a spirit of cooperation and teamwork among students.
   ☐ It allows students to study more than one discipline at the same time.
   ☐ It enables students to design and write their own cases.
   ☐ It develops students' decision-making and problem-solving skills.

▶ Listen to a student giving a presentation in an astronomy class. 🎧

## ASTRONOMY

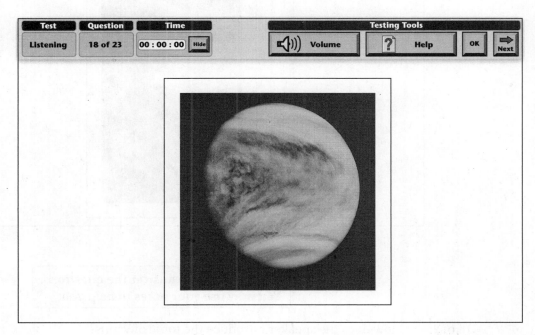

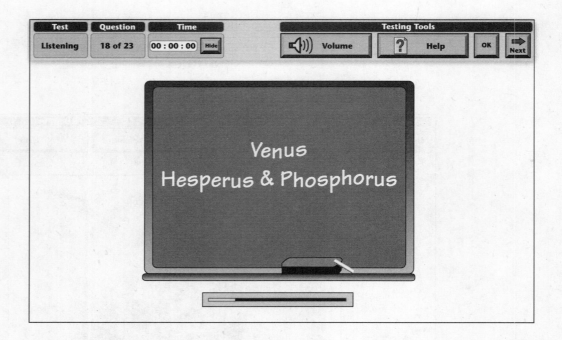

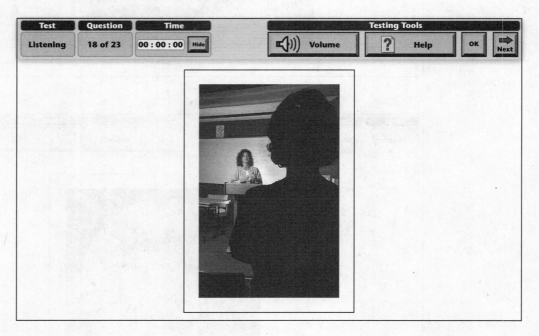

**Now get ready to answer the questions.
You may use your notes to help you.**

18 of 23    How does the speaker introduce the topic of Venus?

○ By comparing Venus with the eight other planets
○ By discussing what people in the past thought of the planet
○ By asking the class what they already know about Venus
○ By listing all of the space probes that have been sent to Venus

19 of 23    According to the speaker, which of the following were once common beliefs
about Venus?

Choose two answers.

☐ That it was not a single object but two objects
☐ That it was actually much colder than the earth
☐ That it had two moons, Phosphorus and Hesperus
☐ That a superior form of life lived under its clouds

20 of 23    In this presentation, the speaker discusses some similarities between Earth and
Venus and some of the differences between the two planets. Indicate which of
the following is a similarity and which is a difference.

Put a check mark (✓) in the proper box for each phrase.

| | Similarity | Difference |
|---|---|---|
| Their ages | | |
| The directions in which they spin around their axes | | |
| Their atmospheric pressures | | |
| The presence of volcanoes | | |
| Their sizes | | |

21 of 23    Which of the following is NOT true about the length of a day on Venus?

○ It is longer than an Earth day.
○ It is longer than an Earth year.
○ It is longer than a Venus year.
○ It is longer than a day on Jupiter.

22 of 23    In what order were these space probes sent to Venus?

Place the letters in the proper boxes.

A.  **Mariner 2**
B.  **Magellan**
C.  **Venus Pioneer 2**
D.  **Venera 4**

| | |
|---|---|
| 1. | |
| 2. | |
| 3. | |
| 4. | |

23 of 23    It can be inferred that the topic of the next student presentation will be about
which of the following?

○ The Moon
○ The Sun
○ Earth
○ Mars

*This is the end of the Listening Preview Test.*

# LESSON 1
## MAIN-TOPIC AND MAIN-PURPOSE QUESTIONS

After each conversation or lecture in the Listening Section, there is a set of questions. The first question of each set is often a **main-topic** question or a **main-purpose** question. To answer these questions, you need to understand the whole conversation or lecture. These questions can be phrased in a number of ways:

### Conversations

What are these people mainly talking about?

What is the main topic of this conversation?

What is this conversation primarily about?

Why is the man/woman talking to the professor?

What is the purpose of this conversation?

### Lectures and Class Discussions

What is the primary topic of this lecture?

What is the main point of this lecture?

What is the purpose of this lecture?

What is the topic of the class discussion?

What is the main subject of this discussion?

What are the students and the professor discussing?

The answer to main-topic/main-purpose questions must correctly summarize the conversation or lecture. Incorrect answers have one of these characteristics:

► They are too general.

► They are too specific, focusing on a detail in the conversation or lecture.

► They are incorrect according to information in the conversation or lecture.

► They are not mentioned in the conversation or lecture.

Although answering these questions will require an overall understanding of the conversations or lectures, the first few sentences often "set the scene" and give you a general idea of what the conversation or lecture will be about. In fact, in some lectures the speaker will actually announce the main topic at the beginning of the talk:

"In our last class, we discussed _____, but today we're going to move on to _____."

"In this class, we're going to focus on _____."

"Today I'd like to introduce the topic of _____."

When you are taking notes, as soon as you become aware of the main topic of the conversation or lecture, you should write it down and underline or circle it.

Pay attention to the "blackboard screens" that are shown before these lectures begin—copy down the information shown on these screens on your note paper. The words that are written on the blackboard are often related to the main idea.

Here is conversation from the Listening Preview Test and a main-topic question about it.

**Sample Item**

▶ Listen to a conversation from the Listening Preview Test and a main-topic question about it. Sample notes on this conversation are also provided. (You can see a script of this conversation in the Audio Scripts and Answer Key part.)

▶ Now start the Audio Program. ⌒

**Sample Notes:**

| | | |
|---|---|---|
| | | Prof. Dixon / student (Brenda Pierce) |
| | S: | In Geol 210 class |
| | P: | Big class + overslp? 8 a.m. |
| | S: | To a'port traffic + need info re rshch paper |
| | P: | no <12 pp no> 25 pp   Biblio: 10 ref srces |
| | | Topic up to stu. |
| | S: | Earthquakes? |
| | P: | Too broad . . . |
| | S: | Using animals predict quakes . . . |
| | P: | Maybe connections animals/quakes? But studies not promising |
| | S: | Saw TV show. In China, animals predicted quake |
| | P: | Haecheng Quake, 30 yrs ago snakes, horses, etc. evac. save 1,000s lives |
| | | But: not able duplic. many quakes not predicted + many false alarms |
| | | (evac. but no quake) |
| | S: | So not good topic? |
| | P: | Maybe OK . . . need look @ serious studies in j'nals, not pop-sci in |
| | | papers or on TV |
| | S: | Will go library, look . . . |
| | P: | Need do formal prop., prelim biblio, due in 1 wk. |
| | | |

**Sample Question:**

What is this conversation mainly about?

○ The student's grade in her geology class
○ The topic of a research paper that the student must write
○ A class assignment that the student did not hand in
○ The reason that the student did not attend class

The subject of the student's grade (choice 1) was barely mentioned in the conversation. The professor simply says that the paper will account for 30% of the student's grade. The conversation does deal with a class assignment (a research paper) but it is an assignment that the student must do in the future, not one that she did not hand in, so choice 3 is not correct. The professor does mention the fact that the student did not attend class yesterday morning (choice 4), but this is only a detail in the conversation. The student and professor are mainly talking about the research paper that the student must complete and about a possible topic for this paper: predicting earthquakes by observing animals' behavior (choice 2).

# EXERCISE 1.1

FOCUS: Answering main-topic/main-purpose questions about conversations.

DIRECTIONS: Listen to the conversations and the main-topic/main-purpose questions about them. Then mark the answer choices that correctly answer the questions. You may take notes on the conversations in the space allowed in the book or on another sheet of paper. As you take notes, try to decide what the main topic/ main purpose of the conversation is and underline it in your notes. You may use your notes to help you answer the questions.

▶ Now start the Audio Program. 🎧

▶ Listen to a conversation between a student and a librarian. 🎧

**Notes:**

_____
_____
_____
_____
_____
_____
_____
_____
_____
_____

> **Now get ready to answer the question.**
> **You may use your notes to help you.**

1. What is the main topic of this conversation?
   ○ Professor Quinn's approach to teaching
   ○ The process of getting a student identification card
   ○ Procedures for checking out reserve materials
   ○ Several recent articles in political science journals

▶ Listen to a conversation between two students. 🎧

**Notes:**

_____
_____
_____
_____
_____
_____

_____

_____

_____

_____

_____

2. What is the main subject of the speakers' conversation?
   ○ Tina's plan for the coming school year
   ○ Tina's volunteer work for Professor Grant
   ○ Tina's vacation in Europe
   ○ An archaeology class that they both took

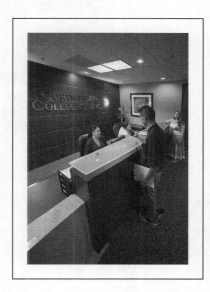

▶ Listen to a conversation between a student and an administrator. 🎧

   **Notes:**

_____

_____

_____

_____

_____

_____

_____

_____

_____

3. Why does Mark Covelli want to speak to Ms. Kirchner?
  ○ He wants to pay for a meal plan that his parents signed him up for.
  ○ He doesn't want to eat in the dormitory at all.
  ○ He wants to change from Meal Plan 1 to Meal Plan 2.
  ○ He wants to eat three meals a day at the dormitory.

▶ Listen to a conversation between two students. 🎧

**Notes:**

_____

_____

_____

_____

_____

_____

_____

_____

_____

> **Now get ready to answer the question.**
> **You may use your notes to help you.**

4. What are these two people mainly discussing?
  ○ A race that the man and his friends will enter
  ○ Some problems that the man has with his car
  ○ A famous race held in Australia
  ○ Difficulties involved in using solar-powered cars

▶ Listen to a conversation between two students. 🎧

**Notes:**

_____

_____

_____

_____

_____

_____

_____

_____

_____

_____

> **Now get ready to answer the question.**
> **You may use your notes to help you.**

5. What is the main topic of this conversation?
   - ◯ The requirements for getting into a photography class
   - ◯ The steps required to put together an art portfolio
   - ◯ Professor Lyle's style of photography
   - ◯ The difference between color and black-and-white photography

## EXERCISE 1.2

FOCUS: Answering main-topic/main-purpose questions about lectures and discussions.

DIRECTIONS: Listen to the lectures/discussions and the main-topic/main-purpose questions about them. Then mark the answer choices that correctly answer the questions. You may take notes on the lectures/discussions in the space allowed in the book or on another sheet of paper. As you take notes, try to decide what the main topic/main purpose of the lecture/discussion is and underline it in your notes. You may use your notes to help you answer the questions.

▶ Listen to a lecture in a dance class. 🎧

## DANCE

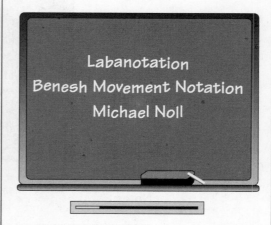

**Notes:**

_____

_____

_____

_____

_____

_____

_____

_____

_____

_____

_____

> **Now get ready to answer the question.**
> **You may use your notes to help you.**

1. What is the main point of this lecture?
   ○ To contrast classical ballet and modern ballet
   ○ To compare two common systems of written dance notation
   ○ To talk about the space program's contribution to computer choreography
   ○ To discuss a problem once faced by choreographers and the means of solving it

▶ Listen to a discussion in a psychology class. 🎧

## PSYCHOLOGY

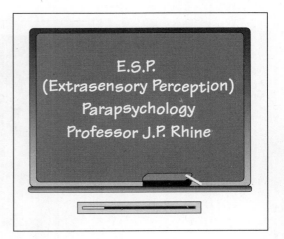

E.S.P.
(Extrasensory Perception)
Parapsychology
Professor J.P. Rhine

**Notes:**

_____

_____

_____

_____

_____

_____

_____

_____

_____

_____

_____

> **Now get ready to answer the question.**
> **You may use your notes to help you.**

2. What are the speakers mainly discussing?
   ○ Reading experiments at Duke University
   ○ Reasons why scientists don't believe ESP is valid
   ○ The accomplishments of Professor Rhine
   ○ The failure of recent experiments in parapsychology

▶ Listen to a lecture in an archaeology class. 🎧

## ARCHAEOLOGY

**Notes:**

_____

_____

_____

_____

_____

_____

_____

_____

_____

_____

**Now get ready to answer the question.
You may use your notes to help you.**

3. What does this lecture mainly concern?
   ○ The archaeological record found in New England shipwrecks
   ○ The rules for a game that the students are going to play
   ○ The leading causes of shipwrecks off the coast of New England
   ○ The role of the State Archaeological Society

▶ Listen to a discussion in an economics class. 🎧

## ECONOMICS

**Notes:**

_____

_____

_____

_____

_____

_____

_____

_____

_____

_____

> **Now get ready to answer the question.**
> **You may use your notes to help you.**

4. What is the main purpose of this discussion?
   ○ To compare regressive and progressive taxes
   ○ To explain the need for a new sales tax
   ○ To discuss the concept of income tax
   ○ To contrast direct and indirect taxation

▶ Listen to a discussion in an art class. 🎧

**ART**

Edward Hopper
*Nighthawks*
*The House by the Railroad*
Film Noir

**Notes:**

_____

_____

_____

_____

_____

_____

_____

_____

_____

_____

> **Now get ready to answer the question.**
> **You may use your notes to help you.**

5.  What is the main topic of this discussion?
    ○ Edward Hopper's early career as a commercial artist
    ○ A style of moviemaking called *film noir*
    ○ Edward Hopper's realistic, bleak style of painting
    ○ Edward Hopper's influence on other painters

▶ Listen to a discussion in an advertising class. 🎧

### ADVERTISING

**Notes:**

_____

_____

_____

_____

_____

_____

_____

_____

_____

_____

> **Now get ready to answer the question.**
> **You may use your notes to help you.**

6. What is the class mainly discussing?
   - ○ Government regulation and self-regulation in the advertising industry
   - ○ A court decision that affected advertising for children in Sweden
   - ○ The problems that a ban on advertising caused the tobacco industry
   - ○ A negative advertising campaign designed to prevent people from smoking

▶ Listen to a lecture in a world literature class. 🎧

**WORLD LITERATURE**

 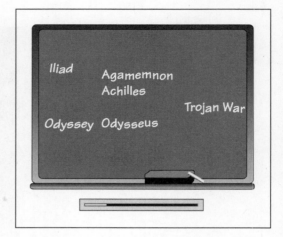

**Notes:**

_____

_____

_____

_____

_____

_____

_____

_____

_____

_____

**Now get ready to answer the question.
You may use your notes to help you.**

7. What is the main point of this lecture?
   - ⭕ To compare the characters of Greek epic poetry and those of modern novels
   - ⭕ To discuss why the professor enjoys the *Iliad* more than the *Odyssey*
   - ⭕ To contrast the main characters of the *Iliad* and the main character of the *Odyssey*
   - ⭕ To explain why the professor is going to have to change the syllabus

▶ Listen to a lecture in a modern history class. 🎧

## MODERN HISTORY

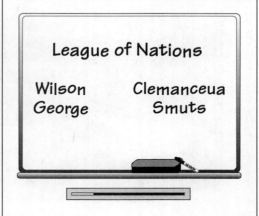

**League of Nations**

Wilson        Clemanceua
George          Smuts

**Notes:**

_____

_____

_____

_____

_____

_____

_____

_____

_____

_____

> **Now get ready to answer the question.**
> **You may use your notes to help you.**

8. What is the main subject of this lecture?
   - ○ The failures of the United Nations
   - ○ The historical role of the League of Nations
   - ○ The origins of World War II
   - ○ The forgotten successes of the League of Nations

▶ Listen to a lecture in an environmental studies class. 🎧

**ENVIRONMENTAL STUDIES**

**Notes:**

_____

_____

_____

_____

_____

_____

_____

_____

_____

_____

> **Now get ready to answer the question.**
> **You may use your notes to help you.**

9. What is the main idea of this lecture?
   ○ Despite certain advantages, there are many problems involved in the use of hot dry rock technology.
   ○ Hot dry rock technology is too expensive to ever be used as a practical energy source.
   ○ The main purpose of hot dry rock technology is to provide pure, clean water.
   ○ Hot dry rock is a potentially important alternative source of energy.

# LESSON 2
## FACTUAL, NEGATIVE FACTUAL, AND INFERENCE QUESTIONS

The three types of Listening questions—factual, negative factual, and inference—are very similar to those that are asked about in the readings in Section 1.

The best way to answer these three types of questions is to take complete, accurate notes on the conversations and lectures. If you are not sure that you remember the answer from the conversation or lecture, refer to your notes for more information. (See the Listening Tutorial on Note Taking, pages 381–393, for more information and practice.) Remember, just as in Reading, the order of these three types of questions follows the order of presentation. In other words, answers for the first few questions will be found in the first part of your notes, answers for the next few will be in the middle, and answers for the last few will be at the end. (To answer some questions, however, such as main-idea or complete-the-chart questions, you must have an understanding of the complete lecture rather than be able to find individual points in your notes.)

### (A) Factual Questions

**Factual questions** ask about supporting ideas and details that are given in the conversation or lecture. These questions ask what, where, when, why, how much, and so on. Another common type of question is "What does the professor say about _____?" Many factual questions begin with one of these phrases:

Conversations

According to the man/woman, . . .

Lectures

According to the professor, . . .

According to the speaker, . . .

To answer these factual questions, you need an understanding of specific points.

If anything in a conversation is repeated or emphasized, it will likely be asked about, as in this portion of a conversation:

*Student A*

My project for my filmmaking class took me six weeks to finish.

*Student B*

*Six weeks!* I can hardly believe it. Doesn't your teacher realize you have other classes too?

You can be fairly sure that there will be a question like this: "How long did the man's project take to complete?"

Here is part of a lecture from the Listening Preview Test and a factual question about it.

### Sample Item 1

▶ Listen to a discussion from the Listening Preview Test and a factual question about it. Sample notes on this lecture are also provided. (You can see a script of this lecture in the Audio Scripts and Answer Key part.)

▶ Now start the Audio Program. 🎧

**Sample Notes:**

Cases = actual bus. sits.
    10-20 pp. of text describing real bus prob
      + 5-10 pp. of exhibits
Exhibits = statist. docs (e.g. spreadshts
                sales reports
                mktg. proj'tions)
  @ center of case: problem
    analyze data
    sometimes collect more data (from Int'net, etc.)
      Then, make decision

**Sample Question:**

What does the professor say about *exhibits*?
- ⭕ They are the center of every case.
- ⭕ They consist of ten to twenty pages of text describing a business situation.
- ⭕ They are generally obtained from the Internet.
- ⭕ They consist of statistical information about a company.

The first choice is not correct. The professor says that at the center of every case is the problem to be solved, not the exhibits. The second choice is not correct. The professor says that there are typically ten to twenty pages of text describing the problem, but that exhibits consist of five to ten pages of statistics. The third choice is not correct. The professor mentions that sometimes it will be necessary to go to the Internet to get more information about a case, but he does not say that the exhibits themselves are taken from the Internet. The best answer is the last one. The professor says that exhibits are "documents . . . statistical documents, really, that explain the situation. They might be oh, spreadsheets, sales reports . . . umm, marketing projections, anything like that."

Some questions will have two correct answers, and a few questions will have five answer choices, three of which will be correct.

Here is an example of a multiple-answer question based on part of a lecture from the Listening Preview Test.

### Sample Item 2

▶ Listen to a lecture from the Listening Preview Test and a multiple-answer question about it. Sample notes on this lecture are also provided. (You can see a script of this lecture in the Audio Scripts and Answer Key part.)

▶ Now start the Audio Program. 🎧

LISTENING

**Sample Notes:**

<table>
<tr><td colspan="2">Conditions in Taiga:</td></tr>
<tr><td></td><td>Very cold    summer shrt</td></tr>
<tr><td></td><td>winter lng</td></tr>
<tr><td colspan="2">Organisms must adapt cold</td></tr>
<tr><td></td><td>Trees: 1) Don't lse lves    evergrn    photosynth right away in</td></tr>
<tr><td></td><td>spng    not need grow new lves</td></tr>
<tr><td></td><td>2) Conical shpe    snow not accum.    slide off, brnches not</td></tr>
<tr><td></td><td>break</td></tr>
<tr><td></td><td>3) Dark grn color absorbs heat</td></tr>
</table>

**Sample Question:**

When discussing needle-leaf trees, which of these adaptations to cold weather does the professor mention?

**Mark three answers.**

- ☐ Their thick bark
- ☒ Their dark green color
- ☐ Their deep root system
- ☒ Their conical shape
- ☒ The fact that they are "evergreen"

The professor does not mention the fact that needle-leaf trees have thick bark that protects them from cold, so choice 1 is not correct. The professor *does* mention the dark green color (2). He says, "And even their color—that dark, dark green—it's useful because it absorbs the sun's heat," so you should mark the second choice as correct. There is no mention of the trees' root system, so choice 3 is not correct. However, choice 4 is correct because he does mention the trees' shape (". . . these trees are conical—shaped like cones—aren't they? This means that snow doesn't accumulate too much on the branches; it just slides off, and so, well, that means their branches don't break under the weight of the snow.). He also mentions the fact that these trees are evergreen (choice 5) (". . . they never lose their leaves—they're "evergreen," right, always green, so in the spring, they don't have to waste time—don't have to waste energy—growing new leaves. They're ready to start photosynthesizing right away.")

Factual questions are the most common type of question in Listening. There are usually two or three factual questions in each set of questions (about twelve to eighteen per Listening Section.) There will probably be three or four multiple-answer factual questions per Listening Section.

### (B) Negative Factual Questions

**Negative, factual questions,** ask you which answer choice is *not* true according to the conversation or lecture or is *not* mentioned in the conversation or lecture.

Here is part of one of the lectures from the Listening Preview Test and a negative factual question about it.

#### Sample Item 3

▶ Listen to part of a student presentation from the Listening Preview Test and a negative factual question about it. Sample notes on this lecture are also provided. (You can see a script of this lecture in the Audio Scripts and Answer Key part.)

▶ Now start the Audio Program. 🎧

**Sample Notes:**

| |
|---|
| Strange fact: Ven. takes 225 E. days to go arnd Sun / E. takes 365 days (= 1 yr.) |
| Ven. turns on axis <u>very</u> slowly          243 days to turn completely |
| E. in 24 hrs. |
| ∴ Venus day > Venus yr. |
| "     "   > days of all planets in sol. sys. |
| All planets in sol. sys. turn same direct EXCPT Ven. |
| (retrgrade spin) |
| |

**Sample Question:**

Which of the following is NOT true about the length of a day on Venus?

○ It is longer than an Earth day.
○ It is longer than an Earth year.
○ It is shorter than a Venus year.
○ It is shorter than a day on Jupiter.

Choice 1 *is* true, and so is not the best answer. An Earth day lasts 24 hours, while a day on Venus lasts 243 Earth days. Choice 2 is the best answer because it is *not* true. An Earth year lasts 365 days, but a day on Venus lasts 243 days. Choice 3 *is* true. A year on Venus lasts 243 Earth days, but a day on Venus lasts 225 Earth days. Choice 4 is also true. The speaker says, "In fact, a day on Venus is . . . longer even than on those big gas planets like Jupiter."

There will probably be two or three negative questions per Listening Section.

## (C) Inference Questions

**Inference questions** ask you to make a conclusion based on information in the conversation or lecture. These questions can be phrased in a number of ways:

Conversations

What does the man/woman imply about _____?

What can be inferred from the man's/woman's comment about _____?

What does the man/woman suggest about _____?

Lectures

What does the professor imply about _____?

What can be inferred from this lecture about _____?

What conclusion can be drawn from the lecture about _____?

Here is a part of a lecture from the Listening Preview Test and an inference question about it.

**Sample Item 4**

▶ Listen to a lecture from the Listening Preview Test and an inference question about it. Sample notes on this conversation are also provided. (You can see a script of this conversation in the Audio Scripts and Answer Key part.)

▶ Now start the Audio Program. 🎧

**Sample Notes:**

Many Taiga animals migrate in wint, but some stay all yr.

Predators:   Arct. foxes, wolves, bears, etc.

<u>All</u> have thick warm coats (keep wrm, but make desirable to

hunters)

Some preds hibernate

"          " change color (e.g. ermine)

Herbivores:  Moose   only yng attacked

Adlt moose biggest, strongest animal of taiga: preds have to be

desperate to attack

Preds mostly eat smaller prey: rabbits, voles, etc.

**Sample Question:**

What does the speaker imply about moose?

○ They are more dangerous to humans than predators.
○ When fully grown, they are in little danger from predators.
○ They have almost vanished from the taiga.
○ Because of the value of their hides, they are often hunted.

There is no information in the lecture to indicate whether or not moose are dangerous to humans, so choice 1 is not correct. The best answer is choice 2. The speaker says, ". . . only young moose are at risk of being attacked. The adult moose is the biggest, strongest animal found in the taiga, so a predator would have to be feeling pretty desperate to take on one of these . . ." This indicates that adult moose are not in much danger from predators. There is no information to support the idea in choice 3, that the moose is endangered in the taiga. The speaker says that the thick fur of predators is prized, but the moose is an herbivore, not a predator, and there is no indication that moose hide is especially valuable to hunters, so choice 4 is not correct.

There will probably be three to five inference questions per Listening Section.

## EXERCISE 2.1

FOCUS: Answering factual, negative factual, and inference questions about conversations.

DIRECTIONS: Listen to the conversations and the questions about them. Then mark the answer choices that correctly answer the questions. You may take notes on the conversations in the space allowed in the book or on another sheet of paper. As you take notes, try to decide what factual, negative factual, and inference questions might be asked about the conversations. You may use your notes to help you answer the questions.

▶ Now start the Audio Program. 🎧

▶ Listen to a conversation between two students. 🎧

**Notes:**

_____

_____

_____

_____

_____

_____

_____

_____

_____

_____

> **Now get ready to answer the questions.**
> **You may use your notes to help you.**

1. What is Cindy's major?

   ○ Education
   ○ Physics
   ○ Mathematics
   ○ Literature

2. What decision about her future has Cindy recently made?

   ○ To change her major
   ○ To try to find a job in a field outside of teaching
   ○ To teach mathematics instead of science
   ○ To look for a job at a middle school

3. What was Cindy's main reason for coming to campus today?

   ○ To apply for a job
   ○ To attend a class
   ○ To arrange her schedule
   ○ To meet with some friends

4. What will Cindy be doing next semester?

   ○ Teaching at a high school
   ○ Taking university classes
   ○ Studying science
   ○ Taking some time off

▶ Listen to a conversation between a student and a visitor to the campus. 🎧

**Notes:**

_____

_____

_____

_____

_____

_____

_____

_____

_____

_____

> **Now get ready to answer the questions.**
> **You may use your notes to help you.**

5. Why was the woman confused at first when the man asked her for directions?

   ○ She didn't know where the art building was located.
   ○ She didn't know about the graduate student art show.
   ○ She was not very familiar with the name "the Reynolds Building."
   ○ She had never been to this campus before.

6. According to the woman, what is directly in front of the art building?

   ○ The library
   ○ A service road
   ○ The chemistry building
   ○ A metal sculpture

7. What was the woman's favorite exhibit at the art show?

   ○ Sculptures made of neon lights
   ○ Abstract paintings
   ○ A large metal sculpture
   ○ The painting of the purple lion

8. What can be inferred from the conversation about the man's sister?

   **Choose two answers.**

   ☐ She works at the gallery in the art building.
   ☐ She is a graduate student.
   ☐ She paints colorful, child-like paintings.
   ☐ She is an old friend of the woman.

▶ Listen to a conversation between two students. 🎧

**Notes:**

_____

_____

_____

_____

_____

_____

_____

_____

_____

_____

> **Now get ready to answer the questions.**
> **You may use your notes to help you.**

9. Which of these courses is required for students in the Semester Abroad program in Greece?

- ◯ Greek history
- ◯ Ancient Greek language
- ◯ Greek drama
- ◯ Modern Greek language

10. Which of these is characteristic of the "island plan" Paul will take part in?

- ◯ He will live and study on one of the Greek islands.
- ◯ His travel and living arrangements will be made by the program.
- ◯ He will live in an apartment surrounded by local people.
- ◯ He will stay with a Greek family.

11. Why did Paul decide NOT to take part in the independent plan?
    - ○ It was too expensive.
    - ○ He thought he would be too isolated.
    - ○ It would require too much of his time.
    - ○ The academic program was too difficult.

12. What does Paul say about Professor Carmichael?

    Choose two answers.

    - ☐ She once taught in a Semester Abroad program in France.
    - ☐ She has taught in the program in Athens many times.
    - ☐ She is no longer his advisor.
    - ☐ She advised him to take part in the program in Greece.

▶ Listen to a conversation between two students. 🎧

**Notes:**

_____

_____

_____

_____

_____

_____

_____

_____

_____

**Now get ready to answer the questions.
You may use your notes to help you.**

13. Why does Steve look tired?

    ○ He stayed up most of the night.
    ○ He had a test last night.
    ○ He's been studying all morning.
    ○ He's been too nervous to sleep lately.

14. How does Steve feel about the grade that he received on the chemistry test?

    ○ It was an improvement.
    ○ It was disappointing.
    ○ It was completely unfair.
    ○ It was a surprise.

15. Who teaches the seminars at the Study Skills Center?

    Choose two answers.

    ☐ Undergraduate students
    ☐ Junior professors
    ☐ Librarians
    ☐ Graduate students

16. Which of the courses at the Study Skills Center will Steve probably be most interested in?

    ○ Basic Internet research methods
    ○ Chemistry
    ○ Business management
    ○ Test-taking skills

17. Where is the Study Skills Center?

    ○ In the library
    ○ In the physics tower
    ○ In a dormitory
    ○ In Staunton Hall

18. What does the woman suggest Steve do now?

    ○ Study for his next exam
    ○ Go directly to the Study Skills Center
    ○ Talk to his chemistry professor
    ○ Get some sleep

▶ Listen to a conversation between a student and a campus housing administrator. 🎧

**Notes:**

_____

_____

_____

_____

_____

_____

_____

_____

_____

**Now get ready to answer the questions.
You may use your notes to help you.**

19. Why does Jeff have to move out of his apartment?

   ○ The building was sold to a new owner.
   ○ He can't find a roommate to share with him.
   ○ The university will not allow him to live off-campus.
   ○ He has not paid his rent for several months.

20. How did Jeff find out about the Resident Advisor position?

   ○ From an ad in the newspaper
   ○ From his landlord
   ○ From another administrator in the housing authority
   ○ From a Resident Advisor

21. What will Jeff receive if he becomes a Resident Advisor?

    **Choose two answers.**

    ☐  A free room in the dormitory
    ☐  Free meals at a cafeteria
    ☐  Free college tuition
    ☐  A monthly salary

22. What does Ms. Delfino suggest Jeff do to get more information about the position?

    ○  Ask Mr. Collingswood for a brochure
    ○  Visit a dormitory and talk to some Resident Advisors
    ○  Take the position on a temporary basis
    ○  E-mail some Resident Advisors and get information from them

# EXERCISE 2.2

FOCUS: Answering factual, negative factual, and inference questions about lectures and academic discussions.

DIRECTIONS: Listen to the lectures and discussions and the questions about them. Then mark the answer choices that correctly answer the questions. You may take notes on the lectures/discussions in the space allowed in the book or on another sheet of paper. As you take notes, try to decide what factual, negative factual, and inference questions might be asked about the lectures and discussions. You may use your notes to help you answer the questions.

▶  Now start the Audio Program. 🎧

LISTENING

▸ Listen to a discussion in an anthropology class. 🎧

**ANTHROPOLOGY**

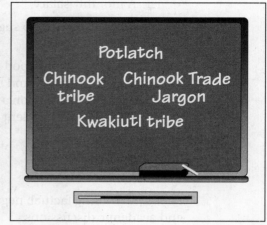

**Notes:**

_____

_____

_____

_____

_____

_____

_____

_____

_____

_____

**Now get ready to answer the questions.
You may use your notes to help you.**

1. What does the professor say about the word *potlatch*?

**Choose two answers.**

☐ It became part of the vocabulary of the Chinook Trade Jargon.
☐ According to some linguists, it originally came from the English word *potluck*.
☐ It was used not just by the Chinooks but by all the Northwestern tribes.
☐ It was originally a word in the language of the Kwakiutl tribe.

2. What was the most common gift at a potlatch?

- ○ Wooden masks
- ○ Fish packed in decorative boxes
- ○ Fishing canoes
- ○ Goat-hair blankets

3. What purpose did seal oil serve at a potlatch?

- ○ It was burned in ceremonial lamps.
- ○ It was used to burn up the host's possessions.
- ○ It was used to flavor foods.
- ○ It heated the building where the potlatch was held.

4. What does Professor Burke imply about the photograph of a potlatch taken in 1900?

- ○ It showed one of the last legal potlatch ceremonies.
- ○ It pictured a gift that the professor considered unusual.
- ○ It indicated that Europeans sometimes attended the ceremony.
- ○ It portrayed typical gifts that would be given away at a potlatch.

5. What does Professor Burke say about the Kwakiutl tribe?

Choose two answers.

- ☐ They held the most elaborate potlatch ceremonies.
- ☐ They were the first tribe to hold potlatches.
- ☐ They held potlatches but did not give away gifts.
- ☐ They used the potlatch to bankrupt their enemies.

6. What does Professor Burke say about potlatch ceremonies held today?

- ○ They are legal in Canada but not in the United States.
- ○ They are illegal but are still held in secret.
- ○ They are still held but are no longer called potlatches.
- ○ They are again an important part of the tribes' culture.

LISTENING

▶ Listen to a lecture in a space science class. 🎧

**SPACE SCIENCE**

 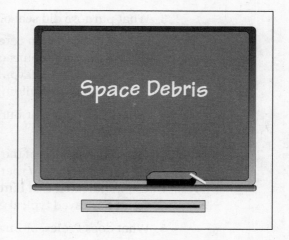

**Notes:**

_____

_____

_____

_____

_____

_____

_____

_____

_____

_____

**Now get ready to answer the questions.
You may use your notes to help you.**

7. What happens to most pieces of orbital debris?

   ○ They burn up in the atmosphere.
   ○ They fly off into deep space.
   ○ They remain in orbit forever.
   ○ They collide with meteors.

8. How many orbital bodies are being monitored today?

   ○ Two hundred
   ○ Three to four hundred
   ○ About thirteen thousand
   ○ Half a million

9. Why is it impossible to monitor most pieces of orbital debris?

   ○ They are too small.
   ○ They are moving too fast.
   ○ They are too far away.
   ○ They are made of reflective material.

10. Which of the following types of orbital debris would NOT be particularly dangerous to astronauts on a spacecraft?

    Choose three answers.

    ☐ A large booster rocket
    ☐ A broken piece of a satellite antenna
    ☐ A lost tool
    ☐ A piece of metal the size of a grain of sand
    ☐ A fleck of paint

11. The professor describes a collision in space between which of the following objects?

    ○ A space shuttle and a space station
    ○ Two rocket parts
    ○ Two surveillance satellites
    ○ A satellite and a rocket

12. What can be inferred about the collector described in this portion of the talk?

    ○ It has been tested on Earth but not in space.
    ○ It is no longer commonly being used.
    ○ It has already been installed on some spacecraft.
    ○ It has not been built yet.

▶ Listen to a discussion in a pharmacy class. 🎧

**PHARMACY**

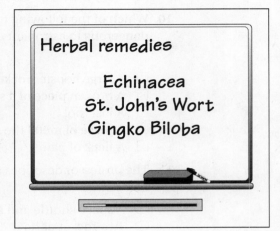

**Notes:**

_____

_____

_____

_____

_____

_____

_____

_____

_____

_____

> **Now get ready to answer the questions.**
> **You may use your notes to help you.**

13. What point does Professor Findlay make about the drugs aspirin and digitalis?
    ○ They are both derived from herbal sources.
    ○ They are much more effective than herbal medicines.
    ○ They can be replaced by safer herbal medicines.
    ○ They should never be taken in combination with herbal medicines.

14. According to Professor Findlay, why do people generally take the herbal remedy Echinacea?

   ○ To prevent colds and the flu
   ○ To treat mild depression
   ○ To improve memory
   ○ To relieve stress

15. Which of the following is the best description of St. John's Wort?

   ○ A fan-shaped leaf
   ○ A yellow flower with five petals
   ○ Small white berries
   ○ Purple flowers that resemble daisies

16. What can be inferred from the professor's remarks about how most herbal medicines are used?

   ○ They are often taken in combination with pharmaceutical drugs.
   ○ They are often taken before people become sick to prevent illnesses.
   ○ They are most often used to treat symptoms of diseases, not their causes.
   ○ They are usually used because a doctor recommends them.

17. In what form are herbal remedies most often taken?
   Choose two answers.

   ☐ In capsules
   ☐ Sprinkled on food
   ☐ Brewed in tea
   ☐ In cold drinks

18. According to the professor, why has research on herbal drugs been limited?

   ○ It requires a very large initial investment.
   ○ It does not interest most research scientists.
   ○ It does not bring drug companies much profit.
   ○ It involves too many variables.

LISTENING

▶ Listen to a lecture in a U.S. history class.

**U.S. HISTORY**

**Notes:**

_____

_____

_____

_____

_____

_____

_____

_____

_____

_____

> **Now get ready to answer the questions.**
> **You may use your notes to help you.**

19. Which of the following caused the decline of roads in the United States in the nineteenth century?

   ○ The effects of the Civil War
   ○ The damage done by horses, carts, and carriages
   ○ The lack of funds caused by economic crises
   ○ The dominance of the railroads

20. How long did it take Dwight David Eisenhower to drive across the United States in 1919?

    ○ Three days
    ○ Sixty-two days
    ○ Seventy-two days
    ○ Almost a year

21. According to the speaker, which of these influenced the way President Eisenhower thought about highways?

    Choose two answers.

    ☐ His experience as a highway engineer
    ☐ His wartime experience with German superhighways
    ☐ His election as president
    ☐ His trip across the United States in 1919

22. When was the Interstate Highway System ORIGINALLY supposed to have been completed?

    ○ 1956
    ○ 1966
    ○ 1972
    ○ 1993

23. Which of the following is NOT given as an effect of the Interstate Highway System?

    ○ Job growth
    ○ Increased safety for motorists
    ○ The decline of the railroads
    ○ The establishment of the first suburb

24. In which of these cities were Interstate highway projects blocked by protests?

    Choose two answers.

    ☐ San Francisco
    ☐ Seattle
    ☐ Washington, D.C.
    ☐ Boston

LISTENING

▶ Listen to a discussion among students preparing a presentation for an architecture class. 🎧

## ARCHITECTURE

**Notes:**

_____
_____
_____
_____
_____
_____
_____
_____
_____
_____

**Now get ready to answer the questions.
You may use your notes to help you.**

25. How did Joyce get most of her information about earthships?

○ From an Internet website
○ From her uncle
○ From a book
○ From her teacher

26. Which of these are NOT one of the main building materials used to construct earthships?

   ○ Wood
   ○ Old tires
   ○ Dirt
   ○ Aluminum cans

27. Which of the walls of an earthship is made of glass?

   ○ The north wall
   ○ The south wall
   ○ The east wall
   ○ The west wall

28. What is meant by the term *nest*?

   ○ A group of earthships
   ○ A large, expensive earthship
   ○ A kind of house similar to an earthship
   ○ A small, basic earthship

29. Why does Joyce call earthships "a real bargain"?

   Choose two answers.

   ☐ Earthships are built in factories, so little construction is necessary.
   ☐ Because earthships are small, owners do not have to purchase much land.
   ☐ Many owners save money by working on the houses themselves.
   ☐ Most of the materials used to build earthships are free or cheap.

30. What will the students probably bring to the presentation?

   ○ A model of an earthship
   ○ A video of an earthship
   ○ A detailed plan for an earthship
   ○ A photograph of earthships

LISTENING

▶ Listen to a lecture in a political science class. 🎧

**POLITICAL SCIENCE**

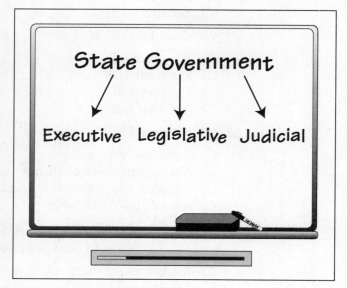

**Notes:**

_____
_____
_____
_____
_____
_____
_____
_____
_____
_____

**Now get ready to answer the questions.
You may use your notes to help you.**

31. What does the professor say about the unitary system of government?

   ○ It involves a single, powerful leader.
   ○ It features a government with only one branch.
   ○ It involves a powerful central government.
   ○ It features a legislature with one house, not two houses.

32. What does the professor say about Switzerland?

   ○ Like Britain and France, it has a unitary form of government.
   ○ Its government served as a model for the government of the United States.
   ○ It has the oldest federalist system of government in the world.
   ○ Like the United States and Canada, it has a federalist system.

33. According to the professor, which of the following is mainly responsible for primary and secondary education in the United States?

   ○ The federal government
   ○ State governments
   ○ Local governments
   ○ Private, nongovernmental agencies

34. Which of these states has the oldest constitution?

   ○ Virginia
   ○ Massachusetts
   ○ Rhode Island
   ○ Oregon

35. What is the maximum time that a governor of Virginia can serve?

   ○ Two years
   ○ Four years
   ○ Eight years
   ○ As many years as he or she wants

36. What is unique about the state legislature of Nebraska?

   ○ It has a single house, not two houses.
   ○ It lacks the power to impeach the governor.
   ○ It is the only legislature that appoints supreme court justices.
   ○ It is appointed, not elected.

LISTENING

▶ Listen to a discussion in a dance class. 🎧

## DANCE

**Notes:**

_____

_____

_____

_____

_____

_____

_____

_____

_____

---

**Now get ready to answer the questions.
You may use your notes to help you.**

---

37. What does the word *hula* mean in the Hawaiian language?
    ○ "Jumping flea"
    ○ "Dance"
    ○ "Graceful ones"
    ○ "Grass skirt"

38. What fact about the hula does the professor particularly emphasize?

    ○ That it is not as old as it was once believed to be
    ○ That it was introduced to the world by visitors from New England
    ○ That it is not as popular with tourists as it once was
    ○ That the current form of the dance differs greatly from the traditional form

39. What roles did the *h'oa-paa,* or "steady ones," play in the performance of the hula?

    Choose two answers.

    ☐ To perform the dance
    ☐ To sing and chant
    ☐ To play musical instruments
    ☐ To direct the dance

40. What did the New England missionaries first do when they arrived in 1820?

    ○ They had the hula completely banned.
    ○ They suggested new themes for the hula.
    ○ They proposed that the hula be performed for visitors.
    ○ They made the hula more conservative.

41. Which of the following would be the most likely theme of a modern hula?

    ○ A tale of a big military victory
    ○ A legend of Laki, goddess of the hula
    ○ The story of a great Hawaiian king
    ○ A description of fish swimming through the sea

42. What will the members of the class do next?

    ○ Attend a live dance performance
    ○ Study another type of traditional dance
    ○ Watch a video of a traditional hula
    ○ Learn to perform the modern hula

LISTENING

# Lesson 3
## Purpose, Method, and Attitude Questions

These three question types are very similar to purpose, method, and attitude questions in the Reading Section.

### (A) Purpose Questions

**Purpose questions** ask *why* a speaker says something or what motivates a speaker to mention something in a conversation or lecture. They may ask you why a speaker presents certain information or gives a certain example.

Here is an example of a purpose question based on part of a lecture from the Listening Preview Test.

### Sample Item 1

▶ Listen to part of a discussion from the Listening Preview Test and a purpose question about it. Sample notes on this conversation are also provided.
(You can see a script of this conversation in the Audio Scripts and Answer Key part.)

▶ Now start the Audio Program. 🎧

**Sample Notes:**

| |
|---|
| Prof Longdell: taught law @ Hvrd, not bus. |
| Case Meth 1st used for law stu. |
| Cple yrs later, used at Columb. U. Law School |
| |
| ± 1910, 1912 Hvrd Bus School |
| Used in other fields as well: e.g. education (Prof. Speed's wife) |

**Sample Question:**

Why does Professor Speed mention his wife?

- ○ She uses case studies in another type of class.
- ○ She also teaches in the business school.
- ○ She studied law by using the case method.
- ○ She disagrees with the professor's opinion of cases.

The student asks if the case method can also be used in fields other than law and business. The professor first gives her a general answer ("it's been used in all sorts of disciplines"). He then gives her a specific example: he mentions his wife, who teaches in the School of Education, and says that she uses cases to train teachers. Choice 1 is therefore best. He does not say that she teaches in the business school (2); he says that she teaches in the School of Education. He does not say that she studied law (3). He also does not say that she disagrees with his own opinion of cases (4); in fact, since she uses cases herself, she probably agrees with his opinion.

You will probably see two to four purpose questions in each Listening Section.

## (B) Method Questions

**Method questions** ask you *how* a speaker introduces an idea, emphasizes an idea, or explains an idea in a conversation or lecture. A speaker may, for instance, indicate cause/effect, contrast two concepts, give reasons, provide statistics, compare an unfamiliar concept with a familiar one, or provide examples to support a general concept.

Here is a portion of a presentation from the Listening Preview Test and a method question about it.

**Sample Item 2**

▶ Listen to part of a student presentation from the Listening Preview Test and a method question about it. Sample notes on this conversation are also provided. (You can see a script of this conversation in the Audio Scripts and Answer Key part.)

▶ Now start the Audio Program. 🎧

**Sample Notes:**

Don: Sun
Lisa: Merc.
Presenter: Venus
1st: What people thght of Venus in past
    Thght Ven. = star
    actually 2 stars: Phosphorus, mrng star
                     Hesperus, eve.
    Named after goddess of love (Why?)

**Sample Question:**

How does the speaker introduce the topic of Venus?

○ By comparing Venus with the eight other planets
○ By discussing what people in the past thought of the planet
○ By asking the class what they already know about Venus
○ By listing all of the space probes that have been sent to Venus

The presenter does not compare Venus with the other planets in the first part of his presentation (although later he does compare specific aspects of Venus with those of certain other planets), so 1 is not correct. The best answer is 2. The student begins by talking about people's ideas of Venus in ancient times ("First off, back in the really . . . in the really ancient days, people thought Venus was a star, not a planet and . . ."). The presenter does *not* ask the other students what they already know about Venus, so choice 3 is not correct. Later in the lecture, he *does* mention a few of the space probes that were sent to Venus, but this is not part of the introduction. Therefore, 4 is not a good answer.

You will probably see one or two method questions per Listening Section.

## (C) Attitude Questions

**Attitude questions** ask you about the speaker's attitude toward something mentioned in the conversation or lecture. What is the speaker's opinion of some concept, person, or thing? The answer to these questions is never given directly in the conversation or lecture. You must infer the answer from the speaker's vocabulary and tone of voice.

Here is a portion of a lecture from the Listening Preview Test and an attitude question about it.

### Sample Item 3

▶ Listen to part of a conversation from the Listening Preview Test and an attitude question about it. Sample notes on this conversation are also provided. (You can see a script of this conversation in the Audio Scripts and Answer Key part.)

▶ Now start the Audio Program. 🎧

**Sample Notes:**

| | |
|---|---|
| ○ | |
| | S. So not good topic? |
| | Prof. Maybe OK . . . need look at serious studies in j'nals, not pop-sci in |
| | papers or on TV |
| | |

**Sample Question:**

What is the professor's attitude toward the topic that the student wants to write about?

- ○ He does not think it is an interesting topic for a research paper.
- ○ He thinks it might be a good topic if the woman researches it carefully.
- ○ He believes students should not write about theories that have not been proved.
- ○ He thinks it is much too narrow a topic for her research paper.

Choice 1 is not correct. After discussing the topic with the student, he says, "It could be a pretty interesting topic." Choice 2 best answers the question. The professor says "just because this theory hasn't been proven doesn't mean you couldn't write a perfectly good paper about this topic . . . on the notion that animals can predict earthquakes. Why not? It could be pretty interesting. But to do a good job, you . . . you'll need to look at some serious studies in the scientific journals . . . ." Choice 3 is not correct. The professor says that the woman *can* "write a perfectly good paper" on a theory that has not been proved. Choice 4 is also incorrect. Earlier in the conversation, the professor seems to think that the woman's topic is too general. However, she then tells him that she is planning to write about a narrower topic, and his response is more positive.

You will probably see one or two attitude questions in each Listening Section.

# EXERCISE 3.1

FOCUS: Answering purpose, method, and attitude questions about conversations.

DIRECTIONS: Listen to the conversations and the questions about them. Then mark the answer choices that correctly answer the questions. You may take notes on the conversations in the space allowed in the book or on another sheet of paper. As you take notes, try to decide what purpose, method, or attitude questions might be asked about the conversations. You may use your notes to help you answer the questions.

▶ Now start the Audio Program. 🎧

► Listen to a conversation between two students. 🎧

**Notes:**

_____

_____

_____

_____

_____

_____

_____

_____

_____

_____

> **Now get ready to answer the questions.**
> **You may use your notes to help you.**

1. Why does the woman mention her father?
   ○ He may help solve the debate team's financial problem.
   ○ Because he went to school in England, he suggested that the woman go there too.
   ○ He advised his daughter to discuss the problem with Dean Metzger.
   ○ Because of his own experience, he persuaded his daughter to join the debate team.

2. How does the man feel about the woman's appointment with Dean Metzger?

○ He doesn't think it will be as useful as a meeting with President Fisher would be.

○ He thinks it will probably hurt the woman's chances of getting what she wants.

○ He thinks it will be useless because he's heard that the dean is unfair.

○ He thinks it is a great idea as long as President Fisher does not attend the meeting.

▶ Listen to a conversation between two students. 🎧

**Notes:**

_____

_____

_____

_____

_____

_____

_____

_____

_____

**Now get ready to answer the questions.
You may use your notes to help you.**

3. How does the man explain his geology mid-term exam to the woman?

- ○ By comparing it with the exams she has taken in math class
- ○ By giving examples of tests that are used to identify minerals
- ○ By comparing it with both multiple-choice and essay exams
- ○ By showing her materials that his professor has prepared

4. What is the woman's attitude toward the taste test?

- ○ She finds it disgusting.
- ○ She realizes it is necessary.
- ○ She thinks it is amusing.
- ○ She doesn't understand it.

5. Why does the man mention quartz?

- ○ It is an example of a mineral that he has previously identified.
- ○ It is an example of a mineral that is softer than gypsum.
- ○ It is an example of a mineral that can be found in various colors.
- ○ It is an example of a mineral with a shiny metallic luster.

6. What is the man's attitude toward his geology mid-term?

- ○ He is hopeful and confident that he will do well.
- ○ He is sure of his abilities but not of his partner's.
- ○ He thinks it will be almost impossible to pass.
- ○ He thinks he needs more time to prepare for it.

## EXERCISE 3.2

FOCUS: Answering purpose, method, and attitude questions about lectures and discussions.

DIRECTIONS: Listen to the lectures and discussions and the questions about them. Then mark the answer choices that correctly answer the questions. You may take notes on the lectures/discussions in the space allowed in the book or on another sheet of paper. As you take notes, try to decide what purpose, method, and attitude questions might be asked about the lectures and discussions. You may use your notes to help you answer the questions.

▶ Now start the Audio Program. 🎧

► Listen to a discussion in a U.S. history class. 🎧

**U.S. HISTORY**

**Notes:**

_____

_____

_____

_____

_____

_____

_____

_____

_____

| **Now get ready to answer the questions. You may use your notes to help you.** |
| --- |

1. Why does Ms. Adams mention the battle of Ivy Station?

   ○ It is not well known, but it was important to the outcome of the war.
   ○ It is an example of a battlefield that has already been lost to development.
   ○ It is a nearby battlefield that is in danger of being developed.
   ○ It is an example of a battlefield that has been adequately protected.

2. How does Ms. Adams make the class aware of the current condition of the Salt Run battlefield?

   ○ She describes the battlefield in detail and urges students to visit it.
   ○ She reads a description of the battle that took place there.
   ○ She asks students to look at a photograph of the site.
   ○ She draws a map of the site on the blackboard.

3. What is Ms. Adams's attitude toward re-enactors?

   ○ She thinks they actually damage the battlefields.
   ○ She disagrees with the methods they use but likes their goals.
   ○ She would like to take part in a re-enactment herself.
   ○ She appreciates the way they help her organization reach its goals.

4. What is David's attitude toward the preservation of Civil War battlefields?

   ○ He doesn't think it is necessary to preserve the sites of unimportant battles.
   ○ He thinks that the only good reason to save battlefields is for re-enactment.
   ○ He doesn't agree that the government needs to protect big, important battlefields.
   ○ He thinks that laws are needed to control further development of battlefields.

LISTENING

▶ Listen to a lecture in an American literature class. 🎧

**AMERICAN LITERATURE**

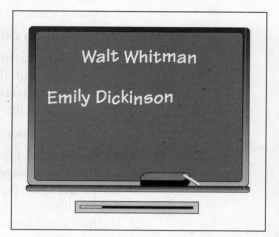

**Notes:**

_____

_____

_____

_____

_____

_____

_____

_____

_____

_____

> **Now get ready to answer the questions.**
> **You may use your notes to help you.**

5. Why does the professor mention the poet Walt Whitman?
   ○ He had a strong influence on Dickinson's poetry.
   ○ He and Dickinson became close friends.
   ○ He criticized Dickinson's lifestyle as well as her poetry.
   ○ He and Dickinson were both influential poets.

6. Why does the professor mention Harvard University?

   ○ Emily Dickinson attended Harvard for one year before her isolation at home.

   ○ Harvard owns the rights to Dickinson's poems and published her complete works.

   ○ Her first poem was published in a Harvard literary magazine.

   ○ A professor at Harvard was the first person to edit one of her poems.

7. Which of the following best summarizes the professor's attitude toward Emily Dickinson?

   ○ She thinks that Dickinson's isolation led her to choose unimportant topics for her poems.

   ○ She agrees with those scholars who say that Dickinson was not at all isolated.

   ○ She thinks Dickinson had a rather strange life but was a major poet.

   ○ She believes scholars pay too much attention to Dickinson's poems and not enough to her lifestyle.

8. How does the professor conclude her discussion of Emily Dickinson?

   ○ By reading part of one of her poems

   ○ By showing the class a picture of her

   ○ By reading what a critic said about her

   ○ By showing the class one of her "fascicles"

LISTENING

▶ Listen to a lecture in an art history class. 🎧

## ART HISTORY

William Rice
Horace Bundy
Rufus Hathaway

**Notes:**

_____
_____
_____
_____
_____
_____
_____
_____
_____
_____

> **Now get ready to answer the questions.**
> **You may use your notes to help you.**

9. How does the professor introduce his discussion of folk art?

○ He compares European folk art and American folk art.

○ He compares folk art of the seventeenth century with that of the eighteenth century.

○ He compares the views of European folklorists with those of American folklorists.

○ He compares folk art created for commercial reasons to that created for artistic reasons.

10. Why does the professor mention wooden carousel horses?

    ○ They were made in factories by groups of workers.
    ○ The Hotchkiss Museum does not consider them to be folk art.
    ○ They were all made by artists from a distinct group.
    ○ European folklorists consider them a fine example of folk art.

11. How does the professor explain the concept of "visual literacy"?

    ○ By contrasting it with other kinds of literacy
    ○ By mentioning examples from the past as well as one from the present
    ○ By giving the definition that appeared in an essay in the catalog
    ○ By showing examples of it that appear in the catalog

12. Why does the professor mention the sign for the King's Inn?

    ○ It is an example of a sign with a shape that indicated a certain type of business.
    ○ It is an example of a trade sign that was used as a landmark in Philadelphia.
    ○ It is an example of a sign used to honor the King of England, George III.
    ○ It is an example of a trade sign with a political message.

13. Why does the professor mention the sign painter William Rice?

    ○ He was once a famous artist but today is almost unknown.
    ○ He painted the only signs in the exhibit that were signed by the artist.
    ○ He is best known for painting portraits, not for painting signs.
    ○ His signs were charming but were not part of the exhibit at the Hotchkiss.

# LESSON 4
## REPLAY QUESTIONS

**Replay questions** ask you to focus on a short portion of a conversation or lecture that you just listened to. You see the photograph of the speaker(s) again, and you hear (but you don't read) a few lines of the conversation or lecture a second time. An icon of headphones 🎧 tells you when you will hear the replayed section.

Replay questions can be phrased in a number of ways:

Why does _____ say this? 🎧

What does _____ mean when s/he says this? 🎧

What does _____ imply when s/he says this? 🎧

Replay questions ask for various types of information.

- Some of these questions ask you about the speaker's motivation for mentioning certain information in the lecture. The answers usually begin with an infinitive explaining possible purposes, such as "To explain . . ." or "To summarize . . ." or "To indicate . . . ," and so on.

- Some of these questions ask you about language "functions": Is the speaker apologizing? Changing the subject? Complaining? Clarifying? Asking for more information? Making a suggestion? Expressing doubt or uncertainty? Interrupting? Showing impatience?

- Some of these questions ask you what the speaker means or implies when s/he says something. These questions often ask you about an idiom or some other set expression that the speaker uses.

### *Example:*

**Student A**

I'm going to ask Michael if he'll help me with these problems.

**Student B**

*Save your breath.* He's way too busy this week.

The idiom "Save your breath" means "Don't waste your time."

- Some of these questions ask you about language that can have different meanings in different circumstances. The context of the conversation or lecture as well as the speaker's tone of voice, stress on a certain word or phrase, or intonation, tells you which meaning the speaker intends.

  Here are four short conversations that all use the phrase "I'm sorry," but in each of the four sentences, the speaker's intention is different.

▷ Listen to these four conversations in the Audio Program. 🎧

- In the first conversation, the student is apologizing for turning in his assignment late and saying that he will not do so again in the future.

- In the second conversation, the student does not understand the phrase "the Krebs cycle" and is asking the professor to repeat the phrase.

- In the third conversation, the woman is turning down an invitation to go skiing.
- In the fourth conversation, the woman is explaining to the man the reason he cannot reserve a tennis court at that time (because the facility isn't open then).

There are two slightly different formats for replay questions.

| | |
|---|---|
| *Replay Question Type 1* | In the first type, the narrator asks a question first. You then hear one line of the conversation or lecture and answer the question. |
| *Replay Question Type 2* | In the second type, the narrator tells you to listen again. You hear a short portion (several lines) of the conversation or lecture. After that, the narrator asks, "What does the speaker mean when s/he says this?" Then you hear one line from the conversation or lecture one more time. |

Replay questions require close, word-for-word listening. And remember: you can (and you should!) take notes during the replay. In fact, you should try to write down as much as possible of what the speakers say during the replay.

Here is an example of a replay question based on part of a lecture from the Listening Preview Test.

**Sample Item**

▷ Listen to a replay question from the Listening Preview Test. Sample notes are also provided. (You can see a script of this part of the lecture in the Audio Scripts and Answer Key part.)

▷ Now start the Audio Program. 🎧

**Sample Notes:**

This sub-zone: If like var'ty, not happy here—
　　see only ½ doz. tree spec. for miles
In few days, talk abt. trop rn forest lot of var'ty there

Why does the professor say this? 🎧

○ To explain why he finds the taiga a less interesting biome than the tropical rain forest

○ To emphasize that this sub-zone is far less varied than the tropical rain forest

○ To explain to students why he is talking about the taiga today, not in a few days

○ To try to encourage students to find out more about different types of biomes

The best choice is 2. The professor is emphasizing that there are very few species of trees in this sub-zone (the closed forest) by comparing it with a tropical rain forest, where there are many species. He does this by saying that a person who likes a variety of trees would be unhappy in this sub-zone. Choice 1 is not correct because the professor does not say he himself thinks the taiga is less interesting than the tropical rain forest. He does not explain why he is discussing the taiga today (choice 3), he simply says that the class will begin to discuss tropical rain forests in a couple of days. He does not, in this part of the lecture, urge students to learn more about different types of biomes (choice 4).

There will probably be four or five replay questions in each Listening Section.

## EXERCISE 4.1

FOCUS: Understanding the language and intonation of replay questions.

DIRECTIONS: Listen to some short conversations and statements followed by replay questions. Then mark the statements below **T** (true) or **F** (false) depending on the information that you hear.

▶ Now start the Audio Program. 🎧

T / F    1. Neither student enjoyed the statistics course.

T / F    2. The woman thinks her lab partner had a good excuse.

T / F    3. Professor White seldom changes his grade.

T / F    4. Greg has already changed his major several times.

T / F    5. The woman thinks the man should move out of his apartment quickly.

T / F    6. Doctor Stansfield does not think Mark should drop the physiology class.

T / F    7. The professor doesn't think he can translate the poem.

T / F    8. The man is already familiar with these terms.

T / F    9. The professor is explaining why the class will be continuing their study of imaginary numbers.

T / F  10. The student is certain that his answer is correct.

T / F  11. The professor is now returning to the main topic.

T / F  12. Most of the students' essays were too short.

## EXERCISE 4.2

FOCUS: Answering replay questions about conversations.

DIRECTIONS: Listen to short portions of conversations and the questions about them. Then mark the answer choices that correctly answer the questions. You may take notes on the conversations in the space allowed in the book or on another sheet of paper. You may use your notes to help you answer the questions.

**Note:** *These short portions of conversations are taken from conversations that you heard in Lessons 1 through 3.*

▶  Now start the Audio Program. 🎧

(Question 1 is from the conversation in Lesson 1 about checking out reserve materials from the library.)

▶ Listen again to part of the conversation. Then answer the question.

**Notes:**

_____

_____

_____

_____

_____

1. What does the woman mean when she says this? 🎧
   ○ That she is willing to risk not seeing the reserve material this evening
   ○ That she is concerned about reading the material before another student checks it out
   ○ That she doesn't plan to eat dinner at her dorm this evening
   ○ That she's certain no other student will check out the reserve material this evening

(Question 2 is from the conversation in Lesson 1 about an archaeological dig.)

▶ Listen again to part of the conversation. Then answer the question.

**Notes:**

_____

_____

_____

_____

_____

2. What does the woman mean when she says this?

   ○ Absolutely no artifacts were found.
   ○ The trip was not fun or interesting.
   ○ All the artifacts that they found were broken.
   ○ The expedition was extremely successful.

(Questions 3 and 4 are from the conversation in Lesson 2 about the graduate art exhibit.)

▸ Listen again to part of the conversation. Then answer the question.

**Notes:**

_____

_____

_____

_____

_____

3. What does the woman imply when she says this? 🎧
   ○ The sculpture is not really very abstract.
   ○ She doesn't like the metal object.
   ○ She wants to know what the man thinks of the object.
   ○ She doesn't know the name of the work of art.

▶ Listen again to part of the conversation. Then answer the question.

**Notes:**

_____

_____

_____

_____

_____

4. What does the man mean when he says this? 🎧
   ○ His sister gets paint on her clothing when she teaches art classes to children.
   ○ The children who are in his sister's class have affected the way she paints.
   ○ His sister has had a strong influence on the way that the children paint.
   ○ He thinks his sister would rather teach art than paint pictures herself.

(Question 5 is from the conversation in Lesson 2 about the Study Skills Center.)

▶ Listen again to part of the conversation. Then answer the question.

**Notes:**

_____

_____

_____

_____

_____

5. What does the man mean when he says this? 🎧

- ○ He's pleased that the class is at a convenient location.
- ○ He doesn't care for the woman's suggestion.
- ○ He doesn't have enough time to take another class.
- ○ He thinks this class sounds perfect for him.

(Question 6 is from the conversation in Lesson 2 about the Resident Advisor position.)

▶ Listen again to part of the conversation. Then answer the question.

**Notes:**

_____

_____

_____

_____

_____

6. What does the man imply when he says this? 🎧

- ○ He is interested in the position but has not definitely decided to apply.
- ○ He is probably not going to apply, but he does not want to be impolite to Ms. Delfino.
- ○ He has definitely decided that he can't accept the position.
- ○ He assumes that he will not be offered the position even though he would like to have it.

(Questions 7 through 9 are from the conversation in Lesson 3 about the problems of the debate team.)

▶ Listen again to part of the conversation. Then answer the question.

**Notes:**

_____

_____

_____

_____

_____

7. **What does the man mean when he says this?** 🎧

○ He doesn't want to discuss the budget cuts.
○ He doesn't have any solution to the woman's problem.
○ He agrees with the woman's ideas but not with her methods.
○ He's afraid the woman will be offended by his opinion.

▶ Listen again to part of the conversation. Then answer the question.

**Notes:**

_____

_____

_____

_____

8. **What does the woman mean when she says this?** 🎧

○ She doesn't know how to respond to the man's question.
○ What the man is asking her is not really clear.
○ There are many reasons why the debate team is worthwhile.
○ She does not wish to begin another discussion with the man.

▶ Listen again to part of the conversation. Then answer the question.

**Notes:**

_____

_____

_____

_____

_____

9. What does the man mean when he says this? ∩

○ He's already convinced by the woman's arguments.
○ He would like to contribute to the debate team.
○ He wants to hear some more reasons.
○ He thinks the woman should quit the debate team.

(Questions 10 through 13 are from the conversation in Lesson 3 about the geology mid-term.)

▶ Listen again to part of the conversation. Then answer the question.

**Notes:**

_____

_____

_____

_____

_____

10. Why does the woman say this? 🎧

    ○ To complain about the fact that the man's test will be so difficult
    ○ To explain similar experiments on mineral samples that she has done herself
    ○ To indicate surprise that one can identify minerals through tests
    ○ To ask about the difference between minerals and rocks

▶ Listen again to part of the conversation. Then answer the question.

    **Notes:**

    _____

    _____

    _____

    _____

    _____

11. What does the woman mean when she says this? 🎧

    ○ She wants to know what other types of tests the man must take.
    ○ She wants to see the scale.
    ○ She doesn't think the man is using the correct name for the scale.
    ○ She's unfamiliar with the Mohs scale.

▶ Listen again to part of the conversation. Then answer the question.

    **Notes:**

    _____

    _____

    _____

    _____

    _____

12. What does the man mean when he says this? 🎧

    ○ He's completely contradicting what he said before.
    ○ He's explaining why he made a mistake earlier.
    ○ He's clarifying what he said earlier with new information.
    ○ He's apologizing for confusing the woman earlier.

▶ Listen again to part of the conversation. Then answer the question.

    **Notes:**

    _____

    _____

    _____

    _____

    _____

13. Why does the woman say this? 🎧

  ○ To indicate that she does not wish to see any more photos of minerals
  ○ To express satisfaction with the man's explanation
  ○ To indicate confusion about the information the man just gave her
  ○ To request more specific examples

## EXERCISE 4.3

FOCUS: Answering replay questions about lectures and discussions.

DIRECTIONS: Listen to short portions of lectures and discussions and questions about them. Then mark the answer choices that correctly answer the questions. You may take notes on the lectures in the space allowed in the book or on another sheet of paper. You may use your notes to help you answer the questions.

**Note:** *These short portions of lectures and discussions are taken from lectures that you previously heard in the Listening Preview Test and in Lessons 1 through 3.*

▷ Now start the Audio Program. 🎧

(Question 1 is from the student presentation about Venus in the Preview Test.)

▷ Listen again to the professor's comment. Then answer the question.

**Notes:**

_____

_____

_____

_____

_____

1. Why does the professor say this? 🎧
   ○ To explain to the class why Venus was the goddess of love
   ○ To contradict what Charlie said about why the planet is named *Venus*
   ○ To urge students to look at Venus both in the morning and in the evening
   ○ To supply some information that was missing from Charlie's presentation

(Question 2 is from the lecture in Lesson 1 about computerized choreography.)

► Listen again to part of the lecture. Then answer the question.

**Notes:**

_____

_____

_____

_____

_____

2. What does the woman mean when she says this? 🎧
   ○ Computers used children's pictures to choreograph dance.
   ○ The first choreography programs used very simple graphic images.
   ○ Computers have been used to choreograph dances for children.
   ○ The dancers used as models for the figures were not very talented.

(Questions 3 and 4 are from the discussion in Lesson 1 about extra-sensory perception [ESP].)

▶ Listen again to part of the discussion. Then answer the question.

**Notes:**

_____

_____

_____

_____

_____

3. What does the professor mean when he says this? ⌒

  ○ He is not sure what most researchers think of the results of Rhine's experiments.
  ○ He thinks the language Rhine used to describe his own experiments was confusing.
  ○ He does not agree with the opinion of most scientists about Rhine's experiments.
  ○ He could use much stronger language to attack Rhine's conclusions.

▶ Listen again to part of the discussion. Then answer the question.

**Notes:**

_____

_____

_____

_____

_____

4. Why does the professor say this?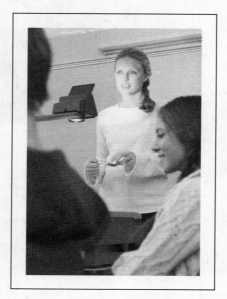

○ To summarize his opinion on the validity of ESP
○ To explain why many people believe in ESP
○ To contradict what he said earlier about ESP
○ To admit that he has never carefully examined the proof for ESP

(Question 5 is from the discussion in Lesson 1 about the painter Edward Hopper.)

► Listen again to part of the discussion. Then answer the question.

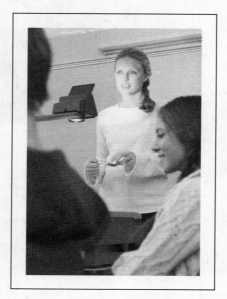

**Notes:**

_____

_____

_____

_____

_____

5. What does the professor mean when she says this?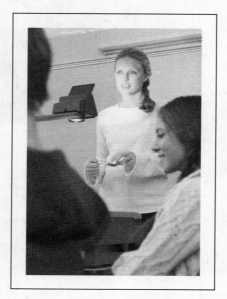

○ She agrees that the man has given the correct name for the painting but prefers to use the shorter name in class.
○ She wants the students to know that the painter himself preferred the title *Nighthawks at the Diner.*
○ She is pointing out that the man has made a common mistake about the title of the painting.
○ She is indicating that she is not sure which of the two titles for the painting is correct.

(Questions 6 and 7 are from the lecture in Lesson 1 about the *Iliad* and the *Odyssey*.)

▷ Listen again to part of the lecture. Then answer the question.

**Notes:**

_____

_____

_____

_____

_____

6. What does the professor mean when she says this? 🎧

   ◯ The point that she makes about epic poems is not important to the lecture.
   ◯ The students are probably familiar with the concept of epic poems.
   ◯ The class has probably already read the epic poems she is discussing.
   ◯ She doesn't have time to discuss the concept of epic poems today.

▷ Listen again to part of the lecture. Then answer the question.

**Notes:**

_____

_____

_____

_____

_____

7. What does the professor mean when she says this? 🎧

   ◯ She is giving a reason why Odysseus is considered a strong warrior.
   ◯ She's telling the class why the Trojan War lasted so long.
   ◯ She's explaining why she prefers the characters in the *Iliad* to Odysseus.
   ◯ She is giving an example of how clever Odysseus could be.

(Question 8 is from the lecture in Lesson 1 about Hot Dry Rocks [HDR].)

▶ Listen again to part of the lecture. Then answer the question.

**Notes:**

_____

_____

_____

_____

_____

8. Why does the professor say this? 🎧

○ To indicate that, in reality, it is not possible to get energy from HDR
○ To stress that the process of obtaining energy from HDR is quite simple
○ To suggest that, in practice, getting energy from HDR might not be easy
○ To indicate that the theory of getting energy from HDR is not hard to understand

(Question 9 is from the discussion in Lesson 2 about potlatches.)

▶ Listen again to part of the discussion. Then answer the question.

**Notes:**

_____

_____

_____

_____

_____

9. What does the student mean when he says this? 🎧

    ○ He still doesn't understand the concept of a potlatch.
    ○ He didn't hear the last thing that the professor said.
    ○ He wants to apologize for making a mistake.
    ○ He thinks the professor must be mistaken.

(Questions 10 and 11 are from the discussion in Lesson 2 about the hula.)

▶ Listen again to part of the discussion. Then answer the question.

**Notes:**

_____

_____

_____

_____

_____

10. What does the student mean when she says this? 🎧

  ○ She thinks that the hula must be an easy dance to perform.
  ○ She finds the professor's question simple to answer.
  ○ She is sure that the topic of traditional dance is easily understood.
  ○ She believes that the professor's explanation is too simplistic.

▶ Listen again to part of the discussion. Then answer the question.

**Notes:**

_____

_____

_____

_____

_____

11. What does the professor mean when she says this? 🎧

  ○ She has absolutely no idea why the ukulele was given its name.
  ○ No one knows why the name "jumping flea" was given to the ukulele.
  ○ She is not sure if *ukulele* really means "jumping flea."
  ○ She is explaining why she has not been telling the truth.

(Questions 12 and 13 are from the discussion in Lesson 3 about Civil War battle sites.)

▶ Listen again to part of the discussion. Then answer the question.

**Notes:**

_____

_____

_____

_____

_____

12. What does the speaker mean when she says this? 🎧

   ○ She is describing the fighting during a Civil War battle.
   ○ She is describing the re-enactment of a Civil War battle.
   ○ She is describing the lack of interest in learning history.
   ○ She is describing the difficulty of saving Civil War battlefields.

▶ Listen again to part of the discussion. Then answer the question.

**Notes:**

_____

_____

_____

_____

_____

13. What does Professor Nugent mean when he says this? 🎧

   ○ He disagrees with Ms. Adams's viewpoint and wants to express his own.
   ○ He wants to respond to what David said before Ms. Adams does.
   ○ He agrees with what David said and wants to add his own comment.
   ○ He wants David to clarify his comment before Ms. Adams responds.

(Questions 14 and 15 are from the lecture in Lesson 3 about Emily Dickinson.)

▶ Listen again to part of the lecture. Then answer the question.

**Notes:**

_____

_____

_____

_____

_____

14. What does the professor mean when she says this? 🎧

   ○ She has talked about Whitman's life, now she wants to discuss his poetry.
   ○ She now wants to talk about the other great voice in nineteenth-century American poetry.
   ○ She is now going to continue her discussion of Walt Whitman.
   ○ She momentarily forgot what she was going to say about nineteenth-century poetry.

▶ Listen again to part of the lecture. Then answer the question.

**Notes:**

_____

_____

_____

_____

_____

15. What does the professor mean when she says this? 🎧

   ○ The poems are not difficult to understand.
   ○ The students don't have to read all of the poems.
   ○ The poems are not very long.
   ○ The students have already read the poems.

# LESSON 5
## ORDERING AND MATCHING QUESTIONS

**Ordering questions** and **matching questions** require a general understanding of the lecture or at least a major section of the lecture. These two types of questions are asked only about the lectures and academic discussions, not about conversations.

### (A) Ordering Questions

**Ordering questions** require you to put four (sometimes three) events or steps in a process into the correct order. Anytime a speaker presents events in chronological order (the order in which they occurred), a biography of a person, the steps of a process, or a ranking of things according to their importance, there will probably be an ordering question. Listen for time words (years, dates) and words that signal a sequence.

| Common Sequence Words | | |
|---|---|---|
| before that | afterwards | first |
| earlier than | next | second |
| previously | after that | third |
| prior to | later | fourth |
| sooner than | subsequent | following that |

As you take notes, use numbers to keep track of the order of events or steps in the sequence. You can circle these numbers to make them easier to find.

Remember: The order in which the speaker *mentions* events or steps is not necessarily the order in which they happened.

To answer ordering questions on the computer, first click on one of the four words, phrases, or sentences in the top half of the screen and then drag and drop it into the appropriate box (labeled 1, 2, 3, and 4) in the lower half of the screen. The expression from the top will then appear in the box that you dropped it into. Do this for all four boxes. If you change your mind, click on the answer that you wish to change and your original choice will disappear from the box.

You need to figure out the correct positions for only three answers because the fourth answer must go in the remaining blank.

### Sample Item 1

Here is a section of a presentation from the Listening Preview Test and an ordering question about it. Sample notes on this section of the lecture are also provided. (You can see a script of this lecture in the Audio Scripts and Answer Key part.)

▷ Now start the Audio Program. 🎧

**Sample Notes:**

| |
|---|
| Important Space Probes: |
| ④ Magellan—'90—4 years—radar, maps—volcanoes |
| ① Mariner 2—'62—1st — (Mariner 1 blew up) |
| ② Venera 4—'67—Sov. Union—dropped instrum—showed how hot— lasted only few secs. |
| ③ Ven. Pioneer 2—'78—discovered $CO_2$ + many others |

**Sample Question:**

In what order were these space probes sent to Venus?

Place the letters in the proper boxes.

A. **Mariner 2**
B. **Venus Pioneer 2**
C. **Magellan**
D. **Venera 4**

| | |
|---|---|
| 1. | |
| 2. | |
| 3. | |
| 4. | |

The speaker mentions the space probe Magellan first. This was launched in 1990. He then goes on to mention the first probe sent to Venus, which was launched in 1962. He next discusses the Soviet Union's probe Venera 4, which was launched in 1967. The last probe he mentions is the Venus Pioneer, launched in 1978. Except for the first probe, Magellan, the speaker lists the probes in chronological order. Magellan is actually the most recent. Therefore, the correct order is A. Mariner 2, D. Venera 4, B. Venus Pioneer 2, and C. Magellan.

You will probably see one or two ordering questions in each Listening Section.

## (B) Matching Questions

**Matching questions** require you to connect three words, phrases, or sentences with three categories somehow related to them. If the lecturer or speaker lists three or more general concepts and then gives definitions, examples, characteristics, or uses of those concepts, you will probably see a matching question.

As you take notes, you should normally list specific characteristics of a general concept under that concept. You can then use your notes to answer the questions.

To answer a matching question on the computer, click on one of the three expressions in the top half of the screen and then drag and drop it into the box below the expression that you think is related to it. That word or phrase will then appear in the box you dropped it into. Do this for all three boxes. If you change your mind, click on the item again and the choice will disappear.

For these questions, you really need to find only two correct choices because the third choice must obviously go in the remaining empty box.

### Sample Item 2

Here is a section of a lecture from the Listening Preview Test and a matching question about it. Sample notes are also provided. (You can see a script of this conversation in the Audio Scripts and Answer Key part.)

▶ Now start the Audio Program. 🎧

▶ Listen to part of a lecture in a biology class. 🎧

**Sample Notes:**

---

Taiga: 3 sub-zones

1. open forest—needle-leaf (= evergrn = connif.)
   small, far apart sim. to tundra w/ few sm. trees

2. closed forest—bigger needle-leaf, closer together
   feels like real forest not much var'ty _ doz. spec.

3. mixed zone—even bigger trees some broadlf (=decid.) trees esp. by
   rivers, etc.
   e.g. larch, aspen
   more like temperate forests

---

**Sample Question:**

The professor discussed three sub-zones of the taiga. Match each sub-zone with its characteristic.

Write the letter of the answer choice in the appropriate box. Use each answer only once.

**A.  Open forest**          **B.  Closed forest**          **C.  Mixed forest**

| Larger needle-leaf trees grow closer together. | Some broad-leaf trees grow here, especially near water. | Widely spaced, small needle-leaf trees grow here. |
|---|---|---|
|  |  |  |

The professor describes open forest as having only needle-leaf trees that grow far apart, so choice A should be placed in the third box. He describes closed forest as having needle-leaf trees larger than those in an open forest. He says it feels more like a real forest and lacks variety. Choice B should therefore be placed in the first box. The professor says that mixed forest contains even bigger trees and some broad-leaf trees, especially along rivers and creeks. Therefore, you should place C in the second box. (Besides, this is the only empty box, so you have to put choice C here!)

You will probably see one or two matching questions per Listening Section.

## EXERCISE 5.1

FOCUS: Answering ordering and matching questions about lectures and academic discussions.

DIRECTIONS: Listen to the lectures and discussions and the questions about them. You may take notes on the lectures in the space allowed in the book or on another sheet of paper. As you take notes, try to decide what ordering and matching questions might be asked about the lectures. You may use your notes to help you answer the questions.

▶ Now start the Audio Program. 🎧

▶ Listen to a lecture in a chemistry class. 🎧

**CHEMISTRY**

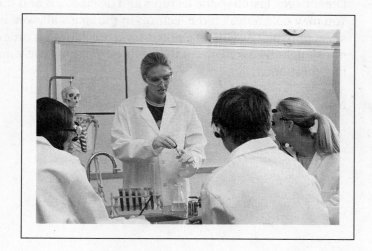

**Notes:**

_____

_____

_____

_____

_____

_____

_____

_____

_____

_____

> **Now get ready to answer the questions.**
> **You may use your notes to help you.**

1. The lecturer discusses the steps involved in the creation of coal. Summarize this process by putting the steps in the proper order.

Place the letters in the proper boxes.

**A. During the decomposition process, plants lose oxygen and hydrogen.**
**B. Layers of sand and mud put pressure on the peat.**
**C. Plants grow in swampy areas.**
**D. Plants die and fall into swampy waters.**

| 1. | |
|----|--|
| 2. | |
| 3. | |
| 4. | |

2. Match the form of coal with the type of industry that primarily uses it.

Put the letters in the proper boxes.

**A. Coal tar**      **B. Bituminous coal**      **C. Coke**

| Electric utilities | Plastic manufacturers | Steel makers |
|--------------------|------------------------|--------------|
| | | |

LISTENING

▶ Listen to a discussion in an accounting seminar. 🎧

### ACCOUNTING

**Notes:**

_____

_____

_____

_____

_____

_____

_____

_____

_____

_____

**Now get ready to answer the questions.**
**You may use your notes to help you.**

3. Match the accounting principle with the appropriate description of it.

Place the letters in the proper boxes.

| A. Matching principle | B. Cost principle | C. Business entity principle |
|---|---|---|
| Owner's and business's accounts must be separate. | Firm must record sales in period when they are made. | Expenses must be recorded at their original price. |
|  |  |  |

▶ Listen to a guest lecture in an agricultural economics class. 🎧

### AGRICULTURAL ECONOMICS

**Notes:**

_____
_____
_____
_____
_____
_____
_____
_____
_____
_____

> **Now get ready to answer the questions.**
> **You may use your notes to help you.**

LISTENING

4. The lecturer mentions four types of crops that are grown in Harrison County. Rank these four types of crops in their order of economic importance, beginning with the *most* important.

Place the letters in the proper boxes.

A. **Heirloom crops**
B. **Wheat**
C. **Corn**
D. **Soybeans**

| | |
|---|---|
| 1. | |
| 2. | |
| 3. | |
| 4. | |

5. Match the type of wheat with the product that is most often made from it.

Place the letters in the proper boxes.

A. **Soft white wheat**     B. **Hard red wheat**     C. **Durum wheat**

| Pasta | Bread flour | Breakfast cereals |
|---|---|---|
| | | |

▶ Listen to a discussion in a modern history class. 🎧

### MODERN HISTORY

**Notes:**

_____

_____

_____

_____

_____

_____

_____

_____

_____

**Now get ready to answer the questions.
You may use your notes to help you.**

LISTENING

6. The professor discusses some of the history of Antarctic exploration. Summarize this history by putting these events in the correct chronological order.

Place the letters in the proper boxes.

A. **Shackleton's expedition approaches the South Pole.**
B. **Scott's party reaches the South Pole.**
C. **Byrd flies over the South Pole.**
D. **Amundsen's party reaches the South Pole.**

| | |
|---|---|
| 1. | |
| 2. | |
| 3. | |
| 4. | |

7. Match these Antarctic explorers with the countries from which they came.

Place the letters in the proper boxes.

A. **Byrd**        B. **Scott**        C. **Amundsen**

| United States | Norway | Britain |
|---|---|---|
| | | |

► Listen to a lecture in a musical acoustics class. 🎧

### MUSICAL ACOUSTICS

**Notes:**

_____

_____

_____

_____

_____

_____

_____

_____

_____

_____

**Now get ready to answer the questions.
You may use your notes to help you.**

8. The professor mentions several conditions caused by excessively loud music. Match the condition to the correct description of it.

Place the letters in the proper boxes.

**A. Tinnitus**          **B. NIHL**          **C. TTS**

| Permanent loss of hearing from loud sounds | Ringing in the ears | Temporary loss of the ability to hear low-volume sounds |
|---|---|---|
|  |  |  |

9. The professor lists several musical events at which her students recorded sound levels. List these events in the correct order based on volume, beginning with the highest volume.

Place the letters in the proper boxes.

A.  Amplified rock music concert at the stadium
B.  Recorded music at Club 1010
C.  Symphony concert
D.  Automotive sound system

| | |
|---|---|
| 1. |  |
| 2. |  |
| 3. |  |
| 4. |  |

► Listen to a lecture in a U.S. literature class. 🎧

## U.S. LITERATURE

**Notes:**

_____

_____

_____

_____

_____

_____

_____

_____

_____

_____

> **Now get ready to answer the questions.**
> **You may use your notes to help you.**

10. The professor gives a brief biography of the writer Edgar Allan Poe. List these events from his life in the order in which they occurred.

Place the letters in the proper boxes.

A. Published his first book of poems
B. Entered the U.S. military academy
C. Worked as a clerk
D. Traveled to England

| 1. | |
|----|--|
| 2. | |
| 3. | |
| 4. | |

11. Match these works by Edgar Allan Poe with the type of writing that they represent.

Place the letters in the proper boxes.

A. "The Gold Bug"     B. "The Raven"     C. "The Fall of the House of Usher"

| Poem | Horror Story | Detective Story |
|------|--------------|-----------------|
| | | |

▶ Listen to a lecture in an anthropology class. 🎧

### ANTHROPOLOGY

**Notes:**

_____
_____
_____
_____
_____
_____
_____
_____
_____

**Now get ready to answer the questions.
You may use your notes to help you.**

12. The professor mentions a number of archaeological finds that were related to the domestication of dogs. Match these finds with their locations.

Place the letters in the proper boxes.

**A. A fragment of a dog's bone**  **B. A rock painting showing hunting dogs**  **C. A rock painting showing herding dogs**

| A cave in Germany | The mountains of Iraq | The desert of Algeria |
|---|---|---|
|  |  |  |

13. The professor mentions a number of roles that dogs have played since they were first domesticated. List these roles in chronological order, beginning with the earliest role that dogs played.

Place the letters in the proper boxes.

A. **Hunter**
B. **Companion**
C. **Guard**
D. **Herder**

| 1. |  |
|---|---|
| 2. |  |
| 3. |  |
| 4. |  |

# LESSON 6
## COMPLETING CHARTS

**Complete-the-chart questions** require an understanding of all or a major part of a lecture. (Chart questions will not be asked about conversations.)

The chart consists of a grid. There are actually several types of grids. One type lists steps in a process. You have to decide if the steps in the grid are actually given in the lecture and then mark each step "Yes" or "No." Another type of grid lists specific characteristics. You have to decide if these characteristics are associated with a certain idea or some general concept, and indicate whether this information was included in the lecture by placing check marks in the appropriate boxes.

Your notes can be very helpful when you answer complete-the-chart questions. During the lecture, listen for the speaker to mention steps in a process or characteristics related to a topic, and then write them down.

### Sample Item

Here is a section of a discussion from the Listening Preview Test and complete-the-chart question about it. Sample notes are also provided. (You can see a script of this part of the lecture in the Audio Scripts and Answer Key part.)

▶ Now start the Audio Program. ⌒

**Sample Notes:**

Cases are <u>real</u> business sits: 10-20 pp. of text describing a prob.
  + 5-10 pp. exhibits"
    (Exhib. = statistic. info: spreadshts, etc.)
      1. Analyze prob and data (get more if needed)
      2. Make decisions about data
      3. Usu. involves role-play (e.g., roleplay CEO, CFO)
      4. Work in grps (4-5 Stu); builds teamwork
      5. Give presentation/write report (group grade based on this)
Not all classes use cases; some lectures, some combin. lect + cases Some
use computer simulations (e.g. World Mktplace)

**Sample Question:**

In this lecture, the professor describes the process of the case study method. Indicate whether each of the following is a step in the process.
Put a check mark (✓) in the proper box for each phrase.

|  | Yes | No |
|---|---|---|
| Analyze the business situation and exhibits |  |  |
| Role-play |  |  |
| Run a computer simulation |  |  |
| Give a presentation and write a report |  |  |
| Visit a real business and attend a meeting |  |  |

    As you can see from the sample notes, the professor did mention the need to analyze the business problem and the data provided in the exhibits. You should therefore check **Yes** for the first step. The professor said that "solving the problem usually involves role-playing," so you should also click on **Yes** for the second step in the list. The professor said that some business classes involve computer simulations, but he was not talking about classes based on case study, so you should click on **No** for the third step. The professor said that a group grade was given for an oral presentation and a written report, so the fourth step should be marked **Yes**. There is no mention in the discussion that visiting a real business and attending a meeting was part of the case study process, so you should click **No** for the fifth step.

You will probably see one or two complete-the-chart questions in each Listening Section.

## EXERCISE **6.1**

FOCUS: Answering complete-the-chart questions about lectures and academic discussions.

DIRECTIONS: Listen to the lectures and discussions and the questions about them. Then complete the chart by placing check marks (✓) in the appropriate boxes. You may take notes on the lectures in the space allowed in the book or on another sheet of paper. As you take notes, try to decide what complete-the-chart questions might be asked. You may use your notes to help you answer the questions.

**Note:** *You will not see more than one complete-the-chart question per lecture on actual tests. However, some of the lectures in this text feature more than one to give you more practice answering this type of question.*

▶ Now start the Audio Program. 🎧

▶ Listen to a discussion in an urban studies class. 🎧

## URBAN STUDIES

**Notes:**

_____

_____

_____

_____

_____

_____

_____

_____

_____

_____

**Now get ready to answer the questions.
You may use your notes to help you.**

1. In this lecture, the professor describes the New Urbanism Movement. Indicate whether each of the following is a principle of this movement.

Put a check mark (✓) in the proper box for each sentence.

|  | Yes | No |
|---|---|---|
| Plentiful parking is provided in large parking lots. |  |  |
| Residents can walk easily to work or shopping areas. |  |  |
| Residences, shops, and offices are all found on the same block. |  |  |
| Communities are located only in large urban centers. |  |  |
| Streets are generally laid out in a grid pattern. |  |  |

2. In this lecture, the professor mentions benefits associated with the New Urbanism Movement. Indicate whether each of the following is a benefit mentioned in the lecture.

Put a check mark (✓) in the proper box for each sentence.

|  | Yes | No |
|---|---|---|
| Housing is less expensive in New Urban communities than in typical suburbs. |  |  |
| There is less crime in New Urban communities. |  |  |
| Most New Urban communities are conveniently located close to large suburban shopping malls. |  |  |
| Residents of New Urban communities get more exercise. |  |  |
| Most houses in New Urban communities feature garages that allow direct access to the house. |  |  |
| There is less air pollution in New Urban communities. |  |  |

LISTENING

▶ Listen to a lecture in a British history class. 🎧

### BRITISH HISTORY

**Notes:**
_____
_____
_____
_____
_____
_____
_____
_____
_____

**Now get ready to answer the question.
You may use your notes to help you.**

3. In this lecture, the professor mentions myths (false stories) and realities (true stories) associated with the Magna Carta. Indicate whether each of the following is considered a myth or a reality.

Put a check mark (✓) in the proper box for each sentence.

|  | Myth | Reality |
|---|---|---|
| It created the first democratic society in England. |  |  |
| It confirmed the rights of the English barons. |  |  |
| It established the "model Parliament." |  |  |
| It established courts in which citizens were tried by their peers. |  |  |
| It was signed by King John himself. |  |  |

LISTENING

▶ Listen to a lecture in a paleontology class. 🎧

### PALEONTOLOGY

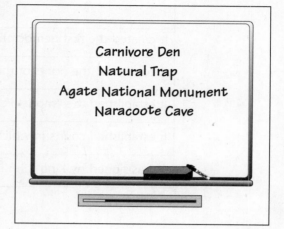

Carnivore Den
Natural Trap
Agate National Monument
Naracoote Cave

**Notes:**

_____

_____

_____

_____

_____

_____

_____

_____

_____

**Now get ready to answer the questions.
You may use your notes to help you.**

4. In this lecture, the professor describes carnivore dens. Decide if the following are characteristics of carnivore dens.

Put a check mark (✓) in the proper box for each phrase.

|  | Yes | No |
|---|---|---|
| Tend to be found in horizontal caves with small entrances |  |  |
| Contain only herbivore fossils |  |  |
| May have had both herbivores and carnivores living in them |  |  |
| Usually have a greater variety of fossils than natural traps |  |  |
| Generally contain well-preserved fossils |  |  |

5. In this lecture, the professor describes important fossil finds at Naricoote Cave, a natural trap. Decide if the following are characteristics of Naricoote Cave.

Put a check mark (✓) in the proper box for each sentence.

|  | Yes | No |
|---|---|---|
| It was discovered by professional palaeontologists. |  |  |
| Animals that fell in here died from the impact of the fall. |  |  |
| Its entrance was covered by plants. |  |  |
| It features the fossil bones of a previously unknown giant cat. |  |  |
| It contains a greater variety of fossils than most natural traps. |  |  |

LISTENING

▶ Listen to a lecture in an astronomy class. 🎧

## ASTRONOMY

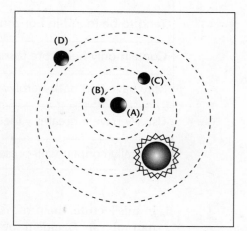

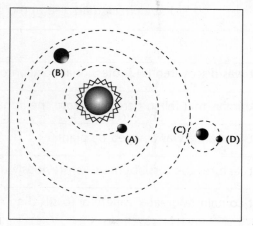

**Notes:**

_____

_____

_____

_____

_____

_____

_____

_____

_____

_____

**Now get ready to answer the question.
You may use your notes to help you.**

6. In this lecture, the professor describes two ways to look at the universe: the Ptolemaic system and the Copernican system. Decide if the following are characteristics of the Ptolemaic system or the Copernican system.

Put a check mark (✓) in the proper box for each sentence.

|  | Ptolemaic System | Copernican System |
|---|---|---|
| This system is also known as the "heliocentric system." |  |  |
| "Epicycles" were used to help explain this system. |  |  |
| This system became part of the medieval system of belief. |  |  |
| This system was disproved by Galileo's discovery of the phases of Venus. |  |  |
| This system provided a good picture of the solar system but not of the universe. |  |  |
| According to this system, music was generated by the movement of crystal spheres. |  |  |

▶ Listen to a lecture in a marketing class. 🎧

**MARKETING**

 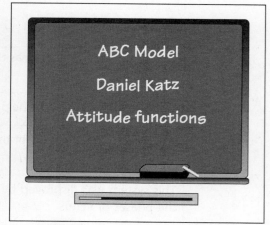

**Notes:**

_____

_____

_____

_____

_____

_____

_____

_____

_____

**Now get ready to answer the questions.
You may use your notes to help you.**

7. The lecturer describes the ABC approach to viewing consumer attitudes. Decide if the following are more closely related to the A component, the B component, or the C component of the ABC approach.

Put a check mark (✓) in the proper box for each sentence.

| | A component | B component | C component |
|---|---|---|---|
| A consumer visits an Internet site to get more information about tires. | | | |
| A man feels a bicycle will make his daughter happy. | | | |
| A customer buys groceries at the store. | | | |
| An investor studies the market for art before buying a painting. | | | |
| A woman orders a sandwich and a drink at a fast-food restaurant. | | | |

8. In this lecture, the professor describes the Katz system of attitude functions. Decide which of the following characteristics is related to which function.

Put a check mark (✓) in the proper box for each phrase.

| | Value-expressive function | Ego-defensive function |
|---|---|---|
| May involve a product that protects a consumer from some threat | | |
| May involve a product that consumers believe will make them more popular | | |
| May involve a product that consumers believe will make people dislike them | | |
| May involve a product that is harmful to the consumer who buys it | | |

## LISTENING REVIEW TEST
### DIRECTIONS

▶ Now start the Audio Program. 🎧

This section tests your understanding of conversations and lectures. You will hear each conversation or lecture only once. Your answers should be based on what is stated or implied in the conversations and lectures.

You are allowed to take notes as you listen, and you can use these notes to help you answer the questions.

In some questions, you will see a headphones icon: 🎧. This icon tells you that you will hear, but not read, part of the lecture again. Then you will answer a question about the part of the lecture that you heard.

Some questions have special directions that are highlighted.

During an actual test, you will not be allowed to skip questions and come back to them later, so try to answer every question that you hear on this test.

There are two conversations and four lectures. Most questions are separated by a ten-second pause.

LISTENING

▶ Listen to a conversation between a student and a professor. 🎧

Now get ready to answer the questions.
You may use your notes to help you.

1 of 34    What course does Scott want to drop?

○ Mathematics
○ Biochemistry
○ Medicine
○ Music

▶ Listen again to part of the conversation. 🎧

2 of 34    What does Professor Calhoun mean when she says this? 🎧

○ She respects Dr. Delaney's academic research.
○ She thinks that Dr. Delaney's advice should be respected.
○ She thinks that Scott should have more respect for Dr. Delaney.
○ She completely disagrees with Dr. Delaney's advice.

3 of 34    What does Professor Calhoun say about her class?

○ The most difficult part of it is already over.
○ It will be ending in a few days.
○ It is not required for students who plan to study medicine.
○ She will not be teaching it next year.

4 of 34    What does Professor Calhoun suggest that Scott do?

○ Wait a few days before he drops her class
○ Speak to Dr. Delaney again
○ Concentrate on his four other classes
○ Work with her teaching assistant

5 of 34    Which of the following best describes Professor Calhoun's attitude towards Scott?

○ Condescending
○ Angry
○ Encouraging
○ Disappointed

► Listen to a conversation between two students. 🎧

**Now get ready to answer the questions.
You may use your notes to help you.**

6 of 34    Why did Martha come to the library?

  ⭕ To look up some terms
  ⭕ To meet Stanley
  ⭕ To get some coffee
  ⭕ To prepare for a test

7 of 34    What did Stanley misplace?

  ⭕ His backpack
  ⭕ A notebook
  ⭕ Some index cards
  ⭕ A library book

► Listen again to part of the conversation. 🎧

8 of 34    What does Martha mean when she says this? 🎧

  ⭕ She thinks that Stanley had better hurry up.
  ⭕ She's surprised he is working on his papers so early.
  ⭕ She thinks she should do some research as well.
  ⭕ She's surprised that Stanley enjoys doing research.

9 of 34    According to Stanley, what does the term *stacks* refer to?

  ⭕ The section of the library where journals are stored
  ⭕ Piles of note cards
  ⭕ The part of the library where books are shelved
  ⭕ A place to get something to eat in the library

10 of 34    Where will Stanley go next?

  ⭕ To the periodicals room
  ⭕ To talk with a librarian
  ⭕ To the snack bar in the basement
  ⭕ To Williams Street

▶ Listen to part of a lecture in an elementary education class. 🎧

### ELEMENTARY EDUCATION

My sister likes to ride her bike.

Pzol2tx
mssrlkrdrbk
mi ster like to rid hir bik
my sistre like to ride her bike.

**Now get ready to answer the questions.
You may use your notes to help you.**

11 of 34    Which of the following activities are signs of "writing readiness" in children?

Choose three answers.

☐  Asking to play with scissors and modeling clay
☐  Making marks on a page that look like writing
☐  Asking adults to guide their hands as they write something
☐  Writing numbers and simple words
☐  Using "invented letters"

12 of 34    What does the speaker imply about the system mentioned in the article that the students read, which was used to describe the development of writing skills?

◯  It is no longer considered valid by most experts.
◯  She does not agree with it at all.
◯  It has fewer stages than some other systems.
◯  It is the only one in common use today.

13 of 34    The speaker mentions four stages in the development of writing skills. Put these stages in the correct order, beginning with the earliest stage.

Put the letters of the stages in the proper boxes.

A.  **Phonemic**
B.  **Symbolic**
C.  **Conventional**
D.  **Transitional**

| | |
|---|---|
| 1. | |
| 2. | |
| 3. | |
| 4. | |

14 of 34    Why does the speaker mention Spanish and Finnish?

○ She thinks that children should learn to write several languages.
○ These languages are easier for young writers because they are phonetic languages.
○ She has learned to write in these languages herself.
○ Children often learn to write these languages without studying the rules of phonics.

15 of 34    Which of the following is the best example of writing done by a child in the transitional stage?

○ ٦ ٥z ؟ ×–M–∞
○ ilketetpzaiskrmevda
○ I lik eat pissa an ise krim ever dae.
○ I'd like to eat piza and ice creem every day.

16 of 34    Which of these statements about writing assignments for young children would the professor probably agree with?

Choose two answers.

☐ They should be designed to increase accuracy and speed of writing.
☐ They should be as enjoyable as possible.
☐ They should emphasize communication skills.
☐ They should be carefully graded by teachers.

▶ Listen to a lecture in an astronomy class. 🎧

## ASTRONOMY

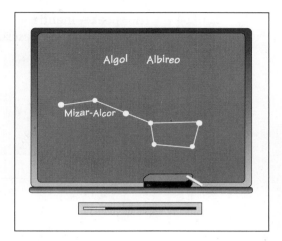

**Now get ready to answer the questions.
You may use your notes to help you.**

17 of 34    What is the main purpose of this lecture?

○ To describe some recent research in astronomy
○ To discuss the first discovery of double stars
○ To give students an assignment to do in the observatory
○ To present a basic description of double stars

18 of 34    According to *most* astronomers, about what percentage of all stars are double stars?

○ 3% to 4%
○ 10%
○ 25%
○ 75%

19 of 34    According to the speaker, what does the term *comes* mean in astronomy?

○ It is the dimmer star in a binary pair.
○ It is one of the stars in a line-of-sight double.
○ It is a system having three or more stars.
○ In an eclipsing binary, it is the star that is eclipsed.

20 of 34    How many stars make up Mizar-Alcor?

○ Two
○ Three
○ Four
○ Eight

21 of 34    How does the speaker describe double stars of contrasting colors?

○ By comparing them to optical pairs
○ By comparing them to familiar objects found on Earth
○ By imagining what a space alien would think of them
○ By providing statistics about their relative ages

22 of 34    The speaker mentions a number of different double-star systems. Match these systems with their descriptions.

Place the letters of the choices in the proper boxes.

**A. Mizar-Alcor**          **B. Algol**          **C. Albireo**

| Two stars of contrasting colors | An eclipsing binary | An optical pair |
|---|---|---|
|  |  |  |

▶ Listen to a lecture in a marketing class. 🎧

**MARKETING**

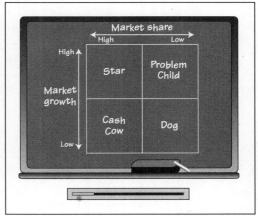

Now get ready to answer the questions.
You may use your notes to help you.

23 of 34    Which of the following is NOT one of the terms for the method the speaker uses for classifying SBUs?

○ The BCG Method
○ The Boston Box
○ The General Electric/Shell Method
○ The Growth-Share Matrix

24 of 34    How does the speaker classify the SBU that makes athletic shoes?

○ As a star
○ As a dog
○ As a problem child
○ As a cash cow

25 of 34    Why is the term *cash cow* used to describe some SBUs?

○ Like actual dairy cows, they require a lot of care and daily attention.
○ They provide nourishment for "problem children."
○ They are often bought and sold as cows are sold at rural markets.
○ They produce a flow of profits as cows produce a flow of milk.

26 of 34    Which of these classification changes would probably most please the marketing manager of the firm that owns this SBU?

○ From star to problem child
○ From dog to cash cow
○ From cash cow to dog
○ From star to dog

27 of 34     In this lecture, the professor describes the marketing strategies of Langfield-Smith. Indicate whether each of the following is a strategy that Smith lists.

Put a check mark (✓) in the proper box for each phrase.

|  | Yes | No |
|---|---|---|
| Increase market share in an SBU and turn a cash cow into a star |  |  |
| Reduce investment in an SBU and collect short-term profits |  |  |
| Buy a well-performing SBU from another company, creating a new star |  |  |
| Sell a poorly performing SBU and get rid of a dog |  |  |
| Raise prices on an SBU's product and change a problem child to a cash cow |  |  |

28 of 34     What is the speaker's opinion of SBUs known as "dogs"?

○ Their products may be a useful part of a product portfolio.
○ They should be traded to other companies as soon as possible.
○ Their products should be aggressively promoted and advertised.
○ They should be "harvested" to increase short-term profits.

▶ Listen to a discussion in a marine biology class. 🎧

## MARINE BIOLOGY

> **Now get ready to answer the questions.**
> **You may use your notes to help you.**

29 of 34    What is NOT known about the songs of the humpback whale?

**Choose two answers.**

- ☐ When humans first became aware of them
- ☐ Exactly how the whales produce them
- ☐ What they mean
- ☐ Who first heard them

30 of 34    In this lecture, the speaker describes two types of calls made by the humpback whale. Indicate whether each of the following is a characteristic of the low-frequency call or of the high-frequency call.

**Put a check mark (✓) in the proper box for each phrase.**

|  | Low-Frequency Sound | High-Frequency Sound |
|---|---|---|
| Travels a long distance |  |  |
| Probably carries a lot of information |  |  |
| Has a simple structure |  |  |
| Is generally considered the "song" of the humpback whale |  |  |

LISTENING

31 of 34    The speaker analyzes the music of the humpback whale by breaking it down into its component parts. Arrange this list of the parts of the humpback's music, beginning with the simplest and shortest part and moving to the longest and most complex.

A. **Theme**
B. **Song**
C. **Element**
D. **Phrase**

Place the letters of the choices in the proper boxes.

| | |
|---|---|
| 1. | |
| 2. | |
| 3. | |
| 4. | |

32 of 34    How long does a humpback whale take to sing a complete song?

○ Three or four minutes
○ Seven or eight minutes
○ Ten to twenty minutes
○ Up to ten hours

33 of 34    When do humpback whales sing the most?

○ During the daytime when they are in warm waters
○ At night when they are feeding
○ During the day when they are migrating
○ On winter nights

▶ Listen again to part of the lecture. 🎧

34 of 34    What does the professor mean when she says this? 🎧

○ She agrees that the humpback songs are a form of oral history.
○ Because no one knows what humpback songs mean, the student's idea might be right.
○ She believes that the student's theory about the humpback songs is better than those of researchers.
○ Although it is not known what the humpback's songs mean, she is sure that they are not singing about their history.

*This is the end of the Listening Review Test.*

# LISTENING TUTORIAL: NOTE TAKING

On the TOEFL iBT, note taking is not only allowed but encouraged. You will be given paper to use for taking notes. After the test, you will have to give your notes to the testing supervisor, but your notes will not be graded.

It certainly makes sense to allow note taking during the test, because the ability to take good lecture notes is an important academic skill. It's not common to take notes on conversations, except sometimes at meetings, but you will have to take notes on both conversations and lectures during this test.

Without notes, the Listening Section of the test is basically a test of memory, and few people have the memory skills to remember all the facts and ideas contained in a lecture lasting five to eight minutes. Research has shown that after twenty minutes has passed, people remember only about 50% of what they hear, and that about 20% of what they hear is remembered incorrectly.

Note taking is a complicated skill, especially note taking in another language. However, note-taking skills can definitely be improved by practice. The more you take notes, the faster and more accurate you will become. During all of the exercises in the Listening Section, you should take notes and use those notes to answer the questions.

## TOEFL NOTE TAKING VS. UNIVERSITY NOTE TAKING

The lectures you hear in the Listening Section simulate (imitate) classroom lectures, but they are not the same. There are two important differences:

1. TOEFL iBT lectures are much *denser* than authentic lectures. From an hour-long classroom lecture, there may be one or two points that will be asked about on tests. On the other hand, there are six questions after a five- to eight-minute TOEFL iBT lecture. Therefore, TOEFL iBT lectures have more facts and information that can be asked about. As a result, your note taking must be more detailed and intensive for the TOEFL iBT than the notes you would take in a lecture class.

2. You may not need to use your notes for a few weeks or even for a few months after you hear a lecture in a classroom. After that much time has passed, you may have forgotten much of the lecture. However, you will use your TOEFL notes immediately after the lecture (and then never again!). Therefore, you can use more abbreviations and omit more words when you take notes on TOEFL lectures. And you don't have to worry too much about writing legibly.

## SOME HINTS ON TAKING NOTES

1. Take notes throughout the lecture. Try to write down as much information as you possibly can.
2. Always write down any terms that are new to you, definitions, specific facts, lists of items, and statistics.
3. Speakers will sometimes give clues telling you which points in a lecture are especially important and will be asked about. Some of the most common clues:
   A. Repetition of a point
   B. Emphasis from tone of voice or from pauses before or after making a point
   C. The amount of time spent on a point
4. Pay attention to the use of signal words or phrases in the lecture, especially ones that indicate the structure of the lecture or a change of topic.

| **Common Signal Words** |
|---|
| **Words and Phrases Indicating the Structure of the Lecture** |
| There are three kinds of . . . |
| We'll be looking at a couple of ways to . . . |
| First, . . . |
| Then, . . . |
| That brings us to . . . |
| There are two points of view . . . |
| Next I want to mention . . . |
| First, let's look at . . . |
| Next, let's consider . . . |
| Okay, now let's talk about . . . |
| Now, what about _____? |
| Finally, . . . |

**Words and Phrases Indicating a Change of Direction**

On the other hand, . . .
However, . . .
But . . .

**Words and Phrases Showing Emphasis or Importance**

Most importantly, . . .
One important point/issue/problem/question/concept is . . .
Especially . . .
Significantly, . . .
Be sure to note that . . .
Pay special attention to . . .

**Words and Phrases Used to Give Examples**

For example, . . .
Take _____ for example . . .
For instance, . . .
Let's consider the case of . . .
Specifically, . . .

5. In academic discussions, important information may be in comments that students make (particularly if the professor agrees with the student).

6. When taking notes on conversations, pay attention to who is saying what. For example, if a professor is speaking to a student, you may want to put the initial **P** before notes on what the professor says and **S** before what the student says.

7. Take notes during replay questions. In fact, try to write down as many words as possible when listening for the second time.

8. Organize your lecture notes according to order of importance. The most important ideas should be on the left side of the page. Indent to the right to show that an idea is subordinate to or supports the more important idea. In other words, ideas on the left side of the page are general divisions of the lecture. As you move to the right, ideas become more specific. You should also skip lines between important parts of the lecture. Writing notes in this way helps you analyze the material that you are listening to and organize your notes in a logical way.

    Main idea

        Supporting idea

        Supporting idea

            Minor point, example, detail, etc.

    Main idea

        Supporting idea

            Minor point, example, detail, etc.

            Minor point, example, detail, etc.

You can indicate ideas that you think are especially important with a box, a circle, an underline, or an exclamation point (!).

Leave plenty of white space around your notes so that, if the speaker returns to a point later, you can add new notes.

9. The average lecturer speaks about 125 to 150 words per minute. The average note taker can write only about 20 to 25 words per minute. Therefore, you need to use abbreviations and other shortcuts to help you get down as much information as possible.

A. Don't write your notes in complete sentences. Write in phrases.

B. Omit unimportant words and words that do not carry information. Suppose the lecturer says this:

> The taiga is the largest of all the world's biomes.

Your note might read:

Taiga largest biome.

Common words that you can generally eliminate:

> *Be* verbs *(is, are, was, were)*, articles *(a, an, the)*, pronouns *(they, his, them)*, determiners *(this, that, these)*, prepositions *(of, with, from)*

C. Use standard symbols and abbreviations:

| | |
|---|---|
| + | or & and |
| = | is, equals, is the same as |
| ≠ | isn't, doesn't equal, is not the same as |
| ≈ | is not quite the same as, is similar to |
| ± | more or less, about, approximately |
| ↑ | increases, goes up |
| ↓ | decreases, goes down |
| / | per |
| % | percent |
| # | number |
| x | times |
| > | more than, bigger than, greater than |
| < | less than, smaller than, fewer than |
| → | causes, leads to, produces |
| $ | money |

| ♂ | man, male |
| ♀ | woman, female |
| @ | at |
| w/ | with |
| w/o | without |
| p. | page |
| pp. | pages |
| re | regarding, about, concerning |
| etc. | and so on, and other things |
| e.g. | for example |
| i.e. | in other words |
| ∴ | therefore |

For example, if the speaker says this:

"The earth is about four times bigger than the moon."

You may take this note:

Earth ± 4 x bigger Moon

Another useful symbol is the ditto mark ( " ). This repeats the words that you wrote on a previous line.

Suppose a professor in a biology class says this:

"There are many types of crustaceans, and they live in many different habitats. Most of them are marine animals—they live in the sea. Some are fresh water animals, and a few types of crustaceans live on the land."

You might take these notes:

Many types of crustaceans
   "    environs.

Most crustac. live in  sea
Some    "     "  "  freshwater
A few   "      "  on land

D.  Besides standard abbreviations and symbols, you often need to create your own abbreviations. There are two common ways to abbreviate words. You can use the first few letters of a word.

| information | info |
| presentation | pres |
| definition | def |
| recommendation | rec |

Another way to abbreviate words is to leave out letters from the middle of words.

| large | lge |
| international | internat'l |
| market | mkt |
| manager | mgr |

Remember, you will be using your notes as soon as the lecture is over. You can probably remember what your abbreviations mean for a few minutes, so abbreviate as much as possible.

10. If you miss a point, don't worry. Just keep taking notes.

11. Don't worry about spelling, punctuation, or correct grammar. Don't worry if your notes are messy.

12. Remember that there are no "perfect" notes. Everyone has his or her own style of taking notes. There are only three important issues in taking notes for the TOEFL test:

    A. Are they accurate?

    B. Do they help you answer the questions?

    C. Can you understand them?

The sample notes that are provided in the *The Complete Guide to the TOEFL Test, iBT Edition* are examples of good note taking, but another person could take good notes in a completely different way.

## NOTE-TAKING EXERCISE 1

▶ Now start the Audio Program. 🎧

DIRECTIONS: Listen to a list of words and phrases. Write down your own abbreviations of these words in the spaces below. (This vocabulary comes from a lecture on business organizations that you will be listening to in order to improve your note-taking skills.) When you have finished, compare your notes with those of a classmate. Check for similarities and differences in what you wrote. You can also compare your notes with those in the Answer Key.

Sample abbreviations appear in the Answer Key.

1. _____ 11. _____

2. _____ 12. _____

3. _____ 13. _____

4. _____ 14. _____

5. _____ 15. _____

6. _____ 16. _____

7. _____ 17. _____

8. _____ 18. _____

9. _____ 19. _____

10. _____ 20. _____

## NOTE-TAKING EXERCISE 2

DIRECTIONS: Working by yourself or with a partner, use the list of abbreviations that you wrote in Exercise 1 to "reconstruct" the full forms of the words and phrases that you heard. Then discuss the meaning of these terms.

1. _____        11. _____
2. _____        12. _____
3. _____        13. _____
4. _____        14. _____
5. _____        15. _____
6. _____        16. _____
7. _____        17. _____
8. _____        18. _____
9. _____        19. _____
10. _____       20. _____

## NOTE-TAKING EXERCISE 3

▶ Now start the Audio Program. 🎧

DIRECTIONS: Listen to the following sentences. Take notes on these sentences using abbreviations and symbols and omitting unimportant words. (These sentences come from a lecture on business organizations that you will be listening to in order to improve your note-taking skills.)

When you have finished taking notes, compare your notes with those of a classmate. Check for similarities and differences in what you wrote. You can also compare your notes with the sample notes in the Answer Key.

1. _____
2. _____
3. _____
4. _____
5. _____
6. _____
7. _____
8. _____
9. _____

LISTENING

## NOTE-TAKING EXERCISE 4

DIRECTIONS: Working by yourself or with a partner, use the notes that you took in Exercise 3 to "reconstruct" the full forms of the sentences that you heard.

1. _____
2. _____
3. _____
4. _____
5. _____
6. _____
7. _____
8. _____
9. _____

## NOTE-TAKING EXERCISE 5

▶ Now start the Audio Program. 🎧

DIRECTIONS: Listen to a lecture on business organizations. The lecture will be given in short sections. Take notes on each section. After each section, answer the questions **Yes** or **No** to find out if you are taking notes on the important points in the lecture. (The more **Yes** answers you have, the more complete your notes are.)

When you have finished taking notes, compare your notes with those of a classmate. Check for similarities and differences in what you wrote. You can also compare your notes with the sample notes in the Answer Key.

**Section 1**

_____

_____

_____

_____

_____

1. Did you note that there were once three main types of business organizations but that now there are four? Yes _____ No _____

2. Did you note the names of the four main types of business organizations? (sole proprietorship, partnership, corporation, and limited liability corporation)? Yes _____ No _____

3. Did you abbreviate the names of the four types? Yes _____ No _____

**Section 2**

_____

_____

_____

_____

_____

4. Did you note that one person is in complete control of a sole proprietorship? Yes _____ No _____

5. Did you note that a sole proprietorship begins when the owner makes the decision to start a business? Yes _____ No _____

6. Did you write down Paul Samuelson's example of when a sole proprietorship begins? Yes _____ No _____
   (This is "extra" information that the speaker uses to clarify how sole proprietorships get started. You probably would not take notes on this during a classroom lecture. However, sometimes TOEFL asks questions such as "Why does the speaker mention Paul Samuelson?" so you may want to make a quick note of this example.)

7. Did you write down the main advantage of a sole proprietorship (that there is no separate tax on it)? Yes _____ No _____

8. Did you write down the main disadvantage of a sole proprietorship (that the owner is legally liable for all the company's debts)? Yes _____ No _____

**Section 3**

_____

_____

_____

_____

_____

9. Did you note that a partnership is similar to a sole proprietorship except that a partnership has more than one owner? Yes _____ No _____

10. Did you note that a partnership has the same tax advantage as a sole proprietorship? Yes _____ No _____

11. Did you note the example the author gave of the problem the two partners had because they were both sole agents? Yes _____ No _____
(This is not a very important point, and in a lecture class you would probably not note this at all. However, the TOEFL iBT sometimes asks you questions such as "Why does the speaker mention the two partners' problem?" Therefore, you may want to make a quick note of this example.)

12. Did you note that some partnerships have _silent partners_ who contribute money but do not take part in management decisions? Yes _____ No _____

**Section 4**

_____

_____

_____

_____

_____

13. Did you write down that the corporation is the most complex and the most expensive business organization? Yes _____ No _____

14. Did you note that the most important feature of a corporation is limited liability and that corporations are distinct legal entities? Yes _____ No _____

15. Did you note in some way (by underlining, circling, etc.) that the professor emphasized the point that corporations are distinct legal entities?
Yes _____ No _____

16. Did you note that double taxation is a disadvantage to corporations and did you define double taxation? Yes _____ No _____

17. Did you write down that there are three important elements in the structure of the corporation (stockholders, the board of directors, and executive officers)? Yes _____ No _____

18. Did you note that shareholders have ultimate control but usually give their votes to the corporate officers (voting by proxy)? Yes _____ No _____

19. Did you write down that the board of directors makes major decisions and sets company policy? Yes _____ No _____

20. Did you note that day-to-day operations of corporations are performed by the executive officers and the corporate bureaucracy? Yes _____ No _____

21. Did you note that the CEO is often the chairman of the board? Yes _____ No _____

**Section 5**

_____

_____

_____

_____

_____

22. Did you note that the limited liability company (LLC) is becoming more popular with smaller businesses? Yes _____ No _____

23. Did you note that an LLC is a hybrid organization with features of both a partnership and a corporation? Yes _____ No _____

24. Did you note that the LLC eliminates double taxation? Yes _____ No _____

## NOTE-TAKING EXERCISE 6

▶ Now start the Audio Program. 🎧

DIRECTIONS: Listen again to the lecture on business organizations and take notes. 🎧 After you have listened to the lecture, use your notes to answer the True/False (T / F) questions and the fill-in-the-blank questions at the end of the lecture. Sample lecture notes appear in the Answer Key.

_____

_____

_____

_____

_____

_____

_____

_____

_____

_____

_____

_____

_____

_____

_____

_____

_____

_____

_____

_____

_____

_____

_____

_____

_____

_____

_____

_____

T / F  1. The lecturer says that he has now added a new form of business organization to his lecture.

2. _____ is a relatively new form of business organization.

T / F  3. The speaker mentions Paul Samuelson in the lecture because Samuelson is an expert on corporate taxes.

4. The chief advantage of a sole proprietorship is that _____

_____.

5. The chief disadvantage of a sole proprietorship is that _____

_____.

6. Partnerships and sole proprietorships are similar except for the fact

that _____.

T / F  7. The speaker gives the example of the two partners who both buy 500 widgets* in order to explain how partners divide up their workload.

T / F  8. A silent partner does not invest money in a partnership.

T / F  9. Corporations cost more than sole proprietorships and partnerships to establish.

10. Corporations are distinct legal entities, so they are sometime called

_____.

T / F 11. In theory, stockholders have ultimate control over a corporation, but they actually have little to do with routine operations.

T / F 12. Board members are appointed by the top executive officers.

T / F 13. Top executive officers are not allowed to serve on the board of directors.

T / F 14. "Double taxation" is a reason for the growing popularity of limited liability corporations.

15. An LLC has features of both a _____ and a _____.

_____

*Widgets do not really exist. A widget is a term used by economists and business experts to mean "an unidentified product."

# COMMUNICATIVE ACTIVITIES FOR LISTENING

Internet activities are marked with this icon: ⌒○

## Activity 1

**Guess Who's Talking?**                                    *Pairs Activity*

The instructor/coordinator writes paired relationships on a slip of paper as well as on the board. S/he gives one slip of paper to each pair of students. Here are some examples of relationships you can choose from (or you can create your own):

student/teacher   motorist/police officer   doctor/patient   journalist/news maker
student/advisor   customer/mechanic   lawyer/client   banker/customer
waiter/customer   librarian/library user   passenger/flight attendant

Together you and your partner will write out a short dialogue (with each person writing half of the dialogue). The dialogue should involve a problem that one of the two people is having and possible solutions for the problem. You and your partner will then perform the dialogue. The rest of the class will take notes on each of the dialogues and answer the following questions:

Who is speaking?

What is the problem?

How are these people trying to solve the problem?

What attitude did the two people take toward each other?

## Activity 2

**Following Directions**                                    *Small-Group Activity*

As a group, create a series of directions for things to do on a piece of paper. Here are some examples:

1. In the left-hand bottom part of the page, write your mother's name.
2. Right above that, write your father's place of birth.
3. In the middle of the page, draw a circle.
4. Find out what movie the person on your left likes best. Write the name of the movie inside the circle.
5. To the right of the circle, draw a diamond.
6. Find out what color the person on your right likes best. Write the color in the diamond.
7. Draw three squares across the top of the page.
8. In the leftmost square, write the name of your favorite food.

After you have completed your directions, read them to the class and have the class follow your directions. After completing the task, exchange your sheet of paper with another student to see if s/he successfully followed all of the directions.

## Activity 3

*Fill-in-the-Lyric*                                      *Small-Group Activity*

Record a song that you like from the radio, a CD, or the Internet. As a group, listen to the song and write down the lyrics that you hear. Next, take out one word from each line. Now make copies of the lyrics (words of the song) and give them to all the students in the class. Play the song and have everyone fill in the missing words. The winner is the student who correctly fills in the greatest number of missing words.

## Activity 4

*Storytelling*                          *Individual Activity/Class Activity*

On the Internet, find a suitable folk tale. Look for one from a country or culture other than your own. You can find many sites featuring folk tales from various countries by typing *folk tales* into your browser, or you can type in the name of a specific type of folk tale (Chinese folk tales, Moroccan folk tales, Navajo folk tales, for example). Bring the story to class and read it aloud. Your classmates will listen and take notes on your folk tale and then guess where the folk tale came from. Afterwards, your class will discuss the meaning of the folk tale.

## Activity 5

*Outside Interview*                    *Small-Group/Individual Activity*

As a group, write out a questionnaire that includes at least five questions about note taking. Then interview a university student, a professor, or anyone else who is familiar with academic lectures. Take notes on this person's responses. Report to the class what you learned from the interview.

## Activity 6

*Half a Class*                                             *Pairs Activity*

To do this activity, you will need to live in a community where there is a university or college in which English is the language of instruction. With a partner, decide what type of class you would like to visit. Then call the department (art, economics, biology, etc.) and try to get permission to visit a class. You or your partner will attend the first half of the class and take notes, and then the other person will attend the second half. Afterwards, use your notes to tell your partner what happened in the half of the class that your partner missed.

## Activity 7

### *Write Your Own TOEFL Items*                 *Small-Group Activity*

Find a suitable lecture and record it. There are many Web sites that feature lectures. One of the best is voanews.com. Listen to the lecture as a group and take notes. Then write five TOEFL-like multiple-choice questions about the lecture. Next, exchange lectures and questions with another group. After you've answered the other group's questions, check with the group that wrote the "test" and see if your group has answered the questions correctly.

## Activity 8

### *Who Are They and What Are They Talking About?*   *Individual/Pairs Activity*

Your instructor or coordinator will record a conversation from a television show or a movie and play it in class. Take notes. Then answer these basic questions about the conversation:

1. Who was speaking?
2. Where were they?
3. What were they talking about?
4. What were their attitudes toward each other?

Compare your answers with those of your partner. Then watch the show again and take further notes. Now you and your partner will write a paraphrase of the conversation. (In other words, you are to rewrite the conversation in your own words.) Perform your paraphrase for the class. The class can then vote on whose paraphrase was closest in meaning and feeling to the original.

## Activity 9

### *Say It with Feeling*                                 *Class Activity*

One student acts as "scribe" (writer). On the board, this student writes as many adverbs (words ending with *-ly*) as possible that describe emotions or attitudes, based on suggestions from the class (*angrily, proudly, nervously,* for example). Next, each student will write a series of sentences, such as the following:

1. Write a sentence about your family.
2. Write a sentence about a trip.
3. Write a sentence about the TOEFL test.

and so on.

Students then read their sentences in a way that demonstrates one of the adverbs written on the board. For example, a student might say "My brother is a good football player" *proudly.* Other students in class then try to guess what feeling/attitude the speaker is expressing.

## Activity 10

***Reduced-Forms Contest***                                        ***Pairs Activity***

Your instructor or coordinator will give you a list of sentences that are missing certain phrases. He or she will then read you a list of sentences with reduced forms. (Reduced forms are two or more words that are pronounced as if they were one word.)

1. <u>Wouldja c'mere</u> for a minute?      _____ for a minute?
2. <u>Howzee</u> doing in that class?      _____ doing in that class?
3. <u>Couldja</u> get me a <u>cuppa</u> tea, please?      _____ get me a
                                            _____ tea, please?

With your partner, decide which words are missing and write the full form of each reduced phrase.

> <u>Would you come here</u> for a minute?
>
> <u>How is he</u> doing in that class?
>
> <u>Could you</u> get me a <u>cup of</u> tea, please?

The pair that correctly writes down the most missing phrases wins.

## Activity 11

***Student Teacher***                                             ***Individual Activity***

Your instructor/coordinator will choose several students to teach one of the five Listening lessons in this text. Students who are selected will go back and study those lessons in detail, write out a lesson plan, and give a five- to ten-minute presentation on the lesson.

LISTENING

# PRACTICE TESTS

# ABOUT TAKING THE PRACTICE TESTS

One of the best ways to prepare for the TOEFL® iBT is to take realistic practice tests. The listening tests included with this program are up-to-date versions that include all the new item types found on the Internet-based test. As closely as possible, they duplicate the actual test in format, content, and level of difficulty.

If possible, take a test all at one time. If you are taking the tests at home, work away from distractions such as televisions or radios.

You can take these tests as paper-and-pencil tests or as computerized tests on the CD-ROM that accompanies *The Guide*.

If you take the tests in the book, you will need to use the Audio Program.

Although this book offers practice listening tests, you should take as many full-length practice tests as possible in preparation for the actual test.

If you take the tests in this book, or other books in this TOEFL iBT series, you should follow these guidelines:

***Reading***  | Please note: Practice for the TOEFL iBT reading section may be found in *The Complete Guide to the TOEFL®: READING Test, iBT Edition* by Bruce Rogers, published by Thomson Heinle.

Time yourself as you take this section (allow yourself 60 minutes). You can skip items in this section and go back to them later, and you can go back and change your answers if you want.

## *Listening*

On the actual test, you will be able to control the speed at which you hear the questions. On the Audio Program, most questions are followed by a pause of 10 seconds. There is a 12-second pause after ordering and matching questions and a 15-second pause after complete-the-chart questions. However, you or your teacher can stop the CD-ROM and give yourself more time. If possible, listen to the Audio Program through headphones.

While the conversations and lectures are being read, you should look only at the photos. Don't look at the questions or the answer choices until the question is read on the Audio Program. Don't skip questions, and don't go back to any questions after you have answered them.

***Speaking***  | Please note: Practice for the TOEFL iBT speaking section may be found in *The Complete Guide to the TOEFL®: SPEAKING Test, iBT Edition* by Bruce Rogers, published by Thomson Heinle.

If possible, listen to the script for the Speaking Section using headphones and record your responses. A beep on the Audio Program tells you when your preparation time is over. Begin speaking then. A second beep tells you when your response time is over.

***Writing***  | Please note: Practice for the TOEFL iBT writing section may be found in *The Complete Guide to the TOEFL®: WRITING Test, iBT Edition* by Bruce Rogers, published by Thomson Heinle.

Time yourself carefully as you write both responses. If possible, write your responses on a computer.

## Scoring the Practice Tests

You can use the charts on the following pages to calculate your approximate scores on the Practice Reading, Listening, Speaking, and Writing Tests found in this book and other books in this series. Keep in mind that your scores on practice tests are not necessarily accurate predictors of what you will score on actual tests.

### *Reading*

To calculate your score on the Reading Section, you must first find your raw score. Simply add up the number of correct answers in the Reading Section for all the questions except the last question in each set of questions (Questions 13, 26, and 39). In both tests, those questions are either summary questions or complete-the-chart questions. Here are the guidelines for scoring these questions:

#### <u>Summary Questions</u>

3 correct choices = 2 points

2 correct choices = 1 point

Fewer than 2 correct choices = 0 points

#### <u>Complete-the-Chart Questions</u>

**Seven-answer chart**

7 correct choices = 4 points

6 correct choices = 3 points

4 correct choices = 1 point

Fewer than 4 correct choices = 0 points

**Five-answer chart**

5 correct choices = 3 points

4 correct choices = 2 points

3 correct choices = 1 point

Fewer than 3 correct choices = 0 points

Your raw score on Reading will range from 0 to 46 (Practice Test 1) or 45 (Practice Test 2). Use this chart to convert your raw score to your scaled Reading Section score.

LISTENING

| Reading | | | |
|---|---|---|---|
| Raw Section Score | Scaled Section Score | Raw Section Score | Scaled Section Score |
| 46 | 30 | 22 | 15 |
| 45 | 30 | 21 | 14 |
| 44 | 29 | 20 | 13 |
| 43 | 29 | 19 | 13 |
| 42 | 28 | 18 | 12 |
| 41 | 27 | 17 | 11 |
| 40 | 27 | 16 | 11 |
| 39 | 26 | 15 | 10 |
| 38 | 25 | 14 | 9 |
| 37 | 25 | 13 | 9 |
| 36 | 24 | 12 | 8 |
| 35 | 23 | 11 | 7 |
| 34 | 23 | 10 | 7 |
| 33 | 22 | 9 | 6 |
| 32 | 21 | 8 | 5 |
| 31 | 21 | 7 | 5 |
| 30 | 20 | 6 | 4 |
| 29 | 19 | 5 | 3 |
| 28 | 19 | 4 | 3 |
| 27 | 18 | 3 | 2 |
| 26 | 17 | 2 | 1 |
| 25 | 17 | 1 | 1 |
| 24 | 16 | 0 | 0 |
| 23 | 15 | | |

### Listening

You must also determine your raw score (number of correct answers) for the Listening Section in order to calculate your scaled Section score. In the Listening Section, all items are worth one point apiece, including two-answer questions, ordering questions, matching questions, and complete-the-chart questions.

Your raw score on the Listening Section will range from 0 to 34. Use the following chart to convert your raw score to your scaled Listening Section score.

| **Listening** | | | |
|---|---|---|---|
| Raw Section Score | Scaled Section Score | Raw Section Score | Scaled Section Score |
| 34 | 30 | 16 | 14 |
| 33 | 30 | 15 | 13 |
| 32 | 29 | 14 | 12 |
| 31 | 28 | 13 | 11 |
| 30 | 27 | 12 | 10 |
| 29 | 26 | 11 | 10 |
| 28 | 25 | 10 | 9 |
| 27 | 24 | 9 | 8 |
| 26 | 23 | 8 | 7 |
| 25 | 22 | 7 | 6 |
| 24 | 21 | 6 | 5 |
| 23 | 20 | 5 | 4 |
| 22 | 20 | 4 | 3 |
| 21 | 19 | 3 | 2 |
| 20 | 18 | 2 | 1 |
| 19 | 17 | 1 | 0 |
| 18 | 16 | 0 | 0 |
| 17 | 15 | | |

LISTENING

## *Speaking*

For the Speaking Section, you (or your instructor, or your classmates) will need to estimate your score on each of the six speaking tasks. The range of scores is from 0 to 4 per task (0 to 24 for the Section). To get your raw score for Speaking, add the six scores. Then use the following chart to calculate your scaled Speaking Section score.

| Speaking | | | |
|---|---|---|---|
| *Raw Section Score* | *Scaled Section Score* | *Raw Section Score* | *Scaled Section Score* |
| 24 | 30 | 12 | 15 |
| 23 | 29 | 11 | 14 |
| 22 | 28 | 10 | 13 |
| 21 | 27 | 9 | 12 |
| 20 | 25 | 8 | 10 |
| 19 | 24 | 7 | 9 |
| 18 | 23 | 6 | 8 |
| 17 | 22 | 5 | 7 |
| 16 | 20 | 4 | 5 |
| 15 | 19 | 3 | 4 |
| 14 | 18 | 1 | 3 |
| 13 | 17 | 0 | 0 |

### Writing

As in the Speaking Section, you must estimate your scores in the Writing Section (or your instructor or classmates can estimate them for you). Each of the two responses is worth 5 points, so the range of raw scores for the Writing Section is 0 to 10. To get your raw score, you simply add your two scores on the responses. Then use this chart to calculate your scaled Writing Section score.

| Writing | | | |
|---|---|---|---|
| Raw Section Score | Scaled Section Score | Raw Section Score | Scaled Section Score |
| 10 | 30 | 4 | 13 |
| 9 | 28 | 3 | 11 |
| 8 | 25 | 2 | 8 |
| 7 | 22 | 1 | 4 |
| 6 | 18 | 0 | 0 |
| 5 | 15 | | |

To calculate your total score on the Practice Test, just add the four scaled Section scores.

### Example

Let's say that your raw score on the Reading Section is 38. Your scaled score (from the chart) is 25.

Your raw score on the Listening Section is 26. Your scaled score for Listening is 23.

Your estimated scores on the six Speaking tasks are 3-4-2-2-3-3, for a raw score of 17. Using the chart, convert that to a scaled score of 22.

Your estimated scores on the two Writing tasks are 4 and 4, for a raw score of 8. Your scaled score is 25.

| | |
|---|---|
| Reading Score | 25 |
| Listening Score | 23 |
| Speaking Score | 22 |
| Writing Score | 25 |
| **Total Score** | **95** |

LISTENING

### *Personal Score Record*

Record your scores on the two Practice Listening Tests below. Use the spaces provided to record scores from other practice tests taken, if applicable.

**Practice Test 1**

Reading Score     _____

Listening Score     _____

Speaking Score     _____

Writing Score     _____

Total Score     _____

**Practice Test 2**

Reading Score     _____

Listening Score     _____

Speaking Score     _____

Writing Score     _____

Total Score     _____

To compare your score with equivalent scores on the computer-based test or the paper test, see the chart in Getting Started: Questions and Answers (pp. xiii–xiv).

# PRACTICE LISTENING TEST 1

## LISTENING SECTION
### DIRECTIONS

▶ Now start the Audio Program. 🎧

This section tests your understanding of conversations and lectures. You will hear each conversation or lecture only once. Your answers should be based on what is stated or implied in the conversations and lectures.

You are allowed to take notes as you listen, and you can use these notes to help you answer the questions.

In some questions, you will see a headphones icon: 🎧. This icon tells you that you will hear, but not read, part of the lecture again. Then you will answer a question about the part of the lecture that you heard.

Some questions have special directions that are highlighted.

During an actual listening test, you will *not* be able to skip items and come back to them later, so try to answer every question that you hear on this practice test.

This test includes two conversations and four lectures. Most questions are separated by a ten-second pause.

▶ Listen to a conversation between a professor and a student. 🎧

**Notes:**

_____

_____

_____

> **Now get ready to answer some questions about the conversation. You may use your notes to help you.**

1 of 34   Why is Ted unable to meet with Professor Jacobs after class?

⃝ He wants to go to a poetry reading.
⃝ He has to attend a meeting.
⃝ He has another class.
⃝ He has to check his e-mail.

▶ Listen again to part of the conversation. Then answer the question.

2 of 34   What does Ted mean when he says this? 🎧

⃝ He is expressing surprise.
⃝ He's showing a lack of interest.
⃝ He's not sure what he is being asked to do.
⃝ He's confused and upset.

3 of 34   What is Ted most interested in reading aloud next Friday?

⃝ Part of a novel
⃝ A newspaper article
⃝ A collection of poems
⃝ A nonfiction guide to fishing

4 of 34   Which of the following can be inferred about Professor Jacobs?

⃝ He likes some of Ted's poems, but not the poem "Northern Lights."
⃝ He doesn't always express his feelings about his students' work in class.
⃝ He prefers teaching graduate students to teaching undergraduates.
⃝ He doesn't like poems in which the imagery is frightening.

5 of 34   Why does Professor Jacobs ask Ted to come to his office?

⃝ To discuss Ted's grade in the creative-writing class
⃝ To help Ted practice for the reading
⃝ To help Ted select some poems to read aloud
⃝ To give Ted a written invitation

▶ Listen to a conversation between a university administrator and a student. ⌒

**Notes:**

_____

_____

_____

> **Now get ready to answer some questions about the conversation. You may use your notes to help you.**

6 of 34     Why does Dana want a work-study position?

    ○ To pay for day-to-day expenses
    ○ To pay for her tuition
    ○ To pay back a bank loan
    ○ To pay for her room and board

7 of 34     What can be inferred about merit-based work-study jobs?

    ○ They are given only to students who receive financial aid.
    ○ They are not arranged by Ms. Fong's office.
    ○ They involve less pay than need-based work-study jobs.
    ○ They are not funded by the government.

8 of 34     Which of these work-study positions does Dana express the most enthusiasm for?

    ○ Cafeteria worker
    ○ Receptionist
    ○ Lab technician
    ○ Museum tour guide

9 of 34     What must Dana do first to apply for the position that she is interested in?

    ○ Arrange an interview with Dr. Ferrara
    ○ Mail an application to the museum
    ○ Fill out some forms
    ○ Meet with Ms. Fong in person

10 of 34    Why does Ms. Fong say this? ⌒

    ○ To encourage Dana to pursue the job.
    ○ To offer Dana an alternative job.
    ○ To suggest reasons for not taking the position.
    ○ To encourage Dana not to work.

▶ Listen to a lecture in an anthropology class. 🎧

## ANTHROPOLOGY

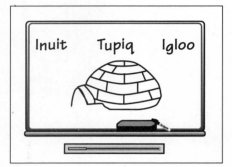

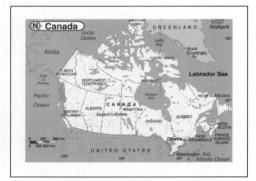

**Notes:**

_____

_____

_____

> **Now get ready to answer some questions about the lecture. You may use your notes to help you.**

11 of 34  The professor mentions three types of winter houses used by the Inuit. Match these three types of houses with the locations where they were used.

A. Snow houses
B. Houses made of driftwood
C. Houses made of stone, earth, and whalebone

**Place the letters of the choices in the proper boxes.**

| Northern Alaska | North Central Canada and Greenland | Labrador (Northeastern Canada) |
|---|---|---|
|  |  |  |

▶ Listen again to part of the lecture. Then answer the question.

12 of 34  Why does the professor say this? 🎧

○ To review part of a lecture he gave earlier
○ To give additional information about one group of Inuit
○ To explain why the Inuit in Greenland were isolated
○ To indicate where Thule is located

13 of 34    What can be inferred about the word *igloo*?

○ Inuit might use this word to talk about a summer house.
○ It is no longer used at all by the Inuit.
○ In Inuit, it refers only to houses made from snow.
○ It was used only in one small part of the Canadian Arctic.

14 of 34    In this lecture, the professor describes the process the Inuit used to build a simple igloo. Indicate whether each of the following is a step in the igloo-building process.

Put a check mark (✓) in the proper box for each phrase.

|  | Yes | No |
|---|---|---|
| Build a framework to support the igloo from inside |  |  |
| Cut blocks of hardened snow with a knife |  |  |
| Dig an entrance tunnel |  |  |
| Stand on top of the igloo in order to compress the snow and make it stronger |  |  |
| Melt snow on the interior surface of the igloo with lamps and then let the water refreeze |  |  |

15 of 34    The professor did NOT mention that larger igloos were used in which of these ways?

Choose two answers.

☐ As a place to dance
☐ As a home for five or more families
☐ As a place to hold wrestling matches
☐ As a location for singing contests
☐ As a storage space for food

16 of 34    According to the professor, what did the Inuit do in the early 1950s?

○ They completely stopped building snow houses.
○ They began making an entirely different type of snow house.
○ They began connecting clusters of igloos with tunnels.
○ They stopped using snow houses except as temporary shelters.

PRACTICE
TEST 1

▶ Listen to a discussion in an astrophysics class. 🎧

## ASTROPHYSICS

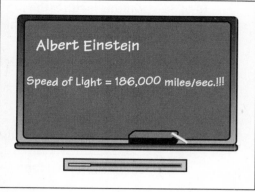

Albert Einstein

Speed of Light = 186,000 miles/sec.!!!

**Notes:**

_____

_____

_____

> **Now get ready to answer some questions about the discussion. You may use your notes to help you.**

17 of 34   What is Professor Fuller's opinion of Albert Einstein?

○ She feels he was mistaken about some key points.
○ She believes he predicted travel to other stars.
○ She thinks that his theories are no longer completely valid.
○ She agrees with him about traveling faster than light.

18 of 34   What powers the "sails" on the ship that the class discusses?

○ Laser light
○ Nuclear reactions
○ Sunlight
○ Wind

19 of 34   According to Professor Fuller, what must be developed before ships can travel to the stars?

○ A deeper understanding of Einstein's theories
○ New materials from which to build spaceships
○ A new means of powering spaceships
○ Another method of calculating the speed of light

20 of 34     Professor Fuller discusses the process by which a new technology evolves. Summarize this discussion by putting these four steps in the proper order.

A. **Technology phase**
B. **Application phase**
C. **Speculation phase**
D. **Science phase**

Put the letters of the stages in the proper boxes.

1. 
2. 
3. 
4. 

21 of 34     What does Professor Fuller say about the planets that have so far been discovered around other stars?

Choose two answers.

☐ Most of them are gas giants.
☐ Some of them are similar to the earth.
☐ Many of them may be inhabited.
☐ A few of them are very close to their stars.

▶  Listen again to part of the discussion. Then answer the question. 🎧

22 of 34     What does Professor Fuller imply about travel to other stars when she says this? 🎧

○ It is strongly inadvisable.
○ It is unlikely in the foreseeable future.
○ It may begin sooner than people realize.
○ It is a complete impossibility.

► Listen to a lecture in an art class. 🎧

## ART

**Notes:**

_____

_____

_____

**Now get ready to answer some questions about the lecture. You may use your notes to help you.**

23 of 34    What does the professor say about Minimalism and Conceptualism?

**Choose two answers.**

☐ They were the dominant schools of art when Photorealism began.
☐ They were very similar in their philosophy and style to Photorealism.
☐ They were abstract schools of art.
☐ They had been influenced by both the Dutch Masters and the *trompe l'oeil* school.

24 of 34    Which of the following did Audrey Flack NOT use when painting *The Farb Family Portrait*?

○ An airbrush
○ A computer
○ A slide projector
○ Acrylic paints

25 of 34   How does the professor explain the subjects that Photorealists painted?

Choose two answers.

- ☐ She quotes two Photorealistic painters on their choice of subjects.
- ☐ She gives specific examples of subjects that Photorealists have painted.
- ☐ She tells her students to read a paper about the topic of Photorealistic paintings.
- ☐ She compares the subjects of Photorealistic paintings to those of famous photographs.

26 of 34   Which of the following would Richard Estes most likely choose to paint?

- ◯ A farmhouse and open fields
- ◯ A woman examining her reflection in a mirror
- ◯ A telephone booth reflected in a large store window
- ◯ A broken window

27 of 34   According to the professor, why are the sculptures of Duane Hanson so remarkable?

- ◯ They are very valuable.
- ◯ They are quite large.
- ◯ They are easy to create.
- ◯ They are extremely lifelike.

28 of 34   In this lecture, the professor gives a number of characteristics of the Photorealistic school of painting. Indicate whether each of the following is a typical characteristic of paintings of that school of art.

Put a check mark (✓) in the proper box for each phrase.

|  | Yes | No |
|---|---|---|
| They feature three-dimensional optical illusions. |  |  |
| Their subjects are ordinary people and scenes. |  |  |
| They are often painted in bright colors. |  |  |
| They may be either representational or non-representational. |  |  |
| They show great attention to detail. |  |  |

▶ Listen to a discussion in a meteorology class. ⌒

**METEOROLOGY**

hail

cumulonimbus clouds

**Notes:**

_____

_____

_____

**Now get ready to answer some questions about the discussion. You may use your notes to help you.**

29 of 34   According to the professor, which of the following are most often damaged by hail?

**Choose two answers.**

☐ Rides at amusement parks
☐ Cars and other vehicles
☐ Farmers' crops
☐ Buildings

30 of 34   According to the professor, which of these methods of preventing damage from hail was used most recently?

○ Banging on pots and pans
○ Dancing
○ Shooting hail cannons
○ Ringing bells

▶ Listen again to part of the discussion. Then answer the question.

31 of 34   What does the professor mean when he says this? ⌒

○ He doesn't understand the student's question and wants her to clarify it.
○ He's unsure, but doesn't think it happens often.
○ He doesn't think there is any way to know the answer.
○ He doesn't think the question makes sense.

32 of 34    Why does the professor compare a hailstone to an onion?

     ○ Because of its size
     ○ Because of its structure
     ○ Because of its color
     ○ Because of its weight

33 of 34    At what time of year are hailstorms most common?

     ○ In the spring
     ○ In the summer
     ○ In the fall
     ○ In the winter

34 of 34    In this lecture, the professor describes the process by which hail is formed. Indicate whether each of the following is a step in that process.

Put a check mark (✓) in the proper box for each phrase.

| | Yes | No |
|---|---|---|
| Hailstones become so heavy that they fall to the ground. | | |
| Water droplets are lifted into the cold region of a thundercloud and freeze. | | |
| Tornado clouds circulate ice crystals inside of thunderclouds. | | |
| Droplets are lifted into the cloud again and again, adding more ice. | | |
| A mass of fast-moving warm air hits a slower-moving mass of cold air. | | |

*This is the end of the Practice Listening Test 1.*

# PRACTICE LISTENING TEST 2

▶ Now start the Audio Program. 🎧

This section tests your understanding of conversations and lectures. You will hear each conversation or lecture only once. Your answers should be based on what is stated or implied in the conversations and lectures.

You are allowed to take notes as you listen, and you can use these notes to help you answer the questions.

In some questions, you will see a headphones icon: 🎧. This icon tells you that you will hear, but not read, part of the lecture again. Then you will answer a question about the part of the lecture that you heard.

Some questions have special directions that are highlighted.

During an actual listening test, you will *not* be able to skip items and come back to them later, so try to answer every question that you hear on this practice test.

This test includes two conversations and four lectures. Most questions are separated by a ten-second pause.

▶ Listen to a conversation between two students. 🎧

**Notes:**

_____

_____

_____

> **Now get ready to answer some questions about the conversation. You may use your notes to help you.**

1 of 34    Why can't Allen vote for Janet?

     ○ Because he is no longer attending the university
     ○ Because she has decided to drop out of the election
     ○ Because they do not attend the same school at the university
     ○ Because she is running for president, not for the Student Council

2 of 34    How many candidates for office is each student allowed to vote for in this election?

     ○ One
     ○ Two
     ○ Three
     ○ Eleven

3 of 34    What is learned about Janet from this conversation?
                        Choose two answers.

     ☐ She is currently a member of the Student Council.
     ☐ She doesn't believe that she has a chance of getting elected.
     ☐ She doesn't think that the president should be directly elected.
     ☐ She may run for Student Council president next year.

4 of 34    According to Janet, what is the most important responsibility of the Student Council?

     ○ To determine how to spend student fees
     ○ To decide when and where to hold concerts
     ○ To attend meetings of the Board of Trustees
     ○ To change the student government charter

   ▶ Listen again to part of the conversation. 🎧

5 of 34    What does Allen imply when he says this? 🎧

     ○ He'll be too busy to vote tomorrow.
     ○ He won't attend tonight's debate.
     ○ He's already decided whom to vote for.
     ○ He hopes the woman gets elected.

▶ Listen to a conversation between two students. 🎧

**Notes:**

_____

_____

_____

> **Now get ready to answer some questions about the conversation. You may use your notes to help you.**

6 of 34　What subject does Professor Marquez probably teach?

- ○ Chemistry
- ○ Filmmaking
- ○ Drama
- ○ Marketing

7 of 34　What will Professor Marquez give the man if he comes to her class the next day?

- ○ Information about what role he will play
- ○ Several types of ice cream
- ○ A list of questions about the product
- ○ Money to pay him for his time

8 of 34　What does the woman imply about focus groups that test Hollywood films?

- ○ They are mainly exploratory focus groups.
- ○ They are used to help select directors for films.
- ○ They are mainly experiential focus groups.
- ○ They are usually used before work on films has begun.

9 of 34　What will Professor Marquez probably pay most attention to during the focus-group activity?

- ○ The knowledge that the moderators have about the product
- ○ The types of ice cream that are used
- ○ The opinions that the volunteers express
- ○ The interaction between focus groups and moderators

▶ Listen again to part of the conversation. 🎧

10 of 34　What does Tony imply when he says this? 🎧

- ○ He wants to take part in the focus-group activity, but he can't.
- ○ He likes mint chocolate-chip ice cream.
- ○ He's already formed his opinion about the product.
- ○ He would like to become a moderator of the focus group.

▶ Listen to a lecture in an American literature class. 🎧

## AMERICAN LITERATURE

**Notes:**

_____

_____

_____

> **Now get ready to answer some questions about the lecture. You may use your notes to help you.**

**11 of 34** Where did Harriet Stowe live when she wrote *Uncle Tom's Cabin?*

○ Cincinnati, Ohio
○ Kentucky
○ Brunswick, Maine
○ Connecticut

**12 of 34** The professor mentions a number of versions of *Uncle Tom's Cabin*. List these in the order in which they were produced, beginning with the earliest.

**A.** The book
**B.** The movie
**C.** The newspaper serial
**D.** The plays

Put the letters of the versions in the proper boxes.

| | |
|---|---|
| 1. | |
| 2. | |
| 3. | |
| 4. | |

13 of 34    Why does the professor mention Charles Dickens?

○ He wrote a book on the same topic as that of Stowe's book.
○ Like Stowe, he wrote about some characters in a sentimental way.
○ His novel *The Old Curiosity Shop* strongly influenced Stowe's writing.
○ He strongly criticized Stowe's novel *Uncle Tom's Cabin*.

14 of 34    What does the professor say about the scene in which Eliza is chased across the icy river by men with dogs?

Choose two answers.

☐ It is considered the most frightening part of the book.
☐ It is one of the scenes that people remember best.
☐ It is a part of the book but not of the play.
☐ It does not appear in the book *Uncle Tom's Cabin*.

15 of 34    In this lecture, the professor mentions a number of criticisms of Harriet Beecher Stowe's novel *Uncle Tom's Cabin*. Indicate whether each of the following is a criticism that was mentioned in the lecture.

Put a check mark (✓) in the proper box for each phrase.

|  | Yes | No |
|---|---|---|
| It is not strong enough in its criticism of slavery. |  |  |
| It treats its characters too sentimentally. |  |  |
| It is not based on the author's first-hand experiences. |  |  |
| It is difficult for modern readers to understand. |  |  |
| It is far too long and repetitive. |  |  |

▶    Listen again to part of the lecture. Then answer the question. 🎧

16 of 34    What does the professor suggest to the students when she says this? 🎧

○ They should read the book several times.
○ They must read the entire textbook.
○ They should read short selections from the novel.
○ They should read all of *Uncle Tom's Cabin*.

▶ Listen to a lecture in a geology class. 🎧

## GEOLOGY

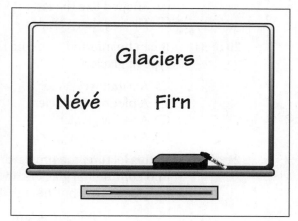

**Notes:**

_____

_____

_____

> **Now get ready to answer some questions about the lecture. You may use your notes to help you.**

17 of 34    The professor discusses four types of materials involved in the formation of a glacier.

Give the order in which these materials appear.

A. **Glacial ice**
B. **Névé**
C. **Firn**
D. **Ordinary snow**

> Put the letters of the materials in the proper boxes.

1. _____
2. _____
3. _____
4. _____

18 of 34    Where can continental glaciers be found today?

> Choose two answers.

☐ West Virginia
☐ Iceland
☐ Greenland
☐ Antarctica

19 of 34    Which of the following describe a valley formed by a valley glacier?

Choose two answers.

☐ Shaped like the letter V
☐ Gently curving
☐ Shaped like the letter U
☐ Having sharp angles

20 of 34    It can be inferred from the lecture that which of the following is the smallest type of glacier?

○ A tributary glacier
○ A piedmont glacier
○ A valley glacier
○ A continental glacier

21 of 34    In this lecture, the professor gives a number of characteristics of valley glaciers and continental glaciers. Indicate whether each characteristic is typical of valley glaciers or continental glaciers.

Put a check mark (✓) in the proper box for each phrase.

| | Valley Glaciers | Continental Glaciers |
|---|---|---|
| Today cover about 10% of the world's landmass | | |
| Flow together to form piedmont glaciers | | |
| As they recede, seem to flow uphill | | |
| About 11,000 years ago, covered 30% of the world's landmass | | |
| As they grow, seem to flow outwards in all directions | | |

22 of 34    What danger does the professor mention?

○ The water from melting glaciers may cause sea levels to rise.
○ Melted ice from glaciers may cause the water in the oceans to cool off.
○ Global warming may cause damaging storms in the Indian Ocean.
○ Glaciers may form in places such as Africa where there are no glaciers today.

▶ Listen to a discussion in an economics class. 🎧

## ECONOMICS

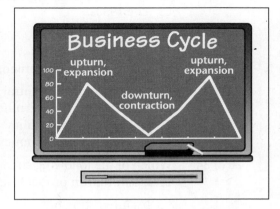

**Notes:**

_____

_____

_____

> **Now get ready to answer some questions about the discussion. You may use your notes to help you.**

23 of 34   What is the main topic of this discussion?

○ The causes of the Great Depression
○ The effects of climate on business cycles
○ The stages of the business cycle
○ Government regulation of business

24 of 34   What does Professor Martin imply when he says this? 🎧

○ These terms are still used but are no longer common.
○ Other terms were more common in the past.
○ These are the correct terms, but they are not very descriptive.
○ He himself prefers to use other terms for the four stages.

25 of 34   In this lecture, the professor describes the business cycle. Indicate whether each of the following is a characteristic of the cycle mentioned by the professor.

Put a check mark (✓) in the proper box for each phrase.

|  | Yes | No |
|---|---|---|
| They vary in length from cycle to cycle. |  |  |
| They are measured from the peak of economic activity to the trough, the lowest point of economic activity. |  |  |
| They vary in intensity from cycle to cycle. |  |  |
| They have involved deeper recessions in recent years because of globalization. |  |  |
| They are sometimes called *fluctuations* because they are irregular. |  |  |

26 of 34    In which of these decades did economic depressions occur?

Choose two answers.

☐ The 1870s
☐ The 1930s
☐ The 1970s
☐ The 1990s

27 of 34    In what ways do governments usually try to affect business cycles?

◯ By reforming the central bank
◯ By hiring more government employees
◯ By spending less money
◯ By controlling the money supply

28 of 34    Which of the following statements about William Jevons's theory would Professor Martin probably agree with?

◯ It's interesting but no longer generally accepted.
◯ It may be valid, but there were never any statistics to support it.
◯ As time has gone by, more and more economists have accepted it.
◯ It was valid when it was first proposed but not today.

▶ Listen to a lecture in a film studies class. 🎧

## FILM STUDIES

Science Fiction Films
(Sci Fi)

Jules Verne    Metropolis
George Méliès   Them!
Sigmund Freud   Forbidden Planet
         Star Wars

**Notes:**

_____

_____

_____

> **Now get ready to answer some questions about the lecture. You may use your notes to help you.**

29 of 34    Why does the professor mention the work of the French director Georges Méliès?

○ To point out that one of the earliest movies was a science fiction movie
○ To give an example of a realistic science fiction movie
○ To discuss the very first use of special effects in any movie ever made
○ To compare the role of a magician with that of a film director

30 of 34    When does the action in the movie *Metropolis* supposedly take place?

○ In 1902
○ In 1926
○ In 1984
○ In 2026

31 of 34    What topic does the movie *Them!* and many other 1950s science-fiction movies deal with?

○ An invasion from outer space
○ An attack by robots
○ The effects of radiation on insects
○ A nuclear war

32 of 34    Which of the following influenced the movie *Forbidden Planet*?
Choose two answers.

☐ The theories of Sigmund Freud
☐ A novel by the French author Jules Verne
☐ A play by William Shakespeare
☐ Movies about the American West

33 of 34    What does the professor think is remarkable about the movie *ET*?

○ That it's considered the most popular science fiction of all time
○ That it features a friendly alien rather than a hostile one
○ That it was popular with audiences but not with critics
○ That it is so similar to other movies about visitors from space

34 of 34    What does the professor imply when she says this? 🎧

○ She prefers recent movies to older movies such as *Forbidden Planet*.
○ She would like to be able to show more of the film *Forbidden Planet*.
○ She doesn't really want to show scenes from any 1950s movies.
○ She doesn't have time to show scenes from her favorite movie today.

**This is the end of Practice Listening Test 2.**

# AUDIO SCRIPTS AND ANSWER KEY

## The Complete Guide to the
## TOEFL® Test: LISTENING, iBT Edition—
## MP3 Tracking List

**MP3**
**Guide to Listening**
01 Track: Announcement
02 Track: Listening Preview Test
03 Track: Lesson 1
04 Track: Lesson 1, Exercise 1.1
05 Track: Lesson 1, Exercise 1.2
06 Track: Lesson 2, Sample Item 1
07 Track: Lesson 2, Sample Item 2
08 Track: Lesson 2, Sample Item 3
09 Track: Lesson 2, Sample Item 4
10 Track: Lesson 2, Exercise 2.1
11 Track: Lesson 2, Exercise 2.2
12 Track: Lesson 3, Sample Item 1
13 Track: Lesson 3, Sample Item 2
14 Track: Lesson 3, Sample Item 3
15 Track: Lesson 3, Exercise 3.1
16 Track: Lesson 3, Exercise 3.2
17 Track: Lesson 4
18 Track: Lesson 4, Sample Item
19 Track: Lesson 4, Exercise 4.1
20 Track: Lesson 4, Exercise 4.2
21 Track: Lesson 4, Exercise 4.3
22 Track: Lesson 5, Sample Item 1
23 Track: Lesson 5, Sample Item 2
24 Track: Lesson 5, Exercise 5.1
25 Track: Lesson 6, Sample Item
26 Track: Lesson 6, Exercise 6.1
27 Track: Listening Review Test
28 Track: Note-taking, Exercise 1
29 Track: Note-taking, Exercise 3
30 Track: Note-taking, Exercise 5
31 Track: Note-taking, Exercise 6

**Practice Test 1**
32 Track: Listening Section

**Practice Test 2**
33 Track: Listening Section

# CONTENTS

# AUDIO SCRIPTS

## MP3

[Track 1]

**Narrator:** Welcome to the Audio Program for *The Complete Guide to the TOEFL Test: Listening iBT Edition,* by Bruce Rogers.

[Track 2]

## Guide to Listening

### Preview Test
Listen as the directions are read to you.

**Narrator:** Directions: This section tests your understanding of conversations and lectures. You will hear each conversation or lecture only once. Your answers should be based on what is stated or implied in the conversations and lectures. You are allowed to take notes as you listen, and you can use these notes to help you answer the questions. In some questions, you will see a headphones icon. This icon tells you that you will hear, but not read, part of the lecture again. Then you will answer a question about the part of the lecture that you heard. Some questions have special directions that are highlighted. During an actual test, you may not skip questions and come back to them later, so try to answer every question that you hear on this test. On an actual test, there are two conversations and four lectures. You will have twenty minutes (not counting the time spent listening) in which to complete this section of the test. On this Preview Test, there is one conversation and three lectures. Most questions are separated by a ten-second pause.

**Narrator:** Listen to a conversation between a student and a professor.

**Student:** Professor Dixon? I'm Brenda Pierce. From your Geology 210 class . . . ?

**Professor:** Yes. I know. That's a big class, but I do recognize you. As a matter of fact, I noticed you weren't in class yesterday morning. Did you oversleep? That's one of the problems with an 8:00 class. I almost overslept myself a couple of times.

**Student:** Oh, uh, no, I didn't oversleep. In fact, I was up at 5:00—one of my roommates had an early flight and I took her to the airport. I thought I'd make it back here in time, but, uh, well, you know . . . you know how traffic can be out on Airport Road at that time of day. Anyway, uh, I know you were going to tell us . . . give us some information about our research paper in class today. Do you have a few minutes to fill me in?

**Professor:** Well, umm, a few minutes, I guess. This isn't my regular office hour. I actually just came by my office to pick up a few papers before the faculty meeting.

**Student:** Okay, well . . . about the research paper . . . how long does it have to be?

**Professor:** Well, as I told the class, the paper counts for 30% of your grade. It should be at least twelve pages, but no more than twenty-five. And your bibliography should contain at least ten reference sources.

**Student:** Will you be assigning the topic, or . . .

**Professor:** I'm leaving the choice of topic up to you. Of course,

it should be related to something we've discussed in class.

**Student:** I, I'm interested in writing about earthquakes . . .

**Professor:** Hmm. Earthquakes . . . well, I don't know, Brenda . . . that sounds like much too broad a topic for a short research paper.

**Student:** Oh, well, I'm planning to choose . . . I plan to get more specific than that. I want to write about using animals to predict earthquakes.

**Professor:** Really? Well, once scientists wondered if maybe. . . if perhaps there was some connection between strange behavior in animals and earthquakes . . . and that maybe animals . . . that you could use them to predict earthquakes. But there have been a lot of studies on this subject, you know, and so far, none of them have shown anything promising . . .

**Student:** But I thought there was this . . . I saw this show on television about earthquakes, and it said that in, uh, China, I think it was, they did predict an earthquake because of the way animals were acting.

**Professor:** Oh, right—you're thinking of the Haecheng earthquake about thirty years ago. Well, that's true. There were snakes coming out of the ground in the middle of winter when they should have been hibernating . . . and supposedly horses and other animals were acting frightened. And there were other signs, too, not just from animals. So the government ordered an evacuation of the area, and in fact, there was an earthquake, so thousands of lives were probably saved.

**Student:** Yeah, that's what I'm thinking of . . . that's what I saw on television.

**Professor:** The problem is that, unfortunately, no one's been able to duplicate that kind of result . . . in China or anywhere else. There have been lots of earthquakes since then that haven't been predicted, and there have been a couple of false alarms when cities were evacuated for no reason . . . and like I said, none of the studies that have been done have shown that animals are any better at predicting earthquakes than people are.

**Student:** So that's . . . so you don't think that's a very good idea for a topic, then, I suppose . . .

**Professor:** I didn't say that . . . just because this theory hasn't been proven doesn't mean you couldn't write a perfectly good paper about this topic . . . on the notion that animals can predict earthquakes. Why not? It could be pretty interesting. But to do a good job, you . . . you'll need to look at some serious studies in the scientific journals, not just some pop-science articles in newspapers, or . . . and you can't get your information from television shows.

**Student:** You really think it might make a good paper? Well, then, I think if I can get enough information from the library or the Internet . . .

**Professor:** Okay, why don't you see what you can find? Oh, I forgot to mention . . . you'll need to write up a formal proposal for your paper, and work up a preliminary bibliography, and hand it in to me a week from tomorrow. I'll need to approve it before you get started. Now, if you'll excuse me, Brenda, I've got to get to that faculty meeting.

**Narrator:** Now get ready to answer the questions. You may use your notes to help you.

**Narrator:** Question 1: What is this conversation mainly about?

**Narrator:** Question 2: Listen again to part of the conversation. Then answer the question.

**Student:** Professor Dixon? I'm Brenda Pierce. From your Geology 210 class . . . ?

**Narrator:** What can be inferred about the student?

**Narrator:** Question 3: What assumption does the professor make about the student?

**Narrator:** Question 4: How did the student first get information about the topic she wants to write about?

**Narrator:** Question 5: What is the professor's attitude toward the topic that the student wants to write about?

**Narrator:** Now listen to a lecture in a biology class.

**Professor:** Okay, everyone . . . if you remember, on Wednesday we talked about the general concept of biomes. So, just to review, biomes are large zones, big sections of the planet that have similar conditions and have the same kinds of plants and animals. Last class, we talked about the tundra, remember? This is a strip of land in the far, far north. We said the tundra consists mainly of open, marshy planes with no trees, just some low shrubs.

So, okay, today, we're going to continue our tour of the world's biomes. The next biome you come to, as you head south from the tundra, is the taiga. That's spelled t-a-i-g-a, taiga. It's also called the "boreal forest." The taiga is the largest of all the world's biomes. About 25% of all the world's forests are found in the taiga.

Now, the word *taiga* means "marshy evergreen forest." It comes from the Russian language, and that's not too surprising, really, because there are huge, I mean, really enormous stretches of taiga in Russia. But taiga isn't just found in Russia. Like the tundra, the taiga is a more-or-less continuous belt that circles the North Pole, running through Russia, Scandinavia, Canada, Alaska. Most of this land was—well, it used to be covered by glaciers, and these glaciers left deep gouges and depressions in the land. And not surprisingly, these filled up with water—with melted snow—so you have lots of lakes and ponds and marshes in the taiga.

Within the taiga itself, you'll find three sub-zones. The first of these you come to, as you're going south, is called open forest. The only trees here are needle-leaf trees—you know, evergreen trees, what we call coniferous trees. These trees tend to be small and far apart. This is basically tundra—it looks like tundra, but with a few small trees. Next, you come to what's called closed forest, with bigger needle-leaf trees growing closer together. This feels more like a real forest. This sub-zone—well, if you like variety, you're not going to feel happy here. You can travel for miles and see only half a dozen species of trees. In a few days, we'll be talking about the tropical rain forest; now, that's where you'll see variety. Okay, finally, you come to the mixed zone. The trees are bigger still here, and you'll start seeing some broad-leafed trees, deciduous trees. You'll see larch, aspen, especially along rivers and creeks, in addition to needle-leaf trees. So this sub-zone feels a bit more like the temperate forests we're used to.

So, what are conditions like in the taiga? Well, to start with, you've gotta understand that it's cold there. I mean, very cold. Summers are short, winters long. So the organisms that call the taiga home have to be well adapted to cold. The trees in the taiga, as I already said, are coniferous trees like the pine, fir, and spruce. And these trees, they've adapted to cold weather. How? Well, for one thing, they never lose their leaves—they're "evergreen," right, always green, so in the spring, they don't have to waste time—don't have to waste energy—growing new leaves. They're ready to start photosynthesizing right away. And then, for another thing, these trees are conical—shaped like cones—aren't they? This means that snow doesn't accumulate too much on the branches; it just slides off, and so, well, that means their branches don't break under the weight of the snow. And even their color—that dark, dark green—it's useful because it absorbs the sun's heat.

What about the animals that live up there? You remember I said there were lots of marshes and lakes. These watery places make wonderful breeding grounds for insects. So naturally, in the summer, you get lots of insects. And insects attract birds, right? Plenty of birds migrate to the taiga in the summer to, uh, to feast on insects. Lots of the mammals that live in the taiga migrate to warmer climates once cold weather sets in. But there are some year-round residents. Among the predators—the animals that hunt other animals—there are Arctic foxes, wolves, bears, martens, oh, and ermines. There's one thing all these predators have in common, the ones that live there all year round . . . they all have thick, warm fur coats, don't they? This heavy fur keeps them toasty in the winter. Of course, on the downside, it makes them desirable to hunters and trappers. Some of these predators survive the winter by hibernating, by sleeping right through it . . . bears, for example. And some change colors. You've heard of the ermine, right? In the summer, the ermine is dark brown, but in the winter, it turns white. That makes it hard to spot, so it can sneak up on its prey.

Then, uh, what sorts of herbivores live up there? What do the predators eat to stay alive? There's the moose, of course, but only young moose are at risk of being attacked. The adult moose is the biggest, strongest animal found in the taiga, so a predator would have to be feeling pretty desperate to take on one of these. Mostly, predators hunt smaller prey, like snowshoe rabbits, voles, lemmings . . .

Okay, the next biome we come to is the temperate forest, where broadleaf trees like, oh, maples and oaks are most common, but before we get to this, I'd like to give you one opportunity to ask me some questions about the taiga.

**Narrator:** Now get ready to answer the questions. You may use your notes to help you.

**Narrator:** Question 6: What does the professor say about the word *taiga*?

**Narrator:** Question 7: Why does the speaker say this:

**Professor:** This sub-zone—well, if you like variety, you're not going to feel happy here. You can travel for miles and see only half a dozen species of trees. In a few days, we'll be talking about the tropical rain forest; now, *that's* where you'll see variety.

**Narrator:** Question 8: The professor discussed three sub-zones of the taiga. Match each sub-zone with its characteristic.

**Narrator:** Question 9: When discussing needle-leaf trees, which of these adaptations to cold weather does the professor mention?

**Narrator:** Question 10: What characteristic do all of the predators of the taiga have in common?

**Narrator:** Question 11: What does the professor imply about moose?

**Narrator:** Listen to a discussion in the first class of a business course.

**Professor:** Well, I guess everyone's here, huh? We may as well get started. Good morning, all. I'm Professor Robert Speed and I'd like you . . . I'd like to welcome you to the Foundations of Business class. The purpose of this class is really to acquaint you with the tools, the various tools, techniques you'll be using in most of your business courses. And we'll concentrate especially on the case study method, because you'll be using that in almost . . . well, in most of the business classes you take.

**Student A:** The . . . case study method, Professor? Is that a new method of teaching business?

**Professor:** Oh, no, no, no. I mean . . . it may seem new to you, but, no, in fact, a professor named Christopher Longdell introduced this system at Harvard University back . . . around the 1870's. And he always insisted that it was based on a system used by Chinese philosophers thousands of years ago.

**Student B:** So then, they've . . . it's been used in business schools ever since the . . . when did you say, the 1870's?

**Professor:** Well, you see, Professor Longdell, he . . . he in fact taught in the law school at Harvard, not in the business school. So the case method first . . . it was first used to train law students. Then, a couple of years after that, they started using it at Columbia University, at the law school there. It wasn't until . . . When was it? Uh, probably about 1910, 1912, something like that, that it was used . . . first used at Harvard Business School.

**Student B:** Then, it's used in other fields? Besides law and business?

**Professor:** Oh sure, over the years, it's been used in all sorts of disciplines. For example, my wife . . . she teaches over at the School of Education . . . she uses cases to train teachers.

**Student A:** Professor Speed, I get that case study has been around awhile, but I still don't quite understand why we're . . . well, why do we study cases, exactly?

**Professor:** Okay, before the case method was introduced, the study of law and business was very . . . abstract . . . theoretical. It was just, just lectures about theory. Professor Longdell thought—and a lot of educators think—that really, the best way to learn law, business, any discipline you can think of, is by studying actual situations and analyzing these situations . . . and learning to make decisions.

**Student A:** That makes sense, but . . . I mean, what does a case look like, exactly . . . I mean, what does it . . . ?

**Professor:** What does a case look like? Well, cases are basically descriptions of actual—let me stress that—of real business situations, chunks of reality from the business world. So, you get typically ten to twenty pages of text that describe the problem, some problem that a real business actually faced. And then there will be another five to ten pages of what are called exhibits.

**Student B:** Exhibits? What are those?

**Professor:** Exhibits . . . those are documents, statistical documents, that explain the situation. They might be oh, spreadsheets, sales reports, umm, marketing projections, anything like that. But as I said, at the center of every case, at the core of every case, is a problem that you have to solve. So, you have to analyze the situation, the data—and sometimes, you'll see you don't have enough data to work with, and you might have to collect more—say, from the Internet. Then, you have to make decisions about how to solve these problems.

**Student B:** So that's why we study cases? I mean, because managers need to be able to make decisions . . . and solve problems?

**Professor:** Exactly . . . well, that's a big part of it, anyway. And doing this, solving the problem, usually involves role-playing, taking on the roles of decision-makers at the firm. One member of the group might play the Chief Executive Officer, one the Chief Financial Officer, and so on. And you . . . you might have a business meeting to decide how your business should solve its problem. Your company might, say, be facing a cash shortage and thinking about selling off one division of the company. So your group has to decide if this is the best way to handle the problem.

**Student B:** So we work in groups, then?

**Professor:** Usually in groups of four or five. That's the beauty of this method. It teaches teamwork and cooperation.

**Student A:** And then what? How are we . . . how do you decide on a grade for us?

**Professor:** You give a presentation, an oral presentation, I mean, and you explain to the whole class what decision you made and . . . what recommendations you'd make . . . and then you write a report as well. You get a grade, a group grade, on the presentation and the report.

**Student B:** Professor, is this the only way we'll be studying business, by using cases?

**Professor:** Oh, no, it's just one important way. Some classes are lecture classes and some are a combination of lectures and case studies and some . . . in some classes you'll also use computer simulations. We have this software called World Marketplace, and using this program, your group starts up your own global corporation and tries to make a profit . . . it's actually a lot of fun.

**Narrator:** Now get ready to answer the questions. You may use your notes to help you.

**Narrator:** Question 12: Professor Speed mentions several stages in the history of the case method. Put these steps in the proper order.

**Narrator:** Question 13: What does Professor Speed say about exhibits?

**Narrator:** Question 14: What does the professor mean when he says this:

**Professor:** It wasn't until . . . when was it? Probably about 1910, 1912, something like that, that it was used . . . first used at Harvard Business School.

**Narrator:** Question 15: Why does Professor Speed mention his wife?

**Narrator:** Question 16: In this lecture, the professor describes the process of the case study method. Indicate whether each of the following is a step in the process.

**Narrator:** Question 17: Which of the following reasons does the professor give for using the case study method?

**Narrator:** Listen to a student giving a presentation in an astronomy class.

**Student Presenter:** Well, uh, hi, everyone . . . Monday, we heard Don tell us about the Sun, and, uh, Lisa talk about Mercury, the planet closest to the Sun. My . . . my, uh, report, what I'm talking about is the next planet, the second planet, Venus. Okay, to start off, I'm going to tell you what people, well, what they used to think about Venus. First off, back in the really . . . in the really ancient days, people thought Venus was a star, not a planet, and . . . well, actually, you know how you can see Venus in the early morning and in the evening? Well, so they thought it was *two* stars, Phosphorus—that was the morning star . . . and, uh, let's see, Hesperus, the evening star. And then, once they figured out it was just one planet, they named it Venus after the goddess of love—I don't really know why, though.

And then later, people started studying Venus through a telescope, and they found out it was covered by clouds. Not partly covered by clouds, like Earth, but completely wrapped up in clouds. And since it was closer to the Sun than Earth, people imagined it was warm there, like it is in the tropics. In the nineteenth century, there was this belief, a lot of people believed, for some reason, that there were these creatures on Venus who were superior to us, almost perfect beings, like angels or something. Then, uh, in the early part of the twentieth century, people imagined that, uh, under the clouds there were swamps and jungles and monsters. There was this guy, this author, um, Edgar Rice Burroughs, he also wrote the Tarzan books, and, uh, he wrote books in the 1930's about . . . well, the series was called "Carson of Venus," and it was about some explorer from Earth having wild adventures and fighting monsters in the jungles. This idea of a "warm" Venus lasted until the 1950's.

Okay, so . . . Venus is the brightest object in the sky, except for the Sun and the moon, and except for the moon it comes closer to the Earth than any other planet, a lot closer than Mars, the, uh, fourth planet. One of the articles I read about Venus said that Venus is Earth's sister . . . Earth's twin, I guess it said. That's because Venus is about the same size as Earth . . . and uh, it's made out of the same basic materials. And Earth and Venus are about the same age; they, uh, were formed about the same time.

But really, we know nowadays that Earth and Venus are not really much like twins. For one thing, the air, the atmosphere of Venus is made out of carbon dioxide and sulfuric acid—not very nice stuff to breathe. And it's really thick, the atmosphere is. It's so thick, it's like being at the bottom of an ocean on Earth, so if astronauts ever went there, they'd have to have a . . . something like a diving bell to keep from getting crushed. And they'd need really good air conditioning, too, because it's really hot down there, not warm the way people used to think. All those clouds hold in the Sun's heat, you see. It's hotter than an oven, hot enough to melt lead, too hot to have any liquid water. So, guess what that means—no jungles, no swamps, and no weird creatures!

Okay, now here's a really strange fact about Venus. It takes Venus only 225 Earth days to go around the Sun, as opposed to the Earth, which of course takes 365 days—what we call a year. But Venus turns around on its axis really slowly. Really slowly. It takes 243 Earth days to spin around completely. The Earth takes—you guessed it—24 hours. This means that a day on Venus is longer than a year on Venus! In fact, a day on Venus is longer than . . . well, than on any planet in the solar system, longer even than on those big gas planets like Jupiter. And here's something else weird. All the planets of the solar system turn on their axis in the same direction as they orbit the Sun. All except Venus, of course! It has what's called a . . . wait, let's see . . . okay, a "retrograde" spin.

Now, there have been quite a few space probes that have gone to Venus, so I'm only going to mention a few of them, the most important ones. I guess, umm, one of the most important was called Magellan. Magellan was launched in 1990 and spent four years in orbit around Venus. It used, uh, radar, I guess, to map the planet, and it found out that there are all these volcanoes on Venus, just like there are on Earth. The first one to go there, the first probe to go there successfully, was Mariner II in, uh, 1962. Mariner I was supposed to go there, but it blew up. There was one, it was launched by the Soviet Union back in the, uh, let's see . . . let me find it . . . hang on, no, here it is, Venera IV in 1967 . . . and it dropped instruments onto the surface. They only lasted a few seconds, because of the conditions, the heat and all, but this probe showed us how really hot it was. Then, there was one called Venus Pioneer II, in 1978. That was the one that found out that the atmosphere of Venus is made of carbon dioxide, mostly. And, uh, well, as I said . . . there were a lot of other ones too.

Well, that's pretty much it—that's about all I have to say about Venus, unless you have some questions.

**Professor:**  Charlie?

**Student Presenter:**  Yes, Professor?

**Professor:**  First, I just want to say . . . good job on your presentation, Charlie; it was very interesting, and then . . . well, I just want to add this. You said you weren't sure why the planet Venus was named after the goddess of love. It's true Venus was the goddess of love, but she was also the goddess of beauty and . . . well, anyone who's ever seen Venus early in the morning or in the evening knows it's a beautiful sight.

**Student Presenter:**  Okay, so, there you have it, everyone—a mystery solved. Thanks, Professor. Well, I don't have anything to add, so unless anyone has any questions . . . no? Well, Caroline will be giving the next report, which is about the third planet, and since we all live here, that should be pretty interesting.

**Narrator:**  Now get ready to answer the questions. You may use your notes to help you.

**Narrator:**  Question 18: How does the speaker introduce the topic of Venus?

**Narrator:**  Question 19: According to the speaker, which of the following were once common beliefs about Venus?

**Narrator:**  Question 20: In this presentation, the speaker discusses some similarities between Earth and Venus and some of the differences between the two planets. Indicate which of the following is a similarity and which is a difference.

**Narrator:**  Question 21: Which of the following is *not* true about the length of a day on Venus?

**Narrator:**  Question 22: In what order were these space probes sent to Venus?

**Narrator:**  Question 23: It can be inferred that the topic of the next student presentation will be about which of the following?

**Narrator:**  This is the end of the Listening Preview Test.

[Track 3]

## Lesson 1: Main-Topic and Main-Purpose Questions

### Sample Item

**Narrator:**  Listen to a conversation between a student and a professor.

**Student:**  Professor Dixon? I'm Brenda Pierce. From your Geology 210 class . . . ?

**Professor:**  Yes. I know. That's a big class, but I do recognize you. As a matter of fact, I noticed you weren't in class yesterday morning. Did you oversleep? That's one of the problems with an 8:00 class. I almost overslept myself a couple of times.

**Student:**  Oh, uh, no, I didn't oversleep. In fact, I was up at 5:00—one of my roommates had an early flight and I took her to the airport. I thought I'd make it back here in time, but, uh, well, you know . . . you know how traffic can be out on Airport Road at that time of day. Anyway, uh, I know you were going to tell us . . . give us some information about our research paper in class today. Do you have a few minutes to fill me in?

**Professor:**  Well, umm, a few minutes, I guess. This isn't my regular office hour. I actually just came by my office to pick up a few papers before the faculty meeting.

**Student:**  Okay, well . . . about the research paper . . . how long does it have to be?

**Professor:**  Well, as I told the class, the paper counts for 30% of your grade. It should be at least twelve pages . . . but no more than twenty-five. And your bibliography should contain at least ten reference sources.

**Student:** Will you be assigning the topic, or . . .

**Professor:** I'm leaving the choice of topic up to you. Of course, it should be related to something we've discussed in class.

**Student:** I, I'm interested in writing about earthquakes . . .

**Professor:** Hmm. Earthquakes . . . well, I don't know, Brenda . . . that sounds like much too broad a topic for a short research paper.

**Student:** Oh, well, I'm planning to choose . . . I plan to get more specific than that. I want to write about using animals to predict earthquakes.

**Professor:** Really? Well, once scientists wondered if maybe . . . if perhaps there was some connection between strange behavior in animals and earthquakes . . . and that maybe animals . . . that you could use them to predict earthquakes. But there have been a lot of studies on this subject, you know, and so far, none of them have shown anything promising . . .

**Student:** But I thought there was this . . . I saw this show on television about earthquakes, and it said that in, uh, China, I think it was, they did predict an earthquake because of the way animals were acting.

**Professor:** Oh, right, you're thinking of the Haecheng earthquake about thirty years ago. Well, that's true. There were snakes coming out of the ground in the middle of winter when they should have been hibernating . . . and supposedly horses and other animals were acting frightened. And there were other signs, too, not just from animals. So the government ordered an evacuation of the area, and in fact, there was an earthquake, so thousands of lives were probably saved.

**Student:** Yeah, that's what I'm thinking of . . . that's what I saw on television.

**Professor:** The problem is, that, unfortunately, no one's been able to duplicate that kind of result . . . in China or anywhere else. There have been lots of earthquakes since then that haven't been predicted, and there have been a couple of false alarms when cities were evacuated for no reason . . . and like I said, none of the studies that have been done have shown that animals are any better at predicting earthquakes than people are.

**Student:** So that's . . . so you don't think that's a very good idea for a topic, then, I suppose . . .

**Professor:** I didn't say that . . . just because this theory hasn't been proven doesn't mean you couldn't write a perfectly good paper about this topic . . . on the notion that animals can predict earthquakes. Why not? It could be pretty interesting. But to do a good job, you . . . you'll need to look at some serious studies in the scientific journals, not just some pop-science articles in newspapers or . . . and you can't get your information from television shows.

**Student:** You really think it might make a good paper? Well, then, I think if I can get enough information from the library or the Internet . . .

**Professor:** Okay, why don't you see what you can find? Oh, I forgot to mention . . . you'll need to write up a formal proposal for your paper, and work up a preliminary bibliography, and hand it in to me a week from tomorrow. I'll need to approve it before you get started. Now, if you'll excuse me, Brenda, I've got to get to that faculty meeting.

**Narrator:** Now get ready to answer the question. You may use your notes to help you.

**Narrator:** Question 1: What is this conversation mainly about?

[Track 4]

**Narrator:** For the Listening exercises in *The Complete Guide*, the directions will not be read aloud on the tape. Therefore, you must read the directions for each exercise and make sure you understand them before you start the Audio Program.

## Exercise 1.1

**Narrator:** Listen to a conversation between a student and a librarian.

**Student:** Hi, I'm in Professor Quinn's Political Science class. She, uh, in class today she said that she'd put a journal on reserve . . . We're supposed to read an article from that journal.

**Librarian:** Okay, well, you're in the right place. This is the reserve desk.

**Student:** Oh, good—I've never checked out reserve materials before. So what do I need? Do I need a library card, or . . . what do I have to do to . . .

**Librarian:** You have your student ID card with you, right?

**Student:** Umm, I think I do . . . I mean, I think it's in my backpack here . . .

**Librarian:** Okay, well, all you really need to do is leave your student ID here with me, sign this form and the journal is all yours—for—let me see—for two hours anyway.

**Student:** Two hours? That's all the time I get?

**Librarian:** Well, when instructors put materials on reserve, they set a time limit on how long you can use them . . . you know, just so all the students in your class can get a chance to read them.

**Student:** I don't know how long the article is, but . . . I guess I can finish it in two hours.

**Librarian:** And, one more thing, you, uh, you'll have to read the article in the library. You're not allowed to check reserve material out of the library, or to take it out of the building.

**Student:** Oh, well, then, . . . maybe I should, uh, maybe I should go back to my dorm and get some dinner . . . before I sit down and read this.

**Librarian:** That's fine, but . . . I can't guarantee the article will be available right away when you come back . . . some other student from your class might be using it.

**Student:** Well, I dunno, I . . . I guess I'll just have to take my chances . . .

**Narrator:** Now get ready to answer the question. You may use your notes to help you.

**Narrator:** Question 1: What is the main topic of this conversation?

**Narrator:** Listen to a conversation between two students.

**Student A:** Tina, hey, how are you?

**Student B:** Hi, Michael. Hey, how was your summer vacation?

**Student A:** Oh, not too bad—mostly I was working. How about you? I, uh, kinda remember you saying that . . . weren't you going to Europe? How was that?

**Student B:** Oh, that fell through. I was going to travel with my roommate, and she changed her mind about going, so . . . well, my parents own a furniture store, and so instead, I was going to work there. But then . . . well, you know Professor Grant?

**Student A:** Oh, uh, from the archaeology department? Sure . . . well, I've heard of her, anyway.

**Student B:** Well, I got a call from her just before the end of the spring semester. She was planning to do this dig in Mexico. So she calls me up and asks if I'd like to be a volunteer, and you know, I've always wanted . . . it's always been a dream of mine to be an archaeologist, so . . . I jumped at the chance.

**Student A:** So, uh, how was it . . . I mean, was it a good dig . . .

**Student B:** Do you mean, did we find any artifacts? No, it . . . it was supposed to be a very . . . promising site. But it turned out to be a complete bust! We didn't find anything . . . not even one single piece of broken pottery. Nothing! Just sand!

**Student A:** Wow, that must have been pretty disappointing.

**Student B:** No, not really. Oh, sure, I mean, I would've liked to have made some amazing discovery, but, well, I still learned a lot about, about archaeological techniques, you know, and I really enjoyed getting to know the people, the other people on the dig, and it . . . well, it was fun!

**Narrator:** Now get ready to answer the question. You may use your notes to help you.

**Narrator:** Question 2: What is the main subject of the speakers' conversation?

**Narrator:** Listen to a conversation between a student and an administrator.

**Administrator:** Yes? Come in.

**Student:** Umm, Ms. Kirchner?

**Administrator:** Yes?

**Student:** I'm, uh, Mark Covelli. I live over in Quincy House?

**Administrator:** Yes, so what can I do for you, Mark?

**Student:** The woman who's in charge of the cafeteria over at Quincy, I talked to her this morning, you see, and . . . well, she told me that I would have to talk to you . . .

**Administrator:** Okay, talk to me about . . . ?

**Student:** Okay, well, I'd like to . . . you see, back at the beginning of the semester, my parents signed me up for Meal Plan 1.You know, the plan where you get three meals a day . . .

**Administrator:** Okay . . .

**Student:** So, well, I've decided it's . . . it was kind of a waste of their money because . . . I mean, I almost never eat three meals there in a day. Three days a week I have early classes and I don't have time to eat breakfast at all, and even on days when I do eat breakfast there, I just have coffee and some yogurt so . . . well, I could do that in my room.

**Administrator:** So what you're saying is, you'd like to be on Meal Plan 2?

**Student:** Yeah, I guess . . . whatever you call the plan where you only eat two meals a day at the dorm . . .

**Administrator:** That's Plan 2. We usually don't make that kind of switch in the middle of a semester . . . you know, if I do approve this, we'd have to make the refund directly to your parents. And it could only be a partial refund . . . since you've been on Plan 1 for a month already.

**Student:** Oh sure, I understand that . . . I just, I just hate to waste my parents' money.

**Narrator:** Now get ready to answer the question. You may use your notes to help you.

**Narrator:** Question 3: Why does Mark Covelli want to speak to Ms. Kirchner?

**Narrator:** Now get ready to listen to a conversation between two students.

**Student A:** Hey, Larry, how are ya? What're ya up to this weekend?

**Student B:** Oh, my friends and I are going to be working on our car, the Sunflower II.

**Student A:** Wait . . . you have a car called . . . the Sunflower?

**Student B:** Yeah, the Sunflower II. Well, it's not a regular car. It's a solar-powered car.

**Student A:** Really? That's why you call it the Sunflower then. Oh, wait, are you entering it in that race next month . . . the . . .

**Student B:** The Solar Derby. Yeah. It's sponsored by the Engineering Department.

**Student A:** I read a little about that in the campus paper. I'm sorry, but the idea of racing solar cars . . . it just sounds a little . . . weird.

**Student B:** I guess, but there are lots of races for solar-powered cars. One of the most famous ones is in Australia. They race all the way from the south coast of Australia to the north coast.

**Student A:** But your race . . . it's not anywhere near that long, right?

**Student B:** No, no, our race is only twenty miles long. We entered the Sunflower I in it last year and . . .

**Student A:** And did you win?

**Student B:** Uh, well, no . . . no, we didn't actually win . . . In fact, we didn't even finish last year. We got off to a good start but then we had a major breakdown. But since then we've made a *lot* of improvements to the Sunflower II, and . . . well, I think we have a pretty good chance this year of . . . well, if not of winning, of finishing at least in the top three.

**Narrator:** Now get ready to answer the question. You may use your notes to help you.

**Narrator:** Question 4: What are these two people mainly discussing?

**Narrator:** Listen to a conversation between two students.

**Student A:** So, Rob, what classes are you taking next semester?

**Student B:** Let's see, uh, I'm taking the second semester of statistics, calculus, German, and . . . oh, I signed up for a class in the art department, a photography class.

**Student A:** Oh? Who with?

**Student B:** Umm, let me think . . . I think her name is . . . I think it's Lyons . . .

**Student A:** Lyons? I don't think . . . oh, you must mean Professor Lyle, Martha Lyle. She's my advisor, and I've taken a coupla classes from her. She's just great. She's not only a terrific photographer, but she's also a, well, just a wonderful teacher. She can take one look at what you're working on and tell you just what you need to do to take a better photograph. I mean, I learned so much about photography from her. And not only about taking color photographs, but also black-and-white—which I'd never done before. She only takes black-and-white photos herself, you know. So what kinds of photos did you show her?

**Student B:** Whaddya mean?

**Student A:** When you got permission to take her class, what kind of photos did you show her? You had to show her your portfolio, didn't you?

**Student B:** No, I . . . I just registered for her class. The registrar didn't tell me I needed permission . . .

**Student A:** Well, for any of those advanced classes, if you're not an art major, or if you haven't taken any other photography classes, you have to get the professor's permission, and usually that involves showing your portfolio.

**Student B:** Oh, see, they didn't tell me that when I registered.

**Student A:** Well, I think it says so in the course catalog. But, you can always sign up for an introductory level photography class. You wouldn't need the instructor's permission to do that.

**Student B:** No, I . . . I don't consider myself a . . . well, not a complete beginner, anyway. I took photos for my school newspaper when I was in high school . . . not just news photos but kind of artistic photos too, you know . . . I could show her those. I'd really like to take her class. From what you said about her, I think I could learn a lot.

**Narrator:** Now get ready to answer the question. You may use your notes to help you.

**Narrator:** Question 5: What is the main topic of this conversation?

[Track 5]

**Exercise 1.2**

**Narrator:** Listen to a lecture in a dance class.

**Professor:** Okay, today we're talking a bit about recording choreography. Let me start with a question for you. Do you know what steps dancers used during the first productions of . . . oh, say, of Swan Lake, or, for that matter, any of the most famous ballets? . . . That's really a trick question because . . . well, in most cases, no one knows, not really. Believe it or not, no written choreography exists for the early performances of most of the world's most famous classical ballets, or, for that matter, even for a lot of modern ballet. So, how did choreographers teach dancers how to perform their dances? Mostly, they demonstrated the steps themselves, or they had one of the dancers model the steps for the other dancers. Sure, systems of written choreography have been around for a long while. Some systems use numbers, some use abstract symbols, some use letters and words, oh, and musical notation, some systems use musical notes. The two most common systems in use are called Labanotation, and, uh, the Benesh system, Benesh Movement Notation it's called. But here's the thing—choreographers don't use these systems all that often. Why not, you ask. Well, because of the time it takes, because . . . Well, because recording three-dimensional dance movements, it's very difficult, very complex, and especially it's very time-consuming. A single minute of dance can take up to maybe, maybe six hours to get down on paper. You can imagine how long recording an entire ballet would take! And choreographers tend to be very busy people. But computer experts came to the choreographers' rescue. Computers have been used since the sixties to record choreography. The first one—well, the first one I know about, anyway, was a program written by Michael Noll . . . and it was . . . oh, I guess by today's standards you'd say it was pretty primitive. The dancers looked like stick figures in a child's drawing. But, uh, since the 1980's, sophisticated programs have been around, programs that . . . uh . . . well, uh, they let choreographers record the dancers' steps and movements quite easily. The only problem with these, these software programs, was that they required very powerful computers to run them . . . and as you no doubt know, not all dance companies have the kind of money you need to buy a mainframe computer. But because personal computers now have more memory, more power, well, now you can choreograph a whole ballet on a good laptop.

Oh, and I meant to mention earlier, we owe a lot of the credit for these improvements in the software for dance choreography to the space program. Back in the sixties and seventies, engineers at NASA needed computerized models . . . three-dimensional, moving models of astronauts' bodies so that the engineers could design spacesuits and spacecraft, and it turned out that the models they designed could be adapted quite nicely to dancers' bodies. So anyway, I've reserved the computer lab down the hall for the rest of this class. We're going to spend the rest of our time today playing around with some of this choreography software, okay? So let's walk over there . . .

**Narrator:** Now get ready to answer the question. You may use your notes to help you.

**Narrator:** Question 1: What is the main point of this lecture?

**Narrator:** Listen to a discussion in a psychology class.

**Student A:** Excuse me . . . excuse me, Professor Mitchie, but . . . I'm a little confused about what you just said.

**Professor:** You're confused? Why is that, Deborah?

**Student A:** Well, you said that you don't . . . well, that most scientists don't think that ESP really exists.

**Professor:** Okay, now you're clear what I'm talking about when I say ESP . . .

**Student B:** It's mind-reading, that kind of stuff. Extrasensory perception.

**Professor:** Well, that's a pretty good definition. It's . . . well, it can be telepathy . . . that's communicating mind to mind. Or telekinesis . . . that's moving things with your mind . . . precognition, which is knowing the future, or seeing the future. Other phenomena, too. And the study of ESP is sometimes called parapsychology.

**Student A:** But you think . . . well, you think all that is nonsense, I guess, right?

**Professor:** Now, I'm not saying there aren't people who have . . . well, remarkable senses of intuition. But I think that's because they're just very sensitive, very tuned in to their environments, to the people around them. I don't think they have any . . . abnormal mental powers beyond that, no.

**Student A:** Well, I was just reading an article about ESP, and it said that there were scientific experiments done at some university, I don't remember where, but the experiments were done with cards, and that they proved that some people could read minds.

**Student B:** She's probably thinking of those experiments at Duke University . . .

**Student A:** Right, it was at Duke.

**Professor:** Well, yes, there were a series of experiments at Duke about seventy years ago. Professor J. P. Rhine—who was, interestingly enough, a botanist, not a psychologist— he founded the Department of Parapsychology at Duke, and he and his wife did a lot of experiments, especially involving telepathy.

**Student B:** He used those cards, didn't he, the ones with, like, stars and crosses?

**Professor:** Yes. Well, at first he used ordinary playing cards, but then he started using a deck of twenty-five cards. There were five symbols on these cards: a star, a cross, some wavy lines, a circle and, ummm, maybe a square?

**Student A:** So how did the experiments work?

**Professor:** Well, basically it went like this. One person turned over the card and looked at it carefully, really trying to focus on it, to . . . to picture it in his mind. This person was called the *sender*. The other person, called the *percipient*, had to guess what symbol the sender was looking at. So . . . if it was just a matter of chance guessing, how many times should the percipient guess correctly?

**Student B:** Five, I guess? I mean, since there are five types of symbols and . . .

**Professor:** And twenty-five cards, yes, that's right, the law of averages says that you should get 20% right even if you have absolutely no ESP talent. So if someone—and they tested thousands of people at their lab—if someone on average got more than 20%, they'd get tested more, and some of these individuals went on to get remarkably high scores.

**Student A:** So, huh, doesn't this prove that some people can . . . that they have powers?

**Professor:** Well, after Rhine did his experiments at Duke, a lot of similar experiments have been done—at Stanford University, in Scotland, and elsewhere, and the conclusion . . . most researchers have decided that Rhine's results were . . . I guess the kindest word I could use is *questionable*. More recent experiments have been done under more carefully controlled conditions, and those, uh, remarkable results, those really high scores that Rhine got have been rare . . . practically nonexistent. And in science, the trend should be the opposite.

**Student B:** What do you mean, Professor?

**Professor:** Well, you know . . . if the phenomenon you're studying is real, and the experiments are improved, are more reliable, then the results you get should be *more* certain, not less certain.

**Student A:** So that's why you don't believe in ESP?

**Professor:** To put it in a nutshell—I've just never seen any experimental proof for ESP that stood up to careful examination.

**Narrator:** Now get ready to answer the question. You may use your notes to help you.

**Narrator:** Question 2: What are the speakers mainly discussing?

**Narrator:** Listen to a lecture in an archaeology class.

**Guest Speaker:** Good afternoon, everyone, I'm Robert Wolf, and I'm president . . . well, I should say past president of the State Archaeological Society. I'd like to thank Professor Kingsly for asking me to, to come in and talk to you all about a subject I'm pretty passionate about: shipwrecks. You see, I'm also a diver, and I'm a member of the International Underwater Archaeology Society, and I've been on a lot of underwater expeditions to investigate shipwrecks.

A lot of times, when someone mentions shipwrecks, you think of pirates and treasures buried under the sea. And in reality, many divers—the ones we call treasure hunters—do try to find shipwrecks with valuables still aboard them. In fact, that's one of the problems we face in this field. Some shipwrecks have literally been torn apart by treasure hunters searching for gold coins or jewelry, even if there wasn't any there, and underwater archaeologists weren't able to get much information from these ships. But, shipwrecks are . . . they can be a lot more than just places to look for treasure. A shipwreck is a time capsule, if you know what I mean, a photograph, a snapshot of what life was like at the moment the ship sank. And unlike sites on land, a shipwreck . . . it's . . . uncontaminated . . . it's not disturbed by the generations of people who live on the site later. Unless, of course, treasure hunters or someone like that has gotten there first. And so, they're valuable tools for archaeologists, for historians. For example, the world's oldest known shipwreck—it sank in about, ummm, 1400 B.C., off the coast of Turkey—the artifacts on that ship completely changed the way we think of Bronze Age civilizations in the Mediterranean.

So, I'm mostly going to stick to shipwrecks that occurred here, that happened off the coast of New England, and I'm going to talk about what we've learned from them, what archaeologists have learned from them. There have been plenty of shipwrecks in this area. Over the years, fog and storms and rocks and accidents and sometimes even war have sunk a lot of ships around New England. I'm going to be showing you some slides of shipwrecks from trading ships that sank in Colonial days, in the 1600's, to the *Andrea Doria*, which went down in the 1950's. The *Andrea Doria*, that's, uh, I suppose that's the most famous shipwreck in the area, the Italian ocean liner, the *Andrea Doria*, and it's a deep, dangerous dive to get to it, I'll tell you. Oh, and after that we're going to play a little game. I'm going to show you some slides of artifacts that were found on board shipwrecks, show them just the way they looked when they were found, and you have to guess what they are.

**Narrator:** Now get ready to answer the question. You may use your notes to help you.

**Narrator:** Question 3: What does this lecture mainly concern?

**Narrator:** Listen to a discussion in an economics class.

**Professor:** Okay, good morning, everyone, I trust everyone had a good weekend and that you managed to read Chapter . . . Chapter 7, on taxation. Friday we talked about the difference between progressive and regressive taxes . . . and, today, we're going to talk about two other types of taxation: direct and indirect. What did the text say about direct taxation? Yes, Troy?

**Student A:** Well, the book . . . according to the chapter that we read, it's, ummm, that's when the person who's being taxed . . .

**Professor:** Well, it could be a person or it could be an organization.

**Student A:** Right. The person or organization who's being taxed pays the government directly. Is that it?

**Professor:** That's great. Now, can you provide an example for us?

**Student A:** Yeah, uh, how about income tax?

**Professor:** Why would you consider income tax a form of direct taxation?

**Student A:** Well, because, um, the person who earns the income pays the taxes directly to the government, right?

**Professor:** Yes, good, Troy. Okay, so, someone else, what is indirect taxation? Cheryl?

**Student B:** Well, if I understand the book correctly, it's when the cost of taxes, of taxation, is paid by someone other than the, uh, the person . . . or organization . . . that is responsible for paying the taxes.

**Professor:** I'd say you understood the book perfectly—that's a good definition. Now, Cheryl, we need an example of indirect taxation.

**Student B:** Okay, let's see . . . what if someone . . . some company . . . brings, oh, say, perfume into the country from France. And let's say there's an import tax on the perfume that the government collects from the company, and then . . . well, the importer just turns around and charges customers more money for the perfume, to, umm, just to pay the import tax.

**Professor:** Good example! Anyone think of another one?

**Student A:** How about this: last year, my landlady raised my rent, and when I asked her why, she said it was because the city raised her property taxes . . . is that an example?

**Professor:** It certainly is. It . . . yes, Cheryl, you have a question?

**Student B:** Yes, Professor, what about sales taxes . . . direct or indirect?

**Professor:** Good question. I'm going to let you all think about it for just a minute—talk it over with the person sitting next to you, if you want—and then . . . then you're going to tell me.

**Narrator:** Now get ready to answer the question. You may use your notes to help you.

**Narrator:** Question 4: What is the main purpose of this discussion?

**Narrator:** Listen to a discussion in an art class.

**Professor:** Hello, everyone . . . today I'm going to be showing you some slides of . . . well, I'm just going to project a slide on the screen and see if you can tell me who the artist is and what the name of the painting is. This is his most famous painting. Here we go. Anyone know?

**Student A:** Yeah, I've seen that painting before . . . I don't remember the name of the artist, but I think the painting is called *Nighthawks at the Diner*.

**Professor:** Yeah, that's . . . well, a lot of people call it that, but the real name of the painting is just *Nighthawks*. Anyone know the artist? Anyone? No? The painter is Edward Hopper. Now tell me . . . what sort of a reaction do you have when you see it?

**Student B:** It's kind of . . . lonely . . . kind of depressing, and, uh, bleak. It's so dark outside, and inside there are these bright lights but . . . but they're kinda harsh, the lights are, and the people in the diner seem . . . well, to me, they look really lonely.

**Professor:** A lot of Hopper's works show . . . loneliness, isolation. He was a very realistic painter. One of the reasons he was so realistic, maybe, is that he started off as an illustrator, a commercial artist, and you know, of course, a commercial artist has to be able to paint and draw realistically. In fact, Hopper spent most of his early career doing illustrations and just traveling around. He didn't develop his characteristic style, his mature style, until, I'd say, not until he was in his forties or maybe fifties. Anyway, most of his paintings show empty city streets, country roads, railroad tracks. There are paintings of storefronts, restaurants, and . . . let me show you another, this is the first one of his mature paintings, and the first one that really made him famous. It's called *The House by the Railroad*. It's pretty bleak, too, isn't it? You'll notice as we look at more slides that, uh, well, there aren't many people in the paintings, and the ones that you do see, they look . . . you could almost say impersonal. Melancholy. That's the . . . mood he tried to convey. Wait, let me back up just a second. He, Hopper, always said he was just painting what he saw, that he wasn't trying to show isolation and loneliness but . . . one look at his paintings tells you he wasn't being completely honest about this.

**Student A:** Some of these paintings remind me of . . . of those old black-and-white movies from, like, the thirties and forties.

**Professor:** Yeah, I agree. That type of movie, that style of moviemaking is called *film noir*. And yeah, it does have that same feel, doesn't it? And it's interesting that you should say that, because Hopper did have an influence on some moviemakers. On the other hand, he did not have much of an influence on his own generation of painters. Nobody else painted the way Hopper did, at least not until . . . well, until the photorealistic painters in the sixties and seventies. But his contemporaries weren't interested in realism. They were . . . well, we'll see some of their works next week when we talk about abstract expressionism.

**Narrator:** Now get ready to answer the question. You may use your notes to help you.

**Narrator:** Question 5: What is the main topic of this discussion?

**Narrator:** Listen to a discussion in an advertising class.

**Professor:** Morning, class. In our last class, we were talking about regulation, about regulation in the advertising industry. In fact, you may remember I said that, in the United States, in some European countries, too, advertising is one of the most heavily regulated industries there is. What did, um, what example did I give of regulation, government regulation of advertising?

**Student A:** Well, you . . . you gave the example of . . . that the United States banned cigarette advertising back in the 1960's . . .

**Professor:** The early 1970's, actually. That's right. Up until then, tobacco companies and their advertising agencies would portray smoking as part of this . . . oh, this carefree, this oh-so-glamorous lifestyle. And then it came out in these scientific studies done by the government that tobacco smoking was really dangerous, really unsafe, and so . . . no more tobacco advertisements. At least, not on television or radio. You could still advertise in magazines, on billboards, and so on, for a long time after that—don't ask me why, but you could. And some studies showed that . . . the studies seemed to indicate that the advertising ban . . . oh, and I might mention, there was also negative advertising by the government and anti-smoking groups telling people not to smoke . . . anyway, these studies showed that smoking, that the use of tobacco actually went down. Okay, there were also some examples in the article I asked you to read for today, other examples of government regulation . . .

**Student:** There was the example from Sweden, about how Sweden completely banned advertisements for children.

**Professor:** Right, for children under twelve. That happened back in 1991. Now . . . not to get too far off track here, but since that article was written, there was a European Court of Justice ruling, and it said that Sweden still has to accept . . . that it has no control over advertisements that target Swedish children, advertisements that come from neighboring countries . . . or from satellite. So this undercuts to a certain extent what the Swedes were trying to do, but still . . . you can see their intent to . . . to protect their children from, uh, from the effects of advertising.

**Student A:** Don't you think that law was . . . a little extreme, maybe?

**Professor:** In my opinion? As a matter of fact, yes, yes, I do. Personally, I think advertisements meant for children should be controlled—maybe controlled more carefully than at present—but not necessarily eliminated. And I . . . speaking for myself still, I think they should be controlled by a combination of government regulation and self-regulation. And that's what we're going to be talking about today. Sometimes self-regulation works well enough, but, but if the idea of self-regulation is to create nothing but honest advertisements, advertisements that are in good taste . . . well, you only have to turn on your TV and you'll see that this system of self-regulation has its faults, right?

**Narrator:** Now get ready to answer the question. You may use your notes to help you.

**Narrator:** Question 6: What is the class mainly discussing?

**Narrator:** Listen to a lecture in a world literature class.

**Professor:** So, for the rest of the class today, we're gonna talk about the two most important poems, epic poems, in Greek literature. And really, not just in Greek literature, but in any literature, anywhere in the world. These are the *Iliad* and the *Odyssey,* written by the blind Greek poet Homer—at least, we think he was blind. Now, if you happen to have a copy of the syllabus that I gave you last week, you'll notice that we're not gonna be able to . . . we just don't have time to read all of these two poems and talk about them. An epic poem . . . I probably don't have to tell you this—is a narrative poem, a really *long* narrative poem. So we're going to read a few passages from the *Iliad,* and we'll read a bit more from the *Odyssey.* What I want to talk about today are some of the . . . the ways these two long poems, especially their main characters, how they're different.

Some people have said that the *Iliad* is the world's greatest war story, and the *Odyssey,* that it's the world's greatest travel story. The *Iliad* tells about the Trojan War, the war between Troy and the various Greek kingdoms. The *Odyssey* tells about a Greek warrior's trip home, and all the amazing adventures he has on the way—and he has some wild ones, too. The warrior's name is Odysseus, hence the name for the poem. I think the reason that I prefer the *Odyssey* to the *Iliad,* myself, is that . . . well, I guess you could say, I just like the main character of the *Odyssey* better than the main characters of the *Iliad.* As I said, the *Iliad* is the story of the Trojan War and about the clash, the personality conflict, between the main characters. The conflict isn't just between warriors from either side—a lot of the story deals with an argument between the two strongest Greek warriors, Achilles and Agamemnon. Anyway, the main characters in the *Iliad,* they're strong, they're great warriors, but you know . . . they're not as clever, not as smart as Odysseus. He's the one who thinks up the plan to end the war—after ten long years—and defeat the Trojans. He's the . . . the mastermind behind the scheme to build the Trojan Horse—you probably know something about that already, the Trojan Horse has been in lots of movies and so on . . . anyway, he helps end the ten-year war, and then he sets off for home and his family. It takes him another ten years to get home, where his wife has been waiting faithfully for him for twenty years, but . . . but like I said, he has plenty of adventures on the way.

Oh, and the other thing about Odysseus that I like is that . . . well, the characters in the *Iliad* are pretty static . . . you know what I mean? They are . . . they don't change much. This is true of most of Homer's characters, in fact. But it's not true of Odysseus. During the course of the epic, on account of the long war and all the, the bizarre experiences he has on the way home . . . he changes. He evolves as a character, just like characters in most modern novels do.

Okay, then, before we go on . . . does anyone have any comments? Comments or questions?

**Narrator:** Now get ready to answer the question. You may use your notes to help you.

**Narrator:** Question 7: What is the main point of this lecture?

**Narrator:** Listen to a lecture in a modern history class.

**Professor:** All right, then, I want to talk about the founding of the United Nations, but before I do, I want to just mention the League of Nations, which was the predecessor of the United Nations. Last week, we talked about the end of the First World War—it ended in 1918, if you remember. Well, right after the war, several leaders of the countries that had won the war, including Wilson of the United States, and Lloyd George of Britain, Clemenceau of France . . . oh, and Jan Smuts of South Africa, and, well, there were others too . . . they recognized the need for an international organization, an organization to keep the peace. So when the agreement that ended the war, the Treaty of Versailles, it was called, was signed, it included a provision that . . . that included formation of the League of Nations. Its headquarters were in Geneva, Switzerland.

But, the problem with the League from the beginning was that some of the most powerful nations of the time never joined. As I said, the, ah, the main drive, the main impetus for forming the League came from Woodrow Wilson, president of the United States. But during the 1920's, the United States went through a period of isolationism. In other words, it just basically withdrew from international affairs. Wilson worked and worked to get the U.S. Senate to agree to join the League, but he never could. Other powerful nations joined but then quit—or were kicked out. This included Brazil, Japan, Germany, the Soviet Union . . . The other problem was, ah . . . the League of Nations never had any power, really, no power to enforce its decisions. It had no armed forces. It could only apply economic sanctions, boycotts, and these were pretty easy to get around.

The League of Nations did have a few successes early on. It helped prevent wars between Bulgaria and Greece, Iraq and Turkey, and Poland and Lithuania in the 1920's. And the League also had some success in refugee work and famine relief and so on. Oh, and it brokered some deals, some treaties to get countries to reduce the size of their navies. But . . . the League was completely, totally powerless to stop the buildup to the Second World War in the 1930's.

So, ah, during the war, during World War II, I mean, the League didn't meet. Then, after the war, it was replaced by the United Nations, which, of course, was headquartered in New York City.

Still, the League of Nations was, ah . . . well, I think it served an important role. It developed a new model of Internationalism. In the late nineteenth and early twentieth century, "Internationalism" really just meant alliances of powerful nations, and these alliances often dragged other countries into conflict—that's what happened, really, that's what led to World War I. But the League was at least an attempt to bring all the nations of the world together to work for peace. True, it didn't work, not really, but at least there was an effort made. Oh, and another thing I meant to add, the structure of the League of Nations, the, ah, administrative structure, the "government," if you will—was very similar to that of the United Nations. The secretary-general, the secretariat, the general assembly, the security council, these are all fixtures of the United Nations that came from the League of Nations.

Okay, we're going to have to wait until next class to discuss the United Nations, but . . . I just wanted you to be aware of the League of Nations because of its role, its, ah . . . place in history, which I think has often been misunderstood . . .

**Narrator:** Now get ready to answer the question. You may use your notes to help you.

**Narrator:** Question 8: What is the main subject of this lecture?

**Narrator:** Listen to a lecture in an environmental studies class.

**Professor:** Let's go ahead and get started. I'd like to finish up our discussion of alternative energy sources this week . . . Remember our definition of an alternative energy source? It has to be environmentally friendly . . . non-polluting, in other words. And what else? Renewable. Not like oil or coal. When you use those, bang, they're gone, they're used up. Renewable sources keep replacing themselves.

Okay, so we discussed solar power and wind power one day . . . and tidal energy, energy from the waves . . . hydro-electric power from waterfalls, we discussed that, too . . . and in our last class we talked about one kind of geo-thermal energy, hydrothermal energy. That's the energy that comes from hot water, from hot springs under the earth. In places like, oh, say, Iceland, parts of New Zealand, where you have these, uh, features, this can be a very good source of heat and power. But unfortunately, hot springs aren't found all over the world. Okay, well, there is *another* source of geothermal power, called "hot dry rock." That's hot dry rock, or HDR. Ever heard of it? No, eh? Well, the chances are, you'll hear a lot about it before long.

How does HDR energy work? Well, in theory, anyway . . . and let me stress, I say in theory . . . it's pretty simple. You use oil-well drilling equipment, big drills, and you punch two holes down into the earth about, oh, maybe two miles—five kilometers, maybe—that's about as far as you can drill into the earth, for now, at least. Down there, deep in the earth, there is this extremely hot cauldron of rock, of granite. So then, you pump water from the surface into the first tube. The water goes down to the hot rock and becomes superheated. Then, the superheated water rises up the second tube—oh, I forgot to mention that these two tubes are interconnected—this hot water rises up the other tube and you use that to heat up a volatile liquid—do I need to go into what I mean by that? No? Okay. So then, this volatile liquid turns into a vapor, a gas, and you use it to turn an electrical turbine, and . . . bingo, you have elec-tricity! And then, when the water has cooled down, you just send it down the first tube again, so that you don't waste water.

So, does HDR technology meet our criteria for alterna-tive energy? Let's see. Is it environmentally friendly? You bet. There are no toxic gases, no greenhouse emissions, no nuclear wastes. Is it renewable? Sure it is, 'cause the earth automatically replaces the heat that is used.

Here's another possibility . . . if you built a big HDR facil-ity by the seacoast, you could pump seawater down one tube. The seawater is heated way past boiling, so you could separate water vapor from the salt and other minerals in the seawater. After you used the hot water vapor to gener-ate electricity, you'd have pure, fresh water for thirsty cities nearby—and as a side effect, you have the salt.

Now, will this work everywhere? No, conditions have to be just right—you have to have really, really hot granite masses no more than about 5 kilometers below the earth. We know there are places like this in Australia, in the south-western United States, in France, a few other places. There are probably a lot of other sites too, that we are not aware of. In fact, there may be a lot of HDR sites, and who knows how important a source of power this may turn out to be. Right now, engineers are building a small, prototype HDR station in southern Australia and one in New Mexico. These could be up and running in a decade or less. Of course, get-ting started will be expensive. Drilling a hole that far into the ground, building generators, all of that will cost lots of money. But, you know, the way oil prices keep going up—HDR energy production could become more and more financially attractive.

Okay, I'm gonna hand out a diagram of what one of these, uh, prototype HDR facilities looks like, the one in Australia, and then once you've had a chance to take a look at it, we'll talk some more about it.

**Narrator:** Now get ready to answer the question. You may use your notes to help you.

**Narrator:** Question 9: What is the main idea of this lecture?

[Track 6]

## Lesson 2: Factual, Negative Factual, and Inference Questions

### Sample Item 1

**Narrator:** Listen to part of a discussion in a business class.

**Professor:** What does a case look like? Well, cases are basi-cally descriptions of actual—let me stress that—of real business situations, chunks of reality from the business world. So, you get typically ten to twenty pages of text that describe the problem, some problem that a real business actually faced. And then there will be another five to ten pages of what are called exhibits.

**Student B:** Exhibits? What are those?

**Professor:** Exhibits . . . those are documents, statistical documents, that explain the situation. They might be oh, spreadsheets, sales reports, umm, marketing projections, anything like that. But as I said, at the center of every case, at the core of every case, is a problem that you have to solve. So, you have to analyze the situation, the data—and sometimes, you'll see you don't have enough data to work with, and you might have to collect more—say, from the Internet. Then, you have to make decisions about how to solve these problems.

**Narrator:** What does the professor say about exhibits?

[Track 7]

### Sample Item 2

**Narrator:** Listen to part of a lecture in a biology class.

**Professor:** So, what are conditions like in the taiga? Well, to start with, you've gotta understand that it's cold there. I mean, very cold. Summers are short, winters long. So the organisms that call the taiga home have to be well adapted to cold. The trees in the taiga, as I already said, are conifer-ous trees like the pine, fir, and spruce. And these trees, they've adapted to cold weather. How? Well, for one thing, they never lose their leaves—they're "evergreen," right, always green, so in the spring, they don't have to waste time—don't have to waste energy—growing new leaves. They're ready to start photosynthesizing right away. And then, for another thing, these trees are conical—shaped like cones—aren't they? This means that snow doesn't accu-mulate too much on the branches; it just slides off, and so, well, that means their branches don't break under the weight of the snow. And even their color—that dark, dark green—it's useful because it absorbs the sun's heat.

**Narrator:** When discussing needle-leaf trees, which of these adaptations to cold weather does the professor mention?

[Track 8]

### Sample Item 3

**Narrator:** Listen to part of a student presentation in an astronomy class.

**Student:**   Okay, now here's a really strange fact about Venus. It takes Venus only 225 Earth days to go around the Sun, as opposed to the Earth, which of course takes 365 days—what we call a year. But Venus turns around on its axis really slowly. Really slowly. It takes 243 Earth days to spin around completely. The Earth takes—you guessed it—24 hours. This means that a day on Venus is longer than a year on Venus! In fact, a day on Venus is longer than . . . well, than on any planet in the solar system, longer even than on those big gas planets like Jupiter. And here's something else weird. All the planets of the solar system turn on their axis in the same direction as they orbit the Sun. All except Venus, of course! It has what's called a . . . wait, let's see . . . okay, a "retrograde" spin.

**Narrator:**   Which of the following is *not* true about the length of a day on Venus?

[Track 9]

### Sample Item 4

**Narrator:**   Listen to part of a lecture in a biology class.

**Professor:**   Lots of the mammals that live in the taiga migrate to warmer climates once cold weather sets in. But there are some year-round residents. Among the predators—the animals that hunt other animals—there are Arctic foxes, wolves, bears, martens, oh, and ermines. There's one thing all these predators have in common, the ones that live there all year round . . . they all have thick, warm fur coats, don't they? This heavy fur keeps them toasty in the winter. Of course, on the downside, it makes them desirable to hunters and trappers. Some of these predators survive the winter by hibernating, by sleeping right through it . . . bears, for example. And some change colors. You've heard of the ermine, right? In the summer, the ermine is dark brown, but in the winter, it turns white. That makes it hard to spot, so it can sneak up on its prey.

   Then, uh, what sorts of herbivores live up there? What do the predators eat to stay alive? There's the moose, of course, but only young moose are at risk of being attacked. The adult moose is the biggest, strongest animal found in the taiga, so a predator would have to be feeling pretty desperate to take on one of these. Mostly, predators hunt smaller prey, like snowshoe rabbits, voles, lemmings . . .

**Narrator:**   What does the speaker imply about moose?

[Track 10]

### Exercise 2.1

**Narrator:**   Listen to a conversation between two students.

**Student A:**   I'm glad we could get together for coffee today, Cindy. You know . . . it just seems like forever since I've seen you.

**Student B:**   I know. It seems . . . I just never see anyone from our freshman dorm days. Ever since I, basically ever since I started student-teaching, I've been just *swamped*. I never knew how much work . . . you know, it always seemed to me that teachers had it pretty easy—short work days, summers off, but . . . I never realized how much work you have to take home. Sometimes I'm grading papers until . . . sometimes until after midnight!

**Student A:**   Wow, no wonder we never see you anymore.

**Student B:**   Yeah, and since I'm not taking any classes, any regular classes, on campus this term, I hardly ever get up here. I seem to be spending my whole life at West Platte Middle School—that's where I'm student teaching.

**Student A:**   So how come you're free today?

**Student B:**   Oh, this week is spring break for the middle school, for the . . . the whole school district. So I came to campus to talk to my academic advisor.

**Student A:**   Oh, I didn't realize that—our spring break isn't until next week. So . . . how's it going? With the teaching, I mean? Except for the long hours . . . do you . . . are you enjoying it?

**Student B:**   Well, let me tell you, at first, I thought it was going to be a disaster! A complete disaster! You know, I, I always saw myself teaching in high school, but . . . there were no student-teaching positions open in any of the high schools in the district. I mean zero, except for one for a German teacher! So that's . . . that's how I ended up at West Platte. And that wasn't the only problem. You know I majored in education but I took lots of classes in physics and chemistry, so I figured they'd put me in a science classroom. But noooo! The only available classes for me to teach were a couple of math classes.

**Student A:**   Wow, so you really . . . you really didn't get anything you wanted, did you?

**Student B:**   As a matter of fact, no! But you know, it's actually turned out okay. For one thing, I had a good background in math, and so, really, teaching math was no problem—although I'd still rather teach science. But, it turns out, I like teaching in a middle school, I like it much more than I thought I would. I like working with kids that age. So . . . guess what, I've decided to look for a job at a middle school instead of at a high school after I graduate.

**Student A:**   So, what do you need to talk to your advisor about?

**Student B:**   Oh, I need to talk to her about next fall, to set up my class schedule for then.

**Student A:**   Really? I thought you were all done. I thought you'd finished all your required classes and you were going to graduate when you finished student teaching.

**Student B:**   Well, I have finished all my required classes, I have all the coursework I need in education and in science but . . . I still don't have enough, not quite enough total credits to graduate. So today, I'm . . . my advisor and I . . . are going to decide which electives I should take next semester. I'm thinking of maybe taking a literature class. I've always wanted to take a Shakespeare class, but I've never had time.

**Student A:**   Oh, well, I'm just glad you'll be around next fall—we can get together more often.

**Narrator:**   Now get ready to answer the questions. You may use your notes to help you.

**Narrator:**   Question 1: What is Cindy's major?

**Narrator:**   Question 2: What decision about her future has Cindy recently made?

**Narrator:**   Question 3: What was Cindy's main reason for coming to campus today?

**Narrator:**   Question 4: What will Cindy be doing next semester?

**Narrator:**   Listen to a conversation between a student and a visitor to the campus.

**Student A:**   Uh, excuse me, but, uh, I'm trying to find my way to the Reynolds Building.

**Student B:**   The Reynolds Building? Hmmm. I'm afraid I don't know where that is.

**Student A:**   Really? But I understand that . . . I was told that there's a graduate student exhibit opening today at the Reynolds Art Building.

**Student B:** Oh, now I know where you mean. I was there earlier today, matter of fact. Yeah, I guess . . . I guess the Reynolds Art Building is its official name, but no one on campus calls it that . . . everyone just calls it the art building.

**Student A:** The art building, okay. So, uh, how do I get there?

**Student B:** Well, just go straight ahead and then . . . first you come to the main library, right? Then you see a walkway leading off to the left. Go that way, and walk past the, uh . . . let's see, the chemistry building . . .

**Student A:** Wait . . . I go to the library, I take the walkway to the right . . .

**Student B:** No, to the left past the chem building. Then you cross a little service road. You just walk a little bit farther, and you see the art building . . . the Reynolds Building. You can't miss it because there's a big metal . . . *thing* on a platform right in front of it.

**Student A:** A thing?

**Student B:** Yeah, there's this . . . this big rusty piece of abstract "art." I guess you'd call it art. Anyway, it's right in front of the doorway.

**Student A:** A big abstract metal sculpture. Okay, I think I've got it.

**Student B:** I think you'll like the exhibit. Like I said, I dropped by there this morning and took a quick look around, because—I'm an art major myself, and because, well, grad student exhibits are usually great. My favorite pieces . . . there's this one little room off the main gallery and it's full of sculptures made all . . . they're all made from neon lights. They're just beautiful, the way they glow. I couldn't believe it wasn't the work of some, some professional artist.

**Student A:** Well, the main reason I'm going is . . . my sister invited me to the opening. She wanted me to see her newest work.

**Student B:** Your sister's an artist?

**Student A:** Yeah, she's a painter. She also, well, she just started volunteering to teach art to kids and . . . I think the way her students paint has sort of rubbed off on her. I think her kids have influenced her more than she's influenced them, as a matter of fact. She's using these bright colors, and . . .

**Student B:** Oh I think I saw her paintings! There was one of a house perched on a hill, and another one of a purple lion. I love the colors she uses!

**Narrator:** Now get ready to answer the questions. You may use your notes to help you.

**Narrator:** Question 5: Why was the woman confused at first when the man asked her for directions?

**Narrator:** Question 6: According to the woman, what is directly in front of the art building?

**Narrator:** Question 7: What was the woman's favorite exhibit at the art show?

**Narrator:** Question 8: What can be inferred from the conversation about the man's sister?

**Narrator:** Listen to a conversation between two students.

**Student A:** So, Paul, figured out where you're gonna live next semester? Are you gonna live in the dorm again or off-campus?

**Student B:** Well, to tell you the truth, I . . .

**Student A:** Because, here's the thing . . . I've leased this big three-bedroom apartment . . . it's within walking distance of campus . . . and I only have one other roommate lined up at the moment . . . and so I was just wondering, if you need a place next semester . . .

**Student B:** It's nice, really nice of you to think of me, Dave, but, I'm not actually going to be living here next fall. I, uh, I'm not going to need a place to live.

**Student A:** What? You're leaving Rutherford? Are you transferring, or . . .

**Student B:** No, uh, actually . . . I've decided to do . . . to take part in a Semester Abroad program. I'm going to spend the semester in Athens.

**Student A:** Really? You mean you're going to be studying in Greece?

**Student B:** Uh huh . . . I'm really excited about it. It's about all I can think of.

**Student A:** But, um, you don't speak any Greek, do you?

**Student B:** No, not a word. But the one and only required course in this program is an intensive language course in modern Greek. So I guess I'll learn some once I get there.

**Student A:** So what . . . what made you decide on Greece?

**Student B:** Well, you know, I'm a history major, and eventually I'd like to teach history at the university level, and so I thought I'd like to study history where a lot of it was made. And Professor Carmichael . . . she's my advisor . . . she said we'd be visiting a lot of historical sites all over Greece. She really talked up the idea of signing up for this program. Also, I'm interested in theater, and I'll be taking a course in, uh, Greek drama too.

**Student A:** You know, I'll bet it's gonna be . . . it's gonna be a real challenge. I mean, it was hard enough for me to find a decent apartment here in town where I've lived for a couple of years and hey, I speak the language. So I can't even imagine looking for an apartment someplace like Athens and not being able to speak Greek . . .

**Student B:** Okay, well, there are actually two kinds of . . . of Semester Abroad programs. One is called an independent program. If you sign up for that kind of program . . . that's the kind of program you're thinking of, probably—then you have to make your own travel plans, you find your own housing, you make your own arrangements for meals, you're . . . you're basically on your own except for the academic program. But the other type of program—they call it an "island plan"—

**Student A:** Why do they call it that?

**Student B:** I dunno. I guess . . . I guess because you're kinda on your own little island even though you're overseas. Anyway, if you go with the island plan, you . . . you stay at a dorm with other students from here at Rutherford College, and you eat with them . . . and the program makes all the airline arrangements, someone meets you at the airport . . . transportation from the dorm to the school—that's all taken care of . . . just about everything is arranged in advance for you. That's the program I . . . that's how I decided to go. I . . .

**Student A:** Oh, that's the way I'd do it too, if I were going. It just sounds . . . so much easier and you wouldn't feel so . . . so isolated, living alone . . .

**Student B:** Well, in a way, I'd rather be in an independent program. It might be a bit tough, but I think I could handle it. And I mean, I think I'd learn more about Greece, and, uh, I'd get to meet more local people. There are some programs, in fact, where they place you with a local family. I'd actually love to live with a family or just out in the community. Plus it's cheaper to go that way.

**Student A:** So . . . why are you doing that island program, then?

**Student B:** Well, the main reason is time. My reason for going over there is to concentrate on classes, and I think I would spend all my time taking care of . . . well, just making living arrangements.

**Student A:** So, will your teachers all be from Greece?

**Student B:** The Greek language professor is, and some of the other teachers too, but some are from here at Rutherford and from other U.S. universities. Professor Carmichael, my advisor, is going to be teaching over there this year. She's never taught in Greece before, but she taught in a similar program in France a couple of years ago.

**Student A:** Well, it sounds great . . . I wish I could go myself!

**Narrator:** Now get ready to answer the questions. You may use your notes to help you.

**Narrator:** Question 9: Which of these courses is required for students in the Semester Abroad program in Greece?

**Narrator:** Question 10: Which of these is characteristic of the "island plan" Paul will take part in?

**Narrator:** Question 11: Why did Paul decide not to take part in the independent plan?

**Narrator:** Question 12: What does Paul say about Professor Carmichael?

**Narrator:** Listen to a conversation between two students.

**Student A:** Morning, Steve . . . boy, you look exhausted!

**Student B:** Do I? Well, guess that's to be expected. I was up almost all night, trying to get ready for my chemistry midterm this morning.

**Student A:** Really? Any idea how you did on it?

**Student B:** Yeah, as a matter of fact, Doctor Porter's already posted grades on her office door, and I . . . well, I could have done a whole lot better.

**Student A:** That really surprises me, Steve. You know so much about science.

**Student B:** Yeah, well, it's not surprising to me. I just . . . I mean, I know the material, but for some reason, when it comes to taking tests . . . I never do well. If a class grade depends on a research paper, I do just fine, but when it comes to taking tests . . . especially multiple-choice tests . . . I just look at the questions and I draw a blank.

**Student A:** Have you ever considered taking some seminars at the Study Skills Center?

**Student B:** Uh, I don't really know anything about it.

**Student A:** Well, the Center's run by some grad students and junior professors that help undergraduates . . . well, help them get organized . . . learn some techniques that help them do better in their classes. When I first got here last year, I took a course from them on . . . on how to do academic research on the Internet, and another one on writing term papers. They were really good, really useful.

**Student B:** Hmmm . . . so, what . . . what other kinds of courses do they offer?

**Student A:** Well, I don't know all the courses they offer, but I know they have a class on test-taking skills.

**Student B:** Wow, that's right up my alley.

**Student A:** And I know there's one on . . . how to, you know, manage your time . . . how to use time efficiently.

**Student B:** Yeah, well . . . I guess that's something I need too.

**Student A:** I should tell you . . . one of the things they're going to tell you is not to stay up all night cramming for a test.

**Student B:** Yeah, I . . . I already know it's not a great idea, but I . . . I just felt like it was the only way I could get ready . . .

**Student A:** As a matter of fact, they'll tell you it's the worst thing you can do . . . you need to be fresh and rested for a test.

**Student B:** Yeah, well . . . I did drink plenty of coffee to keep me alert. So, anyway, where is the Center?

**Student A:** They have a little office in Staunton Hall, across the quadrangle from the physics tower, you know where I mean? That's where you go to sign up. They actually hold their seminars in the main library. I don't know if they're holding any seminars just now, but, uh, I think they start new ones every six weeks or so.

**Student B:** I should go by there now and try to talk to someone.

**Student A:** You know, if I were you, Steve . . . I think I'd go by there tomorrow. Right now, you should go back to your dorm and catch up on your sleep.

**Narrator:** Now get ready to answer the questions. You may use your notes to help you.

**Narrator:** Question 13: Why does Steve look tired?

**Narrator:** Question 14: How does Steve feel about the grade that he received on the chemistry test?

**Narrator:** Question 15: Who teaches the seminars at the Study Skills Center?

**Narrator:** Question 16: Which of the courses at the Study Skills Center will Steve probably be most interested in?

**Narrator:** Question 17: Where is the Study Skills Center?

**Narrator:** Question 18: What does the woman suggest Steve do now?

**Narrator:** Listen to a conversation between a student and a campus housing administrator.

**Student:** Hi, I'm Jeff Bloom. I'm, uh, here to talk to someone about the . . . Resident Advisor position?

**Administrator:** Oh, hi, I'm Frances Delfino. You can talk to me about that. Did you see our ad in the campus paper?

**Student:** No, uh, Mr. Collingswood, down in the off-campus housing office, uh, he suggested I come by and chat with you.

**Administrator:** Oh, okay, so . . .

**Student:** Let me tell you what's happening with me. . . . I've been living off-campus, living by myself in an apartment, right, which is great, but my landlord decided to sell the house I'm living in, and the new owner is . . . well, first she's going to remodel, so I have to move out anyway . . . then she's gonna rent the apartments for a lot more money . . . and, well, to make a long story short, I need a place to live just for one more semester.

**Administrator:** And you're interested in becoming a Resident Advisor?

**Student:** Well, I . . . I came by the housing office today to see if . . . well, the off-campus housing office has a list of apartments available . . . but everything on the list is too expensive, or way too far from campus, or you need to sign a year's lease. There just wasn't anything on the list that interested me so . . . so Mr. Collingswood suggested I come up and see you. He said there were some Resident Advisor positions open at one of the men's dorms and that I, I, uh, could get some information about these positions from you.

**Administrator:** Fine, well, I can tell you a little about the R.A. positions . . . the Resident Advisor positions . . . We do have a couple of openings for grad students or older upperclassmen. If you lived in a dorm yourself, you probably know all about what an R.A. does . . .

**Student:** Well, actually, I never did live in a dorm. I've always lived off-campus so I . . . I have no idea . . .

**Administrator:** Well, there's one R.A. per floor . . . we have openings in Donahue Hall and Hogan Hall . . . and you . . . you inform students of . . . oh, you know, university rules, regulations, policies . . . you organize a few social events for residents . . . and, uh, well, there are a lot of other things you may have to do . . . help students who are locked out of their rooms, uh, in general, you're kind of a mentor, you help students solve their problems . . .

**Student:** Hmmm, that . . . that doesn't sound so bad. And . . . well, my only other option is to share an apartment with a roommate, and I . . . I don't think I want to do that.

**Administrator:** Well, if you took an R. A. position, you wouldn't have to share. You'd have your own room and . . . in fact, the R.A. rooms are actually a little larger than the typical resident rooms.

**Student:** So, how much does it pay?

**Administrator:** Oh, didn't Mr. Collingswood mention that? There's no salary—it's not exactly a paid position. But your room is free and you're entitled to ten meals per week at the cafeteria at Donahue Hall.

**Student:** Really? Hmmm, well, I guess I'd be saving a lot of money on rent and on meals but . . . I . . . well, here's what I'm most worried about—the noise. I'm just afraid it would be too noisy for me to study, to concentrate. See, like I said, I'm in my last semester here, and I'm taking some pretty tough classes this semester. I just . . .

**Administrator:** Well, I'm not going to lie to you and say that the residents will always be quiet and orderly. I mean, come on, they're undergrads, mostly freshmen, so . . . it will probably be noisier than what you're used to, especially on weekends. But during the week, there are quiet hours, from 7 till 10 and then from midnight on . . . in fact, one of your duties is to enforce . . . is to make sure these quiet hours stay quiet.

**Student:** So, suppose I decide I want to . . . to apply for an R.A. position, what, uh, what would I need to do?

**Administrator:** I can give you a form to fill out. You'd also need to get two letters of recommendation . . .

**Student:** Letters? Who from?

**Administrator:** Oh, teachers, administrators, you know, someone like that. Oh, also, I have a pamphlet that describes the position in more detail. You can look that over. And I could give you e-mail addresses for a couple of R.A.s. You could contact them, see how they like the job, see what kinds of experiences they've had.

**Narrator:** Now get ready to answer the questions. You may use your notes to help you.

**Narrator:** Question 19: Why does Jeff have to move out of his apartment?

**Narrator:** Question 20: How did Jeff find out about the Resident Advisor position?

**Narrator:** Question 21: What will Jeff receive if he becomes a Resident Advisor?

**Narrator:** Question 22: What does Ms. Delfino suggest Jeff do to get more information about the position?

[Track 11]

**Exercise 2.2**

**Narrator:** Listen to a discussion in an anthropology class.

**Professor:** Morning, class. I want to start off this morning with a question for you. How many of you have ever been to a potluck dinner? Oh, lots of you, I see. Okay, who can describe a potluck dinner for me? Andy?

**Student A:** It's just a dinner where all the guests bring dishes for . . . well, to share with everyone else. Someone might bring salad, someone might bring dessert . . .

**Student B:** It's a way you can have a dinner party with your friends and not spend a million dollars, because everyone brings something.

**Professor:** You're right. Well, today we're gonna be discussing a ceremony called the *potlatch*.

**Student A:** I'm sorry, the what?

**Professor:** The *potlatch*. Here, I'll put it on the board for you. This is a ceremony held by Native Americans and Native Canadians in the Pacific Northwest—from Washington state north to British Columbia, all the way up to Alaska. Potlatches were held to . . . well, for all kinds of reasons . . . to celebrate births, weddings, naming ceremonies, even a good catch of salmon. Now, some linguists think that the English word *potluck* might be derived from this word *potlatch*. The word *potlatch* is originally from the Chinook language. The Chinooks were a group of Native Americans who lived along the Columbia River. A form of their language, called Chinook Trade Jargon, became a trade language, a language used by tribes all over the region to communicate with one another. So, ah, the word *potlatch* spread, and . . . and before long, it was used by all the tribes in the Pacific Northwest.

**Student B:** Professor Burke, were these potlatches . . . were they sort of like the potlucks we have today?

**Professor:** Well, no, as a matter of fact, they were quite a bit different. I suppose the best way . . . I think the best way to describe a potlatch is as a birthday party in reverse.

**Student B:** Huh? A . . . birthday party in reverse? What do you mean?

**Professor:** Well, at a birthday party, what happens? The guests all bring gifts, right? At a potlatch, it's the host who gives the gifts and the guests who receive them.

**Student A:** Sounds like a pretty good deal for the guests!

**Professor:** In a way it was, but—but in a way it wasn't. Let me describe a typical potlatch to you. A host—it was often a chief or an important person of some kind—would invite people from his tribe or from other tribes in the area. The guests would arrive and there would be some dancing. Then the guests would be seated, and the host and his family, his relatives would serve the guests a huge, formal feast . . .

**Student B:** Professor Burke, excuse me . . . I couldn't help wonder . . . what kind of food would be served at these potlatches?

**Professor:** Well, the tribes that had potlatches all lived near the ocean, so what kind of food do you think they served?

**Student B:** Ummm . . . I'm guessing fish.

**Professor:** Right. Mostly salmon, salmon was the staple food of the Northwest tribes, they spent a lot of their time salmon fishing and then preserving salmon . . . They might also serve whale meat, or seal meat, or venison. They'd dip these foods into pots of seal oil to give them more flavor. And . . . the hosts would always serve more than the guests could possibly eat. Okay, then after the feasting, the host would start distributing gifts.

**Student B:** What kind of gifts would the host give away?

**Professor:** Well, the most common gift was food: salmon. The host would pack smoked fish in these . . . these elaborately carved boxes. Other gifts they might give . . . goat-hair blankets, jewelry, wooden masks. And, and, ah, after these tribes came in contact with Americans and Canadians of European origin, the gifts became more . . . more varied. There might be sacks of flour, dishes, eating utensils. I even remember seeing a photograph of a potlatch from, oh, around 1900, where a guest is receiving a sewing machine!

**Student B:** So, what else happened at a potlatch?

**Professor:** Well, then the host would usually destroy some of his most valuable possessions, such as fishing canoes, and he'd throw coins and . . . and almost anything valuable into the sea . . .

**Student A:**    What?! Excuse me, Professor . . . I just don't get it. It just seems kinda crazy to me. Why would anyone want to host a party like that?

**Professor:**    Okay, well, first off, gift-giving rituals like this are not all that uncommon. I mean, there have been societies all around the world that have gone in for these types of ceremonies, but . . . but having said that, I can't think of any other society where it was such a, such a central part of the culture. See, these tribes . . . to them, status . . . prestige . . . Well, in short, they were highly status conscious. To them, looking good in the eyes of other people was very, very important, and that's what a, a potlatch was all about. It was a means of establishing rank. Status. Power.

**Student A:**    How's that?

**Professor:**    Well, by accepting gifts at a potlatch, the guests . . . they acknowledged the wealth and the generosity of their hosts. And when they were destroying or throwing away valuables, the hosts were really saying, "I'm so important, I'm so wealthy, I can afford to smash up my stuff and throw away my money!"

**Student A:**    Well, I still think it was a much better deal to be a guest than to be a host at these parties.

**Professor:**    Ah, but you see, Andy, there was a catch! In some ways, potlatches were actually a form of . . . of investment.

**Student A:**    Investment?

**Professor:**    Sure. The guests, all the guests at a potlatch were honor-bound to pay the host back by having potlatches of their own and inviting the host.

**Student A:**    Oh, I get it—it was an investment because then the host would be invited to lots of potlatches.

**Professor:**    Right. And the potlatches that the guests held had to be at least as elaborate as the one they'd been invited to. There was this one tribe called the Kwakiutl who lived up on Vancouver Island. Now this group . . . they really turned the potlatch into an art form. They had the most elaborate, most ritualistic potlatches of all the tribes in the Northwest. When the Kwakiutl held potlatches, they would use the ceremony as a . . . as a kind of weapon, a form of revenge against their enemies. They'd throw such extravagant potlatches that their enemies would go broke trying to match them.

**Student A:**    Wow, that was a . . . a clever way to get back at their enemies!

**Student B:**    So, do these tribes still have potlatches?

**Professor:**    That's a really good question. Both the U.S. government and the Canadian government banned potlatches back in the 1880's—although some tribes no doubt held potlatch ceremonies in secret. I suppose government officials just somehow didn't like the idea of people giving away their possessions. At the time, they didn't realize how important potlatches were . . . important culturally, socially, religiously to the tribes. But nowadays—in fact, ever since the 1930's in Canada and the 1950's in the United States—potlatches are legal again. If anything, they're an even more essential element of these societies than they were before.

**Narrator:**    Now get ready to answer the questions. You may use your notes to help you.

**Narrator:**    Question 1: What does the professor say about the word *potlatch?*

**Narrator:**    Question 2: What was the most common gift at a potlatch?

**Narrator:**    Question 3: What purpose did seal oil serve at a potlatch?

**Narrator:**    Question 4: What does Professor Burke imply about the photograph of a potlatch taken in 1900?

**Narrator:**    Question 5: What does Professor Burke say about the Kwakiutl tribe?

**Narrator:**    Question 6: What does Professor Burke say about potlatch ceremonies held today?

**Narrator:**    Listen to a lecture in a space science class.

**Professor:**    As I said at the end of our class on Tuesday, today I'm going to talk about a growing problem in the sky. You can call it . . . call it space junk, space debris, orbital litter, whatever you like—it's basically the leftovers from the thousands of satellites and spacecraft that have been sent into orbit over the last fifty years or so.

The problem started back in the late 1950's. The Soviet Union launched the first satellite—Sputnik, it was called—in 1957. And that's, that's when a tracking network was first set up, too, to monitor bodies in orbit. Today, there's a worldwide network of 21 telescopes and radar stations called the, umm, the Space Surveillance Network, that keeps track of all this stuff, all these items in space.

Almost every launch contributes to the problem, contributes to the amount of junk up there circling the earth. There are non-functioning satellites, food wrappers, an astronaut's glove, the lens cap from a camera, broken tools, bags of unwashed uniforms. Luckily, most of this junk burns up when it re-enters the atmosphere, just like little meteors. And although old pieces fall out of the sky, new pieces are launched. On average, there's a net increase of around 200 pieces per year.

Today there are around 13,000 pieces of . . . 13,000 separate bodies that are monitored from Earth. And of those, only about 400 are still active, still useful pieces of equipment. Most of it is in what is called low-Earth orbit, within . . . well, that's defined as within 1,200 miles of the earth. There are also about a thousand pieces in high orbit. It's in a very thin, very narrow ring, shaped like a bicycle tire, about 22,000 miles above the Equator.

The, uh, Surveillance people can only monitor objects bigger than about a baseball. There are probably, I'd say about half a million pieces of debris that are just too small to be monitored. Most of these small objects are tiny flecks of paint or little pieces of metal, say around the size of a grain of sand. Some orbital debris is huge—big as a bus! The smallest pieces are not that dangerous, not usually. When they hit a spacecraft, they only cause, oh, just some surface damage. Several times outer windows on the space shuttle have had to be replaced because of collisions with micro-objects in space, but there was no real danger. And the really big pieces—those are mostly empty booster rockets or other rocket parts—they're not necessarily all that dangerous either. Why not? Because these large objects can be detected by radar and so . . . so they can be avoided fairly easily. Several times shuttles have had to maneuver to avoid getting close to large pieces of debris. But it's the medium-sized pieces that represent the biggest danger. These objects are so dangerous, of course, because of their tremendous speed. They can be moving up to 12 miles per second. That's way faster than a bullet . . . your typical bullet doesn't even travel 1 mile per second. If one of these flying pieces of debris—say, a lost screwdriver, or a piece of an antenna that broke off a satellite—if one of these hit a space shuttle or the International Space Station—it could puncture the outer hull. Then what would happen? You'd have de-pressurization—all of the air inside would rush out into the vacuum of space, and then, you'd have a disaster on your hands. So far—fortunately—there has never been a major collision involving a manned spacecraft but . . . but space debris has damaged the solar panels on an unmanned communications satellite. And there, there have also been some collisions of these pieces of debris themselves. In January of 2005, the engine from a Thor rocket launched by the United States thirty years ago and a fragment of a Chinese rocket that blew up five years ago met over Antarctica. The event was recorded by a camera on a surveillance satellite. The collision produced even more pieces of space junk.

So, what can we do, what can be done about this problem? Well, a couple of years ago, space engineers came up with an idea, a possible way to solve this, uh, this debris problem. Here's what they suggested. You build a "junk collector," a large cone or group of cones that fits on the front of a spacecraft. The cone is full of sticky plastic fibers that trap debris inside it. This invention is still in its conceptual stage, but . . . there are two ways it might be used. You could launch unmanned satellites equipped with these devices and radar sensors and you could actively hunt down dangerous pieces of space junk. Or you could put one of these on the front of a manned spacecraft and use it as a defensive shield. Oh, and another possible solution . . . you could use laser guns, either on a space-based platform or based here on earth, to shoot some of the smaller pieces out of the sky. Okay, anyone have any questions for me?

**Narrator:**  Now get ready to answer the questions. You may use your notes to help you.

**Narrator:**  Question 7: What happens to most pieces of orbital debris?

**Narrator:**  Question 8: How many orbital bodies are being monitored today?

**Narrator:**  Question 9: Why is it impossible to monitor most pieces of orbital debris?

**Narrator:**  Question 10: Which of the following types of orbital debris would not be particularly dangerous to astronauts on a spacecraft?

**Narrator:**  Question 11: The professor describes a collision in space between which of the following objects?

**Narrator:**  Question 12: What can be inferred about the collector described in this portion of the talk?

**Narrator:**  Listen to a discussion in a pharmacy class.

**Professor:**  Good morning, all. This is our last class before the final, you know, and I told you I'd give you a little more information about the test today, but . . . before I do that, I want to talk about a different class of drugs. This term we've been discussing, mmmm, different types of, of pharmaceutical drugs. Today, though, I'd like to spend a little time discussing another class of drugs. You could lump them all together and call them herbal drugs or herbal remedies.

**Student:**  Oh, I just read a magazine article about herbal drugs. It said that herbal remedies were becoming more and more popular.

**Professor:**  That's probably true. I've heard that, oh, something like 12 million people in the United States use herbal drugs and . . . worldwide—well, there are countries where herbal remedies are as important . . . maybe even more important than pharmaceutical drugs.

**Student B:**  So, Professor Findlay—why do you think—why is it important for pharmacists to know about herbal medicines? I mean, usually patients don't get prescriptions and come to pharmacists for herbal remedies, do they? They just buy them at . . . I don't know, health food stores and so on, right?

**Professor:**  Well, there are several reasons, Thomas. For one thing, pharmaceutical and herbal medicine have a lot . . . they share a lot of history. I mean, think about it, at one time all drugs came from herbs and other plants. At one time, the "pharmacist" was just some guy, well, usually some woman, who knew what herbs were helpful and knew where to look for them. Also, a lot of pharmaceutical drugs in use today, they, mmm, originally came from herbal sources.

**Student B:**  Really? Which ones?

**Professor:**  Well, the most commonly taken drug of all—good old aspirin—is one example. The active ingredient in aspirin originally came from the bark of a tree—the white willow tree. And anyone remember a drug we talked about last month called digitalis?

**Student A:**  I do. It's used to . . . to treat heart problems, right?

**Professor:**  You're correct. And digitalis originally came from a plant called foxglove. Anyway, to introduce you to alternative medicine, I brought along some samples of plants that are often used in herbal medicines. See this flower that looks like a purple daisy?

**Student A:**  It's a pretty little flower. What is it?

**Professor:**  Well, some people call it the herbal equivalent of a flu shot. It's called Echinacea.

**Student A:**  Oh, I read about that—doesn't it work on the immune system?

**Professor:**  Right. Well, lots of people think it does, anyhow. It's one of the most commonly taken herbal remedies. A lot of people, when they feel a cold or the flu coming on, will take Echinacea.

**Student A:**  What are those yellow flowers with the five petals?

**Professor:**  Those are called St. John's Wort. St. John's Wort. It's used to reduce stress and for mild depression. Now, here's a plant you uh you might find of interest at this time of year, with finals coming on. See this fan-shaped leaf? It's from the Ginkgo Biloba tree.

**Student B:**  What's that one for?

**Professor:**  Ginkgo Biloba is thought to improve memory and to help you be more alert, more focused.

**Student A:**  Is that right? Wow, we really should try some of that! So, Professor, how do you . . . how do most people take these drugs? Do they just . . . swallow them?

**Professor:**  I'd imagine the most common way to take them is in powdered form—the leaves or flowers are crushed and powdered and put in a capsule, and people swallow the capsule. Another way . . . some people make tea from the plants and drink the tea, although I'm told that most of these herbs taste pretty nasty.

**Student B:**  Here's what I don't understand—why would someone use herbal drugs when there are regular drugs, pharmaceutical drugs that do the same thing?

**Professor:**  Well, Thomas, for one thing, a lot of herbal drugs are a form of preventative medicine. In other words, people tend to take these drugs to avoid getting sick. On the other hand, most prescription drugs are used after someone gets sick . . . I mean, to treat some specific problem. Then, for another thing, people—a lot of people that use these drugs, they think that herbs . . . that, umm, herbal remedies have fewer side effects and are generally—well, safer than prescription drugs.

**Student B:**  What do you think, Professor? Do you think that's true? Are they safer?

**Professor:**  Well, I'd have to say, not always. There are some herbs I would never recommend, and then there are definitely some herbal drugs that some people—for example, pregnant women, people with high blood pressure—these folks should definitely not take these drugs.

**Student B:**  But Professor, do you think they work? I mean, are most herbal remedies as effective as prescription drugs?

**Professor:**  I don't really have a simple answer for that question, Thomas. I think that in some cases, they might be. But not all that much research has been done on herbal drugs, so there isn't that much scientific proof.

**Student A:**  Why is that, Professor? Why no research?

**Professor:**  That's easy. Because drug research, most of the research done on drugs is done by pharmaceutical companies that hope to patent the drug and then to make a profit on it. But, guess what, you can't patent an herb, since, well, since it's a natural substance. So . . .

**Student B:**  Professor, as a pharmacist, would you recommend . . . would you ever tell a patient to take herbal medicine instead of a prescription drug?

**Professor:**  Mmm, well, I might, depending on the medical situation, but there are several considerations. Patients need to take a few precautions. First, they should be sure that they get herbs from a reputable company, a dependable company, to make sure the herbs they are taking are pure. They should also talk to their doctors and their pharmacists—*especially* if they are taking any other drugs, because there is always the possibility drugs and herbs . . . well, there could be a serious drug-herb interaction. Finally, I'd remind patients not to, not to expect miracles from herbs. I mean, let's face it, no herbal remedy can take the place of exercise and a healthy diet.

**Narrator:**  Now get ready to answer the questions. You may use your notes to help you.

**Narrator:**  Question 13: What point does Professor Findlay make about the drugs aspirin and digitalis?

**Narrator:**  Question 14: According to Professor Findlay, why do people generally take the herbal remedy Echinacea?

**Narrator:**  Question 15: Which of the following is the best description of St. John's Wort?

**Narrator:**  Question 16: What can be inferred from the professor's remarks about how most herbal medicines are used?

**Narrator:**  Question 17: In what form are herbal remedies most often taken?

**Narrator:**  Question 18: According to the professor, why has research on herbal drugs been limited?

**Narrator:**  Listen to a lecture in a U.S. history class.

**Professor:**  Good afternoon, class. Today I want to talk a little about something that's done more, I think, to shape the landscape of the United States as it is today than, uh, well, probably more than just about any other phenomenon: the Interstate Highway System. The Interstate System has been called the largest public works project in the history of the country—maybe in the history of the world—and it's definitely one of the world's great engineering wonders. When the, uh, the Century Highway in Los Angeles was completed in 1993, it marked the end—well, almost the end, there were still some bits and pieces that weren't finished—but it effectively marked the end of a forty-year project that cost hundreds of billions of dollars.

Okay, let's take a trip back in time; let's go back to the early part of the twentieth century. Let's say you've just bought a brand-new automobile—maybe a shiny new Model A Ford. Here's your problem: you can drive your car around the city, but if you want to go from city to city, there are no roads to speak of. When the weather is bad, well, people joke about losing automobiles in the mud. In fact, in many places, roads are probably worse than they were a hundred years before. Anyone guess why? No? Okay, remember a couple of weeks ago, we talked about how, after the Civil War, the railroad became dominant, the dominant form of transportation? Does that ring a bell? So, what was one of the side effects of this? The roads meant for horses, for carts, for carriages, these all fell into disrepair because—well, because passengers and goods all moved by railroad. There was no reason to maintain roads. Anyway, you've got these terrible roads, no way to . . . to get from place to place, so what do you motorists do? You organize, you form groups, and then you ask, you demand that the government build roads. These groups of motorists went by a lot of different names, depending on where they were, but collectively, they were known as the Better Roads Movement. And the government responded. It responded slowly, but it responded. Roads were built, but it would be years, many years before there was a comprehensive highway system.

Okay, let's move ahead in time a few years. It's 1919, and a young army officer, whose name is Dwight David Eisenhower, is ordered to lead a military convoy of trucks and motorcycles across the country, from Washington, D.C., to San Francisco, California. He's ordered to get there as soon as possible. It takes him . . . you might find this hard to believe, but it took him sixty-two days. Sixty-two days!

Okay, now it's the 1930's . . . the time of the Great Depression, as I know you'll remember, and there are millions of unemployed workers—millions—and President Roosevelt puts some of them to work on public works projects. These projects include road building. In 1938, the first "superhighway" opens. It's called the Pennsylvania Turnpike. You may have traveled on it yourself and not found it . . . well, not found it all that exciting. However, at the time it opened, it was known as "the dream road." This four-lane highway became a model for the highways of the future.

So . . . after World War II, the United States really and truly enters the automobile age. By 1950, there are over 50 million vehicles on the road. In 1954, Dwight David Eisenhower—he's the president of the United States by now—he proposes a system of superhighways. This system would basically connect all of the major cities in the United States. Of course, Eisenhower has been interested in roads for a long time. There were two events that . . . two major events in his life that influenced the way he thinks about highways. One is his wartime experience. He was commander of the Allied forces in Europe during World War II, and he saw, uh, the advantage that the efficient German autobahn system—the German superhighway system—he saw the advantage this gave Germany during the war. The other event? It's that long, hard trip he took across the country back in 1919.

So, in 1956 Congress passes the Federal Highway Act, and the first section of the Interstate system is built in Kansas—Eisenhower's home state. The system is supposed to be completed by 1972, but it's not finished, as I said, until the 1990's.

The Interstate Highway System has had just a . . . just an enormous impact on life in the United States. It's created millions of jobs. It's provided an incredibly efficient system for moving people and transporting goods around the country—and because of that, it's contributed to the decline of the railroads. Because of the safety factors that were built into the system, it's probably saved thousands of lives. It's helped create the suburbs that surround every U.S. city. Now, it's true, there were suburbs before there were Interstate highways, but the Interstate system has helped accelerate their growth because . . . well, it's just so easy to travel from suburb to central city.

Now don't get me wrong—not all the effects of this superhighway system have been, well, positive, especially in urban areas. There have been whole neighborhoods destroyed to make way for roads. Just in Seattle, for example, thousands of homes were destroyed to make way for Interstate 5. Whole neighborhoods were . . . well, it was like having a river, a concrete river, a river of traffic cut through a neighborhood, or cut off from other neighborhoods. There was opposition, there were protests. In Boston in 1966, an anti-highway group successfully blocked the building of a highway called the Inner Belt. Another group stopped the building of an Interstate highway through San Francisco.

Still, for better or worse, the Interstate Highway System has changed the face of the United States. And remember that trip from Washington to San Francisco in 1919 that took Eisenhower 62 days? Today, you can make that same trip in just 72 hours!

**Narrator:** Now get ready to answer the questions. You may use your notes to help you.

**Narrator:** Question 19: Which of the following caused the decline of roads in the United States in the nineteenth century?

**Narrator:** Question 20: How long did it take Dwight David Eisenhower to drive across the United States in 1919?

**Narrator:** Question 21: According to the speaker, which of these influenced the way President Eisenhower thought about highways?

**Narrator:** Question 22: When was the Interstate Highway system originally supposed to have been completed?

**Narrator:** Question 23: Which of the following is not given as an effect of the Interstate Highway System?

**Narrator:** Question 24: In which of these cities were Interstate Highway projects blocked by protests?

**Narrator:** Listen to a discussion among students preparing a presentation for an architecture class.

**Student A:** Okay, so . . . the presentation on alternative housing in Professor Maxwell's class is going to be . . . what, the 21st?

**Student B:** Umm, let me check . . . no, it's, uh, not until the 23rd. But we have to hand in a . . . a preliminary outline next Tuesday.

**Student C:** And this presentation counts for . . . I think it's a fourth of our grade, so we need to do a good job.

**Student A:** Right. So, either of you do any research, or decide what kind of housing we should talk about?

**Student C:** Well, I . . . I looked at a couple of Web sites on the Internet, and paged through some journals, but . . . I didn't really come up with much of anything. How about you, Joyce?

**Student B:** As a matter of fact, ummm, I have some . . . I guess you could call it indirect experience with one type of alternative housing. I think I told you my uncle owns a construction company, and, okay, last year, he had these clients, this couple come to him and say they wanted him to help them build the kind of house called an earthship. They showed him the plans and . . . at first he thought they were nuts, but, well, he needed the business and so . . . he helped them build the house, the earthship . . . and he ended up thinking . . . well, he's actually thinking of building an earthship for himself.

**Student C:** An earthship! Huh! That sounds like . . . like something from a science fiction movie!

**Student B:** Yeah, I guess it does!

**Student A:** So, uh, what's so interesting about earthships?

**Student B:** Well, for one thing, they're made almost entirely out of recycled materials. In fact, the main building materials are old tires and aluminum cans. The outer walls consist of used tires packed with soil. Then you take the aluminum cans and tuck them between the tires and then . . .you cover the walls with cement.

**Student C:** You're kidding. I mean, I . . . hate to say this but . . . used tires, old cans, dirt, cement . . . . those aren't the most attractive building materials.

**Student B:** I know, I know, they don't sound that attractive, not at all, but, uh, you can finish the interior, the inside of the earthship any way you want. You can finish the walls with plaster and paint them, or you can use wood panels . . . I've seen pictures of the one my uncle built, and it's full of plants and art and, and believe me, it looks really nice.

**Student A:** Well, Maxwell should love them—you know how she feels about building with recycled materials . . .

**Student B:** Yeah, but that's not all . . . earthships are not only made from recycled materials. They also use . . . very, very little power. They generate their own electricity from solar panels—these are up on the roof . . . and they use, uh, passive solar heating to provide heat in the winter.

**Student A:** Really? How do they do that?

**Student B:** Well, earthships are basically shaped like the letter U. The three walls made of tires are on the west, north, and east sides. The open part of the U, which is on the south side, is made of glass windows, and they're . . . they're angled upward to catch the winter sunlight.

**Student A:** Yeah, this definitely sounds like the kind of house Maxwell would love.

**Student C:** What about costs? How much does an earthship cost?

**Student B:** Well, you know . . . dirt, aluminum cans . . . a lot of the materials are either free or almost free . . . and a lot of times, the owners help build the houses themselves. Earthships are a real bargain. My uncle's clients got a small "nest" for . . . well, I'm guessing, but it probably only cost them about $40,000, not counting the land it was built on.

**Student C:** Umm, what do you mean, a "nest?"

**Student B:** Oh, that's what . . . that's the most basic form of earthship, the smallest type. Course, you can spend a lot more if you build a big, fancy one.

**Student C:** Well, I vote we do our presentation on earthships, then, since Joyce already knows a lot about them, and they, uh, they sound pretty interesting to me too.

**Student A:** I'll go along with that. Like I say, I think Maxwell will love them, and she's the one who gives the grade.

**Student C:** Joyce, if you can get me some plans, I bet I could build a small model before we give our presentation.

**Student B:** Well, detailed plans are pretty expensive, but I can probably get you some photos of the earthship that my uncle helped build.

**Student C:** That's probably all I'd need, as long as they show the house from all sides . . .

**Student A:** But would you have time to make a model before the presentation?

**Student C:** Oh, I'm sure I can. I can make a simple architectural model of just about anything in a coupla days.

**Narrator:** Now get ready to answer the questions. You may use your notes to help you.

**Narrator:** Question 25: How did Joyce get most of her information about earthships?

**Narrator:** Question 26: Which of these are not one of the main building materials used to construct earthships?

**Narrator:** Question 27: Which of the walls of an earthship is made of glass?

**Narrator:** Question 28: What is meant by the term *nest?*

**Narrator:** Question 29: Why does Joyce call earthships "a real bargain"?

**Narrator:** Question 30: What will the students probably bring to the presentation?

**Narrator:** Listen to a lecture in a political science class.

**Professor:** Afternoon. How's everyone today? Good. So, we've spent the best part of the last couple weeks going over the structure of the federal government . . . and talking about the document that, that provides the basis for government structure, the U.S. Constitution. Today, as promised, we're going to take a look at the structure of the states, of the individual state governments in the United States.

There are two main types of government . . . two main systems of governing in the world. Under the *unitary* system, the national government, the central government has a great deal of control over the regional and local governments. For example, the central government may completely control the budgets of the provinces, the states, the departments, whatever the political subdivisions are called. The national president may appoint the governors of these regional units. Actually, most of the national governments in the world are of this type: unitary. The other type, the other system of government is the *federal* system. Under this system, the constituent parts of the nation have a great deal of power. Only about twenty-four, twenty-five nations in the world are considered to have federal systems. The oldest one of these is the United States.

The reason that the U.S. has a federal system . . . it's because of our history. Before independence, the thirteen British colonies were ruled separately. People from the colony of Virginia, for example, considered themselves Virginians, really, not Americans. So then, after the Revolutionary War, the former colonies . . . well, as you can imagine, they each jealously guarded their own independence. When the states signed the Constitution, they surrendered some of their sovereign powers but . . . here's the thing: the Constitution says that, whatever powers are not given directly to the federal government belong to the state governments. So . . . compared to other countries . . . well, there may be a few countries that have an equally decentralized system . . . Switzerland comes to mind, the Swiss states, they're actually called cantons there, they have a great deal of power, too . . . and so do the Canadian provinces. But, if you look at other countries . . . France has always had a very centralized system of government. Paris has traditionally controlled everything. Now, this may be becoming less true—there's been some decentralization in recent years—but still, it's a unitary system. And if you look at the United Kingdom, well, local governments there have a fair amount of power, but . . . but there is nothing comparable, really, to state governments. Britain is divided into regions, but these regions have no real governments to speak of. Again, maybe someday soon they will, but for now, we'd have to consider the U.K.'s system of government more or less a unitary system. So anyway, my point here is, compared to most comparable political units around the world, the U.S. states are pretty powerful.

What kind of powers do the states have? They collect taxes . . . they regulate businesses that operate within the state . . . they issue licenses, like drivers' licenses, marriage licenses . . . they build roads. What else? Well, they're involved in education. Mostly with higher education. All the states operate a state university system. Elementary schools, secondary schools, those are mostly controlled by local school boards.

Now, as we said earlier, the structure of the federal government, the rules for operating the federal government, these are determined by the U.S. Constitution. Likewise, each state has its own constitution that determines its structure. Massachusetts has the oldest constitution. In fact, it's older than the national constitution. Granted, it's been changed some since then, but it's, it's really the same document that was adopted in 1780.

We said the federal government was divided into three branches: executive, legislative, and judicial. Same is true of the states. The chief of the executive branch is called the governor, as you no doubt know. The governor—this is true in all the states—is elected for a four-year term. In about half the states, the governor can serve only two terms, in about half he can serve as many as he wants. In one state— Virginia—the governor can only serve one term.

The state legislatures serve the same purpose as the U.S. Congress. Members of the legislature are elected. They make laws, they set tax rates, and in all of the states except Oregon, they can impeach—know what I mean, they can throw out the governor. Like the U.S. Congress, state legislatures have a . . . a bicameral structure. This means they are divided into two bodies, two houses. The upper house is called the state senate, the lower house, well, it has different names, depending on what state you're in . . . Oh, and, uh, when I said every state has a bicameral legislature, I should have said all but one of them do. Nebraska is the exception, Nebraska is unique because it has only one house . . . so its, it has a unicameral system . . . just one house.

State supreme courts . . . those represent the judicial branch . . . their job is to interpret the state constitution . . . just like the U.S. Supreme Court does . . . and to try various cases. In some states, they are elected, in some states they are appointed by the governor or the legislature. In most states, they serve terms of 8 to 10 years, but in Rhode Island, they're appointed for life.

Next up . . . we're going to take an in-depth look at the structure of our own state government. I'm going to pass out copies of the Ohio State Constitution in just a minute but . . . anyone have any questions first?

**Narrator:** Now get ready to answer the questions. You may use your notes to help you.

**Narrator:** Question 31: What does the professor say about the unitary system of government?

**Narrator:** Question 32: What does the professor say about Switzerland?

**Narrator:** Question 33: According to the professor, which of the following is mainly responsible for primary and secondary education in the United States?

**Narrator:** Question 34: Which of these states has the oldest constitution?

**Narrator:** Question 35: What is the maximum time that a governor of Virginia can serve?

**Narrator:** Question 36: What is unique about the state legislature of Nebraska?

**Narrator:** Listen to a discussion in a dance class.

**Professor:** Okay, everyone. We've been talking about traditional forms of dance. Today, umm, we're going to shift our attention to the islands of Hawaii, and the most famous form of dance that's associated with those beautiful islands. Anyone know what that is? Laura?

**Student A:** Oh, that's an easy one—it's the hula dance.

**Professor:** Yeah, you're right, it's the hula—um, you don't have to say hula *dance*, actually, because the word hula means dance in Hawaiian, in the Hawaiian language. Has anyone ever seen this dance performed, or know anything about it? James?

**Student B:** Well, I've seen a coupla TV shows and movies about Hawaii, and, um, it seems to me, that usually when you see the hula, it's done by women in long grass skirts.

**Professor:** Laura?

**Student A:** When I was a little kid, I . . . my parents took me to Hawaii, and there were hula dancers who'd perform at our hotel. I remember being fascinated by . . . by how gracefully they moved their bodies and their hands.

**Professor:** Yeah, and you know, those body movements and gestures, they all have meaning. The dancers use those to tell stories. But, uh, what I want to emphasize, really emphasize, is the fact that the hula that's performed today for tourists, the one you see at hotels and cultural shows, is very different from the traditional hula, the one that was performed hundreds of years ago. Modern hula is called *hula auane*. The old style, traditional hula, is called *hula kahiko*.

**Student A:** Hundreds of years ago . . . I didn't realize it was such an old dance!

**Professor:** Yeah, and as a matter of fact, we don't even know exactly how old the hula is. We do know that when Captain Cook visited the islands in the 1770's—he was the first European to go there . . . , he was allowed to see a hula on the island of Kauai. He wrote in his journal how much he enjoyed it. We also know that one of the queens of Hawaii established a royal school of hula over 500 years ago. Back then, both men and women took part in the dance. There were two types of performers. There were young performers, called *olapa*, which means "graceful ones" in Hawaiian. These were the dancers, the ones that actually performed the dance. Then there were older performers called *h'oa-paa*, which means "steady ones." They chanted and sang, and they also played musical instruments. Apparently back then hula ceremonies could get quite wild! But all that changed in 1820.

**Student B:** Why? What happened then?

**Professor:** That was the year that religious missionaries came to Hawaii from the United States—from New England, to be specific. They found the original form of the hula to be a little . . . well, shocking, so they arranged to have the hula completely banned for around fifty years. Then, when it came back, it was a much tamer version, a much more conservative dance—the *hula auane*.

**Student B:** So, how was it different?

**Professor:** Well, remember I told you that the hula tells stories through movements? In the old days, the hula . . . well, probably the most important story was the story of how the islands rose up out of the sea. Also, there were dances about the . . . the Hawaiian gods and goddesses, especially the goddess Laki, who was the special goddess of the hula. Some dances told the stories of brave Hawaiian kings and queens . . . stories of Hawaiian history. But, uh, in the modern version of the dance, the movements of the dance . . . they usually represent some, uh, some natural phenomenon such as palm trees swaying in the wind, or waves crashing on the beach, or birds flying across the sky.

**Student B:** Professor, what about the music for the hula? It's, uh, a lot of times you hear it played on the ukulele, right? Has that always been true? Is the ukulele a traditional instrument?

**Professor:** No, no, not at all. There was a group of Portuguese workers who came to Hawaii around 1870, and they brought with them these small guitars that were common in Portugal back then. These little guitars eventually evolved into ukuleles. By the way, in Hawaiian, the word *ukulele* means "jumping flea."

**Student B:** Jumping flea? Yeah? Why did they call it that?

**Professor:** Hmmmmm. Probably it was because . . . well, to tell you the truth, I don't have a clue. I'll try to find out for you, though.

**Student A:** So . . . how did the hula . . . how did it get to be a tourist attraction?

**Professor:** In the 1950's, tourism became a major industry in Hawaii, and tourists wanted to see . . . to see samples of "authentic" Hawaiian culture. Even though the modern hula is . . . well, it's not really an expression of Hawaiian culture, not the way the traditional hula was, but then, most tourists probably didn't know the difference.

**Student B:** Well, personally, I think it's too bad that you can't see what the hula was like back in the old days. I'll bet it was a lot more interesting than what you see now.

**Professor:** Yeah, I have to agree with you on that, but actually, you can. These days, there are several groups of Hawaiian dancers that have gotten together to perform the *hula kahiko* the way it was originally performed. In fact, I have a video of one of their performances, and we'll be taking a look at that next.

**Narrator:** Now get ready to answer the questions. You may use your notes to help you.

**Narrator:** Question 37: What does the word *hula* mean in the Hawaiian language?

**Narrator:** Question 38: What fact about the hula does the professor particularly emphasize?

**Narrator:** Question 39: What roles did the *h'oa-paa*, or "steady ones," play in the performance of the hula?

**Narrator:** Question 40: What did the New England missionaries do when they arrived in 1820?

**Narrator:** Question 41: Which of the following would be the most likely theme of a modern hula?

**Narrator:** Question 42: What will the members of the class do next?

[Track 12]

## Lesson 3: Purpose, Method, and Attitude Questions

### Sample Item 1

**Narrator:** Listen to a part of a discussion from the Listening Preview Test.

**Professor:** Well, you see, Professor Longdell, he, he in fact taught in the law school at Harvard, not in the business school. So the case method first . . . it was first used to train law students. Then, a couple of years after that, they started using it at Columbia University, at the law school there. It wasn't until . . . when was it, probably about 1910, 1912, something like that, it was used, first used at Harvard Business School.

**Student B:** Then, it's used in other fields? Besides law and business?

**Professor:** Oh, sure, over the years, it's been used in all sorts of disciplines. For example, my wife, she teaches over at the School of Education, she uses cases to train teachers.

**Narrator:** Why does Professor Speed mention his wife?

[Track 13]

## Sample Item 2

**Narrator:** Listen to a part of a student presentation from an astronomy class.

**Student Presenter:** Well, uh, hi, everyone . . . Monday, we heard Don tell us about the Sun, and, uh, Lisa talk about Mercury, the planet closest to the Sun. My . . . my, uh, report, what I'm talking about is the next planet, the second planet, Venus. Okay, to start off, I'm going to tell you what people, well, what they used to think about Venus. First off, back in the really . . . in the really ancient days, people thought Venus was a star, not a planet, and . . . well, actually, you know how you can see Venus in the early morning and in the evening? Well, so they thought it was two stars, Phosphorus—that was the morning star . . . and, uh, let's see, Hesperus, the evening star. And then, once they figured out it was just one planet, they named it Venus after the goddess of love—I don't really know why, though.

**Narrator:** How does the speaker introduce the topic of Venus?

[Track 14]

## Sample Item 3

**Narrator:** Listen to part of a conversation from the Listening Preview Test.

**Student:** So that's . . . so you don't think that's a very good idea for a topic, then, I suppose . . .

**Professor:** I didn't say that . . . just because this theory hasn't been proven doesn't mean you couldn't write a perfectly good paper about this topic . . . on the notion that animals can predict earthquakes. Why not? It could be pretty interesting. But to do a good job, you . . . you'll need to look at some serious studies in the scientific journals, not just some pop-science articles in newspapers, or . . . and you can't get your information from television shows.

**Narrator:** What is the professor's attitude toward the topic that the student wants to write about?

[Track 15]

## Exercise 3.1

**Narrator:** Listen to a conversation between two students.

**Student A:** So, Joan, your roommate told me that you had a meeting with Dean Metzger this morning.

**Student B:** Well, actually, it's later this afternoon—I'm meeting her at four today.

**Student A:** How come?

**Student B:** Well, I'm sure you've been hearing and reading about the cuts in the university budget, right? Well, the budget for the university debate team was really slashed. In fact, it was cut more than in half. And it was already a bare-bones budget! To tell you the truth, I don't know if . . . well, I don't really think we'll be able to keep debating.

**Student A:** Really? So how do you . . . what does the debate team spend its money on? The coach's salary, or . . .

**Student B:** No, as a matter of fact, my friend Kurt Wyndham is our coach, and he volunteers his time. Kurt's a graduate student now, but when he was an undergrad, he was a debater himself.

**Student A:** So, then, how do you spend your money?

**Student B:** Well, mostly, we spend it on travel expenses. We take four or five trips a semester to other campuses, and we need money for bus fares or gas money, hotel rooms, meals, things like that.

**Student A:** Well, I—I kinda hate to say this, but . . . would it really be the end of the world if the debate team couldn't keep going? I mean, does anyone really care all that much about debate?

**Student B:** The people on the team do! Most of us have been debating since high school, and it's really important to us. And you know, it can be really good career preparation. You learn research skills, you learn . . . well, to communicate . . . to think on your feet—you learn teamwork. My father's a lawyer, you know, and when he was in college—he went to college over in England—he was involved in debate, and he says it was a wonderful way to train for the courtroom. He's the one who talked me into joining the team.

**Student A:** Well, I'm just saying . . . except for a few people on the team . . . how does having a debate team really benefit the university?

**Student B:** Oh, don't even get me started! For one thing, there's the whole matter of school tradition. I mean, did you know that this school has had a debating team for over a hundred years? And over the years, we've won a dozen or more regional tournaments and a couple of national tournaments. Then there's the prestige. We haven't had a good football or basketball team for . . . for years, but our debate team is always one of the best in the region. A good debate team attracts people who debated in high school, and they're always some of the top students. And you know, a lot of famous people were on college debate teams . . . President John F. Kennedy, for one, and . . .

**Student A:** Okay, okay, you've sold me!

**Student B:** And we're not even asking for that much. It's like a, like a millionth of what the school spends on football and basketball! I mean, I don't have anything against sports teams, but . . .

**Student A:** Still, I can't see why you're going to talk to Dean Metzger. She's . . . she's Dean of the School of Arts and Sciences. She's not in charge of the university budget.

**Student B:** No, I know, you're right. And we tried to get an appointment with President Fisher, but his assistant kept saying he was too busy right now and wasn't able to meet with us. So Kurt came up with the idea of our talking to Dean Metzger. He said Dean Metzger is fair—she has that reputation, anyway—and she's, you know, willing to listen. So, I don't know, maybe if we can convince her, then she can persuade President Fisher and the Board of Chancellors not to cut our budget so much.

**Student A:** Well, if anyone can convince her, you can! I'll tell you, though . . . if I were you, I'd keep trying to get a meeting with President Fisher. Talking to Dean Metzger won't hurt, but really, President Fisher is the person whose mind you have to change.

**Narrator:** Now get ready to answer the questions. You may use your notes to help you.

**Narrator:** Question 1: Why does the woman mention her father?

**Narrator:** Question 2: How does the man feel about the woman's appointment with Dean Metzger?

**Narrator:** Listen to a conversation between two students.

**Student A:** Hey, Julie, want to go see a movie tonight?

**Student B:** Oh, wish I could, but I'm on my way home to study. I have a mid-term in my math class tomorrow.

**Student A:** How are your mid-terms going?

**Student B:** So far, so good . . . the only one I'm at all worried about is the math exam tomorrow. How about you? Don't you have any mid-term exams?

**Student A:** As a matter of fact, I do have one in geology class tomorrow, but there's nothing I can do tonight to get ready for it.

**Student B:** What sort of test is it? Multiple-choice or essay?

**Student A:** Neither, actually. Doctor Fowles gives us a mineral sample and we have an hour to figure out what it is—we work in teams of two.

**Student B:** How on earth do you do that? I mean, a rock's a rock, isn't it?

**Student A:** Actually, there are a number of tests you can perform on minerals to, ah, figure out what they are. First off, you just look carefully at the sample.

**Student B:** Okay . . . what do you look for?

**Student A:** Well, you check the mineral's color . . . although that's one of the most unreliable tests.

**Student B:** Why? Why would that be unreliable?

**Student A:** Because a lot of minerals have impurities that change their color. For example, pure quartz is clear, but then you also have white quartz, rose quartz, smoky quartz—it's all the same, the same mineral, but different colors. Another thing to look for is luster . . .

**Student B:** You mean, how shiny it is?

**Student A:** That's right. The way light reflects off the mineral. Most minerals that contain metals tend to have a shiny, metallic luster. Non-metallic rocks often look dull. Then, you can do a taste test . . .

**Student B:** Ewww, yuck! I wouldn't taste a mineral sample! Who knows where that mineral sample has been!

**Student A:** Well, it can help you identify certain minerals—for example, halite has a salty taste. Probably the most useful test of all is the hardness test. Have you ever heard of the Mohs scale?

**Student B:** Huh? The what scale?

**Student A:** It's a scale that indicates how hard a mineral is. We have a kit that we use that contains samples of minerals, of known minerals that, ah, have a certain hardness. It goes from talc at number 1—talc is so soft you can scratch it with your fingernail—to diamonds at number 10. Diamonds are the hardest . . .

**Student B:** I know, I know, they're the hardest substance in the world. Do you actually have a diamond in your kit?

**Student A:** Yeah, sure, a tiny little industrial diamond. So, let's say you can scratch your sample with fluorite, which is number 4 on the scale, but not with, umm, gypsum, that's number 2, then on the Mohs scale, you, ah . . .

**Student B:** Then the sample must be about 3 on that scale, right?

**Student A:** Right! So you look on the list that comes with the kit and you know it's one of those minerals that is about 3 on the scale. Another good test is the streak test, which tells you the true color of a mineral . . .

**Student B:** I thought you said color is unreliable . . .

**Student A:** Uh, right, I did, but, ah, see, the streak test shows you the true color of the mineral. You take your sample and rub it against a piece of unglazed porcelain, okay, and look at the color of the streak on the porcelain. Remember all those different colors of quartz I mentioned? Well, if you do a streak test on those, the streak on the porcelain looks the same, no matter what color the mineral appears to be. Oh, and my favorite is the acid test. You pour a little bit of acid, of vinegar, say, on the sample, and, sometimes, with a certain kind of mineral, one that contains calcium, it fizzes and foams. It's really cool. And then there's the specific gravity test, the ultraviolet test—that one's kinda fun too—oh, and the blowpipe test, and then . . .

**Student B:** Wait, stop, I get the picture! And after . . . after you've done all these tests, you can identify any mineral?

**Student A:** Well, usually . . . not always, but usually. My partner and I have done a couple of practice runs, and we didn't have any trouble figuring out what mineral we were looking at. So, I'm pretty sure we can do the same tomorrow.

**Narrator:** Now get ready to answer the questions. You may use your notes to help you.

**Narrator:** Question 3: How does the man explain his geology mid-term exam to the woman?

**Narrator:** Question 4: What is the woman's attitude towards the taste test?

**Narrator:** Question 5: Why does the man mention quartz?

**Narrator:** Question 6: What is the man's attitude toward his geology mid-term?

[Track 16]

**Exercise 3.2**

**Narrator:** Listen to a discussion in a U.S. history class.

**Professor:** Morning, everyone. We've been discussing the Civil War for the last coupla weeks . . . talking about some of the major battles of the war. So today, I've, uh, invited a guest to come to our class. I'd like all of you to meet Ms. Frances Adams. She's the state coordinator of the Civil War Heritage Society, which is involved in preserving battlefields all over the eastern part of the country. Ms. Adams . . . .

**Guest Speaker:** Thank you, Professor Nugent, thanks for inviting me. I always appreciate the chance to talk to students . . . to anyone who'll listen, for that matter . . . about our disappearing battlefields. The organization I work with is trying to save battlefields from development. It's an uphill struggle. By one estimate, twenty-five acres of Civil War battlefield are being lost every day. That's like an acre an hour. In fact, we're trying to save one battlefield right here in our state . . . you may have read about it in the newspapers. There's a site, oh, only about 100 miles from here called Ivy Station where a small battle was fought in the closing days of the war, in 1864. A development company wants to build a 300-unit apartment complex where that battle was fought and we—the Society, that is—we're trying to stop them.

**Student A:** Ms. Adams, I understood . . . I mean, I always assumed, I guess, that battlefields are protected by the government. A few years ago, I went with my family to the battlefield at Gettysburg, and it seemed pretty well protected to me.

**Guest Speaker:** You're right, the Gettysburg battlefield is well protected. After all, Gettysburg was the largest battle of the whole war, and so . . . well, the sites of most important battles—Gettysburg, Antietam, Shiloh, Vicksburg—they're all national historical sites, and they're under the protection of the National Park Service. But, have you ever heard of, oh, say the Battle of Salt Run in Virginia?

**Student A:** Ummm, no.

**Guest Speaker:** Well, that's not too surprising, as it wasn't a turning-point battle, but . . . it involved several thousand Union and Confederate troops . . . Okay, now when I came in I put one of our society's brochures on each of your desks. I want to show you . . . just take a look at the cover of the brochure. What do you see?

**Student B:** Ummm, a shopping mall?

**Guest Speaker:** Right. It's called the Salt Run Mall. And it's located right . . . right smack in the middle of what was the Salt Run battlefield. Now, take a look inside the brochure. There's a list of almost 400 Civil War battlefields. As you see, these are classified in, uh, one of three ways. Do you see what I mean? They're classified as "Adequately Protected," "At Risk," or "Lost to Development." Only about 70 are Adequately Protected. About 180 are endangered. You'll find the Ivy Station battlefield on this list. Then there are 150 that have already been developed, that are completely gone. The Salt Run battlefield is on this list, you'll notice.

**Professor:** David, I see you have a question for Ms. Adams.

**Student B:** Thanks, Professor. Yeah, Ms. Adams, I'm just wondering—is your organization—is it made up of re-enactors?

**Guest Speaker:** Of re-enactors? No, not at all. I mean, a few members of the Society may be involved in re-enactment, but not many . . .

**Student B:** I read somewhere that most of the, ah, pressure to save Civil War battlefields, that it comes from re-enactors.

**Student A:** Hold on! What are . . . who are . . . re-enactors?

**Student B:** They're people who pretend the Civil War is still going on . . .

**Guest Speaker:** Well . . . I don't know if I'd go so far as to say *that*, but . . . they're people who enjoy . . . re-enacting, re-living the Civil War experience. They wear the uniforms of the northern and the southern soldiers—some of them have equipment and wear uniforms that are amazingly authentic—and they . . . well, they fight Civil War battles all over again. Without real bullets, of course. And naturally, they prefer to stage these, umm, re-enactments on authentic—on the actual battlefields where the original battle took place.

**Student A:** So they're interested in the same thing you are, right?

**Guest Speaker:** Well, yes, their goals and ours certainly overlap. Now, personally, I have no interest in spending my weekends dressed up as a Civil War nurse and sleeping in a tent on a battlefield. My interest, the Society's interest, is to preserve these battlefields as places of historical . . . of cultural significance. But . . . several of the re-enactment organizations are . . . well, I guess you'd call them our allies . . . yeah, our allies in the fight to save these sites.

**Student B:** I'm just wondering why it's necessary to save all these sites. The big battlefields, sure, but . . . some of these sites are . . . . well, they weren't all that important to the way the war turned out, and, well—they may have been in the middle of nowhere during the Civil War, but now they're on some pretty valuable suburban real estate, and hey, they're privately owned. Can't we just read about these little battles in history books?

**Professor:** I'm going to jump in here, Frances, and comment on what David just said. Geography and . . . topography shape a battle. The patterns of uh, hills, valleys, rocks, rivers, streams . . . these are all important. And if future historians, military historians, if they don't have access to these battlefields, they won't be able to understand what really happened back in the 1860's.

**Guest Speaker:** And I'd just like to add . . . for those of us who are non-historians, who are not professional historians, well, I think it is important for us, too, that these sites be preserved. If you walk around on a Civil War battlefield, and you imagine what happened there, well, you have an emotional, um, connection, an emotional empathy with those who fought there. You can't get that walking around a parking lot! And also, well, I think we owe those soldiers,

the ones who fought and died in these places, I think we owe them a measure of respect for their courage. For their sacrifices. No matter how unimportant the battle was to the outcome of the war.

**Student A:** So, what does your society do, Ms. Adams, to save battlefields?

**Guest Speaker:** Well, one of the things we do is what I'm doing today—making people like you aware, educating people about the the, uh, the problem of disappearing battlefields. And then, as I said, we work with other groups—re-enactment groups and historical societies and so forth—to coordinate our efforts. We meet with government officials—state, local, federal—and try to persuade them to buy battlefield land in order to preserve it. And, when we can afford it, we buy up land ourselves and keep it free of commercial or industrial development. The Society owns and maintains about 3,000 acres of battlefield land in seven states.

**Student B:** Well, I'm still of the opinion that . . . that you can't really stop progress. Sometimes you shouldn't even try.

**Professor:** Well, David, you're certainly entitled to your opinion. But I . . . I can't imagine giving up our own heritage, our own history without a fight. Anyway, if any of you are interested in joining the Society and helping preserve these sites, personally, I think it's a wonderful idea. I've been a member myself for about five years.

**Guest Speaker:** Inside the brochure I gave you, there's a form you can fill out, if you're interested in joining. There's a special membership for students that's not as expensive as a regular membership.

**Narrator:** Now get ready to answer the questions. You may use your notes to help you.

**Narrator:** Question 1: Why does Ms. Adams mention the battle of Ivy Station?

**Narrator:** Question 2: How does Ms. Adams make the class aware of the current condition of the Salt Run battlefield?

**Narrator:** Question 3: What is Ms. Adams' attitude toward re-enactors?

**Narrator:** Question 4: What is David's attitude toward the preservation of Civil War battlefields?

**Narrator:** Listen to a lecture in an American Literature class.

**Professor:** Okay, for the last few minutes of class, I'd like to introduce you to the poet Emily Dickinson. A couple of days ago, we were talking about the poet Walt Whitman, and if you recall, I said that he was one of the two great voices in American poetry in the nineteenth century. Today, I'm going to drop the other shoe and talk about the other great poet, Emily Dickinson.

The poetry of Emily Dickinson and the poetry of Walt Whitman couldn't have been more different, as we'll see. Dickinson claimed that she never . . . never even read Whitman's poems. And their lifestyles . . . again, couldn't have been more different. But they were both innovators, important innovators, and they both had a major role in shaping American poetry.

I said Monday that Whitman became famous all over the country and in Europe as well. He was really the first American poet who was read much outside the United States. Dickinson was well known only in her own small town—in those days, it was just a village—Amherst, Massachusetts. But she wasn't known there for her poetry. Oh, no! She was known for her . . . her odd, her mysterious ways. You see, after she finished high school she went to the Mount Holyoke Female Seminary—today, it, uh, it's called Mount Holyoke College—but she only went there for one year. She didn't get along with the headmistress, apparently. After that, she returned to her father's house in Amherst—and she hardly ever left. In fact, she hardly left her own bedroom. And when she did leave the house, she always wore white dresses like a bride. Outside of her family, her only person-to-person contact with others was with the children who lived in her neighborhood. This, uh, may not seem all that odd to us today, but . . . in Amherst, Massachusetts, in the 1800's, this was considered . . . well, pretty strange behavior.

For a woman who lived such an uneventful life—at least, her life was uneventful on the surface—she wrote amazingly perceptive poems about nature, love, and death. Her poems are all quite short and are all untitled. What I like about them the most is their economy. She was able to say so much, to express so much in so few words. She was an extremely prolific poet. Just in one year alone, 1874—that was the year her father died—she wrote, like, 200 poems. But she never wanted her poems to be published. Well, she did engage in a kind of self-publishing. She assembled collections of her poems in packets that were called "fascicles," which she bound herself with needle and thread. There were some forty of these booklets. But she never tried to have these . . . these fascicles published, seldom even showed them to anyone else. She did send a few of her poems to friends and relatives, and somehow, six or seven of these found their way into print in magazines or newspapers during her lifetime. You can imagine, though, how she felt when she heard that her poems had been published.

After Emily Dickinson died in 1886, her family discovered that she had written over 1,700 poems. Her sister Lavinia edited three volumes of Emily's poetry. They were popular as soon as they were published, but it was not until the twentieth century that critics recognized her as one of the top American poets. Martha Dickinson Bianchi, the poet's niece, brought out several more books of poems in the early 1900's. Eventually all of them appeared in print. In 1950, Harvard University bought all of her manuscripts and acquired the publishing rights to all of her poems. Harvard published a complete three-volume collection of her poems and letters five years later.

Okay, for Friday, I'd like you to read all of Dickinson's poems that are in our textbook. There are about twenty, maybe twenty-five of her poems in there. Don't worry, though. That may sound like a lot of reading, but it shouldn't take you long! Friday, we'll take a closer look at her poems.

Before we move on to another topic, I'd just like to say this: These days, a lot of scholars downplay Dickinson's, um, eccentric lifestyle. They point out that she was not as intellectually cut off as people used to think, that she had a lively relationship with others through her letters—and that she was quite learned about other writers, such as John Keats and John Ruskin. But, there's no doubt that she lived in relative isolation and that she did not want to be in the public eye. I'm going to leave you with the first verse of one of her most famous poems:

I'm nobody! Who are you?
Are you nobody, too?
Then there's a pair of us—don't tell!
They'd banish us, you know.

**Narrator:** Now get ready to answer the questions. You may use your notes to help you.

**Narrator:** Question 5: Why does the professor mention the poet Walt Whitman?
**Narrator:** Question 6: Why does the professor mention Harvard University?
**Narrator:** Question 7: Which of the following best summarizes the professor's attitude toward Emily Dickinson?
**Narrator:** Question 8: How does the professor conclude her discussion of Emily Dickinson?

**Narrator:** Listen to a lecture in an art history class.
**Professor:** Morning. Today I'm going to take a few minutes to talk about folk art. I, uh, know this isn't on your syllabus, but I saw a wonderful exhibit of folk art from the eighteenth and nineteenth century at the Hotchkiss Museum over the weekend, and I'd like to share my impressions of this exhibit with you.

First off, I should tell you that there's, umm, some disagreement in the art world about what is meant by the term *folk art*. European folklorists, in particular, take the position that folk art must be part of a . . . of some long-standing artistic tradition. They say it must have been created by artists from a distinct group, say, oh, American Indians, Australian aborigines—or that it must have been made by people from some particular occupation—say, uh, sailors on whaling ships. These European folklorists would generally not say . . . they wouldn't categorize pieces made for commercial reasons as folk art. They would also, um, disqualify pieces made by groups, not by individuals.

Folklorists in the United States, though—not just folklorists, also museums and galleries—don't take such a narrow view—and I must say, I think the European way of looking at folk art is way too restrictive. Among most American folklorists . . . well, they define a folk artist as simply someone who . . . someone who creates art without any formal artistic training. And, uh, in the catalogue for this exhibit, there's a little essay written by the curator of the Hotchkiss, and he says, "A folk artist is someone who would be surprised to find his or her pieces on display in a museum." That's a definition I like! Anyway, lots of pieces on display at the museum would probably be considered crafts by European folklorists. Some pieces were made by groups, some were even made in factories—for example, the wooden animals for carousels.

The exhibit features lots of different kinds of folk art. There are paintings—portraits and landscapes—that were created to be works of art. But most of the pieces have some utilitarian, some commercial purpose. There's furniture, plates and pots, clothing, clocks. There are ships' figureheads, circus carvings, duck decoys, fish lures . . . lots of weathervanes. Then there's a *wonderful* collection of trade signs. You know what I mean, doncha? Signs advertising shops, taverns, hotels, restaurants . . . As a matter of fact, I spent most of my time at the exhibit looking at trade signs. I found them just fascinating . . . charming.

Now, here's something to keep in mind. It wasn't until 1870 that most people in America could read. Signs had to appeal to both readers and non-readers. Sometimes the shape of the sign told you what kind of business was inside. There's a sign in the shape of a tea kettle that was once in front of a tea shop in Boston . . . a sign in the shape of a pocket watch that was in front of a jeweler's shop . . . a boot-shaped sign from a shoe store—you didn't have to be literate to understand these. More often, there were painted images . . . a sign for a blacksmith shop featured a picture of a horseshoe . . . a bookshop sign showed a picture of a man reading a book . . . well, you get the idea.

Sometimes the images weren't so . . . so obvious. For example, there were signs that pictured an American Indian, a Turkish sultan, a, let's see, an exotic Cuban lady, and a racetrack gambler. All of these images symbolized the same kind of shop . . . tobacco shops. At the time, people instantly recognized these symbols. Maybe they couldn't read, but they had what's called *visual literacy*. Visual literacy. These symbols were as meaningful to them . . . well, just like today, we know we can get hamburgers and French fries when we see golden arches . . . it was the same sort of thing.

Sometimes signs contained political messages. There was an inn in Philadelphia called King's Inn, and its sign showed a picture of King George III on a horse. Well, this was just before the Revolutionary War and George III wasn't too popular with the colonists . . . they weren't real fond of him. So, the king is pictured on this sign as a clumsy fool practically falling off his horse.

Oh, another thing to keep in mind: back in Colonial times, many streets didn't have names, and most buildings didn't have numbers . . . street addresses. Trade signs served as landmarks. People would say, "Meet me by the sign of the Lion and the Eagle," or "by the sign of the Dancing Bear".

If you go to the exhibit and you look at the trade signs, you'll notice that there are almost no plaques that tell you who painted the signs. There are maybe three, four signed pieces in the show—the sign-painter William Rice of Hartford, Connecticut was one of the few who signed his work. A few of the signs in the exhibit were done by fairly well-known portrait artists. Horace Bundy, Rufus Hathaway, who made signs for extra money. Their styles are distinctive, and the signs they made can be easily identified. But most of the sign painters . . . they were mostly itinerant artists, traveling from town to town on horseback, painting a few signs in each town . . . anyway, their names have been long forgotten.

Well, I want to get back to our discussion of Renaissance art, but I do hope all of you get a chance to see the exhibit at the Hotchkiss . . . it will be there another six weeks.

**Narrator:** Now get ready to answer the questions. You may use your notes to help you.

**Narrator:** Question 9: How does the professor introduce his discussion of folk art?

**Narrator:** Question 10: Why does the professor mention wooden carousel horses?

**Narrator:** Question 11: How does the professor explain the concept of "visual literacy"?

**Narrator:** Question 12: Why does the professor mention the sign for the King's Inn?

**Narrator:** Question 13: Why does the professor mention the sign painter William Rice?

[Track 17]

## Lesson 4: Replay Questions

**Narrator:** Listen to the following short conversations. Pay special attention to the way the phrase "I'm sorry" is used.

### Conversation Number 1

**Professor:** You know, Donald, that's the, uh, the second or third time you've turned in an assignment after the due date.

**Student:** I know, Professor Dorn, and I'm sorry, I really am. I won't . . . I'll try not to let it happen again.

### Conversation Number 2

**Professor:** Next, I want to talk about a process that's important, that's of central importance to all living things . . . to all living things that breathe oxygen, anyway. That's the Krebs cycle.

**Student:** I'm sorry, Professor, the *what* cycle?

### Conversation Number 3

**Student A:** Hey, Laura, you wanna go skiing up at Snowbury this weekend with my roommate and me?

**Student B:** I'm sorry, I wish I could, but I've gotta hit the books this weekend. I have a big test in my calculus class on Monday.

### Conversation Number 4

**Employee:** University Recreation Center, Jill speaking.

**Student:** Yeah, hi, I'm calling to reserve a tennis court on Friday morning at 6:30 A.M.

**Employee:** At 6:30 in the morning? I'm sorry, but we don't even open until 7:30.

[Track 18]

## Sample Item

**Narrator:** Why does the speaker say this:

**Professor:** This sub-zone—well, if you like variety, you're not going to feel happy here. You can travel for miles and see only half a dozen species of trees. In a few days, we'll be talking about the tropical rain forest; now *that's* where you'll see variety.

[Track 19]

## Exercise 4.1

**Narrator:** Number 1

**Student A:** Oh, that statistics course I'm taking is just *loads* of fun!

**Student B:** Didn't I tell you it would be?

**Narrator:** Number 2

**Student A:** So did you and your lab partner get together and write up your experiment?

**Student B:** No, and wait till you hear his latest excuse. You're going to *love* it!

**Narrator:** Number 3

**Student A:** Does Professor White ever change his grades?

**Student B:** Oh, sure, about once a century!

**Narrator:** Number 4

**Student A:** Did you know Greg has changed his major?

**Student B:** Oh, no, not again.

**Narrator:** Number 5

**Student A:** So, you're moving out of your apartment?

**Student B:** Yeah, I got a place closer to campus. I just hope the landlady here gives me all of my security deposit back.

**Student A:** Well, you'd better leave the place spic-and-span.

**Narrator:** Number 6

**Student A:** Doctor Stansfield, I've decided to drop my physiology class. It just meets too early in the morning for me.

**Professor:** Do you *really* think that's a good reason, Mark?

**Narrator:**  Number 7
**Student:**  Professor McKee, I know you speak Spanish. I wonder if you could translate this poem for me?
**Professor:**  Let me have a look. Hmmm. Well, I'm afraid this is written in Catalan, not Spanish.

**Narrator:**  Number 8
**Professor:**  Next, next we'll be taking a look at Japanese theater. Kabuki Theater and, uh, Noh Theater . . .
**Student:**  Professor, could you, uh, put those terms on the board?

**Narrator:**  Number 9
**Professor:**  Today we were going to uh, continue to . . . continue our discussion of complex numbers. In our last class, we spent quite a bit of time talking about imaginary numbers, but, uh, I must say, I noticed a few . . . a few puzzled expressions as you filed out. Part of the problem, I think, is the name *imaginary numbers*. They are *not* imaginary, they are as real as any other kind of number. So, here's the thing, we really can't go on to complex numbers until we get this right . . .

**Narrator:**  Number 10
**Professor:**  So, who can tell me who wrote the Brandenburg Concertos?
**Student:**  I *think* . . . umm, was it Bach?

**Narrator:**  Number 11
**Professor:**  Okay, well, uh, I've been digressing . . . no more about my childhood experiments with rockets!

**Narrator:**  Number 12
**Professor:**  Now, I *know* I didn't give you a set number . . . a *maximum* number of words or pages for your term paper . . . I only said it had to be more than ten pages. I didn't really want to discourage anyone from fully exploring the topic you chose. But, uh, I must say, some of these were well, almost ridiculous!

[Track 20]

**Exercise 4.2**
**Narrator:**  Listen again to part of the conversation. Then answer the question.
**Student:**  Oh, well, then, . . . maybe I should, uh, maybe I should go back to my dorm and get some dinner . . . before I sit down and read this.
**Librarian:**  That's fine, but . . . I can't guarantee the article will be available right away when you come back . . . some other student from your class might be using it.
**Student:**  Well, I dunno, I, I guess I'll just have to take my chances . . .
**Narrator:**  Question 1: What does the woman mean when she says this:
**Student:**  I guess I'll just have to take my chances . . .

**Narrator:**  Listen again to part of the conversation. Then answer the question.
**Student A:**  So, uh, how was it . . . I mean, was it a good dig?
**Student B:**  Do you mean, did we find any artifacts? No, it . . . it was supposed to be a very . . . promising site. But it turned out to be a complete bust! We didn't find anything . . . not even one single piece of broken pottery. Nothing! Just sand!
**Narrator:**  Question 2: What does the woman mean when she says this:

**Student B:**  But it turned out to be a complete bust!

**Narrator:**  Listen again to part of the conversation. Then answer the question.
**Student B:**  You just walk a little bit farther, and you'll see the art building . . . the Reynolds Building. You can't miss it because there's a big metal . . . *thing* on a platform right in front of it.
**Student A:**  A thing?
**Student B:**  Yeah, there's this . . . this big rusty piece of abstract "art." I *guess* you'd call it art. Anyway, it's right in front of the doorway.
**Narrator:**  Question 3: What does the woman imply when she says this:
**Student B:**  Yeah, there's this . . . this big rusty piece of abstract "art." I *guess* you'd call it art. Anyway, it's right in front of the doorway.

**Narrator:**  Listen again to part of the conversation. Then answer the question.
**Student B:**  Your sister's an artist?
**Student A:**  Yeah, she's a painter. She also, well she just started volunteering to teach art to kids and . . . I think the way her students paint has sort of rubbed off on her. I think her kids have influenced her more than she's influenced them, as a matter of fact. She's using these bright colors, and . . .
**Narrator:**  Question 4: What does the man mean when he says this:
**Student A:**  I think the way her students paint has sort of rubbed off on her.

**Narrator:**  Listen again to part of the conversation. Then answer the question.
**Student B:**  Hmmm, so, what . . . what other kinds of courses do they offer?
**Student A:**  Well, I don't know all the courses they offer, but I know they have a class on test-taking skills.
**Student B:**  Wow, that's right up my alley.
**Narrator:**  Question 5: What does the man mean when he says this:
**Student B:**  . . . that's right up my alley.

**Narrator:**  Listen again to part of the conversation. Then answer the question.
**Student:**  So, suppose I decide I want to . . . to apply for an R.A. position, what, uh, what would I need to do?
**Administrator:**  I can give you a form to fill out. You'd also need to get two letters of recommendation . . .
**Narrator:**  Question 6: What does the man imply when he says this:
**Student:**  So, suppose I decide I want to . . . to apply for an R.A. position?

**Narrator:**  Listen again to part of the conversation. Then answer the question.
**Student A:**  So then, how do you spend your money?
**Student B:**  Well, mostly, we spend it on travel expenses. We take four or five trips a semester to other campuses and we need money for bus fares or gas money, hotel rooms, meals, things like that.
**Student A:**  Well I—I kinda hate to say this, but . . . would it really be the end of the world if the debate team couldn't keep going?
**Narrator:**  Question 7: What does the man mean when he says this:
**Student A:**  Well, I—I kinda hate to say this . . .

**Narrator:**  Listen again to part of the conversation. Then answer the question.

**Student A:**  Well, I'm just saying . . . except for a few people on the team . . . how does having a debate team really benefit the university?

**Student B:**  Oh, don't even get me started! For one thing, there's the whole matter of school tradition. I mean, did you know that this school has had a debating team for over a hundred years? And over the years, we've won a dozen or more regional tournaments and a couple of national tournaments. Then there's the prestige. We haven't had a good football or basketball team for . . . for *years,* but our debate team is always one of the best in the region. A good debate team attracts people who debated in high school, and they're always some of the top students. And you know, a lot of famous people were on college debate teams . . . President John F. Kennedy, for one, and . . .

**Narrator:**  Question 8: What does the woman mean when she says this:

**Student B:**  Oh, don't even get me started!

**Narrator:**  Listen again to part of the conversation. Then answer the question.

**Student B:**  Oh, don't even get me started! For one thing, there's the whole matter of school tradition. I mean, did you know that this school has had a debating team for over a hundred years? And over the years, we've won a dozen or more regional tournaments and a couple of national tournaments. Then there's the prestige. We haven't had a good football or basketball team for . . . for *years,* but our debate team is always one of the best in the region. A good debate team attracts people who debated in high school, and they're always some of the top students. And you know, a lot of famous people were on college debate teams . . . President John F. Kennedy, for one, and . . .

**Student A:**  Okay, okay, you've sold me!

**Narrator:**  Question 9: What does the man mean when he says this:

**Student A:**  Okay, okay, you've sold me!

**Narrator:**  Listen again to part of the conversation. Then answer the question.

**Student B:**  What sort of test is it? Multiple-choice or essay?

**Student A:**  Neither, actually. Doctor Fowles gives us a mineral sample and we have an hour to figure out what it is—we work in teams of two.

**Student B:**  How on earth do you do that? I mean, a rock's a rock, isn't it?

**Narrator:**  Question 10: Why does the woman say this:

**Student B:**  How on earth do you do that? I mean, a rock's a rock, isn't it?

**Narrator:**  Listen again to part of the conversation. Then answer the question.

**Student A:**  Probably the most useful test of all is the hardness test. Have you ever heard of the Mohs scale?

**Student B:**  Huh? The what scale?

**Narrator:**  Question 11: What does the woman mean when she says this:

**Student B:**  Huh? The what scale?

**Narrator:**  Listen again to part of the conversation. Then answer the question.

**Student A:**  Another good test is the streak test, which tells you the true color of a mineral . . .

**Student B:**  I thought you said color is unreliable . . .

**Student A:**  Uh, right, I did, but, ah, see, the streak test shows you the true color of the mineral.

**Narrator:**  Question 12: What does the man mean when he says this:

**Student A:**  Uh, right, I did, but, ah, see, the streak test shows you the true color of the mineral.

**Narrator:**  Listen again to part of the conversation. Then answer the question.

**Student A:**  And then there's the specific gravity test, the ultraviolet test, that one's kinda fun too . . . oh, and the blowpipe test, and then . . .

**Student B:**  Wait, stop, I get the picture! And after . . . after you've done all these tests, you can identify any mineral?

**Narrator:**  Question 13: Why does the woman say this:

**Student B:**  Wait, stop, I get the picture!

[Track 21]

**Exercise 4.3**

**Narrator:**  Listen again to the professor's comment. Then answer the question.

**Professor:**  First, I just want to say . . . good job on your presentation, Charlie, it was very interesting, and then . . . well, I just want to add this. You said you weren't sure why the planet Venus was named after the goddess of love. It's true Venus was the goddess of love, but she was also the goddess of beauty and, well, anyone who's ever seen Venus early in the morning or in the evening knows it's a beautiful sight.

**Narrator:**  Question 1: Why does the professor say this:

**Professor:**  . . . well, I just want to add this.

**Narrator:**  Listen again to part of the lecture. Then answer the question.

**Professor:**  Computers have been used since the sixties to record choreography. The first one—well, the first one I know about, anyway, was a program written by Michael Noll . . . and it was . . . Oh, I guess by today's standards you'd say it was pretty primitive. The dancers looked like stick figures in a child's drawing.

**Narrator:**  Question 2: What does the woman mean when she says this:

**Professor:**  The dancers looked like stick figures in a child's drawing.

**Narrator:**  Listen again to part of the discussion. Then answer the question.

**Professor:**  Well, after Rhine did his experiments at Duke, a lot of similar experiments have been done—at Stanford University, in Scotland, and elsewhere, and the conclusion . . . most researchers have decided that Rhine's results were, I guess the kindest word I could use is *questionable.*

**Narrator:**  Question 3: What does the professor mean when he says this:

**Professor:**  . . . most researchers have decided that Rhine's results were, I guess the kindest word I could use is *questionable.*

**Narrator:**  Listen again to part of the discussion. Then answer the question.

**Student A:**  So that's why you don't believe in ESP?

**Professor:** To put it in a nutshell—I've just never seen any experimental proof for ESP that stood up to careful examination.

**Narrator:** Question 4: Why does the professor say this:

**Professor:** To put it in a nutshell . . .

**Narrator:** Listen again to part of the discussion. Then answer the question.

**Student A:** Yeah, I've seen that painting before . . . I don't remember the name of the artist, but I think the painting is called *Nighthawks at the Diner.*

**Professor:** Yeah, that's . . . well, a lot of people call it that, but the real name of the painting is just *Nighthawks.*

**Narrator:** Question 5: What does the professor mean when she says this:

**Professor:** . . . a lot of people call it that, but the real name of the painting is just *Nighthawks.*

**Narrator:** Listen again to part of the lecture. Then answer the question.

**Professor:** Now, if you happen to have a copy of the syllabus that I gave you last week you'll notice that we're not gonna be able to . . . we just don't have time to read all of these two poems and talk about them. An epic poem—I probably don't have to tell you this—is a narrative poem, a really long narrative poem.

**Narrator:** Question 6: What does the professor mean when she says this:

**Professor:** . . . I probably don't have to tell you this . . .

**Narrator:** Listen again to part of the lecture. Then answer the question.

**Professor:** Anyway, the main characters in the *Iliad,* they're strong, they're great warriors, but you know . . . they're not as clever, not as smart as Odysseus. He's the one who thinks up the plan to end the war—after ten long years— and defeat the Trojans. He's the . . . the mastermind behind the scheme to build the Trojan Horse.

**Narrator:** Question 7: What does the professor mean when she says this:

**Professor:** He's the . . . the mastermind behind the scheme to build the Trojan Horse.

**Narrator:** Listen again to part of the lecture. Then answer the question.

**Professor:** How does HDR energy work? Well, in theory, anyway . . . and let me stress, I say in theory . . . it's pretty simple. You use oil-well drilling equipment, big drills, and you punch two holes down into the earth about, oh, maybe two miles—five kilometers, maybe—that's about as far as you can drill into the earth, for now, at least. Down there, deep in the earth, there is this extremely hot cauldron of rock, of granite. So then, you pump water from the surface into the first tube. The water goes down to the hot rock and becomes superheated. Then, the superheated water rises up the second tube—oh, I forgot to mention that these two tubes are interconnected—this hot water rises up the other tube and you use that to heat up a volatile liquid— do I need to go into what I mean by that? No? Okay. So then, this volatile liquid turns into a vapor, a gas, and you use it to turn an electrical turbine, and . . . bingo, you have electricity!

**Narrator:** Question 8: Why does the professor say this:

**Professor:** How does HDR energy work? Well, in theory, anyway . . . and let me stress, I say in theory . . . it's pretty simple.

**Narrator:** Listen again to part of the discussion. Then answer the question.

**Student B:** So, what else happened at a potlatch?

**Professor:** Well, then, the host would usually destroy some of his most valuable possessions, such as fishing canoes, and he'd throw coins and . . . and almost anything valuable into the sea . . .

**Student B:** What?! Excuse me, Professor . . . I just don't get it. It just seems kinda crazy to me. Why would anyone want to host a party like that?

**Narrator:** Question 9: What does the student mean when he says this:

**Student A:** Excuse me, Professor . . . I just don't get it.

**Narrator:** Listen again to part of the discussion. Then answer the question.

**Professor:** Okay, everyone. We've been talking about traditional forms of dance. Today, umm, we're going to shift our attention to the islands of Hawaii, and the most famous form of dance that's associated with those beautiful islands. Anyone know what that is? Laura?

**Student A:** Oh, that's an easy one—it's the hula dance.

**Narrator:** Question 10: What does the student mean when she says this:

**Student A:** Oh, that's an easy one . . .

**Narrator:** Listen again to part of the discussion. Then answer the question.

**Professor:** By the way, in Hawaiian, the word *ukulele* means "jumping flea."

**Student B:** Jumping flea! Yeah? Why did they call it that?

**Professor:** Hmmmmm. Probably it was because . . . well, to tell you the truth, I don't have a clue. I'll try to find out for you, though.

**Narrator:** Question 11: What does the professor mean when she says this:

**Professor:** . . . to tell you the truth, I don't have a clue.

**Narrator:** Listen again to part of the discussion. Then answer the question.

**Guest Speaker:** Thank you, Professor Nugent, thanks for inviting me. I always appreciate the chance to talk to students . . . to anyone who'll listen, for that matter, about our disappearing battlefields. The organization I work with is trying to save battlefields from development. It's an uphill struggle. By one estimate, twenty-five acres of Civil War battlefield are being lost every day. That's like an acre an hour.

**Narrator:** Question 12: What does the speaker mean when she says this:

**Guest Speaker:** It's an uphill struggle.

**Narrator:** Listen again to part of the discussion. Then answer the question.

**Student A:** Can't we just read about these little battles in history books?

**Professor:** I'm going to jump in here, Frances, and comment on what David just said.

**Narrator:** Question 13: What does Professor Nugent mean when he says this:

**Professor:** I'm going to jump in here, Frances, and comment on what David just said.

**Narrator:** Listen again to part of the lecture. Then answer the question.

**Professor:** A couple of days ago, we were talking about the poet Walt Whitman, and if you recall, I said that he was one of the two great voices in American poetry in the nineteenth century. Today, I'm going to drop the other shoe and talk about the other great poet, Emily Dickinson.

**Narrator:** Question 14: What does the professor mean when she says this:

**Professor:** Today, I'm going to drop the other shoe . . .

**Narrator:** Listen again to part of the lecture. Then answer the question.

**Professor:** Okay, for Friday, I'd like you to read all of Dickinson's poems that are in our textbook. There are about twenty, maybe twenty-five of her poems in there. Don't worry, though. That may sound like a lot of reading, but it shouldn't take you long! Friday, we'll take a closer look at her poems.

**Narrator:** Question 15: What does the professor mean when she says this:

**Professor:** Don't worry though, that may sound like a lot of reading, but it shouldn't take you long!

## [Track 22]

## Lesson 5: Ordering and Matching Questions

### Sample Item 1

**Narrator:** Listen to part of a presentation in an astronomy class.

**Presenter:** Now there have been quite a few space probes that have gone to Venus, so I'm only going to mention a few of them, the most important ones. I guess, umm, one of the most important was called Magellan. Magellan was launched in 1990 and spent four years in orbit around Venus. It used, uh, radar, I guess, to map the planet, and it found out that there are all these volcanoes on Venus, just like there are on Earth. The first one to go there, the first probe to go there successfully was Mariner 2 in, uh, 1962. Mariner 1 was supposed to go there, but it blew up. There was one, it was launched by the Soviet Union back in, the, uh, let's see . . . let me find it . . . hang on, no, here it is, Venera 4 in 1967 . . . and it dropped instruments onto the surface. They only lasted a few seconds, because of the conditions, the heat and all, but this probe showed us how really hot it was. Then, there was this one called Venus Pioneer 2, in 1978. That was the one that found out that the atmosphere of Venus is made of carbon dioxide, mostly. And, uh, well, as I said . . . there were a lot of other ones too.

**Narrator:** In what order were these space probes sent to Venus?

## [Track 23]

### Sample Item 2

**Narrator:** Listen to part of a lecture in a biology class.

**Professor:** Within the taiga itself, you'll find three sub-zones. The first of these you come to, as you're going south, is called open forest. The only trees here are needle-leaf trees—you know, evergreen trees, what we call coniferous trees. These trees tend to be small and far apart. This is basically tundra—it looks like tundra, but with a few small trees. Next, you come to what's called closed forest, with bigger needle-leaf trees growing closer together. This feels more like a real forest. This sub-zone—well, if you like variety, you're not going to feel happy here. You can travel for miles and see only half a dozen species of trees. In a few days, we'll be talking about the tropical rain forest; now,

that's where you'll see variety. Okay, finally, you come to the mixed zone. The trees are bigger still here, and you'll start seeing some broad-leafed trees, deciduous trees. You'll see larch, aspen, especially along rivers and creeks, in addition to needle-leaf trees. So this sub-zone feels a bit more like the temperate forests we're used to.

**Narrator:** The professor discussed three sub-zones of the taiga. Match each sub-zone with its characteristic.

## [TRACK 24]

### Exercise 5.1

**Narrator:** Listen to a lecture in a chemistry class.

**Professor:** Okay, last class, we were considering various hydrocarbon compounds, and today, we're focusing on the most . . . well, definitely one of the most useful hydrocarbon compounds of all, at least from a commercial . . . an economic point of view. That's right, I'm talking about coal. You know, there probably . . . you probably would never have seen an Industrial Revolution in the eighteenth century without coal. Coal provided the fuel, the power for the Industrial Revolution. And even today, life would be very different if we didn't have coal. You may not know this, but in most countries around the world, electricity is still mostly produced by burning coal.

So, where does coal come from? Well, imagine what the earth was like, oh, say 300 million years ago, give or take a few million years. We call this time the Carboniferous Period. Get the connection? Carboniferous . . . coal forming? Most of the land was covered with . . . with luxuriant vegetation, especially ferns—ferns big as trees. Eventually, these plants died and were submerged in the waters of swamps, where they gradually decomposed. And we've seen what happens when plants decompose—the vegetable matter loses oxygen and hydrogen atoms, leaving a deposit with a high percentage of carbon. When this happens, you get peat bogs—in other words, you, uh, you get wetlands full of this muck, this, umm, partly decayed vegetable matter that's called peat. Okay, so now you've got these great peat bogs and over time, layers of sand and mud from the water settle over this gooey mass of peat. The deposits grow thicker and thicker and this in turn means the pressure gets . . . it increases on the peat. The water is squeezed out, the deposits are compressed and, uh, hardened . . . because of this pressure. And so you have—coal!

There are different grades of coal. Lignite—it's also called brown coal—is the lowest grade. By lowest grade, I mean it has the lowest percentage of carbon. Lignite has a lot of moisture, it can be up to 45% water, and has a fairly high amount of sulfur as well. It's often burned in furnaces to produce heat and to make electricity. Bituminous coal has a higher carbon content—and of course, less moisture. Bituminous coal is usually used for generating electricity. Anthracite is the highest . . . the highest grade of naturally occurring coal. It's used mainly to produce coke. The anthracite is baked and, uh, distilled to make coke. Everyone knows what coke is, right? It's almost pure carbon and is used in the manufacture of steel, mainly. One of the byproducts of . . . of the process of making coke is coal tar. Coal tar is used to make a lot of different types of plastic. It's also used to make some types of soap and shampoo. Oh, and I almost forgot about jet. Jet is a kind of compact lignite, and it's used to make jewelry.

OK, we're going to talk about oil, about petroleum, next, but, uh, any questions about coal first?

**Narrator:** Now get ready to answer the questions. You may use your notes to help you.

**Narrator:** Question 1: The lecturer discusses the steps involved in the creation of coal. Summarize this process by putting the steps in the proper order.

**Narrator:** Question 2: Match the form of coal with the type of industry that primarily uses it.

**Narrator:** Listen to a discussion in an accounting seminar.

**Professor:** Hello, everyone. As you can see from our course syllabus, our topic today is something called "GAAP, G-A-A-P." Anyone have any idea what we mean by that acronym, GAAP? Yes, Jennifer?

**Student A:** Ummm, I think it means "General Accepted Accounting Practices."

**Professor:** Almost right. Anyone else? Yeah, Michael?

**Student B:** Generally Accepted Accounting Principles, I think.

**Professor:** Bingo, you got it. So, what are these? What do we mean by Generally Accepted Accounting Principles? Well, they are basically a set of rules, of, uh, concepts, assumptions, conventions, whatever you want to call them, for measuring and, um, for reporting information in financial forms.

**Student A:** What kind of financial forms?

**Professor:** Almost any kind of form—balance sheets, income statements, cash flow statements, you name it. There are different kinds of GAAP. There are GAAP for government organizations, for non-profit organizations, and for profit-making businesses. The principles we'll be looking at deal with for-profit entities, but they are really general principles that apply to almost any accounting system.

**Student A:** And so, the purpose of GAAP is to . . .

**Professor:** It has the same purpose as standards in any field. If every business in one field used different standards—okay, imagine this. You go to the store to get a pound of coffee. Then you go to another store and get another pound of coffee, and it weighs more than the first pound. Or you get a liter bottle of milk from one store, and it's much smaller than the liter bottle from another store. That's what it would be like. There'd be no, uh, no basis for comparison . . .

**Student A:** That would be pretty confusing!

**Professor:** You bet. It would be sheer chaos. Now, GAAP includes a lot of concepts, but to get us started, we'll, uh, we'll focus on these three important ones, these three basic ones today. Okay, first off, the business entity principle. Who wants to take a swing at explaining that concept? Jennifer?

**Student A:** Uh, that means . . . well, a business has to keep its accounts . . . has to keep them separate from its owners' account . . . from their personal accounts.

**Professor:** Exactly. It means that, for accounting purposes, a business and its owners are separate entities. The assets and liabilities of a business have to be kept separate from the assets and liabilities of any other entity, including the owners and the creditors of the business. This means that if you own a business, and you have a dinner date one night, you can't finance your date with funds from your business. It means that, uh, you can't list your collection of baseball cards as corporate assets—those are your *personal assets.* So, everybody got that? Pretty simple concept . . . the business entity principle. Okay, onward to the next principle, the cost principle. What do you think that might be?

**Student B:** The cost principle. Hmmm. I don't know, Professor . . . Um, does it just mean that, when your business has a cost, you have to record it in the books?

**Professor:** Well, not just that you have to record it . . . it means that assets have to be recorded in the company accounts at the price at which they were originally purchased—not at today's perceived market value. Let's say, umm, you bought ten computers five years ago for $1,000 each, and that today they're worth about half that. This principle says that you have to record them on your books at the original price. We'll talk more about that later, but before we do, let's just quickly mention the *matching* principle. Anyone know what that is? Jennifer?

**Student A:** No idea, Professor.

**Professor:** Anyone else? No? Well, this principle . . . it simply states that a firm has to record any expenses that it incurs in the period when the sale was made. Say, uh, you own a used car lot, and your books say that you sold ten cars in June. Okay, then you have to record the salespersons' June salaries along with those sales. You have to include the rent you paid for the land that your used car lot is standing on. You have to include the expense of the helium that you used to blow up the balloons that lured the customers onto your car lot, and the money you spent for advertising your wonderful deals on cars on late-night cable television. Okay, now I'm going to give you a handout that explains GAAP in more detail, and we're going to see how these principles actually affect the way you enter information in accounts, but . . . before we go on, anyone have any questions?

**Narrator:** Now get ready to answer the question. You may use your notes to help you.

**Narrator:** Question 3: Match the accounting principle with the appropriate description of it.

**Narrator:** Listen to a guest lecture in an agricultural economics class.

**Guest Lecturer:** Hi there, I'm Floyd Haney. I'm your U.S. Department of Agriculture's county agent for Harrison County, have been for some twenty-two years. Professor Mackenzie was kind enough to ask me over to the school here today to chat with you about the, uh, agricultural situation in Floyd County today. Now, you probably know, your main crop here in Harrison County has always been wheat, wheat followed by corn. Been that way for, well, likely since the Civil War, I guess . . . maybe even longer. Wheat is still your most important crop here, but, this may come as a bit of a shocker to some of you, in the last few years, soybeans have actually outstripped corn. Soybeans are now more economically important than corn. Imagine.

Now, down in the southern part of the county, you've got a real interesting phenomenon with your heirloom crops, your heirloom fruit and vegetables. Anyone know what those are? Heirloom crops?

**Student A:** Well, I've heard of heirloom breeds of animals—breeds of animals that were common a long time ago, but they're really rare today. Some farmers are trying to bring these animals back now.

**Guest Lecturer:** Right, well, heirloom crops—they're also called heritage crops—they're exactly the same. These are varieties of plants that were grown 20, 40, 100 years ago, but these days, only a few people grow them. Down in the southern part of Harrison County there are, oh, half a dozen small farms—Rainbow Valley, Cloverleaf Farms, Underwood Acres, and a handful of others—that are growing these heirloom crops. They're growing this variety of watermelon, it's called Moon and Star melon—that was popular around 1910. I'll tell you, those melons are so sweet and juicy, you wonder why farmers ever stopped growing them! What else . . . they grow heirloom tomatoes, cucumbers, peppers, squash, just all kinds of fruits and vegetables. These farmers are selling seeds over the Internet and they're selling their vegetables at farmers' markets, mostly. Now, these heirloom crops, they're not as important yet as the other three crops I mentioned, but I'll tell you what, sales of these seeds and veggies are so hot right now that you've got a lot of other farmers in the area thinking about growing some heirlooms themselves.

All right, then, let's talk a bit about our top crop, which is wheat, as I said earlier. Now, according to the Department of Agriculture, there are seven types of wheat, depending on their texture and color. You'll find three or four of those growing here in Harrison County. You get a lot of durum wheat here, that's probably the most common kind you'll see. Durum is used for, mainly used for making pasta—spaghetti, macaroni, linguini, and so on, all your types of pasta. Then there's soft white wheat, which is usually bought up by companies that make breakfast cereals. The next time you're having your Toasty Wheat Squares in the morning, just think, they might be made with Harrison County wheat. And of course, you have hard red wheat, which is wonderful bread flour.

By the way, I brought some packets of tomato seeds from Rainbow Valley Farms—these are seeds for heirloom tomatoes called Better Boy Tomatoes—you'll notice the seed packages look like they came from around 1910, too. If any of you want to try your hand at growing some of these babies in your backyard, come on up after class and I'll give you a free packet of seeds.

**Narrator:**  Now get ready to answer the questions. You may use your notes to help you.

**Narrator:**  Question 4: The lecturer mentions four types of crops that are grown in Harrison County. Rank these four types of crops in their order of economic importance, beginning with the most important.

**Narrator:**  Question 5: Match the type of wheat with the product that is most often made from it.

**Narrator:**  Listen to a discussion in a modern history class.

**Professor:**  Okay, we're going to continue with "Explorers and Exploration Week." Today we're talking about twentieth-century explorers. Usually, you know, when we, uh, mention twentieth-century exploration, people naturally think about astronauts, cosmonauts. We think about the first man in orbit, the first man to walk on the moon, and so on. And, in fact, we will take a look at space exploration in our next class, but today, we're going to talk about explorers in the early part of the twentieth century. Back then, the place to go if you were an explorer was . . . Antarctica. Tell me, has anyone ever read anything about the early exploration of Antarctica?

**Student A:**  A coupla years ago, I read a book by, umm, Richard Byrd, Admiral Byrd, called *Alone*.

**Professor:**  That's a remarkable book . . . about endurance . . . about courage.

**Student A:**  Oh, I know—it was just incredible how he could survive in that cold, dark place all by himself.

**Student B:**  I've never read that book—what's it about?

**Professor:**  Well, it's about Richard Byrd's second trip to Antarctica, in 1934. He established this advance weather station about 100 miles from his main base. It was basically just a wooden hut, and it was soon completely covered in snow and ice. There were supposed to be three people working there, but because of bad weather, Byrd was cut

off from the main base and got stuck there for the whole winter. And at that time of year in Antarctica, it's dark all day long.

**Student A:**  Yeah, and at first he didn't realize it, but his heater . . . it was poisoning him. The, uh, fumes from the heater were toxic . . .

**Professor:**  That's right. It was carbon monoxide poisoning.

**Student A:**  But he kept sending messages back to the main base saying that everything was okay so that they wouldn't try to come rescue him and maybe die themselves in the winter storms. He barely survived.

**Student B:**  So, Professor, was Byrd the first person to go to the South Pole?

**Professor:**  No, no, not by a long shot he wasn't. He was the first person to fly to the South Pole. Well, he didn't actually land there, but he flew over the Pole, he and his pilot Bernt Balchen. That was in 1929. That same year he also established the first permanent . . . the first large-scale camp in Antarctica. Since he was from the United States, he named it Little America. Some people called Byrd "the mayor of Antarctica."

**Student B:**  So then, if it wasn't Byrd, who was it?

**Professor:**  I'm glad you asked that! Years before, about twenty years before Byrd came to Antarctica, there was a race, an international race to see who could get to the South Pole first. The newspapers called it "the race to the bottom of the world." The two main players were Norway and Britain. It was a little like the race to the moon in the 1960's, like the . . . like the space race between the U.S. and the U.S.S.R. The first expedition to get near the South Pole was led by a British explorer, Ernest Shackleton. That was in 1909. He was less than a hundred miles from the Pole when he had to turn around and go back to his base.

**Student B:**  Why did he turn around if he was so close?

**Professor:**  Well, he was running low on supplies, and as happens so often in Antarctica, the weather turned bad. Then, things got really exciting in 1911. Two expeditions left their base camps and headed for the Pole. The race was on. The first one to leave was under the Norwegian explorer Roald Amundsen. The other one was under the British explorer Robert Scott, who had been, um, on Shackleton's expedition a couple of years earlier.

**Student A:**  C'mon, Professor, don't keep us in suspense. Tell us who won!

**Professor:**  Well, in January of 1912—

**Student B:**  January? Wouldn't that be the worst time to travel in Antarctica . . . in the middle of winter?

**Professor:**  You're forgetting, it's in the southern hemisphere, December, January, those are the warmest months, the middle of summer. Of course, anywhere near the South Pole, the middle of summer is hardly tropical. Anyway, the British expedition reached the Pole in January 1912, thinking they were going to be the first. And what do you suppose they found there? The Norwegian flag, planted in the ice. Amundsen's party had reached the Pole about, oh, a few weeks earlier, in late December, 1911.

**Student B:**  Oh, the British team must have been really disappointed, huh?

**Professor:**  No doubt. In fact, there's a picture of the Scott expedition taken at the Pole, and they look exhausted, and terribly disappointed, and dejected, but that was just the beginning of their troubles.

**Student A:**  Oh, no. What else happened?

**Professor:**  Their trip back to their base turned into a—into just a nightmare. The expedition suffered setback after setback. They weren't as well equipped or as well supplied as the Norwegian expedition, either. This being Antarctica, the weather was frightful, there were terrible storms. Then they ran out of food and . . . ironically, they were just 11 miles from where they had left a cache of food, but . . . sadly, none of Scott's men made it back to their base.

**Narrator:** Now get ready to answer the questions. You may use your notes to help you.

**Narrator:** Question 6: The professor discusses some of the history of Antarctic exploration. Summarize this history by putting these events in the correct chronological order.

**Narrator:** Question 7: Match these Antarctic explorers with the countries from which they came.

**Narrator:** Listen to a lecture in a musical acoustics class.

**Professor:** Anyone know what this little electronic device is? No? It's a sound-level meter, a digital sound-level meter. It measures intensity of sound . . . what we usually call volume. Loudness. The read-out gives you the decibel level. By the way, I'm lecturing at about 61, 62 decibels. Now, we've been hearing a lot about decibel levels lately. The City Council has been considering a law to regulate the sound levels outside of clubs, and you know, student hangouts along State Street. This law, the one they're thinking about passing, says the decibel level just outside the doorways of these places has to be 70 or below from 10 P.M. until 7 A.M. and 80 or below any other time. If, uh, the police or environmental officers record decibel levels higher than that, they'll give a warning the first time and after that, they could give the business owners a fine. And there's already a law that controls the decibel level for concerts at the stadium. After years of complaining that their window panes rattled during rock concerts, the people who live in the Stone Hill neighborhood over by the stadium, those neighbors got together and got the City Council to limit the sound level just outside the stadium to a maximum of 100 decibels.

And, you know, there are good reasons why we should be concerned about high sound levels. About 10 million people in the United States have some sort of hearing loss due to excessive noise. A lot of this, it's caused by . . . well, there are occupational reasons. People who operate heavy equipment, who work in noisy factories, farmers, miners . . . they all have to deal with high decibel levels. But some of the problem comes from loud, loud music. The thing is, hearing loss is incremental, it, uh, it happens bit by bit, so it's . . . well, you don't usually notice it happening, although sometimes . . . have you ever been to a concert and when you came out, your ears were ringing? Or you hear a buzzing sound? This is called tinnitus. Tinnitus. Now, if you are at a really loud concert, or you go to a number of concerts in a short period, you may experience TTS—Temporary Threshold Shift. This means that you, uh, well, it means that you lose the ability to hear low-volume sounds. Everything sounds . . . muffled, like you had cotton in your ears. This can last a couple of hours or it can last all day. And unfortunately, noise exposure over a prolonged period can cause TTS to turn into a permanent condition called NIHL—noise-induced hearing loss.

Anyway, what I wanted to tell you about today is an experiment that a group of students in my class did a couple of years ago. It was their final project for my class. They borrowed this little sound-level meter of mine and took it to all sorts of musical venues. They went to a rock concert at the stadium—this was before the law was passed regulating sound levels there. There was a band called the Creatures playing, I think it was the Creatures. From the

seats they had—they sat pretty close to the stage—they measured a maximum decibel level of about 110 when the band was playing. This level, 110 decibels, is the high end of what is considered "musically useful." Now, 110 decibels is loud, no doubt about it. It's about as loud as a jet taking off when you're 100 meters away. Of course, the sound didn't just come from the music—the meter also measured the crowd noise, too, and rock concert crowds can get pretty loud. Still, I was a little surprised—I mean, given the size of these bands' amplifiers, I was a bit surprised that the sound levels weren't even higher.

The students also took the meter to a classical concert, the University Philharmonic Symphony. I'd estimate that if a full symphony orchestra plays flat-out as loud as they possibly can, you might get levels of about, oh, 95, 100 decibels. The night the students went, though, the loudest level they recorded was only 85 decibels. During a violin solo, the level from their seats was only about 55 decibels. That's at the very low end of the "musically useful" range. At that level, you can barely hear the music over the sound of the ventilating system, and the, uh, the occasional cough. Of course, at a classical concert, you're not going to have the audience noise that you would at a rock concert. Beethoven fans are usually a little more restrained than rock fans.

The loudest music the students recorded in a public place wasn't even live music. It was at a club over on State Street, Club 1010. I think it's closed now. Anyway, as I said, it wasn't live music, it was a disc jockey playing recorded music but . . . well, that club must have had a very powerful sound system, practically a nuclear-powered sound system, because the sound level on the dance floor was 117 decibels. That's not considered "musically useful." That's considered "painfully loud."

One time, the students were on their way to a jazz club downtown, and one of their friends gave them a ride in his van. The friend didn't realize they had their sound-level meter with them. Anyway, he was playing a CD and cranked up the sound system to the maximum volume . . . and guess what? This was the highest reading of all! It was over 125 decibels, which is just this side of being considered "unbearable." It must have been loud enough to shake the fillings out of their teeth!

Okay, well, I'm going to pass out a copy of the students' paper so you can see for yourself just how noisy your favorite places to hear music are . . .

**Narrator:** Now get ready to answer the questions. You may use your notes to help you.

**Narrator:** Question 8: The professor mentions several conditions caused by excessively loud music. Match the condition to the correct description of it.

**Narrator:** Question 9: The professor lists several musical events at which her students recorded sound levels. List these events in the correct order based on volume, beginning with the highest volume.

**Narrator:** Listen to a lecture in a U.S. literature class.

**Professor:** Well, I told you at the end of the last class that I thought you would enjoy the reading assignment that I gave you—was I right? . . . Yeah, I thought so . . . most students like reading the works of Edgar Allan Poe—maybe in part because so many of his works have been turned into spooky movies!

Let's, um, take a brief look at Poe's early life. He was born in Boston in 1809. He was an orphan, he was orphaned at an early age. A businessman named John Allan unofficially adopted him. Allan took him to England when he was six, and Poe went to private school there. He came back to the United States in 1820 and in 1826 he went to the University of Virginia in Charlottesville for a year. However, his adoptive father John Allan wasn't happy about the way Poe carried on at the university. He kept hearing stories that Poe was drinking and gambling all his money away. Allan came to Charlottesville and made Poe drop out and go to work as a bank clerk—as a bookkeeper, more or less.

Well, Poe was young and artistic—he already considered himself a poet—and, as you can imagine, he hated this boring bank job. He did everything he could to get himself fired. It didn't take long. After leaving his job, he wrote and published his first book of poems. Right after this, Poe returned to Boston and reconciled with John Allan. Allan decided that all Poe needed was some discipline, so he arranged for Poe to enter the U.S. military academy at West Point. Now, do you think Poe enjoyed the life of a cadet at the academy? You're right, he didn't like it any more than he'd liked working as a bank clerk, and he was tossed out of the school after just a few months for disobeying orders and for, um, generally neglecting his duties. After this . . . well, John Allan was fed up. He figured he'd done everything he could for his adopted son and so Allan completely disowned him. Poe was on his own. He moved to Baltimore—that's the city he's most closely associated with—and devoted himself to his writing.

Now, I'm not going to talk about Poe's later life right now, not until after we've had a chance to talk about some of his works, because . . . well, the tragic events of his later life deeply influenced his writing.

Poe's first love was poetry. He considered himself mainly a poet. In fact, he said that he wrote other works just to make money, money to live on while he wrote his poems. The poem that I asked you to read for this class is "The Raven," and it's definitely one of his most famous pieces. Isn't it amazing how Poe creates such a sad and mysterious and downright scary mood in this poem? Then I also asked you to read Poe's horror story, "The Fall of the House of Usher." Poe wrote a lot of horror stories. Several of them—including this one—are considered classics of that genre. Today's horror writers, like Stephen King, owe Poe quite a debt. Again, in this story, Poe creates a gloomy, haunting mood, but the plot and characterization are outstanding. Finally, I asked you to read the short story "The Gold Bug." This is a detective story, a mystery, a "whodunit." Who do you think invented the detective story? It was none other than Edgar Allan Poe. A lot of people think it was Arthur Conan Doyle, who wrote the Sherlock Holmes stories, but Poe was writing this kind of story years before Doyle.

Okay, I'm going to read Poe's poem "The Raven" aloud. I want you to listen carefully to the rhythm of the poem, the rhymes, the sounds, just the sounds of Poe's words, and see how all these contribute to the meaning of the poem, how he builds this gloomy, almost desperate mood. Okay, ready?

**Narrator:** Now get ready to answer the questions. You may use your notes to help you.

**Narrator:** Question 10: The professor gives a brief biography of the writer Edgar Allan Poe. List these events from his life in the order in which they occurred.

**Narrator:** Question 11: Match these works by Edgar Allan Poe with the type of writing that they represent.

**Narrator:** Listen to a lecture in an anthropology class.

**Professor:** All right, today, our class is going to the dogs! Last week, we talked about the process of domesticating animals in general. Today, we're going to talk about the first animal to be domesticated—man's best friend, the dog!

There's a lot we don't know about the domestication of dogs. For one thing, we don't know when it happened. For a long time, scientists thought that it occurred about 10,000 years ago. Then, some scientists—scientists who study dog DNA, like Robert Wayne of UCLA—they tried to push that date way back in time. They said that domestication occurred about 100,000 years ago. We now know, know for sure that it happened at least 14,000 years ago. A fragment of a bone that has definitely been identified as belonging to a dog was found in a cave in Germany, and it's 14,000 years old. Domestication probably took place around 20,000 years ago.

We don't know where dogs were first domesticated either. By the fifteenth century, the dog was found all over the world—the first domestic animal with a global range. The most likely point of origin is Southwest Asia, but some scientists think that it was in East Asia, while others think maybe Europe or North Africa. We know it wasn't in the Western Hemisphere because the DNA of dogs in the Americas is more closely related to Eurasian wolves than it is to American wolves, so dogs must have followed humans to Alaska across the land bridge from Siberia.

Then we also don't know exactly how humans domesticated dogs, although there are various theories. One theory is that dogs figured out early on that they could feed pretty well just by hanging around humans and eating the scraps of food that were, you know, just thrown out or left sitting around. But, to have access to these morsels, dogs had to get over their natural fear of humans, and so, according to this theory, dogs more or less domesticated themselves. Another theory is that dogs were domesticated from wolves by means of selective breeding. There was an experiment done by a Russian scientist, Dmitri Balyaev, in the 1940's. He bred a group of wild Siberian foxes. The only characteristic he was interested in when he was breeding these foxes was tameness, friendliness towards humans. In only six generations of foxes—only six generations, mind you!—he had bred foxes that weren't afraid of humans, that wagged their tails when they saw their keepers, that even licked their keepers' faces. If he could do this with foxes in six generations, early humans surely could have done it with wolves over thousands of generations.

We do know what animal domestic dogs come from. There are almost 400 breeds of dogs today, but all of them, from Chihuahuas to great Danes, are descendants of the Eurasian grey wolf. Because there are so many differences among types of dogs—size, shape, color, temperament—scientists once wondered if some were related to other types of wild dogs, like African jackals, Australian dingoes, or American coyotes. DNA tests, though, showed that all dogs are related to wolves. But, uh, there are some dogs, like German shepherds, that are closer to wolves than others. This indicates that domestication may have taken place in various stages—you know, some breeds may have been domesticated more recently than others.

Dogs were first domesticated during humankind's earliest stage of development—the hunter-gatherer period. Apparently, umm, their first job was to serve as guards. With their keen sense of smell and hearing, dogs made it almost impossible for strangers to come up to a sleeping village by surprise. Later, humans took advantage of dogs' hunting ability. Dogs helped humans get hold of meat and skins from wild animals. Take a look at this rock painting that was found in the Jaro Mountains in Iraq—it's maybe

8,000 years old. It shows people with spears hunting deer, getting some help from dogs with curly tails. Still later, after humans domesticated herd animals—goats, cattle, sheep—well, dogs helped gather up these animals and move them from place to place by barking and nipping at their heels. Take a look at this fresco. It's from the wall of a sandstone grotto in the desert in Algeria. It's probably 5,000 years old. The herders are driving their oxen home from the fields while their "best friends" are helping them out.

Today, of course, most dogs have taken on another role. Sure, some dogs are still working dogs. They help hunters, they herd animals, they pull loads, they find survivors of natural disasters. Most dogs, though, are not valued so much for the work they do as for the company they provide. But that doesn't mean their ability to perform these earlier roles has been completely bred out of them. My two dogs, Raisin and Cosmo—they still perform guard duty. No way will they let the mail carrier sneak up to my house! And, last weekend, I was at the park with my little nieces and nephew, and the kids were running around the playground. Raisin and Cosmo—they're both border collies, which are herding dogs—they were actually out there herding these kids! I mean, they were barking and jumping around and trying to keep the kids from running off. They still have that herding instinct!

All right, next I'm going to talk a little about horses, about domesticating horses, and what a huge impact that had on humans, but first, any questions about domesticating dogs?

**Narrator:** Now get ready to answer the questions. You may use your notes to help you.

**Narrator:** Question 12: The professor mentions a number of archaeological finds that were related to the domestication of dogs. Match these finds with their locations.

**Narrator:** Question 13: The professor mentions a number of roles that dogs have played since they were first domesticated. List these roles in chronological order, beginning with the earliest role that dogs played.

[Track 25]

## Lesson 6: Completing Charts

### Sample Item

**Narrator:** Listen to part of a discussion in a business class.

**Professor:** What does a case look like? Well, cases are basically descriptions of actual—let me stress that, of real business situations, chunks of reality from the business world. So, you get typically ten to twenty pages of text that describe the problem, some problem that a real business actually faced. And then there will be another five to ten pages of what are called exhibits.

**Student B:** Exhibits? What are those?

**Professor:** Exhibits . . . those are documents, statistical documents, that explain the situation. They might be oh, spreadsheets, sales reports, umm, marketing projections, anything like that. But as I said, at the center of every case, at the core of every case, is a problem that you have to solve. So, you have to analyze the situation, the data—and sometimes, you'll see you don't have enough data to work with, and you might have to collect more—say, from the Internet. Then, you have to make decisions about how to solve these problems.

**Student B:** So that's why we study cases? I mean, because managers need to be able to make decisions . . . and solve problems?

**Professor:** Exactly . . . well, that's a big part of it, anyway. And doing this, solving the problem, usually involves role-playing, taking on the roles of decision-makers at the firm. One member of the group might play the Chief Executive Officer, one the Chief Financial Officer, and so on. And you . . . you might have a business meeting to decide how your business should solve its problem. Your company might, say, be facing a cash shortage and thinking about selling off one division of the company. So your group has to decide if this is the best way to handle the problem.

**Student B:** So we work in groups, then?

**Professor:** Usually in groups of four or five. That's the beauty of this method. It teaches teamwork and cooperation.

**Student A:** And then what? How are we . . . how do you decide on a grade for us?

**Professor:** You give a presentation, an oral presentation, I mean, and you explain to the whole class what decision you made and . . . what recommendations you'd make . . . and then you write a report as well. You get a grade, a group grade, on the presentation and the report.

**Student B:** Professor, is this the only way we'll be studying business, by using cases?

**Professor:** Oh no, it's just one important way. Some classes are lecture classes and some are a combination of lectures and case studies and some . . . in some classes you'll also use computer simulations. We have this software called World Marketplace, and, using this program, your group starts up your own global corporation and tries to make a profit . . . it's actually a lot of fun.

**Narrator:** In this lecture, the professor describes the process of the case study method. Indicate whether each of the following is a step in the process.

[Track 26]

## Exercise 6.1

**Narrator:** Listen to a discussion in an urban studies class.

**Professor:** Okay, I guess most of you are familiar with the, uh, with the commercial section of Harmony Road, right? Who can describe that area for me?

**Student A:** Well it's . . . there are a couple of big shopping centers and a few strip malls . . . lots of fast food places and motels, uh, big box stores . . . used car lots . . .

**Professor:** Right. And, suppose you had to sum up that sort of development, what would you call it?

**Student A:** I guess you'd call it . . . sprawl. Suburban sprawl.

**Professor:** Right. And the residential suburbs out in that area, how would you describe them?

**Student B:** Well, they're fairly nice . . . nice big houses, big yards . . .

**Professor:** Now, say you lived in one of those neighborhoods and you ran out of bread . . . would you walk to the market?

**Student B:** No way. Most places there don't even have sidewalks. And . . . everything is so far apart.

**Professor:** Exactly right. Those suburbs, and that commercial section, represent what we call Conventional Suburban Design, or CSD. Today I want to talk about a theory of urban design, a movement called New Urbanism that challenges CSD. In a New Urban community, you can walk to the store to buy a loaf of bread.

Although this movement, this philosophy is called New Urbanism, in a way, it should be called traditional urbanism because it looks to the past, it models today's communities on the way communities looked in the past. Think about a typical town in the United States a hundred years ago. You had a central business area, a downtown surrounded by residential neighborhoods. That all changed in the fifties and sixties. That's when the "flight to the suburbs" took place. A lot of suburban shopping malls were built. Huge areas of land, usually farmland, were developed. Automobile use soared. Downtowns deteriorated or died, and the old neighborhoods in the city center, mostly they became slums.

Today over 500 "New Urbanist" communities have been built or are being constructed, and most of these feature an old "Main Street" style business center . . . a "downtown," if you will.

Okay, here are some core principles of New Urbanism. First, walkability. Streets are pedestrian friendly and lined with trees. Just as in older cities, streets are laid out on a grid. Actually, New Urbanists generally use a "modified" grid, with "T" intersections and some diagonals to, uh, calm traffic and increase visual interest. There's a mix of narrow streets, wider boulevards, walkways, and alleys between streets. Some streets are designated car-free. You wouldn't get any big surface parking lots. Parking is in underground lots or in garages behind houses, out of sight. And there are some great benefits to this. With more people walking the streets, communities are safer, there's less crime. And fewer cars means less pollution.

Another principle is mixed use. On one block, even in one building, there may be a mix of shops, restaurants, offices, and apartments. A big family house may be right next to a moderately-priced apartment building. Shop owners live upstairs from their shops. This kind of development encourages a diverse population—a mix of ages, classes, cultures, races.

Another principle: increased density. Residences, shops, and services, all of these are closer together than in a CSD, especially around the community center. This helps with the ease of walking I mentioned before—no residences should be more than a ten-minute walk from the community center. But, increased density doesn't mean eliminating open space. New Urban communities are dotted with little parks, pocket parks, and ideally there is a community space, an open plaza, a village green in the center of town where people can gather.

You also want to emphasize smart transportation, and, uh, of course that means de-emphasizing the car. Ideally, there is a train or a light-rail system for transport in and out of the community. Within the community, as I said, you want to encourage walking and bicycling. Of course, this gives you exercise, and it's healthier than driving everywhere.

**Student B:** Professor, do the, uh, houses, the residences in these New Urban places, ummm, New Urban communities, do they look any different from houses in regular suburbs?

**Professor:** Well, there's an emphasis on comfort . . . on creating attractive, comfortable houses. I already mentioned that parking spaces, garages are typically behind the house. So, the front of the house is not taken up with two- or three-car garages that are part of the house. Houses are closer to the street. And a common feature is a big front porch, often with a porch swing. This is a, uh, well, an inviting space to get together, to sit around with neighbors. Sometimes, too, you'll get a theme going in a New Urban community. I have some slides that I'm going to show you later. In some East Coast communities, there's a Colonial look to all the buildings. Some communities have a neo-Victorian look. In other communities, all the houses are painted in bright colors.

**Student A:** You said there were about 500 New Urban communities around the country. Where are they mostly?

**Professor:** Well, there are some in almost every state. Some are built in undeveloped areas. Those are called "greenfield sites." Others are in run-down urban areas. Those are "grayfield sites." Oh. And some of the most promising sites for future projects are what are called "grayfield malls."

**Student A:** What are those?

**Professor:** Well, about 2,000 major shopping malls have been built in the United States. Of these, 8% are closed—and another 11% are in danger of closing. Many of these would make ideal New Urban communities. Well, next I want to show you some slides of some New Urban communities: Seaside in Florida, Kentlands in Maryland, Prospect in Colorado, Plum Creek in Texas. Would someone in the back there dim the lights?

**Narrator:** Now get ready to answer the questions. You may use your notes to help you.

**Narrator:** Question 1: In this lecture, the professor describes the New Urbanism Movement. Indicate whether each of the following is a principle of this movement.

**Narrator:** Question 2: In this lecture, the professor mentions benefits associated with the New Urbanism Movement. Indicate whether each of the following is a benefit mentioned in the lecture.

**Narrator:** Listen to a lecture in a British History class.

**Professor:** Good morning. In our last class, we were discussing King Richard. Richard the Lionhearted. We talked, as you'll no doubt recall, about his role in the Third Crusade, how he was kidnapped on his way home to England, how he died fighting in France—although, if he'd just remembered to put his armor on, he probably would have been just fine. Now, after Richard, we have John, John Lackland, the King John. Actually, Richard's nephew Arthur was supposed to become king, he was next in line, but Richard had signed an agreement with John, and so John became king.

Now, there is a tendency, rather an unfortunate tendency, to consider Richard the good king and John the evil one. Frankly, Richard was not all that great although he was a fairly decent military leader. He was more interested in being the subject of songs than he was in ruling England. He was intolerant, and he practically bankrupted the country to pay for his wars. Of course, John was supposedly so wicked that no other British king has ever been named John. It's true, he was no prize, but he was probably no worse than most other medieval rulers.

Like Richard, John spent almost no time in England. The war in France was still going on and John was still bleeding England white to pay for it. England at that time still controlled some odd bits, some dribs and drabs of France— Normandy, Brittany, umm, Anjou—but King Philip of France was trying to take them away. In 1214, at the battle of Bouvines, Philip decisively defeated John. So, defeated and broke, John returned to England hoping to raise some funds. He insisted that the nobles, the barons and dukes and so on, that they pay a kind of tax called *scutage*—this was a payment the barons could make rather than go fight the war in France, a kind of bribe to avoid military service. But the barons, a substantial number of them, anyway, were fed up. They were tired of being taxed whenever John needed some money. There was a Civil War. Barons chose sides, for the king or against him. The anti-John barons were able to capture London. On June 15, 1215, they forced John to meet with them. They confronted him on a green meadow southwest of London. They demanded that their traditional rights be written down and that John sign this document. The result was the Magna Carta—the Great Charter.

Now, one of the great myths about the Magna Carta is that it was some kind of a constitution, that it created a democratic society. There were no democratic societies in Europe in the thirteenth century! Really, it was . . . a feudal document, an agreement between the king and the barons, the aristocracy. It gave rights really to just a few powerful families. In fact, it barely mentions the ordinary people. The, uh, the majority of the English population gained little from the Charter and wouldn't have an active voice in government for hundreds of years. Another myth is that the Charter established the parliamentary system of government. It did create a council of twenty-five barons to see that the articles of the Magna Carta were observed, but the first recognizable English Parliament—it was called "the model Parliament"—did not come for almost a hundred years.

Now I said that the Magna Carta didn't have much immediate influence on the ordinary Englishman. That doesn't mean it wasn't a document of great importance. In its own time, the greatest value of the Magna Carta was that it limited royal power . . . and made it clear that even the king had to obey the law. Think about that. Before this time, the King's word was law, but the Magna Carta stated that no one—no one—was above the law. That's pretty revolutionary, eh? And, over time, the charter took on even more significance. Some articles that in 1215 applied only to the powerful barons later applied to the whole nation. For example, one article of the Charter says that no tax can be imposed by the king without the barons' consent. Eventually, this came to be interpreted as "no taxation without the consent of Parliament." Another article says that no freeman can be put in jail, deprived of property, exiled, or executed without the lawful judgment of his *peers,* his equals. Now, in John's time, there was no such thing as trial by jury in criminal cases, but the Magna Carta . . . well, it sort of set this system up.

Now, I'd like everyone to take a look in your textbook, ah, let me see, on page 184. We'll take a quick look at a few more of the most important provisions of the Charter.

**Narrator:**   Now get ready to answer the question. You may use your notes to help you.

**Narrator:**   Question 3: In this lecture, the professor mentions myths (false stories) and realities (true stories) associated with the Magna Carta. Indicate whether each of the following is considered a myth or a reality.

**Narrator:**   Listen to a lecture in a paleontology class.

**Professor:**   In our last class, we were talking about the tar pits at Rancho La Brea in Los Angeles, and, uh, what a great source of fossils, fossil information these, uh, tar pits have been. There have been . . . well, millions, literally millions of fossils, of bones of Ice Age mammals that were, uh, trapped in the asphalt ponds there. It's an ideal place for fossil hunters . . . the sticky asphalt trapped the animals, and then the asphalt helped preserve their bones.

Of course, um, tar pits are not the only place to look for fossil bones. Many are found in stream beds, lake beds, deserts. Another good place for paleontologists to look for remains is in caves.

There are really two types of caves where fossils can be found. One type is the carnivore den, places where carnivores lived. Carnivore dens tend to be small horizontal caves. They're generally about one to three meters in height, and maybe thirty meters in length. They typically have small entrances. These caves often contain the remains of both the herbivores that the, uh, predators dragged into the den and, uh, the remains of the carnivores themselves. Now, with many carnivore dens, you, uh, uh, you often will have multiple occupants of the same den over the centuries. The occupants might not even be the same species. Those dens, they're kinda like dormitory rooms. You get a couple of roommates who live there for a year or two, they move on, then someone else moves in, so sometimes, there's a real jumble of bones in a carnivore's den—the bones of fish, rodents, birds, antelopes, all kinds of creatures. Then, too, most of the time, caves get flooded, and the flood waters wash all the bones and the dirt into one corner of the cave, so you have a pile of sediment-embedded bones. Sorting out these bones of extinct animals—some of which might be from completely unknown species—well, this can be a pretty big challenge for paleontologists.

A good example of a carnivore den was, uh, discovered at Agate National Monument in Nebraska. It was excavated by paleontologists from the University of Nebraska in the 1980's. It's actually a whole complex of dens used by Miocene carnivores about, um, 22 million years ago, more or less. Several types of carnivores used this complex, but the most important was the beardog—a kind of extinct wild dog. There are fragments of the bones of their prey, parts of bones from juvenile camels, woolly rhinoceroses—did you know that there once were camels and rhinos in Nebraska? Pretty hard to picture, isn't it? Giant ground sloths, lots of oreodonts—little raccoon-size mammals that lived in herds. There are the remains of young, mature, and aged beardogs. There's some evidence that they all died off about the same time, possibly because of a prolonged drought. After their death, their skeletons were covered up with sand and silt that blew into the caves.

Now, uh, the second type of cave where you find fossils is called a natural trap. Natural traps are pit caves—holes in the ground, really. Large mammals sometimes fall right into these holes. Generally, natural traps tend to have a lower diversity of fossils than den sites.

One of the most incredible collections of cave fossils was found in a natural trap in the, uh, Naracoote Cave in Australia, in the state of Western Australia. It was found by a group of amateur cave explorers and this site was explored—is still being explored—by paleontologists from a university in Adelaide. This whole area in Australia is riddled with caves, but this is the first time that there's been a major find of fossils there. The hole leading to the cave was covered with vegetation. This is true of most natural traps—vegetation hides the hole and makes it almost invisible. There is a 15-meter drop down to the cave floor. Animals fell in and couldn't get out. Even with that long drop, though, most of the animals that fell into the cave didn't die on impact, apparently. How do we know? Specimens were found in all three rooms of the cave. They probably wandered around for several days, looking for a way out, before eventually dying of dehydration or starvation. If the animals had died on impact, all the bones would have been found in a heap directly below the hole in the ceiling. Now, remember I said that there were usually fewer species in a natural trap than in a den? Not true at the Naracoote Cave. There have been some amazing finds there. Some, uh, ten species of giant kangaroos have been found there. These guys were, like, five meters tall. Then there was a giant wombat. There were Tasmanian tigers. Oh, and one of the most exciting finds was an "Australian lion," a predator about the size of a modern leopard. The Australian lion, though, isn't related to big cats, it's a marsupial, it has a pouch like a kangaroo or a koala.

So, caves. Caves, uh, present a window to the past. Sometimes the view is a . . . a bit murky. Sometimes, like the Naracoote Cave, you get this unbelievably clear look at animal life long ago.

**Narrator:**  Now get ready to answer the questions. You may use your notes to help you.

**Narrator:**  Question 4: In this lecture, the professor describes carnivore dens. Decide if the following are characteristics of carnivore dens.

**Narrator:**  Question 5: In this lecture, the professor describes important fossil finds at Naricoote Cave, a natural trap. Decide if the following are characteristics of Naricoote Cave.

**Narrator:**  Listen to a lecture in an astronomy class.

**Professor:**  Now, ancient Greek astronomers believed that the Earth was the center of the universe. This model is called the *geocentric* model—*geo*, of course, is Greek for *Earth*. Why, you ask, did they think the Earth was at the center of everything? Well, let's think about it a little. Ummm, they were on the Earth and the Earth, obviously, was not moving. I mean, if the Earth moved below our feet, clouds and birds would be "left behind" as we moved, right? If we jumped into the air, we wouldn't land at exactly the same place that we jumped from. We'd feel a constant breeze on our cheeks caused by the Earth's movement. And then, of course, when the Greeks looked up at the sky, it seemed that all the bodies they saw were revolving around the Earth. So you see, this was really a very sensible theory, a theory that was confirmed by observation.

Around the second century, Ptolemy, a Greek astronomer living in Egypt, collected all the ideas of Greek astronomers in a book called *Almagest*, which means "Great Treatise." This Ptolemy, by the way, was quite a genius—he also wrote books about optics and geography. So anyway, he developed, um, an elegant model of a universe that worked like clockwork. This model is so associated with Ptolemy that it's . . . we call it the Ptolemaic model. In this model, the planets are points of light attached to crystal spheres, the "celestial spheres," they're called. These spheres fit one inside another and move in perfect harmony. Their circular movements were believed to create a kind of music called "the music of the spheres." I always liked that idea—heavenly music. So, anyway, in this system, the Earth is immobile and is located at the very heart of things. The moon is attached to the closest sphere, followed by the inner planets, Mercury and Venus. Then came the Sun, followed by the rest of the known planets—Mars, Jupiter, Saturn. The stars are attached to the outermost crystal sphere. All of these heavenly bodies are made out of some glowing substance called "perfect matter."

Now, there were problems with this model. One was the retrograde movement of planets. Sometimes, planets such as Mars seem to slow down and then change direction, they actually seem to go backwards and then loop around and go the other way. That's why the Greeks called them *planets*—*planet* is Greek for *wanderer*. Actually, this is an optical illusion caused by the fact that the various planets don't take the same amount of time to orbit the Sun. Ptolemy theorized that . . . well, he devised a trick to

explain this abnormality. He invented the idea of *epicycles*. I'm not going to bother explaining epicycles because they are very, very complicated. In fact, hardly anyone completely understands this system today. But his system was remarkably accurate. It could predict the future positions of planets and even predict solar and lunar eclipses.

Well, this Earth-centered model was accepted by almost everyone for well, almost 1,500 years. By the Middle Ages, the Ptolemaic system had become part and parcel of the medieval worldview, part of religion, philosophy, science. The planets and stars were believed to have all kinds of powers to influence events on Earth, to shape people's destinies. Then, in the sixteenth century Nicolas Copernicus, a scientist from East Prussia—now part of Poland—came up with a revolutionary theory. It was the heliocentric model—*helios* is Greek for *Sun*. It's also called the Copernican model. In this model, the Sun is the center of the universe, and all the planets circle it, moving in the same direction—first Mercury, then Venus, then Earth. The moon, naturally, circles the Earth. Farther out from the sun are the orbits of Mars and the other planets.

It wasn't until a century later, when Galileo built a telescope and turned it on the planets, that the Ptolemaic model could be definitely proven false. Galileo learned that Venus has phases, just like the moon: crescent, full, crescent, then it disappears. In the Ptolemaic system, Venus should always look like a crescent when viewed from the Earth, but because actually it is lit from the center of its orbit by the Sun, Venus has a complete set of phases. So, Galileo proved Ptolemy was wrong.

Of course, nowadays we know that the Copernican system presents a reasonably accurate picture of our solar system but not of the universe. Copernicus didn't know what to make of the stars. He said they were faraway points of light of an unknown nature. It was impossible for him to know that they were much like our Sun, only unthinkably farther away. Today we know that the Sun is only one of billions of stars in our galaxy. We're not even in the center of that galaxy, but way out in one arm, out in the suburbs. And not only that, we now know that our galaxy is only one of billions, maybe trillions of galaxies. So, in a couple of thousand years, we've moved from being right smack in the center of the universe to living on a rather insignificant piece of real estate.

**Narrator:**  Now get ready to answer the question. You may use your notes to help you.

**Narrator:**  Question 6: In this lecture, the professor describes two ways to look at the universe: the Ptolemaic system and the Copernican system. Decide if the following are characteristics of the Ptolemaic system or the Copernican system.

**Narrator:**  Listen to a lecture in a marketing class.

**Professor:**  All right, then, next topic. I want to talk a bit about attitude, consumer attitude and how it affects consumer behavior. Before we get ahead of ourselves, though, we should define attitude. Attitude is an opinion, or evaluation, of a person, an issue, or—and this is how we'll generally use it—of a product. And anything you have an attitude towards, that's called an object.

Okay, then, one fairly traditional approach to viewing attitude is called the ABC model. In this model, attitude is made up of three parts, three components. The *A* component, that's the *affective* component, the, shall we say, emotional part of the formula. It reflects the consumer's feelings towards the object. If you look at a product, if you consider a product, how does it make you feel? Does the idea of owning this product give you a warm, happy, glowing feeling or a cold, negative feeling? If you buy it for Aunt Sally, will she be pleased?

The *B* component is the *behavioral* component. This is . . . it's not *just* actual behavior . . . it's both actual behavior and potential behavior . . . . It's . . . it's how you might act and how you do act. For us in marketing, this basically means, do you want to buy something and if you do, do you actually buy it? That's the B in the ABC model.

The C component, now that's the *cognitive* component. That's the consumer's knowledge, intellectual knowledge, ideas, and thoughts about the object. Where does this information come from? How do consumers get knowledge about a product? Well, there are lots of sources. There are consumer magazines that compare products. There's word of mouth . . . your brother-in-law Bob just bought a new digital camera and he tells you how great it is. But of course, these days, most people get product information from advertising, advertising on television, on the radio, in newspapers and magazines . . . on the Internet . . . advertising is everywhere!

So, in marketing, what you are trying to do, obviously, is to influence consumer attitude towards a product. You can do that in an affective way—you can appeal to consumers' emotions—or you can do it in a cognitive way, you can sway consumers' opinion by appealing to their good sense, or you can use a combination of A and C, but what you want to do, bottom line, is to affect behavior. You want consumers to buy your products.

Now, according to the social psychologist Daniel Katz—he did this classic study on attitude in 1960—attitudes are functional. In other words, we have an attitude towards something because it serves some purpose. Katz identified a number of attitude functions. Two of these are especially useful for marketers to understand. The first one is called the value-expressive function. This has to do with how people think about you—or rather, your *perception* of how people think about you. You might not really be able to afford a sleek little sports car, or expensive designer shoes from Italy, or a big flat-screen TV, but perhaps you buy these products anyway. Why? Because you believe that the people you come in contact with will think you look really stylish in those shoes, or they'll think you must be rich if you own that TV, or that you're cool if you drive around in that sports car. Conversely, the value-expression function can work the opposite way. You might *not* buy a perfectly good product because, well, you think it will make you seem . . . what, unsophisticated, unpopular, out of touch, boring.

The second function to consider is the ego-defensive function. These products appeal to your desire to be safe, to minimize threats. You are responding to this function when you buy car insurance, homeowners' insurance, health insurance . . . Also if you buy an alarm system for your house or car . . . if you, if you buy deodorant, you are responding to this function. Again, this function can also cause you not to buy a product. You don't buy it because you think it is dangerous. This could be why you don't buy cigarettes, why you don't buy a car that is known to be unsafe, to roll over. Again, you're responding to this ego-defensive function.

Okay, coming up in our next class, we'll look at some examples of real advertisements and see how they change attitudes and influence behavior. And don't forget to finish reading Chapter 7 before then.

**Narrator:** Now get ready to answer the questions. You may use your notes to help you.

**Narrator:** Question 7: The lecturer describes the ABC approach to viewing consumer attitudes. Decide if the following are more closely related to the A component, the B component, or the C component of the ABC approach.

**Narrator:** Question 8: In this lecture, the professor describes the Katz system of attitude functions. Decide which of the following characteristics is related to which function.

[Track 27]

## Listening Review Test
Listen as the directions are read to you.

**Narrator:** This section tests your understanding of conversations and lectures. You will hear each conversation or lecture only once. Your answers should be based on what is stated or implied in the conversations and lectures. You are allowed to take notes as you listen, and you can use these notes to help you answer the questions. In some questions, you will see a headphones icon. This icon tells you that you will hear, but not read, part of the lecture again. Then you will answer a question about the part of the lecture that you heard. Some questions have special directions that are highlighted. During an actual test, you will not be allowed to skip questions and come back to them later, so try to answer every question that you hear on this test. There are two conversations and four lectures. Most questions are separated by a ten-second pause.

**Narrator:** Listen to a conversation between a student and a professor.

**Student:** Hi, Professor Calhoun. May I come in?

**Professor:** Oh, hi, Scott, sure. What's up?

**Student:** Oh, well, I've decided, uh, I'm going to drop your biochemistry class.

**Professor:** Oh? Well, we'll just have to see about that! Why ever would you want to do such a thing?

**Student:** Well, you know, on the last test . . .

**Professor:** Oh, I know, you blew that last unit test! But you still have a . . . hang on a second, let me take a look on my computer . . . Well, you had a B+ average on your first two unit tests, so, you still have a C average . . .

**Student:** Well, I talked it over with my advisor, Doctor Delaney, and he said, since I'm taking five classes this semester, he thought it would be a good idea if I dropped this one and concentrated on my four other classes . . .

**Professor:** Did he now. Well, with all due respect to Doctor Delaney, I couldn't agree with him less. You've already put a lot of work into this class, you're not doing that badly, and . . . well, I'm just not of the opinion that you should drop it. Tell me, what's your major, Scott?

**Student:** Pre-medicine. But . . .

**Professor:** There you are! You've got to have a good grade in biochemistry if you're majoring in pre-med, and if you want to be a doctor, you need to know this stuff!

**Student:** I know, and I know I have to take biochem at some point. It's just that . . . well, for the first few weeks of this class, I felt like I pretty much understood what you were talking about. It was hard, yeah, but I was keeping up. Then we got to that unit on atomic structure, molecular structure, and . . .

**Professor:** You're right, that's . . . there are some difficult concepts in that unit. But . . . here's the good news! That's as hard as it gets! It's all downhill from there!

**Student:**  Well, my math skills are, um, a little weak, and . . . well, I never realized how much math you need to do biochemistry . . .

**Professor:**  Of course you should have realized that. Trying to understand science without understanding math . . . it's like trying to study music without being able to read notes.

**Student:**  Right. So . . . here's what I'm thinking. I drop biochemistry now, take a couple of math courses, and then I'll retake your class in a year or so . . .

**Professor:**  Listen, Scott, I think all you really need is a little help. Do you know my teaching assistant, Peter Kim? No? Well, he does some tutoring. I think if you spent an hour or two a week working with Peter, he could get you over the rough patches. We still have four more unit tests and a final exam, so there are plenty of opportunities for you to get your grades up.

**Student:**  Well, I . . . the thing is . . . today is the last day I can drop a class and not get a grade . . . I just worry that . . . if I don't do well . . .

**Professor:**  Stop thinking those negative thoughts, Scott! You're going to get a little help and you're going to do just fine!

**Narrator:**  Now get ready to answer the questions. You may use your notes to help you.

**Narrator:**  Question 1: What course does Scott want to drop?

**Narrator:**  Listen again to part of the conversation.

**Professor:**  Did he now? Well, with all due respect to Doctor Delaney, I couldn't agree with him less. You've already put a lot of work into this class, you're not doing that badly, and . . . well, I'm just not of the opinion that you should drop it. Tell me, what's your major, Scott?

**Narrator:**  Question 2: What does Professor Calhoun mean when she says this?

**Professor:**  . . . with all due respect to Doctor Delaney, I couldn't agree with him less.

**Narrator:**  Question 3: What does Professor Calhoun say about her class?

**Narrator:**  Question 4: What does Professor Calhoun suggest that Scott do?

**Narrator:**  Question 5: Which of the following best describes Professor Calhoun's attitude towards Scott?

**Narrator:**  Listen to a conversation between two students.

**Student A:**  Hi, Martha. What brings you up to the library?

**Student B:**  Oh, I've just been using the *Encyclopedia of Art,* looking up some terms for my art history class. What about you, Stanley?

**Student A:**  Well, I've got these two papers due at the end of this term, and I, uh, I've been trying to get an early start on them by collecting some references and getting some data.

**Student B:**  Really? For the end of the term? Wow, you really like to get a jump on things, don't you!

**Student A:**  Yeah, well, I just know how crazy things get at the last moment. Matter of fact, I've spent most of the day here.

**Student B:**  Well, you oughta be ready for a break then. Wanna go get some coffee and grab something to eat?

**Student A:**  Sure, that, uh, that sounds pretty good. I could use some caffeine, actually. Let me just get my stuff together and . . . hey, where are my notes?

**Student B:**  What notes?

**Student A:**  The notes I spent all day working on—I thought they were in my backpack.

**Student B:**  You mean you lost your notebook?

**Student A:**  No, uh, I don't use a notebook—I take notes on index cards. That's really the best way to . . .

**Student B:**  Okay, well, just think about where you could've left them, Stanley. Focus. Retrace your steps in your mind since you came in the library.

**Student A:**  Uhhh, let's see. I think I came in here, first, to the reference room, and I was using one of those computers over against the other wall there . . . but I don't think I made any notes when I was down here. After that . . . let's see, I, uh, think I went up to the stacks . . .

**Student B:**  Stacks? What do you mean, the stacks?

**Student A:**  You know, the, uh, book stacks . . . that's what they call the main part of the library, where most of the books are shelved.

**Student B:**  Okay, well, maybe your cards are up there, then.

**Student A:**  I don't think so. No. After that, I was in the periodicals room up on the third floor. I was sitting in a cubicle up there, looking at some journals, some psychology journals, and . . . well, I definitely remember I was taking notes then . . .

**Student B:**  And you haven't had them since then?

**Student A:**  No, no, I don't think so. Let me run up to the periodicals room and check. I'll bet they're still in that cubicle. When I get back, we can go down to the snack bar in the basement and get some coffee.

**Student B:**  Are you kidding? They have some of the worst coffee on campus—maybe in the world—down there. It tastes like mud! Let's walk over to Williams Street and find some decent coffee.

**Student A:**  All right, wherever. I'll be right back.

**Narrator:**  Now get ready to answer the questions. You may use your notes to help you.

**Narrator:**  Question 6: Why did Martha come to the library?

**Narrator:**  Question 7: What did Stanley misplace?

**Narrator:**  Listen again to part of the conversation:

**Student A:**  Well, I've got these two papers due at the end of this term, and I, uh, I've been trying to get an early start on them by collecting some references and getting some data.

**Student B:**  Really? For the end of the term? Wow, you really like to get a jump on things, don't you!

**Narrator:**  Question 8: What does Martha mean when she says this?

**Student B:**  Wow, you really like to get a jump on things, don't you!

**Narrator:**  Question 9: According to Stanley, what does the term "stacks" refer to?

**Narrator:**  Question 10: Where will Stanley go next?

**Narrator:**  Listen to part of a lecture in an elementary education class.

**Professor:**  Okay, in the time we have left today, I wanna talk about the article I asked you to read over the weekend, the one, um, about writing and reading skills. First we'll talk about writing skills, then, uh, later, if we have time, we'll talk about reading too.

One point I want to make before we begin . . . when we talk about stages of writing development, these stages are not associated with grade levels. A child doesn't necessarily enter the first stage in, ummm, say, kindergarten. Children develop these skills at their own pace, in their own way. But, a little encouragement from parents and teachers helps children move through these stages faster.

Well, as you remember, the article first talked about "writing readiness." This is behavior that . . . well, these are ways that children tell us they're almost ready to start writing.

There are several signs of this. One early sign is making random marks on the page, sometimes accompanied by drawings. To the child, these marks and drawings may represent a story or a message. Another sign is *mock handwriting*. Mock handwriting. Some children create lines of wavy scribbles, pages and pages of them, sometimes. These look like cursive writing, and children may move their hands from left to right, the way they've seen adults do. The scribbles consist of lots of loopy o's, often, and dashes and, and dots and squiggles. Some kids produce symbols that look more like printing, but with *invented letters,* marks that look like letters but aren't, really. Another sign of writing readiness—the author doesn't mention it, but I remember my own kids did this when they were preschoolers—they ask adults to help them write something by guiding their hands. Oh, and I wanted to mention that one thing you want to do at this stage is to build children's fine motor skills, build up their finger muscles. One good way to do this is to have children use scissors and play with modeling clay—this builds up those muscles.

So, the system that the author uses to describe the stages of learning to write, it's not the only one you'll encounter. Many experts divide the process into more stages, and they use different names for the stages. The system used in this article, though . . . it's pretty clear, don't you think, and it's pretty easy to understand for both teachers and parents.

In this system, the first stage is the symbolic stage. In this stage, children string together pretty much random letters and numbers that they happen to be familiar with. Let's say a child wants to write this sentence. I'll put it on the board.

MY SISTER LIKES TO RIDE HER BIKE.

A child in the symbolic stage may try to write this sentence by writing a series of random letters or numbers. The child may write oh, "PZOL2TX," for example. Children at this stage, they've figured out that letters are symbols for sounds, they just haven't figured out which letters go with which sound. Writing in this stage is, uh, intelligible only to the writer. It doesn't mean anything to anyone else. It could mean "pizza," it could mean "Big Bird." Sometimes it doesn't even make sense to the writers. Sometimes, kids write something like this and then ask an adult, "What did I write?"

The next stage of writing is called the phonemic stage. Children in this stage are beginning to understand letter-sound relationships, so they write the most distinct sounds, the dominant sounds they hear in a word, usually the first consonant sound, and sometimes the final consonant sound in a word. A child in the phonemic stage might write our sentence this way:

MSSRLKRDRBK

After this comes the transitional stage. Children at this stage of writing record every speech sound they hear when they sound out words to themselves. They're often able to distinguish where one word ends and another begins. Children may also use words that are familiar to them from their own reading. I'll put an example of this on the board.

MI STER LIK TO RID HIR BIK

My sister likes to ride her bike. Of course, children who are learning to write English . . . well, they learn basic phonics rules, basic word-attack skills, and they tend to think that those rules work all the time. In fact, they only work about 65% of the time in English. It's easier for kids to learn to write in say, Finnish, or Spanish, which are more or less phonetic languages. The relationship between written symbols and sounds is closer in those languages. Of course, it's much harder in languages like Chinese, where there is virtually no relationship between written symbols and sounds.

Okay, the fourth stage is called the conventional stage. In this stage, children apply their knowledge of vocabulary, spelling, grammar . . . the basic rules of writing. Children in this stage sometimes make mistakes, but in general their writing is effective and correct. Let me write that on the board and you'll see . . .

MY SISTRE LIKE TO RIDE HER BIKE.

A couple of points I want to make about the teaching of writing skills, and I'll have to make them quickly—one is, communication should be the main focus for writing. If children can express what they're thinking through their writing, then the writing activity is a success. Another point: writing activities should be fun. Most young kids love to write, and the best way to keep them interested in writing over the years is to make writing enjoyable.

Well, obviously I'm not going to have enough time in this class to discuss what the article says about reading skills, so I'm going to save that for our next meeting. I want to give that discussion the time it deserves. Any comments before we stop for the day?

**Narrator:** Now get ready to answer the questions. You may use your notes to help you.

**Narrator:** Question 11: Which of the following activities are signs of "writing readiness" in children?

**Narrator:** Question 12: What does the speaker imply about the system mentioned in the article that the students read, which was used to describe the development of writing skills?

**Narrator:** Question 13: The speaker mentions four stages in the development of writing skills. Put these stages in the correct order, beginning with the earliest stage.

**Narrator:** Question 14: Why does the speaker mention Spanish and Finnish?

**Narrator:** Question 15: Which of the following is the best example of writing done by a child in the transitional stage?

**Narrator:** Question 16: Which of these statements about writing assignments for young children would the professor probably agree with?

**Narrator:** Listen to a lecture in an astronomy class.

**Professor:** Did you know that, when you look up into the night sky, a lot of the stars you see are actually not single stars? To the naked eye, they look like one star, but they're actually double stars.

So, what are double stars? Well, first you should realize that there are two types of double stars. One is called an optical pair, or a line-of-sight double. These are two stars that just seem to be close together when we look at them from Earth. They might really be thousands of light years away from each other. The other type is a true double star, a binary-star system. These consist of two or more stars that are in each other's gravity fields. They, uh, in other words, they orbit each other. Sir William Herschell, in 1803, was the first to discover that some stars were really double stars, and he coined the term "binary star."

There are a lot of double stars out there. A surprising number. Most astronomers think about a quarter of all stars are binary stars, and some astronomers estimate as many as 75% of all stars will turn out to be binary stars. Well, I say binary, but actually, probably 10% of all multiple-star systems have more than two stars. Some have three stars—ternary stars, they're called—and some have four, five, even more.

Some astronomers think that binary stars are more likely to have planets than single-star systems. I've always wondered what it would be like to live on a planet in a solar system around one of these stars. Maybe you'd have two suns in the sky at the same time. Maybe you'd have a sunset and a sunrise at the same time. Imagine that! Or maybe one of the stars would always be in the sky, and there would never be any night on your planet. Aliens from a double-star system who visited Earth would probably find our skies . . . pretty boring.

One of the nice things about double stars is that many are visible with just binoculars or a small telescope. They're among the most interesting objects that an amateur can look at—and . . . uh, I think they're also among the prettiest sights in the night sky. Some binaries, though, are impossible to see as double stars unless you have a powerful telescope. This is either because the two stars are really close together or because one star is much brighter than its companion. By the way, when you have one star brighter than the other, that star's called the *primary*, and the dimmer one is called the *comes*, which means "companion" in Latin.

One of the most famous of all double-star systems is made up of the stars Mizar and Alcor. It's the second-to-the-last star in the handle of the Big Dipper, the one at the bend of the handle. If you get away from city lights, both stars are clearly visible through binoculars, or even with the naked eye. In fact, in ancient times, it was a test of excellent vision to be able to see both stars.

As it turns out, though, Mizar-Alcor is not a true binary-star system at all. It's one of those optical pairs I was talking about. The two stars are quite far apart and don't orbit each other. However, much to astronomers' surprise, when they looked at Mizar-Alcor with a spectroscopic telescope, they discovered that in fact, it was a "double-double" star system. In other words, both Mizar and Alcor, they're . . . uh, actually both binary stars.

One type of binary star is called an eclipsing binary. The star Algol is one of those—don't confuse Algol with the star Alcor in the Big Dipper that we already discussed. Anyway, Algol is usually a fairly bright star, but for a few hours every three days it dims to one-third its normal brightness. That's because the dimmer secondary star—the *comes*—moves between the brighter primary star and the Earth.

One of the reasons I like double stars is because I like to check out the colors. I said before that binary stars are pretty sights. They are particularly pretty, I think, when the pair of stars are of contrasting colors. You often get this when the two stars are of different ages. Think of two jewels of different colors lying on a piece of black velvet! That's what they look like to me. There's a double star named Albireo. One of the stars in this system is gold and the other blue, at least to my eyes. Other people have told me that, to them, the stars appear yellow and green, or even white and purple. Next week, when we visit the observatory again, you'll have a chance to look at Albireo for yourself, and you can let me know what colors you see.

**Narrator:** Now get ready to answer the questions. You may use your notes to help you.

**Narrator:** Question 17: What is the main purpose of this lecture?

**Narrator:** Question 18: According to most astronomers, about what percentage of all stars are double stars?

**Narrator:** Question 19: According to the speaker, what does the term *comes* mean in astronomy?

**Narrator:** Question 20: How many stars make up Mizar-Alcor?

**Narrator:** Question 21: How does the speaker describe double stars of contrasting colors?

**Narrator:** Question 22: The speaker mentions a number of different double-star systems. Match these systems with their descriptions.

**Narrator:** Listen to a lecture in a marketing class.

**Professor:** Okay, next we're going to talk about a process that's important to all marketing managers—it's called product portfolio analysis. First off, what do we mean by a *product portfolio?* Well, a product portfolio is the combination of all the products that a firm sells when considered in terms of their performance. It's a little like, well, like an investment portfolio. You know, investors want a balanced group of stocks: some stocks that are safe but always productive, some that are high-risk but have the chance of making lots of money quickly. So, the marketing manager wants this same kind of balance—some good old standbys, some products that show promise, and some products that may still be under development but have a good payoff potential.

There are a couple of methods used to analyze product portfolios. One's the General Electric/Shell method. Another is the BCG method, which we'll be looking at today. This system was devised by the Boston Consulting Group—that's why it's called the *BCG* method. It's also called the Boston Box or, uh, sometimes the Growth-Share Matrix. This method uses a grid, a box divided into four quadrants. Each quadrant has a rather . . . well, picturesque name: Star, Cash Cow, Problem Child, and Dog.

Okay, to get this into perspective, let's imagine we all work in the marketing department of a big corporation. We want to analyze our product portfolio. Our first step is to identify the various SBUs—those are Strategic Business Units. You can define an SBU as a unit of a company that has its own separate mission, its own . . . goals, if you will. An SBU can be a division of a company, a line of products, even an individual brand—it all depends on how the company is organized. So, now, we can classify our SBUs according to this grid.

Let's say we have four SBUs. SBU #1 makes digital cell phones. The market for this product is hot and SBU #1 has a nice share of this market. SBU #1's product is a *star.* Then let's say that SBU #2 makes chicken soup. There's no growth in the chicken soup market right now, but SBU #2's good old chicken soup is a steady performer. It provides a dependable flow of "milk" for our company, so this SBU is a *cash cow.* Okay, then let's say there is a growing demand for a new kind of athletic shoe, and SBU #3 makes this kind of shoe. Unfortunately, SBU #3's shoes aren't selling all that well. This SBU is called a *problem child.* Finally, let's say SBU #4 makes shaving cream, and there's no growth in that area. SBU #4's shaving cream is not exactly a hot product anyway; it has only a small fraction of the shaving cream market. So SBU #4, it's what's called a *dog.*

Now, once we've classified our SBUs, is the portfolio analysis over? No, it's just starting. We have to decide what to do with this information—whether to commit more of the company's resources into marketing a product, or less, or the same as before. A few years ago, the Australian marketing expert Langfield-Smith identified four basic strategies that companies can adopt to deal with SBUs. We can *build* by aggressively trying to increase market share . . . even if it means lower short-term profits. We'd use this strategy to try to turn a cash cow into a star. We can *hold,* preserving our market share. This strategy tries to ensure that cash cows remain cash cows. We can *harvest.* This means that we reduce the amount of investment in an SBU. Why? To maximize short-term profits. This may actually turn stars into cash cows. The last strategy is to *divest.* In other words, the company sells off or kills off dogs, and possibly some problem children.

Of course, all companies want to market stars—who wouldn't? But stars are vulnerable—all competing companies are trying to knock our telephone out of its role as a star and replace it with their own. How do we maintain our product's star status? More advertising? Lower prices? New features? And what do we do to move our athletic shoes from problem child position to star position? How much are we willing to spend to make that happen?

And what about cash cows? Not all SBUs can become stars—but cash cows have value too. Chicken soup may not be an exciting, high-growth market, but it does provide us with a stream of cash. Maybe we can use the cash flow from our cow to finance the development of stars.

Then there are dogs. Now, some marketing experts think a company should get rid of dogs and concentrate on projects that are more profitable. In my opinion, though, dogs may have a place in a portfolio. Products with low share of low-growth markets may appeal to customers who, uh, buy just because of price—bargain-hunters, in other words. And dogs don't cost a company much. There's little or no money spent on advertising dogs or on improving the product. Our SBU #4 can simply place its shaving cream on the shelves of retail stores.

Well, when we meet again—Monday, I guess—I'm going to give you the product portfolios of some real companies. We'll break into small groups and classify SBUs according to the system we talked about today, and make recommendations about how company resources should be spent to market these products.

**Narrator:**  Now get ready to answer the questions. You may use your notes to help you.

**Narrator:**  Question 23: Which of the following is *not* one of the terms for the method the speaker uses for classifying SBUs?

**Narrator:**  Question 24: How does the speaker classify the SBU that makes athletic shoes?

**Narrator:**  Question 25: Why is the term *cash cow* used to describe some SBUs?

**Narrator:**  Question 26: Which of these classification changes would probably most please the marketing manager of the firm that owns this SBU?

**Narrator:**  Question 27: In this lecture, the professor describes the marketing strategies of Langfield-Smith. Indicate whether each of the following is a strategy that Smith lists.

**Narrator:**  Question 28: What is the speaker's opinion of SBUs known as "dogs"?

**Narrator:**  Listen to a discussion in a marine biology class.

**Professor:**  Good afternoon. In today's lecture, we'll be talking about a, umm, a truly remarkable creature, the humpback whale. The humpback, as you may know, is not the largest member of the whale family. That distinction belongs to the blue whale, which is, in fact, the largest animal on earth. But humpbacks *do* have an amazing talent. Anyone know what that is?

**Student A:**  Are they the ones that, uh, sing?

**Professor:**  That's right, they're the opera singers of the animal kingdom. People first became aware of this in the late sixties, in 1968, when a marine biologist by the name of Roger Payne lowered a microphone into the ocean. He really didn't know what to expect. It turns out, the ocean is a very noisy place. He heard all kinds of sounds, sounds from dolphins, from other types of whales, but . . . the weirdest, most complex songs of all came from humpback whales. Hang on a minute . . . okay, um, listen to this: . . . Isn't that haunting, mournful music?

**Student B:**  Professor, how do they do that? How do they make those noises?

**Professor:**  Good question, because, well, we know that whales don't have vocal cords. We know that no air escapes during their songs. We know that their mouths don't move when they sing. But we still aren't exactly sure how they produce the sounds.

Humpbacks actually have two kinds of calls. One is a low-frequency sound, a sound with a relatively simple structure with just a few variations. These low-pitched sounds can be heard from . . . well, at least a few hundred kilometers away, and quite possibly, from much farther than that. These calls probably carry very little information. They probably just mean, "Hey! There's a humpbacked whale here!" It's the other kind of call, the high-frequency sounds that have a lot of variation, that seem to contain a lot of information. These are meant for whales in the . . . well, whales that are right in the neighborhood. This type of call is what we generally think of when we think of humpbacks' songs.

The most basic unit of humpback music is a single sound, or *element.* That might be a low moan, a chirp, a roaring sound, a trill, a grunt, a whistle, a shriek. These elements are arranged into simple repeating patterns called *phrases,* which generally consist of three or four elements. Phrases are repeated several times. A collection of phases are . . . they're called a *theme.* The singer moves from one theme to the next without even pausing. There can be up to seven or eight themes in a song, and they're always sung in exactly the same order. The songs last from ten to twenty minutes. After singing the last theme, the whale surfaces for a breath and then he—it's generally the young males who sing—then he starts all over again. Sometimes they'll do this for up to ten hours at a time!

**Student B:**  So they sing all the time?

**Professor:**  No, you see, whales migrate thousands of miles each year. During the summer they migrate to their cold-water feeding grounds. During their winter breeding season, they travel to the warm waters around Hawaii, in the Caribbean, off the coast of Mexico. They only sing during their four-month breeding season, and then they sing more at night than during the day. The other eight months of the year, when they're migrating or in their feeding grounds . . . they're practically silent then.

Members of the same group of whales always sing the same song. Atlantic whales have one song, northern Pacific whales another, and southern Pacific whales still another. But what's surprising is that these songs evolve from year to year. Isn't that incredible! After eight months of traveling and feeding, the whales return to the warm waters where they mate, and they're all singing a new song. The new song has echoes of the previous year's song, some of the themes are the same, but each year there are also completely new themes. And each whale in the group sings the new song the same way. Within about eight years, the whales create a totally new song. None of the themes are the same as they were eight years previously.

**Student A:** I'd like to know what these songs mean. Or do they mean anything?

**Professor:** Well, you're not the only one who would like to know that! Some researchers think the males are singing to attract females. Some think they are singing to warn off other males that get too close.

**Student A:** Since the humpbacks change their songs every year, well, maybe they're singing about what they've done that year, about where they've been, what they've seen. Do you think that's possible?

**Professor:** You mean, that their songs are some form of oral history? Well . . . frankly, your guess is as good as anyone else's!

**Narrator:** Now get ready to answer the questions. You may use your notes to help you.

**Narrator:** Question 29: What is not known about the songs of the humpback whale?

**Narrator:** Question 30: In this lecture, the speaker describes two types of calls made by the humpback whale. Indicate whether each of the following is a characteristic of the low-frequency call or of the high-frequency call.

**Narrator:** Question 31: The speaker analyzes the music of the humpback whale by breaking it down into its component parts. Arrange this list of the parts of the humpback's music, beginning with the simplest and shortest part and moving to the longest and most complex.

**Narrator:** Question 32: How long does a humpback whale take to sing a complete song?

**Narrator:** Question 33: When do humpback whales sing the most?

**Narrator:** Listen again to part of the lecture.

**Student A:** Since the humpbacks change their songs every year, well, maybe they're singing about what they've done that year, about where they've been, what they've seen. Do you think that's possible?

**Professor:** You mean, that their songs are some form of oral history? Well . . . frankly, your guess is as good as anyone else's.

**Narrator:** Question 34: What does the professor mean when she says this?

**Professor:** Well . . . frankly, your guess is as good as anyone else's!

**Narrator:** This is the end of the Listening Review Test.

[Track 28]

## Listening Tutorial: Note Taking

### Note-taking Exercise 1

**Narrator:** Directions: Listen to a list of words and phrases. Write down your own abbreviations of these words in the spaces below. This vocabulary comes from a lecture on business organizations that you will be listening to in order to improve your note-taking skills. When you have finished, compare your notes with those of a classmate. Check for similarities and differences in what you wrote. You can also compare your notes with those in the Answer Key.

1. business organizations
2. sole proprietorship
3. partnership
4. corporation
5. limited liability company
6. advantage
7. corporate tax
8. sole agent
9. responsibility
10. legal documents
11. distinct legal entities
12. artificial persons
13. stockholders
14. profit
15. investments
16. double taxation
17. executive
18. board of directors
19. popular
20. hybrid

[Track 29]

### Note-taking Exercise 3

**Narrator:** Directions: Listen to the following sentences. Take notes on these sentences using abbreviations and symbols and omitting unimportant words. These sentences come from a lecture on business organizations that you will be listening to in order to improve your note-taking skills. When you have finished taking notes, compare your notes with those of a classmate. Check for similarities and differences in what you wrote. You can also compare your notes with the sample notes in the Answer Key.

1. Today we're going to talk about the most common forms of business structures, of, uh, business organizations.
2. So first, let's, um, discuss the sole proprietorship, the sole proprietorship . . . did you know it's the most common form of business organization? Also the simplest.
3. Basically, there's not much difference between a sole proprietorship and a partnership except that a partnership is owned by more than one person.
4. In some partnerships, there are *silent partners,* partners who invest money in the company but have nothing to do with management decisions.
5. Corporations are . . . this is an important concept . . . distinct legal entities. They're even called "artificial persons."
6. Most shareholders don't bother to attend, and often give their votes . . . uh . . . assign their votes to the top corporate officers. This is called *voting by proxy.*
7. The day-to-day operations of the corporation are performed by the executive officers, and by the corporate bureaucracy.
8. By the way, the CEO is often the chairman of the board as well as being the top executive officer.
9. An LLC, as it's called, it's a . . . a hybrid organization, it combines some of the best features of a partnership and those of a corporation.

[Track 30]

### Note-taking Exercise 5

**Narrator:** Directions: Listen to a lecture on business organizations. The lecture will be given in short sections. Take notes on each section. After each section, answer the questions *Yes* or *No* to find out if you are taking notes on the important points in the lecture. (The more *Yes* answers you have, the more complete your notes are.) When you have finished taking notes, compare your notes with those of a classmate. Check for similarities and differences in what you wrote. You can also compare your notes with the sample notes in the Answer Key.

**Narrator:** Section 1

**Professor:** Today we're going to talk about the most common forms of business structures, of, uh, business organizations. When I used to give this lecture, oh, just a few years ago, really, I would have said the, uh, the *three* most common forms of businesses: the sole proprietorship, the partnership, and the corporation. Now, though, you . . . uh . . . you really need to add limited liability company to that list. It's . . . it's a new animal, a new way to structure a business that's becoming more and more popular.

**Narrator:** Section 2
**Professor:** So first, let's, um, discuss the sole proprietorship, the sole proprietorship . . . did you know it's the most common form of business organization? Also the simplest. As the term *sole proprietorship* implies, there's one owner, and he or she is the boss, period. There may be many employees, but only one boss. You may be wondering, how does someone start up a sole proprietorship? Well, the economist Paul Samuelson, in his textbook, he gives the example of a person who wakes up one morning and says, "I think I'll start making toothpaste in my basement." Samuelson says a sole proprietorship begins with that moment of decision. One advantage of this form of organization is that there is no separate tax on the sole proprietorship, and that's a *huge* advantage. A sole proprietorship is taxed at personal income rates and those . . . those are generally lower than the, uh, the corporate tax rate. Now, the main *dis*advantage of a sole proprietorship is that the owner is legally liable for all the company's debts. If, say, a company gets sued, or, uh, can't pay back a loan, then the owner is liable. The people suing the company can come after the owner's personal assets, like his or her house or car.

**Narrator:** Section 3
**Professor:** Now, another type of business organization is the partnership. Basically, there's not much difference between a sole proprietorship and a partnership except that a partnership is owned by more than one person. The tax advantage of operating as a partnership is the same as you'd get as a sole proprietorship.

How about liability? Each partner has the right to act as the sole agent for the partnership. How does this work? Say one partner signs a contract to buy, oh, 500 widgets from company A. He tells his partner what a great deal he got on the widgets, and she says, "Oh no! I just signed a contract to buy 500 widgets from Company B!" Are those contracts legally binding? You bet, because both partners can act as sole agents. So . . . in a partnership, one partner is liable not only for his own actions, but also for the actions of all the other partners.

Who's in charge in a partnership? In most partnerships, partners share responsibility for day-to-day operations. In some partnerships, there are *silent partners,* partners who invest money in the company but have nothing to do with management decisions.

**Narrator:** Section 4
**Professor:** Okay, then, that brings us to the corporation. This is the most complex form of business organization, also the most expensive to set up. You need to fill out legal documents called *articles of incorporation* and pay a fee, and it can be . . . well, pretty expensive. Still, almost all large business are organized as corporations.

The most important thing about a corporation is the concept of *limited liability.* Corporations are . . . this is an important concept . . . distinct legal entities. They're even called "artificial persons." What's that mean? Well, a corporation can open a bank account, own property, get sued, all under its own name, just like a person, an individual.

The owners—they're called *stockholders*—share in the company's profits, but their liability is limited to what they invest. See the advantage? If a corporation goes broke, then, sure, stockholders lose their investment, the money they invested in the company's stock—but not their personal property, not their cars or houses.

Now, unlike sole proprietorships and partnerships, corporations have to pay taxes, taxes on their profits. Not only that, but stockholders, they have to pay taxes on dividends, on the money that corporations pay them. This is . . . uh . . . it's really double taxation, and it's one of the disadvantages of organizing your business as a corporation.

Let's, uh, talk about the structure of corporations. There are three important elements. The owners—that is, the shareholders, have ultimate control. There are regular meetings of shareholders, usually once a year, and they vote on important issues. But, in reality, you usually get only the biggest shareholders at these meetings. Most shareholders don't bother to attend, and often give their votes, uh, assign their votes to the top corporate officers. This is called *voting by proxy.* Okay, now, corporations also have a board of directors. This board—oh, and I should mention this, the board is elected by the shareholders—it's responsible for making major decisions. The board appoints the chief executive officer . . . and it, uh, sets policy. However, the day-to-day operations of the corporation are performed by the executive officers and by the corporate bureaucracy. By the way, the CEO is often the chairman of the board as well as being the top executive officer.

**Narrator:** Section 5
**Professor:** Now, remember I said that today there are four important forms of business organization. An increasingly popular form of organization for smaller businesses is the limited liability company. An LLC, as it's called, it's a . . . a hybrid organization, it combines some of the best features of a partnership and those of a corporation. It eliminates that double taxation I mentioned. But, uh, I'm afraid I'll have to wait till our next meeting to talk about the LLC because we're out of time today . . .

[Track 31]

**Note-taking Exercise 6**
**Narrator:** Directions: Listen again to the lecture on business organizations and take notes. After you have listened to the lecture, use your notes to answer the True/False questions and the fill-in-the-blank questions at the end of the lecture. Sample lecture notes appear in the Answer Key.

**Professor:** Today we're going to talk about the most common forms of business structures, of, uh, business organizations. When I used to give this lecture, oh, just a few years ago, really, I would have said the, uh, the *three* most common forms of businesses: the sole proprietorship, the partnership, and the corporation. Now, though, you, uh, you really need to add limited liability company to that list. It's . . . it's a new animal, a new way to structure a business that's becoming more and more popular.

So first, let's, um, discuss the sole proprietorship, the sole proprietorship . . . did you know it's the most common form of business organization? Also the simplest. As the term *sole proprietorship* implies, there's one owner, and he or she is the boss, period. There may be many employees, but only one boss. You may be wondering, how does someone start up a sole proprietorship? Well, the economist Paul

Samuelson, in his textbook, he gives the example of a person who wakes up one morning and says, "I think I'll start making toothpaste in my basement." Samuelson says a sole proprietorship begins with that moment of decision. One advantage of this form of organization is that there is no separate tax on the sole proprietorship, and that's a huge advantage. A sole proprietorship is taxed at personal income rates and those . . . those are generally lower than the, uh, the corporate tax rate. Now, the main disadvantage of a sole proprietorship is that the owner is legally liable for all the company's debts. If, say, a company gets sued, or, uh, can't pay back a loan, then the owner is liable. The people suing the company can come after the owner's personal assets, like his or her house or car.

Now, another type of business organization is the partnership. Basically, there's not much difference between a sole proprietorship and a partnership except that a partnership is owned by more than one person. The tax advantage of operating as a partnership is the same as you'd get as a sole proprietorship.

How about liability? Each partner has the right to act as the sole agent for the partnership. How does this work? Say one partner signs a contract to buy, oh, 500 widgets from company A. He tells his partner what a great deal he got on the widgets, and she says, "Oh no! I just signed a contract to buy 500 widgets from Company B!" Are those contracts legally binding? You bet, because both partners can act as sole agents. So . . . in a partnership, one partner is liable not only for his own actions, but also for the actions of all the other partners.

Who's in charge in a partnership? In most partnerships, partners share responsibility for day-to-day operations. In some partnerships, there are *silent partners,* partners who invest money in the company but have nothing to do with management decisions.

Okay, then, that brings us to the corporation. This is the most complex form of business organization, also the most expensive to set up. You need to fill out legal documents called *articles of incorporation* and pay a fee, and it can be . . . well, pretty expensive. Still, almost all large business are organized as corporations.

The most important thing about a corporation is the concept of *limited liability.* Corporations are . . . this is an important concept . . . distinct legal entities. They're even called "artificial persons." What's that mean? Well, a corporation can open a bank account, own property, get sued, all under its own name, just like a person, an individual. The owners—they're called *stockholders*—share in the company's profits, but their liability is limited to what they invest. See the advantage? If a corporation goes broke, then, sure, stockholders lose their investment, the money they invested in the company's stock—but not their personal property, not their cars or houses.

Now, unlike sole proprietorships and partnerships, corporations have to pay taxes, taxes on their profits. Not only that, but stockholders, they have to pay taxes on dividends, on the money that corporations pay them. This is, uh, it's really double taxation, and it's one of the disadvantages of organizing your business as a corporation.

Let's, uh, talk about the structure of corporations. There are three important elements. The owners, that is, the shareholders, have ultimate control. There are regular meetings of shareholders, usually once a year, and they vote on important issues. But, in reality, you usually get only the biggest shareholders at these meetings. Most shareholders don't bother to attend, and often give their votes . . . uh . . . assign their votes to the top corporate

officers. This is called *voting by proxy.* Okay, now, corporations also have a board of directors. This board—oh, and I should mention this, the board is elected by the shareholders—it's responsible for making major decisions. The board appoints the chief executive officer . . . and it, uh, sets policy. However, the day-to-day operations of the corporation are performed by the executive officers and by the corporate bureaucracy. By the way, the CEO is often the chairman of the board as well as being the top executive officer.

Now, remember I said that today there are *four* important forms of business organization. An increasingly popular form of organization for smaller businesses is the limited liability company. An LLC, as it's called, it's a . . . a hybrid organization, it combines some of the best features of a partnership and those of a corporation. It eliminates that double taxation I mentioned. But, uh, I'm afraid I'll have to wait till our next meeting to talk about the LLC because we're out of time today . . .

**Narrator:** This is the end of the Guide to Listening.

[Track 32]

## Practice Listening Test 1

### Listening Section

**Narrator:** Directions: This section tests your understanding of conversations and lectures. You will hear each conversation or lecture only once. Your answers should be based on what is stated or implied in the conversations and lectures. You are allowed to take notes as you listen, and you can use these notes to help you answer the questions. In some questions, you will see a headphones icon. This icon tells you that you will hear, but not read, part of the lecture again. Then you will answer a question about the part of the lecture that you heard. Some questions have special directions that are highlighted. During an actual listening test, you will *not* be able to skip items and come back to them later, so try to answer every question that you hear on this practice test. This test includes two conversations and four lectures. Most questions are separated by a ten-second pause.

**Narrator:** Listen to a conversation between a student and a professor.
**Professor:** Ted, did you get my e-mail?
**Student:** Umm, no, I, actually I haven't had a chance to check my e-mail yet today, sorry.
**Professor:** Well, I just wanted to see if I could have a quick word with you after this class.
**Student:** Well, the thing is, professor, I'm working on the campus newspaper and . . . and I need to get over there right after class for a meeting . . .
**Professor:** Well, this won't take long . . . let's just chat now before class starts . . .
**Student:** Sure, what's up, Professor Jacobs?
**Professor:** Well, next week, the students in my graduate Creative Writing seminar are going to be reading aloud from their works at the Student Union.
**Student:** Yeah, I saw a poster about that on the bulletin board down the hall.
**Professor:** Yes, well, anyway, Ted, I'm also inviting a few students from my undergraduate class to take part, and I'd like one of them to be you, if you're willing.
**Student:** Me? Seriously? I don't know what to say . . .
**Professor:** Well, just say you'll do it, then. The reading will be in the ballroom of the Student Union at noon next

Friday.

**Student:** You know . . . I'd really like to read the first two or three chapters of this novel I've been working on . . .

**Professor:** I was thinking that you could read some of your poems. In fact, I didn't even realize that you were writing a novel. What's it about?

**Student:** Umm, well, I . . . it's about the commercial fishing business, about working on a fishing boat . . .

**Professor:** Really? Do you know a lot about that topic?

**Student:** Well, I grew up in Alaska, and my grandfather owned a fishing boat, and I worked on it one summer. Plus my grandfather told me a million stories about fishing. Of course, I've changed the stories some and fictionalized all the characters.

**Professor:** I was hoping you'd read that poem about spending the night alone in the forest . . . what was it called? *Northern Lights*, I think . . .

**Student:** That poem? Huh! When I read it in class, you didn't say much about it at all, so I figured . . . I figured you didn't much like it.

**Professor:** Well, I wanted to hear what the other students in class thought of it . . . but, yes, I quite liked it. The language was very strong and in particular I found the imagery . . . powerful. Almost a little frightening.

**Student:** How about this, then . . . I'll read just one chapter from the novel, the first one's pretty short, and then a couple of poems as well. Will that be okay?

**Professor:** I think that should work. Drop by my office sometime this week and we'll figure out which poems you should read.

**Student:** Okay, and Professor Jacobs, thanks . . . I'm really flattered that you'd ask me to take part.

**Narrator:** Now get ready to answer some questions about the conversation. You may use your notes to help you.

**Narrator:** Question 1: Why is Ted unable to meet with Professor Jacobs after class?

**Narrator:** Listen again to part of the conversation.

**Professor:** Yes, well, anyway, Ted, I'm also inviting a few students from my undergraduate class to take part, and I'd like one of them to be you, if you're willing.

**Student:** Me? Seriously? I don't know what to say . . .

**Narrator:** Question 2: What does Ted mean when he says this?

**Student:** Me? Seriously? I don't know what to say . . .

**Narrator:** Question 3: What is Ted most interested in reading aloud next Friday?

**Narrator:** Question 4: Which of the following can be inferred about Professor Jacobs?

**Narrator:** Question 5: Why does Professor Jacobs ask Ted to come to his office?

**Narrator:** Listen to a conversation between a university administrator and a student.

**Administrator:** Hello, Financial Aid Office, Connie Fong speaking.

**Student:** Hi, Ms. Fong. My name's Dana Hart and I'm a second-year student. I'm, uh, just calling to see if I can get some information on your . . . on the work-study program?

**Administrator:** Sure, happy to help you. What would you like to know?

**Student:** Well, what do you . . . what are the requirements for . . .

**Administrator:** The eligibility requirements? Okay, first off, are you taking at least 60% of a full-time academic load?

**Student:** Yeah, a hundred percent—I'm a full-time student.

**Administrator:** Okay, that's fine. Then, let me ask you this,

are you qualified to receive financial aid?

**Student:** Ummm, I have no idea. I'm not getting any financial aid now. See, I have a personal bank loan to pay for my tuition, and my parents are helping me out with my room-and-board expenses. But I really have no money for living expenses, so, uh, that's why I'm hoping to land a part-time job.

**Administrator:** Well, you'd need to fill out some financial aid forms to see if you qualify . . . it depends on your level of income and on your parents' level of income.

**Student:** So, if I fill out these forms and . . . and I don't qualify for financial aid, then . . . then there's no way I could get a work-study job?

**Administrator:** No, uh, no, that's not necessarily true. You see, there are two kinds of work-study positions. There are needs-based positions—those are the ones funded by the government, and for those, yes, you have to qualify for financial aid, but there are also what we call merit-based work-study positions. These positions are available regardless, uh, regardless of financial need, as long the financial aid office determines that a work-study position helps you meet your educational goals, if it's a . . . a . . . you know, useful supplement for your formal classes. It's even possible that you could earn academic credit for some of these positions.

**Student:** So, what sorts of positions do you have open right now?

**Administrator:** Well, it depends on your interests, your experience.

**Student:** The only job I've ever had, I worked in a restaurant but . . . I don't want anything in food service, food preparation . . . no cafeteria job.

**Administrator:** Well, we try to find you jobs related to your educational goals. Say, for example, if you're studying biology, we might try to place you as a technician in a biology lab.

**Student:** I'm an art major, and I was wondering . . . are there any jobs in the art gallery at the Student Union?

**Administrator:** Hang on a sec. No, no positions at all at the Student Union . . . but, uh, okay, here's a position at the Metropolitan Art Museum . . . it's as a tour guide there.

**Student:** Really? Wow, that sounds fabulous. But, uh, I thought work-study jobs were all on campus.

**Administrator:** Oh, no, about 25% of all our positions are off-campus . . . they're positions with foundations or organizations that we think perform some worthwhile community service.

**Student:** So, how many hours a week is this job?

**Administrator:** I'll check . . . uh, it looks like they want someone there for around twenty to twenty-five hours a week.

**Student:** Really? I don't know if I could put in that much time and still . . . still do okay in my classes.

**Administrator:** Well, don't give up on the position for that reason. Y' know, we really encourage job-sharing—two students working one position. It's possible that we could arrange something where you'd only work about half that much time.

**Student:** That sounds more like what I had in mind: ten, twelve hours a week or so. So what do I do to apply for this job?

**Administrator:** Well, the first step is to fill out the Financial Aid forms I mentioned. You can come down and get them from the receptionist at the front desk, or you can fill them out online if you like. Then I'll call the contact person at the museum. Let's see . . . oh, okay, it's, uh, it's a Doctor Ferrarra, he's the personnel director at the museum. I'll call him and set up an interview for you. And you understand that he's the one . . . the one who makes the hiring decision, not anyone in our office, right?

**Student:** Sure. Okay, then, thanks a lot for all the information. I'll get those forms from your Web site and send them back to you this afternoon or tomorrow.

**Narrator:** Now get ready to answer some questions about the conversation. You may use your notes to help you.

**Narrator:** Question 6: Why does Dana want a work-study position?

**Narrator:** Question 7: What can be inferred about merit-based work-study jobs?

**Narrator:** Question 8: Which of these work-study positions does Dana express the most enthusiasm for?

**Narrator:** Question 9: What must Dana do first to apply for the position that she is interested in?

**Narrator:** Question 10: Why does Ms. Fong say this?

**Administrator:** Well, don't give up on the position for that reason.

**Narrator:** Listen to a lecture in an anthropology class.

**Professor:** Okay, class, we've been talking about traditional types of shelters . . . about the, uh, styles of houses used by traditional people, and today . . . today I'd like to talk a bit about the homes of the Inuit people, the Eskimos, the people who live in the far north, in the Arctic regions of North America. Now, *all* the Inuit used to have two types of houses, summer houses and winter houses. Their summer houses were called *tupiq,* and they were originally made of animal skins and, later, canvas. There were various types of winter houses, though. The Inuit who lived in northern Alaska, where there was plenty of driftwood, built their winter houses from wood they found on the shore. The Inuit who lived in Labrador—that's in Northeastern Canada—now, they built their winter houses from stone and earth and supported them with whalebones. It was only in the north central part of Canada and in one place in Greenland that the Inuit built their winter houses from snow. Oh, and by the way, the Inuit who lived up in Greenland, in a place called Thule, they were some of the most isolated people in the world. Until sometime in the early nineteenth century, in fact, they thought they were the only people in the world. Imagine how surprised they were the first time they met outsiders!

Anyway, when the first Canadians of European descent arrived in northern Canada, and they saw these houses made of snow, they asked what they were called. The Inuit replied, "Igloos," and so that's what we call them now. In English, the word *igloo* means a dome-shaped house made of snow. However, it turns out, the word *igloo* in Inuit just means *house,* any sort of house—a house of wood, a house of snow, whatever.

How did the Inuit make these snow houses? They used knives made of bone or ivory to cut wind-packed snow into blocks. They arranged these in a circle and then kept adding smaller and smaller blocks in a rising spiral until a dome was formed. Then they'd pack the cracks between the blocks with loose snow. A skilled igloo-builder could put up a simple igloo in a couple of hours, and you know what? He could do it in a blizzard!

The igloo was the only dome-shaped traditional housing that was built without internal support. It didn't need any interior support because, well, because it was so strong. The bitter Arctic winds caused the outside of the igloo to freeze solid. Then, the interior was "set" with a seal-oil lamp. What I mean is, they used these lamps to melt a little bit of the snow blocks, and then the water refroze into ice. So you had a layer of ice on the outside of the dome and

one on the inside, and like I say, it was strong. In fact, it would support the weight of a man standing on top of it.

Igloos were remarkably warm inside. I mean, given that they were made out of snow, they were surprisingly cozy. Snow is actually a good insulator, believe it or not, and it keeps the intense cold out. Igloos were usually small enough so that body heat warmed them up pretty quickly. The Inuit slept on platforms of packed snow covered with furs. Oh, and the entrance tunnel to the igloo was dug out so that it was lower than the igloo floor, and cold air got trapped in the tunnel. Seal-oil lamps were usually used to heat igloos, so there had to be a hole at the top of the dome to let out stale air and smoke.

If igloos were to be used for a fairly long time, they, uh, they naturally tended to be more elaborate. Sometimes circular walls of snow were built around igloos to shield them from the wind. Sometimes these walls were even built into a second dome around the first one, and the layer of air between the two domes provided even more insulation. These semi-permanent igloos had windows and skylights made of freshwater ice or translucent seal gut. And sometimes you'd have clusters of igloos. They were connected by tunnels. Sometimes five or more Inuit families lived in these clusters. And, uh, sometimes the Inuit built larger snow domes that could be used more or less as . . . uh, community centers. You know, the nights are long up there in the Arctic, so they needed some entertainment. They held dances and wrestling matches and their famous singing competitions in these larger igloos.

In the early 1950's, the Inuit began living in permanent, year-round housing. They only used igloos when they went on overnight hunting trips. Today, they don't use these wonderful snow-domes for shelter at all, not even as temporary housing. But, uh, sometimes they'll build igloos for special exhibits, and sometimes you'll see little igloos in their yards that they build as playhouses for their children.

**Narrator:** Now get ready to answer some questions about the lecture. You may use your notes to help you.

**Narrator:** Question 11: The professor mentions three types of winter houses used by the Inuit. Match these three types of houses with the locations where they were used.

**Narrator:** Question 12: Why does the professor say this?

**Professor:** Oh, and by the way, the Inuit who lived up in Greenland, in a place called Thule, they were some of the most isolated people in the world. Until sometime in the early nineteenth century, in fact, they thought they were the only people in the world. Imagine how surprised they were the first time they met outsiders!

**Narrator:** Question 13: What can be inferred about the word *igloo*?

**Narrator:** Question 14: In this lecture, the professor describes the process the Inuit used to build a simple igloo. Indicate whether each of the following is a step in the igloo-building process.

**Narrator:** Question 15: The professor did *not* mention that larger igloos were used in which of these ways?

**Narrator:** Question 16: According to the professor, what did the Inuit do in the early 1950's?

**Narrator:** Listen to a discussion in an astrophysics class.

**Student A:** Ah, excuse me, Professor Fuller . . . ?

**Professor:** Yes, Mark?

**Student A:** You just said . . . you just told us that it's impossible to travel faster than light . . .

**Professor:** Well, that's according to the theories of Albert Einstein, as I said. And who am I to argue with Einstein?

**Student A:** So that means . . . well, doesn't that mean people can never travel to other stars in spaceships?

**Professor:** Well, let's think about it . . . how fast does light travel?

**Student A:** Wait, you just told us . . . let me find it in my notes . . . . Okay, 186,000 miles an hour.

**Professor:** That's miles per *second*, Mark—186,000 miles per second. Almost 6 *trillion* miles per hour! And how far is it to the nearest star?

**Student A:** I think you told us it's four light years . . .

**Professor:** It's a little more, but that's close enough . . . so, think about that. Moving at 6 trillion miles per hour, it takes about four years to get to the closest star. And of course, we can't travel anywhere near as fast as light. A couple of years ago, the Voyager spacecraft left our solar system, and it was traveling faster than any man-made object ever. And you know what? It would take Voyager 80,000 years at that speed to get to the closest star.

**Student A:** Wow. If you brought along sandwiches for the trip, they'd get pretty stale before you arrived, wouldn't they?

**Professor:** No doubt they would! Now, of course, Voyager isn't accelerating, it's just coasting; it's traveling through space like a bullet that was shot from a gun. What you need is a ship that constantly accelerate and keep increasing its speed. Clearly, rockets won't work . . .

**Student A:** What's wrong with rockets?

**Student B:** I think I know . . . they couldn't carry enough fuel, right?

**Professor:** Right. It takes an enormous rocket full of fuel just to lift one of the shuttles into Earth orbit. You could *never* carry enough to get to another star. Even if you used nuclear-powered engines, you just couldn't bring enough mass.

**Student B:** Professor, I read an article about a space ship that used sails to propel itself through space.

**Student A:** You couldn't use sails in space, it's a vacuum . . . no air . . .

**Professor:** No, Liza's right. These aren't conventional sails, of course. A scientist named Robert Forward came up with this idea. He said you could launch a ship with rockets, and then unfurl these *giant* sails made of thin plastic—I mean, many square kilometers of thin plastic sails. Then you fire intense bursts of laser beams at the sails, and since lasers travel at light speed, pretty soon, you're scooting along at close to the speed of light.

**Student B:** I thought it was a brilliant idea . . .

**Professor:** There's a catch, though . . .

**Student A:** What's the catch?

**Professor:** Well, you'd still need huge amounts of fuel to power the lasers—more than you could carry. No, to reach the stars, you need some revolutionary drive system that requires little or no fuel.

**Student B:** Is anyone even working on something like that?

**Professor:** As a matter of fact, yeah, there are teams of some cutting-edge physicists who are looking at things like anti-gravity, anti-matter, artificial wormholes, things called negative mass and zero-point energy—as possible ways to power ships. But these concepts are all in the speculation phase . . .

**Student B:** What do you mean, they're in the speculation phase?

**Professor:** Well, any workable technology goes through at least four phases of development. There's the speculation phase—that's where you figure out what your need is and dream up a system or a device that can fill that need. Next is the science phase, where you basically do experiments and see if the technology you dreamed up might possibly work. After this comes the technology phase. You bring in the engineers, tell them what you need, and they build it

for you. Finally, you put the technology to work. That's the application phase. But all these technologies that I mentioned, they're just in the speculation phase.

**Student A:** Okay, professor, let's say, for the sake of argument, that scientists dream up a way to travel *half* as fast as light, and engineers manage to build it . . . then it would only take about eight years to get to the nearest star and eight years to get back. That's . . . isn't that just a sixteen-year trip?

**Professor:** Well, possibly. But 4.2 light years is the distance to the *nearest* star, *not* to the nearest star with planets. We don't know if any of the stars in our immediate neighborhood have planets. Suppose you went all that way and just found empty space! The closest star with planets—at least with earthlike planets—may be *much* farther away.

**Student B:** Professor, I thought you said that, these days, scientists could detect planets around other stars.

**Professor:** Well, yes, that's true, I did say that . . . there have been hundreds of what are called "extra-solar" planets discovered, but if you remember, I said that almost all of them are huge planets, gas giants, a lot like Jupiter, probably. And a few that were discovered recently are smaller, rocky planets but they are *very* close to their stars, closer than the planet Mercury. We still don't have the know-how to detect earth-like planets. Maybe the closest earth-like planet is dozens, even hundred of light years away.

**Student A:** Well, professor, I guess you're saying that we'll never be able to visit other stars. I just think that's too bad. I love science fiction books and movies, and I always hoped that people would one day be able to whiz around the galaxy the way people travel around our planet today.

**Professor:** You know, Mark, I don't think that trips to the stars will be practical unless we develop a way to travel faster than light, or close to that, and I don't think that will ever happen. So . . . I don't want to rule out anything . . . who knows what kind of scientific breakthroughs we might have in the future. But Mark, I don't think I'd pack my bags and head for the spaceport any time soon.

**Narrator:** Now get ready to answer some questions about the discussion. You may use your notes to help you.

**Narrator:** Question 17: What is Professor Fuller's opinion of Albert Einstein?

**Narrator:** Question 18: What powers the "sails" on the ship that the class discusses?

**Narrator:** Question 19: According to Professor Fuller, what must be developed before ships can travel to the stars?

**Narrator:** Question 20: Professor Fuller discusses the process by which a new technology evolves. Summarize this discussion by putting these four steps in the proper order.

**Narrator:** Question 21: What does Professor Fuller say about the planets that have so far been discovered around other stars?

**Narrator:** Listen again to part of the discussion.

**Professor:** You know, Mark, I don't think that trips to the stars will be practical unless we develop a way to travel faster than light, or close to that, and I don't think that will ever happen. So . . . I don't want to rule out anything . . . who knows what kind of scientific breakthroughs we might have in the future. But Mark, I don't think I'd pack my bags and head for the spaceport any time soon.

**Narrator:** Question 22: What does Professor Fuller imply about travel to other stars when she says this?

**Professor:** But Mark, I don't think I'd pack my bags and head for the spaceport any time soon.

**Narrator:** Listen to a lecture in an art class.

**Professor:** Morning, class. Okay, so today we're gonna continue our study of twentieth-century art with a discussion of photorealism. This, ah, style of art—it was also called hyperrealism or superrealism—it was popular in the late 1960's and the 1970's. Painters who worked in this style, they . . . they portrayed their subjects down to the smallest detail, and so their paintings look like photographs, they resemble photographs in many respects.

Now, you have to keep in mind that at this time, in the 60's and 70's, art was dominated by Minimalism and Conceptual Art, which were very *non*-representational types of art, very abstract, and so this was . . . this incredible realism was kind of a reaction to that.

Okay, I'm going to show you a slide of a painting by the photorealist Audrey Flack. It's called *The Farb Family Portrait.* When she painted this, she used the same techniques that a lot of Photorealists used. First, she took a photo of the family. Next she drew a grid on her canvas, dividing the whole surface of the canvas into little squares. Then she made a slide from the photo and projected the picture onto her canvas. One by one, she systematically painted what was projected onto each of the little squares. Each square was really its own tiny work of art. Audrey worked with an airbrush, and she used acrylic paints. The acrylic paints account for the bright, luminous colors that you see in most of her works. In fact, most Photorealist paintings tend to be bright and colorful.

So, ah, where did this style of painting come from? You might say, what's the big deal, people have been painting realistically for hundreds of years. The Dutch Masters were obsessed with getting details right. And in the eighteenth century there was a European school of painting called *trompe l'oeil,* and painters who worked in this style were as interested as Photorealists in . . . in capturing every detail of what they saw, in . . . ah, making their subjects look real. However, these painters were . . . they were also interested in creating optical illusions, three-dimensional optical illusions—the phrase *trompe l'oeil* means "trick of the eye." For example, one of the paintings from this school pictures a boy who appears to be climbing out of the painting, climbing right out of the frame. That's not . . . not one of the interests of Photorealism, creating optical illusions.

Anyway. What sort of subjects did the Photorealists paint? Photorealists painted still-lifes, portraits, landscapes—although there are not many paintings of rural scenes, mostly they show urban scenes. The subjects of Photorealist paintings are interesting only because they are so . . . just so ordinary. One Photorealist, the painter Chuck Close, once said the subjects of his paintings were "so normal that they are shocking." Another one, a painter named Richard Estes, said, "I don't enjoy looking at the things I paint, so why should you enjoy it?" What he meant there, I think, is that the *technique* of painting is the important thing, that the subject itself means little. *How* one painted was much more important than *what* one painted. In a little while, when we look at some more of the slides I brought, you'll see typical Photorealist subjects. There's one of a gas station . . . one of an elderly man waiting at a bus stop . . . let's see, there's one of an old, closed-down drive-in movie. Weeds are growing up between the speaker stands and the screen is practically falling down.

Some painters specialized in painting one type of subject. Richard Estes, for example, liked to paint urban scenes, ordinary city sights, reflected in sheets of window glass. For example, he might paint a parking lot reflected in glass, or a drug store reflected in big plate-glass windows. There was one Photorealist who only painted neon signs and one who painted only trucks. The point is, Photorealists never chose grand, inspiring subjects to paint. They always painted ordinary, everyday, banal subjects.

Now I'm going to show you another slide. This picture was taken at the museum where Duane Hanson's works were on display. Looks like a photo of the museum security guard, doesn't it? That's ah, what a lot of the visitors to the museum thought too. They would come up to the "guard" and ask him questions. But this isn't a photo of a flesh-and-blood person; it's a photo of one of Hanson's sculptures. Hanson was a Photorealist sculptor. He fashioned human-size statues of people from plastic. He then painted them to make the plastic look like human skin, and he added hair, clothing, shoes, jewelry, sometimes props—one of his sculptures features a man riding on a lawn mower. Again, his subjects were ordinary people—a car salesman, a homeless person, a student, a child putting together a puzzle. As you'll see in a couple of minutes, all of these statues are as realistic as this one of the security guard.

Okay, as promised, I'm, uh, going to have a little slide show for you. While you're viewing these works of Photorealistic art, I'd like you to take notes on what you think of them. Then, over the weekend, I'd like you to write a short paper—really short, just a page or two—that describes your reactions to these works.

**Narrator:** Now get ready to answer some questions about the lecture. You may use your notes to help you.

**Narrator:** Question 23: What does the professor say about Minimalism and Conceptualism?

**Narrator:** Question 24: Which of the following did Audrey Flack *not* use when painting *The Farb Family Portrait*?

**Narrator:** Question 25: How does the professor explain the subjects that Photorealists painted?

**Narrator:** Question 26: Which of the following would Richard Estes most likely choose to paint?

**Narrator:** Question 27: According to the speaker, why are the sculptures of Duane Hanson so remarkable?

**Narrator:** Question 28: In this lecture, the professor gives a number of characteristics of the Photorealistic school of painting. Indicate whether each of the following is a typical characteristic of paintings of that school of art.

**Narrator:** Listen to a discussion in a meteorology class.

**Professor:** Afternoon, everyone. So, um, in our last class, we talked about thunderstorms. Today, I want to talk about a similar phenomenon: hailstorms. Anyone here ever been caught in a hailstorm?

**Student A:** As a matter of fact, last year, I was driving home from the university one weekend—my parents live about seventy miles from here—and the sky got really dark, and it started to rain. And then, all of a sudden—it, well, it was like . . . like little pebbles were pounding on the car, and there were balls of ice as big as marbles bouncing around on the highway.

**Student B:** So what did you do, Mike?

**Student A:** Well, as soon as I could, I pulled off the road and parked under a highway bridge until the storm was over. But it was too late—I had lots of little dents in my car.

**Student B:** I remember when I was in high school, there was a bad hailstorm, and it wiped out my parents' garden. They were really upset, because they love gardening.

**Professor:** Well, that's interesting, those two examples you gave—because every year, hailstorms cause more than a billion dollars worth of damage, and you know what? By far the most damage is done to vehicles and plants—not gardens, really, but farmers' crops.

**Student A:** There's nothing farmers can do? Can't they cover their crops with plastic sheets or . . .

**Professor:** No, there's no . . . no practical way to protect crops, although farmers can buy insurance against hail damage. Now, back in the fourteenth century in Europe, farmers tried to ward off hail by ringing church bells, banging on pots and pans, and firing cannons. Hail cannons were common in wine-producing regions, at least through the nineteenth century. And . . . uh, in the Soviet Union, as late as the 1950's, the government used cannons to shoot silver iodide crystals into clouds. This . . . uh, was supposed to make the hailstones smaller so they wouldn't do as much damage, but it didn't really work too well.

**Student B:**   Professor, are people . . . do they get hurt by hailstorms very often?

**Professor:**   Hurt? Hmmm, well, it doesn't . . . it doesn't really seem like it to me. Sometimes you'll hear about a person stuck up in a Ferris wheel or some other ride at an amusement park being injured, or something like that, but . . . uh, it doesn't seem to happen very often, does it? And that's . . . well, it's kind of surprising, isn't it, considering that hailstones can be as big as baseballs—sometimes even bigger—and can travel like, a hundred miles an hour. So, uh, I don't really have any statistics about that, but I'll try to get some information. Okay, now, another question—has anyone ever cut a hailstone in half to see what it looks like? No? No one? Well, what do you *think* it would look like? Penny?

**Student B:**   Well, I dunno. I suppose . . . it must look like a little snowball cut in half . . .

**Professor:**   No, as a matter of fact, it looks more like an onion cut in half—lots of layers. And what does it usually mean when you find layers in something? Mike?

**Student A:**   Um, well . . . I guess that it wasn't formed all at once.

**Professor:**   Exactly. Here's how you get hailstones. A hailstone starts off as a droplet of water in a cumulonimbus cloud—that's a thundercloud. Then—remember, last class, we said there were a lot of strong updrafts of warm air and strong downdrafts of cold air inside a thunderstorm? Well, one of these updrafts picks up the droplet and lifts it high into the cloud, where the air is cold, and it freezes. Then, because of gravity and cold downdrafts, it falls.

**Student B:**   Professor? Wouldn't it melt when it falls . . . I mean when it gets into the warmer air?

**Professor:**   Yeah, when it hits the warmer air at the bottom of the thundercloud, it might start to thaw—but then, our little half-frozen droplet gets picked up by another updraft, carrying it back into very cold air and refreezing it. This happens again and again. With each trip above and below the freezing level, the hailstone adds another layer of ice. Eventually, the hailstone gets so heavy that the updrafts can't lift it anymore, so it drops out of the cloud and . . . bingo, you've got hail!

**Student A:**   So, Professor, you said that you only get hail when there's a thunderstorm—is that right?

**Professor:**   Well, hail only forms in cumulonimbus clouds, which are the only kind of clouds that generate thunderstorms—though you don't always get thunder and lightning when you have hail.

**Student B:**   Sometimes, I've seen on weather reports, you get a lot of hail just before tornadoes.

**Professor:**   Well, that's true. But hail isn't always associated with tornadoes, and . . . uh, not all tornadoes are accompanied by hail.

**Student A:**   So if you just look at a thundercloud from the ground, can you tell if you're going to have hail?

**Professor:**   No, not just by looking. But a meteorologist can tell by using Doppler radar. Doppler radar can "look" inside a cloud. Okay, we said thunderstorms are most common in summer. How about hailstorms? When are they most common?

**Student B:**   I'd guess in the winter.

**Professor:**   Nope, afraid not.

**Student A:**   The hailstorm I was caught in was in April, maybe early May, so I'd guess spring.

**Professor:**   You're right. And the part of the United States where they're most common is along the Rocky Mountains . . . in Colorado, Wyoming, Montana . . . In fact, the most costly hailstorm in U.S. history was in Denver, Colorado. Just that one storm caused over . . . I believe it was about $750 million dollars' worth of damage.

**Narrator:**   Now get ready to answer some questions about the discussion. You may use your notes to help you.

**Narrator:**   Question 29: According to the professor, which of the following are most often damaged by hail?

**Narrator:**   Question 30: According to the professor, which of these methods of preventing damage from hail was used most recently?

**Narrator:**   Listen again to part of the discussion.

**Student B:**   Professor, are people . . . do they get hurt by hailstorms very often?

**Professor:**   Hurt? Hmmm, well, it doesn't . . . it doesn't really seem like it to me. Sometimes you'll hear about a person stuck up in a Ferris wheel or some other ride at an amusement park being injured, or something like that, but, uh, it doesn't seem to happen very often, does it?

**Narrator:**   Question 31: What does the professor mean when he says this?

**Professor:**   Hurt? Hmmm, well, it doesn't . . . it doesn't really seem like it to me.

**Narrator:**   Question 32: Why does the professor compare a hailstone to an onion?

**Narrator:**   Question 33: At what time of year are hailstorms most common?

**Narrator:**   Question 34: In this lecture, the professor describes the process by which hail is formed. Indicate whether each of the following is a step in that process.

**Narrator:**   This is the end of the Listening Section of Practice Listening Test 1.

[Track 33]

# Practice Listening Test 2

## Listening Section

**Narrator:**   Directions: This section tests your understanding of conversations and lectures. You will hear each conversation or lecture only once. Your answers should be based on what is stated or implied in the conversations and lectures. You are allowed to take notes as you listen, and you can use these notes to help you answer the questions. In some questions, you will see a headphones icon. This icon tells you that you will hear, but not read, part of the lecture again. Then you will answer a question about the part of the lecture that you heard. Some questions have special directions that are highlighted. During an actual listening test, you will not be able to skip items and come back to them later, so try to answer every question that you hear on this practice test. This test includes two conversations and four lectures. Most questions are separated by a ten-second pause.

**Narrator:**   Listen to a conversation between two students.

**Student A:**   Hey, Allen, have you decided who you're going to vote for tomorrow? In the student government election?

**Student B:**   Oh, that's tomorrow?

**Student A:** Yeah, haven't you seen the posters all over campus?

**Student B:** Tell you the truth, there're always a lot of posters around campus, and I never pay much attention to any of them. So are you running for office again, Janet?

**Student A:** As a matter of fact, yeah, I am, I'm running for re-election for the seat on the Student Council that belongs to the School of Business. But you can't vote for me, because you're in the School of Engineering.

**Student B:** Oh, that's how it works? You can only vote for someone from your own school?

**Student A:** Right. Each of the ten schools on campus—the Engineering School, the Law School, the School of Arts and Sciences, the Business School, all ten of them—has one representative on the Student Council, and you can only vote for someone from your own school. Except for the Student Council President and Vice President. All the students at the university get to vote for those two offices. So you'll be voting for council member, president, and V.P. tomorrow.

**Student B:** Oh, I thought I read somewhere that first the council was elected and that then they voted for president and vice president.

**Student A:** Uh, well, you're right, it *used* to be that way. But last year the Student Council voted to change the student government charter. We decided it was more . . . well, more democratic if all the students could directly elect the president and vice president.

**Student B:** Why didn't you run for president then? Almost everyone on campus knows you, and . . .

**Student A:** I want to serve one more year on the council . . . and then, well, I'm thinking that next year, I'll try to get elected president.

**Student B:** Well, if I can't vote for you tomorrow, Janet, I don't think there's much point in voting. I don't know anything about any of the other candidates.

**Student A:** You should vote anyway, Allen. You may not think so, but student government's important.

**Student B:** Why? Why should it matter to me who's on the Student Council?

**Student A:** Well, the most important thing is—the Council gets to decide how to spend your money. Fifteen dollars from each student's fees goes into the Student Council's general fund. That's a budget of, like, a hundred and fifty thousand dollars. The Council decides how much each campus organization can spend, it decides what concerts we're going to have.

**Student B:** Tell you the truth, Janet, I'm too busy to join any organizations or go to any concerts—most engineering students are. Besides, everyone knows that student government doesn't have any real power. Real power on this campus belongs to the Board of Trustees.

**Student A:** Yeah, but the president of the Student Council goes to the Trustees' Meetings. Now it's true, he or she doesn't get to vote, but that doesn't mean that the Trustees don't listen to the Council President's concerns sometimes. Just last year . . .

**Student B:** Well, I have my doubts—I think the Trustees do what they want to do. But I'll tell you what, Janet—since you asked me, I'll vote in the election tomorrow.

**Student A:** Great! Then you should also go to the debate tonight, to figure out who's the best candidate for you to vote for.

**Student B:** Don't push your luck! I have a quiz tomorrow that I have to study for.

**Narrator:** Now get ready to answer some questions about the conversation. You may use your notes to help you.

**Narrator:** Question 1: Why can't Allen vote for Janet?

**Narrator:** Question 2: How many members of the council is each student allowed to vote for?

**Narrator:** Question 3: What is learned about Janet from this conversation?

**Narrator:** Question 4: According to Janet, what is the most important responsibility of the Student Council?

**Narrator:** Listen again to part of the conversation.

**Student B:** Well, I have my doubts—I think the Trustees do what they want to do. But I'll tell you what, Janet—since you asked me, I'll vote in the election tomorrow.

**Student A:** Great! Then you should also go to the debate tonight, to figure out who's the best candidate for you to vote for.

**Student B:** Don't push your luck! I have a quiz tomorrow that I have to study for.

**Narrator:** Question 5: What does Allen imply when he says this?

**Student B:** Don't push your luck!

**Narrator:** Listen to a conversation between two students.

**Student A:** Hi, Tony. Hey . . . I wonder if you could . . . uh, do me a little favor tomorrow afternoon?

**Student B:** Oh, hi, Alison. Well . . . depends on what the favor is.

**Student A:** Okay, you know that class I'm taking with Professor Marquez? Well, she's asked us to try to find some volunteers to . . . uh, well, to take part in a role play . . .

**Student B:** And so what sort of a role would I have to play?

**Student A:** Well, you won't find out until tomorrow. See, we're learning about focus groups and how they work and how to be a moderator of a focus group. You and the other volunteers from outside our class will be members of the focus groups. The students in my class will take turns being moderators. In real life, there's only one moderator for each focus group, usually, but Professor Marquez wants everyone to have a chance to play the role of moderator. Now, since a good focus group has people from different backgrounds, uh, when you come in the classroom tomorrow, Professor Marquez will give you a little card that tells you your vital information: your age, your occupation, how much education you have, that sort of thing . . . and that's the role you play when you're pretending to be in this focus group.

**Student B:** Tell me a little about focus groups. I mean, I've heard of them, but . . .

**Student A:** All right. Well, according to Professor Marquez, there are two basic types. There's . . . uh, the exploratory group . . . the moderator asks the focus group if a company should market a new product at all, if there would be any demand for it. Then there's the experiential group—you'll be in an experiential group tomorrow. Experiential groups, they try out several versions of a product. People in the group tell the moderator which version of the product they like better. This helps the company decide which one of these versions of the product to market.

**Student B:** Don't they use focus groups a lot in Hollywood? To make movies?

**Student A:** Yeah, they do. I mean, a movie's a product, too, and film companies want to know which version of a movie to market. So a lot of times, a director will make several different versions of a movie. Usually each version has a different ending. The focus group watches them all and then says which one they like best.

**Student B:** So, what product will the groups in your class be testing?

**Student A:** Well, different teams will have different products. My team, the three students I'm working with, we're . . . uh, pretending that a client company, an imaginary food company came to our marketing agency and said, "We're thinking about adding a new flavor of ice cream to our product mix, and we've come up with a half-dozen recipes for this ice cream flavor, and we want you to help us figure out which of these we should market."

**Student B:** Ice cream, huh. So where are you getting the ice cream?

**Student A:** We're just gonna buy different brands of the same flavor of ice cream at the supermarket.

**Student B:** So, you get a grade for this project?

**Student A:** Yeah, and it's actually a fairly important part of our total grade. Professor Marquez says that . . . that the chemistry, the uh, interaction between the moderator and the focus group, is key in making sure a focus group goes well. You have to be sure that the people in the group feel free to give their opinions, but you have to keep them on topic. And you want to help the group develop a . . . a group identity, a group spirit, you know? But at the same time you don't want them to fall into the "group think" trap, where the members say things just to be going along with the group . . . being a moderator's not all that easy, I guess.

**Student B:** Well, I'm pretty sure I'm free tomorrow afternoon. Oh, and . . . uh, what flavor ice cream are we going to be tasting?

**Student A:** Umm, mint chocolate chip.

**Student B:** Okay, that settles it . . . I'm in!

**Narrator:** Now get ready to answer some questions about the conversation. You may use your notes to help you.

**Narrator:** Question 6: What subject does Professor Marquez probably teach?

**Narrator:** Question 7: What will Professor Marquez give the man if he comes to her class the next day?

**Narrator:** Question 8: What does the woman imply about focus groups that test Hollywood films?

**Narrator:** Question 9: What will Professor Marquez probably pay most attention to during the focus group activity?

**Narrator:** Listen again to part of the conversation.

**Student B:** Well, I'm pretty sure I'm free tomorrow afternoon. Oh, and . . . uh, what flavor ice cream are we going to be tasting?

**Student A:** Umm, mint chocolate chip.

**Student B:** Okay, that settles it . . . I'm in!

**Narrator:** Question 10: What does Tony imply when he says this?

**Student B:** Okay, that settles it . . . I'm in!

**Narrator:** Listen to a lecture in an American Literature class.

**Professor:** Today I'd like to continue our discussion of nineteenth-century literature by talking about the novelist Harriet Beecher Stowe. She was born Harriet Beecher in Connecticut in 1811. When she was 21, she moved to Cincinnati, Ohio. Now, Cincinnati's on the border between the Northern states and the Southern states. In those days, before the Civil War, Ohio was one of the free states—slavery wasn't permitted there—but right across the river is Kentucky, where slavery *was* permitted. Stowe said that when she lived in Cincinnati, she met people who gave her ideas and she heard stories that she used in her book. However, she never really lived *in* the South, and that's one of the criticisms that Southerners directed at her—that she had no firsthand knowledge of slavery, of life in the South, because she'd never spent time there.

Okay, Harriet Beecher was what we call an Abolitionist—a person who was utterly opposed to slavery . . . uh, to the whole idea of owning slaves. In Cincinnati, she met another Abolitionist, a man named Calvin Stowe. They got married, and she became Harriet Beecher Stowe. After a while,

Stowe and her husband moved back to New England, to Brunswick, Maine. He encouraged her to write a book that showed the evils of slavery. So, Stowe wrote *Uncle Tom's Cabin,* by far her most famous work. This novel was first published in an Abolitionist newspaper, the *National Era,* in 1851. It didn't attract a lot of attention at first. Then in 1852, *Uncle Tom's Cabin* was published in book form. It became extremely popular in the United States—at least in the Northern half of the United States—and also in Britain. Harriet Stowe became a celebrity and gave readings all over the North. If she were writing today, no doubt we'd see her all the time as a guest on television talk shows.

*Uncle Tom's Cabin's* true historical impact has been debated. Southerners hated it and said it presented an unfair, overly negative view of slavery. On the other hand, some Northern Abolitionists thought that it didn't go far enough, that it painted too soft a picture of slavery. But there's no doubt that it, uh, stirred up lots of opposition to slavery and played a role in causing the Civil War. Supposedly, when Abraham Lincoln met Stowe during the Civil War, he said to her, "So you're the little lady whose book started this great war."

Basically, *Uncle Tom's Cabin* is the story of a group of slaves. When the book opens, they're owned by a fairly humane, kind farmer, but for business reasons, he has to sell them to new masters. Some—like the character Eliza—escape and, even though they are chased by hired slave hunters, they make their way with the help of Abolitionists to Canada, where they're safe. Other slaves from this group—including kindly old Uncle Tom, whom the book is named for—are taken to the Deep South and are treated miserably, horribly, and come to tragic endings.

One strange thing about *Uncle Tom's Cabin* is that some of the most famous scenes aren't in the original book. Soon after the book was published, it began to inspire theatrical versions, little dramatic plays called "Tom Shows." These were mostly of pretty bad quality and didn't follow the plot of the book very carefully. Anyway, one of most famous of these Tom Shows was directed by George Aiken. It featured a scene where the slave Eliza is chased by men with dogs, with bloodhounds, across the ice of a frozen river. This scene was also featured in the movie *Uncle Tom's Cabin,* which was made later, in, like 1927. That's probably why this scene sticks in people's minds, but it wasn't in the book at all.

Now, the novel has come in for its share of criticism since it was written. I've already mentioned a few of these criticisms. Another criticism is that Stowe's treatment of her characters is overly sentimental, overly emotional. But remember, Stowe lived in a sentimental age. Even some great writers of the time, like the British author Charles Dickens, treated his characters sentimentally—think about Little Nell in his book *The Old Curiosity Shop.*

Anyway, sentimental or not, *Uncle Tom's Cabin* is still an important book. I don't think you can understand the pre–Civil War era in the U.S. without reading it. Now, our textbook has some short selections from the novel, but I really suggest you go to the library and get a copy and read it cover to cover.

**Narrator:** Now get ready to answer some questions about the lecture. You may use your notes to help you.

**Narrator:** Question 11: Where did Harriet Stowe live when she wrote *Uncle Tom's Cabin*?

**Narrator:** Question 12: The professor mentions a number of versions of *Uncle Tom's Cabin.* List these in the order in which they were produced, beginning with the earliest.

**Narrator:** Question 13: Why does the professor mention

Charles Dickens?

**Narrator:** Question 14: What does the professor say about the scene in which Eliza is chased across the icy river by men with dogs?

**Narrator:** Question 15: In this lecture, the professor mentions a number of criticisms of Harriet Beecher Stowe's novel *Uncle Tom's Cabin*. Indicate whether each of the following is a criticism that was mentioned in the lecture.

**Narrator:** Listen again to part of the lecture. Then answer the question.

**Professor:** Anyway, sentimental or not, *Uncle Tom's Cabin* is still an important book. I don't think you can understand the pre–Civil War era in the U.S. without reading it. Now, our textbook has some short selections from the novel, but I really suggest you go to the library and get a copy and read it cover to cover.

**Narrator:** Question 16: What does the professor suggest to the students when she says this?

**Professor:** But, I really suggest you go to the library and get a copy and read it cover to cover.

**Narrator:** Listen to a lecture in a geology class.

**Professor:** Morning, everyone. Everyone have a good weekend? As I said on Friday, I want to talk some about glaciers today. Now, glaciers just start with ordinary snow, but in some parts of the world—in . . . uh, polar and mountainous regions—snow builds up, it accumulates faster than it is removed by melting in the summer. Now, ordinary snow is about 80% air and about 20% solids. This snow melts and refreezes several times, and becomes a dense, more compact form of snow. There's less air and more solids. It's then called *névé*. Now, um, when névé doesn't melt for a whole year, when it goes all summer without melting, it becomes what's called *firn*. Firn is a type of ice, a granular ice that looks a lot like wet sugar. It's even more compressed, even denser than *névé*. Then, every year, more and more snow falls, and the most deeply buried firn becomes even more tightly compressed, it becomes about 90% solid. This type of ice is called *glacial ice*. As the weight of accumulated snow and ice builds, the ice on the underside becomes pliable, it becomes elastic enough to flow, and a glacier is born. The glacier flows just like a river, but a glacier moves only about three centimeters a day.

There are two main types of glaciers, the valley glacier and the continental glacier, plus a couple of minor types. Valley glaciers usually form near the top of a mountain. They flow down the mountainside. Valley glaciers follow a V-shaped valley carved by an old stream of water or else they, um, well, they cut their own path. The glacier is gonna pick up rocks as it moves downhill, and carry them along with it. These rocks that the glacier drags along round out the bottom of the valley, and the V-shaped stream bed becomes U-shaped. Because they're rigid, glaciers don't take sharp corners very well, so their downhill paths are generally gonna be a series of gentle curves. In some cases, valley glaciers are fed by little glaciers, called tributary glaciers, that form in smaller valleys that lead into the main valley. And sometimes, you get one or more valley glaciers that flow together, forming what are called piedmont glaciers.

Now, uh, the second major type of glacier is called the continental glacier. It's a lot larger than a valley glacier. The average continental glacier is about the size of the state of West Virginia. Today, continental glaciers are found only on the island of Greenland and on the continent of Antarctica, but still, they cover almost 10% of the world's land area.

During the Ice Ages—and remember, we said the last one of those was only about eleven thousand years ago—an additional 20% of the world was buried under these giant continental glaciers. Most of North America—most of the northern hemisphere, for that matter—was covered by continental glaciers.

Now, a continental glacier moves, too, but not down a slope the way a valley glacier does. In fact, most continental glaciers were on relatively flat land. Still, they move at a . . . uh—well, you can measure their movement. As ice piles up to a greater and greater thickness—it can be 1,000 meters deep or more—you get a tremendous amount of pressure inside the ice sheet. This force is so powerful that it causes the interior ice to practically liquefy, and so a continental glacier moves out in all directions from the glacier's central point.

At some point, glaciers, all types of glaciers, become stationary. In other words, they appear to stop growing. That's because they're melting at the same rate at which new ice is being added. Then they begin to recede. When they recede, valley glaciers seem to be moving uphill. Continental glaciers seem to be retreating towards their central point. What's really happening is that they are melting faster than they are adding new materials.

A lot of glaciers around the world these days are receding—the glaciers in the high mountains of Africa, Mt. Kenya, Mt. Kilimanjaro, for example, are noticeably smaller every year. A lot of scientists are afraid that the reason behind this is global warming. If glaciers melt—especially the continental glaciers in Greenland and Antarctica—the level of the sea will rise. A lot of great beaches around the world will disappear, some cities will be underwater—some low-lying island nations like those in the Indian Ocean may completely disappear.

Now, I'm gonna talk about the effects of glaciers on the landscape, about some of the geological features that are a result of glaciers, but first, questions or comments, anyone?

**Narrator:** Now get ready to answer some questions about the lecture. You may use your notes to help you.

**Narrator:** Question 17: The professor discusses four types of materials involved in the formation of a glacier. Give the order in which these materials appear.

**Narrator:** Question 18: Where can continental glaciers be found today?

**Narrator:** Question 19: Which of the following describe a valley formed by a valley glacier?

**Narrator:** Question 20: It can be inferred from the lecture that which of the following is the smallest type of glacier?

**Narrator:** Question 21: In this lecture, the professor gives a number of characteristics of valley glaciers and continental glaciers. Indicate which type of glacier each of the following is typical of.

**Narrator:** Question 22: What danger does the professor mention?

**Narrator:** Listen to a discussion in an economics class.

**Student A:** Professor Martin, you said that there would be an essay question on the mid-term exam about the business cycle. I wonder if we can go over the . . . ah, well, the whole concept of the business cycle again . . .

**Professor:** Umm, well, Donald, we only have a few minutes left, but we can do a quick review, sure. Let's see what you remember from that lecture. Who knows what the names of the four stages of the business cycle are?

**Student B:** Umm, let's see . . . I think it's . . . expansion, downturn, contraction, upturn, right?

**Professor:** Yes, those are the most common names for the four stages these days. And the highest point of the expansion is . . .

**Student A:** The peak. And, uh, the lowest part, the lowest point of the, uh, contraction is called the trough, I believe.

**Professor:** Yes, you're right. And as I said, we measure a cycle from the peak of one cycle to the peak of the next. Now, what's going on during the expansion phase of the business cycle?

**Student B:** Uh, that's when things are going pretty good, when the economy is just humming along.

**Professor:** Exactly. Business profits are up . . . wages are high . . . economic output is growing . . . then what happens?

**Student A:** Well, you have a downturn . . . there are economic problems . . . uh, the economy stops growing.

**Professor:** Right, and eventually the economy enters a contraction. Usually, during a contraction, you have a recession. Demand for goods is down, and . . . well, you know what a recession is like. Businesses close, people are laid off. It's a painful period for many people. After a while, though, things start to improve. Sometimes the government steps in. Or sometimes this just happens on its own. Demand picks up again, and businesses' inventories shrink, so manufacturers have to hire people to produce more goods . . .

**Student A:** Professor? What can a government do to stop a recession?

**Professor:** Well, there may not be *anything* a government can do to completely prevent recessions. What they usually do is, the government . . . the Central Bank, really . . . manipulates the money supply. This doesn't really stop recessions from occurring, but it may make these dips in business activity less severe. Anyway, as I said, after a while, the economy starts to improve. The recovery is usually slow at first, then it picks up speed, it improves, and you have an upturn. Pretty soon the economy is back in the expansion phase and the cycle starts all over.

**Student B:** Professor, what I'd like to know is . . . is this oversimplified? I mean, is the business cycle really this regular?

**Professor:** That's a good question. It's a useful model, but you're right, no business cycle is exactly the same. They vary in length, for example. In fact, they are so irregular in length that some economists prefer to talk about business *fluctuations* rather than a business cycle.

**Student A:** So how long does the typical cycle last?

**Professor:** Well, since the end of World War II, there've been ten cycles. That averages out to six years a cycle. But some were quite a bit longer than others. For example, the U.S. economy was in an expansion phase throughout most of the 1990's. Some economists even said that, because of globalization, recessions were a thing of the past. Then, sadly, along came the recession of 2001 to prove them wrong.

**Student A:** Don't they also vary by . . . uh, how bad they are? How bad the recession is?

**Professor:** That's right, they do vary in intensity. For example, the downturn in the early 90's was quite mild, but some recessions have been so serious that they were called *depressions*. We haven't had a depression recently, though. The last one was in the 1930's—that one was so bad we call it the *Great Depression*. There was another one in the 1870's.

**Student B:** Professor Martin, I never really understood— what causes business cycles anyway?

**Professor:** Well, if I could answer that, I'd probably win a Nobel Prize in economics. There are a lot of theories—there are several in your book. I always thought one of the most interesting theories was the one that the economist William Jevons came up with back in the nineteenth century. The way he explained it, business cycles were caused by sunspots.

**Student B:** Sunspots? How could something happening on

the sun cause business cycles?

**Professor:** Well, he thought that sunspots affected the climate. A lot of sunspots cause the weather to be cooler, and this affects both the quality and the quantity of agricultural production, and this in turn causes a drop in economic activity.

**Student A:** And this theory . . . a lot of people believed it?

**Professor:** Yeah, at the time, it was widely accepted. And as a matter of fact, there were a lot of statistics that seemed to back it up. Today, though, it's no longer considered a valid theory. Still, you have to admit, it's an interesting one!

**Narrator:** Now get ready to answer some questions about the discussion. You may use your notes to help you.

**Narrator:** Question 23: What is the main topic of this discussion?

**Narrator:** Listen again to part of the discussion.

**Professor:** Who knows what the names of the four stages of the business cycle are?

**Student B:** Umm, let's see . . . I think it's . . . expansion, downturn, contraction, upturn, right?

**Professor:** Yes, those are the most common names for the four stages these days.

**Narrator:** Question 24: What does Professor Martin imply when he says this?

**Professor:** Yes, those are the most common names for the four stages these days.

**Narrator:** Question 25: In this lecture, the professor describes the business cycle. Indicate whether each of the following is a characteristic of the cycle mentioned by the professor.

**Narrator:** Question 26: In which of these decades did economic depressions occur?

**Narrator:** Question 27: In what ways do governments usually try to affect business cycles?

**Narrator:** Question 28: Which of the following statements about William Jevons's theory would Professor Martin probably agree with?

**Narrator:** Listen to a lecture in a film studies class.

**Professor:** OK, settle down, everyone, let's get started, lots to do today. If you remember, in our last class, we were discussing movies about the American West, and we saw some scenes from some classic westerns. Today we're going to shift our attention to another genre of film, science fiction, or "sci-fi" as a lot of people call it. Sci-fi movies are about aliens from outer space, they're about people from Earth traveling to other planets, they can be about time travel, about robots. They're often set in the future—sometimes the far future, sometime the near future, but sometimes they're set in the present and sometimes even in the distant past—like the *Star Wars* films.

Now, most people think of sci-fi as being a fairly recent phenomenon, a contemporary kind of film, but . . . uh, in fact, some of the very first movies ever made were science fiction films. The very first one was probably *Voyage to the Moon*, made way back in 1902 by the pioneering French director Georges Méliès—who, by the way, was also a magician. It's . . . uh, it's loosely based on a novel by the French science fiction novelist Jules Verne, and given that it was made over a hundred years ago, it has some pretty amazing special effects. There . . . uh, there's this bullet-shaped rocket that's shot to the moon by a giant cannon. In fact, it hits the Man in the Moon right in the eye!

Probably the first really great science fiction film was the 1926 film *Metropolis*. It involves a sinister, industrialized city of the future—it was set a hundred years in the future, in the year 2026. It features a beautiful but evil robot named Maria—the first robot to ever appear in a movie. It has these wonderful futuristic sets. The themes this movie explores—well, they seem as up-to-date now as they did then. In fact—this is kinda interesting—it was re-released in 1984 with a rock-and-roll music soundtrack.

The 1950's—that's the . . . the so-called Golden Age of sci-fi movies. Hundreds, maybe thousands of sci-fi movies were made then. Most of them, frankly, were pretty awful. About the only reason to watch them today is that they can be unintentionally funny because of their terrible dialogue, bad acting, and really low-budget special effects. Now, the 1950's was the height of the Cold War between the Soviet Union and the United States. It was a really anxious time, there was the danger of nuclear war, and both the U.S. and the Soviet Union were testing nuclear weapons. So, uh, Hollywood responded to this fear of atomic energy by making a lot of movies about the, about . . . ummm, about the mutations atomic energy could cause. One of the first of these was the movie *Them!,* which was about ordinary ants that are exposed to atomic radiation during a test in the desert. These ants grow into giant ants and they attack the city of Los Angeles. There were movies about lots of big bugs—about giant scorpions, about huge spiders, crabs, grasshoppers. The famous Japanese movie *Godzilla* was about a bad-tempered, prehistoric lizard who's brought back to life by an atom bomb test.

Of course, there *were* a few good sci-fi movies made during the Golden Age. My favorite science fiction movie of all time is *Forbidden Planet,* which is, interestingly enough, based on William Shakespeare's play *The Tempest.* It also makes use of ideas from the theories of the famous psychologist Sigmund Freud.

Now, most sci-fi movies of the 50's were seen by small audiences and were either ignored or attacked by critics. The first science fiction movie that was a hit with both the public and with critics came along in 1969. It was the brilliant movie *2001: A Space Odyssey.* Then, in 1977, came the most popular science fiction movie of all time, the first *Star Wars* movie—eventually there would be a series of six of these. The director got his ideas for this film from . . . from everywhere: from western movies, Japanese samurai movies, 1930's serials, Greek mythology, you name it. This first *Star Wars* movie had awesome special effects, and people fell in love with the characters, like Luke Skywalker, the evil Darth Vader . . . and especially those robots.

Another important sci-fi movie was 1982's *ET.* Think about most of the movies you've seen about visitors from space: there's *Independence Day,* and *War of the Worlds,* and *Predator,* and oh, of course, *Alien.* These visitors are horrible invaders that want to kill us or enslave us or . . . or eat us. But in *ET,* the space creature is cute, he's cuddly, he's smart, he makes friends with a young Earth boy—he's much nicer than most Earth people!

Okay, well, for the rest of the class, let's look at some clips from science fiction films. Today I brought along some scenes from the really early sci-fi moves I mentioned: *A Trip to the Moon* and *Metropolis.* Then, uh, unfortunately, we just have time for a few quick scenes from my favorite, *Forbidden Planet,* then we'll look at some bits from some slightly more recent movies, like the latest *Star Wars* film.

**Narrator:**  Now get ready to answer some questions about the lecture. You may use your notes to help you.

**Narrator:**  Question 29: Why does the professor mention the work of the French director Georges Méliès?

**Narrator:**  Question 30: When does the action in the movie *Metropolis* supposedly take place?

**Narrator:**  Question 31: What topic does the movie *Them!* and many other 1950's science fiction movies deal with?

**Narrator:**  Question 32: Which of the following influenced the movie *Forbidden Planet?*

**Narrator:**  Question 33: What does the speaker think is remarkable about the movie *ET?*

**Narrator:**  Question 34: What does the professor imply when she says this?

**Professor:**  Then, uh, unfortunately, we just have time for a few quick scenes from my favorite, *Forbidden Planet,* then we'll look at some bits from some slightly more recent movies, like the latest *Star Wars* film.

**Narrator:**  This is the end of the Listening Section of Practice Listening Test 2.

# ANSWER KEY

## Guide to Listening

(The TOEFL iBT does not use the letters A, B, C, and D for the multiple-choice items. However, in these answer keys, *A* corresponds to the first answer choice, *B* to the second, *C* to the third, and *D* to the fourth.)

### Listening Preview Test

**Answer**  **Explanation**

**1.** B   The student gets some basic information from the professor about the research paper that she must write for her geology class. The student then discusses a possible topic for that paper (predicting earthquakes through animal behavior) with the professor.

**2.** C   The student says, "Professor Dixon? I'm Brenda Pierce. From your Geology 210 class . . . ?" Her questioning tone of voice indicates that she is not sure if Professor Dixon recognizes her. (Professor Dixon says that it is a large class.)

**3.** A   The professor asks, "Did you oversleep? That's one of the problems with an eight o'clock class. I almost overslept myself a couple of times." This indicates that the professor assumes (believes) that the student missed class because she got up too late.

**4.** D   The student says, "I saw this show on television about earthquakes, and it said that in uh, China, I think it was, they *did* predict an earthquake because of the way animals were acting."

**5.** B   The student worries that the professor thinks her topic is not a good one. However, the professor says, ". . . just because this theory hasn't been proven doesn't mean you couldn't write a perfectly good paper about this topic . . . on the notion that animals can predict earthquakes. Why not? It could be pretty interesting. But to do a good job, you . . . you'll need to look at some serious studies in the scientific journals . . ."

**6.** D   The professor says that the taiga is ". . . also called the 'boreal forest.' "

**7.** B   The professor says, "This sub-zone—well, if you like variety, you're not going to feel happy here. You can travel for miles and see only half a dozen species of trees. In a few days, we'll be talking about the tropical rain forest; now *that's* where you'll see variety." The professor is emphasizing that there are very few species of trees in the closed forest by comparing it with tropical rain forests, where there are many species.

**8.** B, C, A   The professor says that the closed forest, choice B, has "bigger needle-leaf trees growing closer together." In the mixed forest, choice C, "The trees are bigger still here, and you'll start seeing some broad-leafed trees, deciduous trees. You'll see larch, aspen, especially along rivers and creeks, in addition to needle-leaf trees." In the open forest, choice A, "The only trees here are needle-leaf trees—you know, evergreen trees, what we call coniferous trees. These trees tend to be small and far apart."

**9.** B, D, E   The professor mentions the trees' dark green color (which absorbs the sun's heat), their conical shape (which prevents too much snow from accumulating on their branches), and the fact that they are "evergreen" trees (which allows them to start photosynthesizing right away in the spring) as adaptations to the cold. There is no mention of their bark or of their root systems.

**10.** B   According to the professor, "There's one thing all these predators have in common, the ones that live there all year round . . . they all have thick, warm fur coats . . ."

**11.** C   The professor says, ". . . only young moose are at risk of being attacked. The adult moose is the biggest, strongest animal found in the taiga, so a predator would have to be feeling pretty desperate to take on one of these."

**12.** C, D, B, A   According to Professor Speed, Professor Longdell, who invented the case study method, "insisted that it was based on a system used by Chinese philosophers thousands of years ago." Professor Longdell first began using the case study method at Harvard School of Law in the 1870's. It was first used at Columbia University Law School "a couple of years after that." It was not used at Harvard School of Business until "probably about 1910, 1912, something like that."

**13.** D   Professor Speed explains exhibits this way: "Exhibits . . . those are documents, statistical documents, that explain the situation. They might be, oh, spreadsheets, sales reports, umm, marketing projections, anything like that."

**14.** B   The best answer is B; the professor is not *exactly* sure when case study was first used at Harvard Business School. That's why he says, ". . . When was it? Uh, probably about 1910, 1912, something like that . . ." Notice that choice A is not correct because, although he does ask a question ("When was it?"), he does not ask the class, he asks himself.

**15.** A   Professor Speed says that the case study method is used in many fields of study. "For example, my wife . . . she teaches over at the School of Education . . . she uses cases to train teachers."

**16.**

|  | Yes | No |
|---|:---:|:---:|
| Analyze the business situation and exhibits | ✓ | |
| Role-play | ✓ | |
| Run a computer simulation | | ✓ |
| Give a presentation and write a report | ✓ | |
| Visit a real business and attend a meeting | | ✓ |

The first phrase should be marked **Yes** because it *is* part of the process of case study. Professor Speed says that ". . . you have to analyze the situation, the data . . . Then you have to make decisions about how to solve these problems." The second phrase should also be marked **Yes** because the professor says, ". . . solving the problem usually involves role-playing, taking on the roles of decision-makers at the firm." The third phrase should be marked **No.** Computer simulation is *another* method of studying business; it is not part of the case study method. The fourth phrase should be marked **Yes.** When Professor Speed is asked by a student how grades are calculated, Professor Speed tells him, "You give a presentation, an oral presentation . . . and then you write a report as well. You get a grade, a group grade, on the presentation and the report." The last phrase should be marked **No.** Professor Speed does not mention that students will be visiting real businesses or attending meetings as part of the case study process.

**17.** A, D Choice A is correct because Professor Speed says, "That's the beauty of this method. It teaches teamwork and cooperation." Choice D is also a correct answer because a student asks the professor, "So *that's* why we study cases? I mean, because managers need to be able to make decisions . . . and solve problems?" and the professor responds, "Exactly . . . well, that's a big part of it, anyway."

**18.** B The presenter introduces the topic of Venus by saying, "Okay, to start off, I'm going to tell you what people, what they used to think about Venus." He goes on to explain several old beliefs about the planet.

**19.** A, D Choice A is correct. The presenter explains that, in the distant past, people thought that the object we now know as Venus was once thought to be two stars, Phosphorus, the morning star, and Hesperus, the evening star. Choice D is also correct. The speaker says, "a lot of people believed, for some reason, that there were these creatures on Venus who were superior to us, almost perfect beings, like angels or something."

**20.**

|  | Similarity | Difference |
|---|---|---|
| Their ages | ✓ | |
| The directions in which they spin around their axes | | ✓ |
| Their atmospheric pressures | | ✓ |
| The presence of volcanoes | ✓ | |
| Their sizes | ✓ | |

The first phrase is a **similarity.** The presenter says, "Venus is about the same size as Earth." The second phrase should be considered a **difference** between the two planets. The presenter says, "All the planets of the solar system turn on their axis in the same direction as they orbit the Sun. All except Venus, of course!" The third phrase is also a **difference.** According to the presenter, the atmosphere on Venus is "really thick . . . so thick, it's like being at the bottom of an ocean on Earth." The fourth phrase should be considered a **similarity.** The presenter says that the space probe Magellan "found out that there are all these volcanoes on Venus, just like there are on Earth." The last phrase should likewise be considered a **similarity** because the presenter says that "Venus is about the same size as Earth."

**21.** B Choice A *is* true, so it is not the right answer. On Earth, a day lasts 24 hours, but a day on Venus lasts 243 Earth days. Choice B is *not* true and is the best answer. A year on Venus lasts 225 Earth days, but an Earth year last 365 Earth days. Choice C is true. A year on Venus lasts 225 Earth days, but a day on Venus lasts 243 Earth days. Choice D is also true. According to the speaker, a day on Venus is longer than a day on any planet in the solar system, including giant gas planets such as Jupiter.

**22.** A, D, C, B The presenter says that "The first one to go there, the first probe to go there successfully was Mariner 2 in, uh, 1962," so choice A should be listed first. Choice D should be placed in the second box. According to the presenter, the Soviet probe Venera 4 was sent to Venus in 1967. The presenter says Choice C, Venus Pioneer, was launched in 1978. Choice B, Magellan, should be placed in the last box because this probe went to Venus in 1990. However, although Magellan should be listed last, it is mentioned first in the presentation.

**23.** C The presenter says, "Well, Caroline will be giving the next report, which is about the third planet, and since we all live here, that should be pretty interesting." Since Caroline's presentation is about the planet where we all live, it must be about the Earth.

## Lesson 1: Main-Topic and Main-Purpose Questions

### Exercise 1.1

| | | | |
|---|---|---|---|
| **1.** C | **3.** C | **4.** A | **5.** A |
| **2.** B | | | |

### Exercise 1.2

| | | | |
|---|---|---|---|
| **1.** D | **4.** D | **6.** A | **8.** B |
| **2.** B | **5.** C | **7.** C | **9.** D |
| **3.** A | | | |

## Lesson 2: Factual, Negative Factual, and Inference Questions

### Exercise 2.1

| | | | |
|---|---|---|---|
| **1.** A | **7.** A | **13.** A | **19.** A |
| **2.** D | **8.** B, C | **14.** B | **20.** C |
| **3.** C | **9.** D | **15.** B, D | **21.** A, B |
| **4.** B | **10.** B | **16.** D | **22.** D |
| **5.** C | **11.** C | **17.** D | |
| **6.** D | **12.** A, D | **18.** D | |

### Exercise 2.2

| | | | |
|---|---|---|---|
| **1.** A, C | **12.** D | **23.** D | **34.** B |
| **2.** B | **13.** A | **24.** A, D | **35.** B |
| **3.** C | **14.** A | **25.** B | **36.** A |
| **4.** B | **15.** B | **26.** A | **37.** B |
| **5.** A, D | **16.** B | **27.** B | **38.** D |
| **6.** D | **17.** A, C | **28.** D | **39.** B, C |
| **7.** A | **18.** C | **29.** C, D | **40.** A |
| **8.** C | **19.** D | **30.** A | **41.** D |
| **9.** A | **20.** B | **31.** C | **42.** C |
| **10.** A, D, E | **21.** B, D | **32.** D | |
| **11.** B | **22.** C | **33.** C | |

## Lesson 3: Purpose, Method, and Attitude Questions

### Exercise 3.1

| | | | |
|---|---|---|---|
| **1.** D | **3.** B | **5.** C | **6.** A |
| **2.** A | **4.** A | | |

### Exercise 3.2

| | | | |
|---|---|---|---|
| **1.** C | **5.** D | **8.** A | **11.** B |
| **2.** C | **6.** B | **9.** C | **12.** D |
| **3.** D | **7.** C | **10.** A | **13.** B |
| **4.** A | | | |

## Lesson 4: Replay Questions

### Exercise 4.1
| | | | |
|---|---|---|---|
| 1. T | 4. T | 7. T | 10. F |
| 2. F | 5. F | 8. F | 11. T |
| 3. T | 6. T | 9. T | 12. F |

### Exercise 4.2
| | | | |
|---|---|---|---|
| 1. A | 5. D | 8. C | 11. D |
| 2. A | 6. A | 9. A | 12. C |
| 3. B | 7. D | 10. C | 13. B |
| 4. B | | | |

### Exercise 4.3
| | | | |
|---|---|---|---|
| 1. D | 5. C | 9. A | 13. B |
| 2. B | 6. B | 10. B | 14. B |
| 3. D | 7. D | 11. A | 15. C |
| 4. A | 8. C | 12. D | |

## Lesson 5: Ordering and Matching Questions

### Exercise 5.1
| | | |
|---|---|---|
| 1. C, D, A, B | 6. A, D, B, C | 11. B, C, A |
| 2. B, A, C | 7. A, C, B | 12. A, B, C |
| 3. C, A, B | 8. B, A, C | 13. C, A, D, B |
| 4. B, D, C, A | 9. D, B, A, C | |
| 5. C, B, A | 10. D, C, A, B | |

## Lesson 6: Completing Charts

### Exercise 6.1

1.

| | Yes | No |
|---|---|---|
| Plentiful parking is provided in large parking lots. | | ✓ |
| Residents can walk easily to work or shopping areas. | ✓ | |
| Residences, shops, and offices are all found on the same block. | ✓ | |
| Communities are located only in large urban centers. | | ✓ |
| Streets are generally laid out in a grid pattern. | ✓ | |

2.

| | Yes | No |
|---|---|---|
| Housing is less expensive in New Urban communities than in typical suburbs. | | ✓ |
| There is less crime in New Urban communities. | ✓ | |
| Most New Urban communities are conveniently located close to large suburban shopping malls. | | ✓ |
| Residents of New Urban communities get more exercise. | ✓ | |
| Most houses in New Urban communities feature garages that allow direct access to the house. | | ✓ |
| There is less air pollution in New Urban communities. | ✓ | |

3.

| | Myth | Reality |
|---|---|---|
| It created the first democratic society in England. | ✓ | |
| It confirmed the rights of the English barons. | | ✓ |
| It established the first British Parliament. | ✓ | |
| It established courts in which citizens were tried by their peers. | ✓ | |
| It was signed by King John himself. | | ✓ |

4.

| | Yes | No |
|---|---|---|
| Tend to be found in horizontal caves with small entrances | ✓ | |
| Contain only herbivore fossils | | ✓ |
| May have had both herbivores and carnivores living in them | | ✓ |
| Usually have a greater variety of fossils than natural traps | ✓ | |
| Generally contain well-preserved fossils | | ✓ |

5.

| | Yes | No |
|---|---|---|
| This cave was discovered by professional palaeontologists. | | ✓ |
| Animals that fell in here died from the impact of the fall. | | ✓ |
| Its entrance was covered by plants. | ✓ | |
| This cave features the fossil bones of a previously unknown giant cat. | | ✓ |
| This cave contains a greater variety of fossils than most natural traps. | ✓ | |

6.

| | Ptolemaic System | Copernican System |
|---|---|---|
| This system is also known as the "heliocentric system." | | ✓ |
| "Epicycles" were used to help explain this system. | ✓ | |
| This system became part of the medieval system of belief. | ✓ | |
| This system was disproved by the discovery of the phases of Venus. | ✓ | |
| This system provided a good picture of the solar system but not of the universe. | | ✓ |
| According to this system, music was generated by the movement of crystal spheres. | ✓ | |

**7.**

|  | Component | | |
|---|:---:|:---:|:---:|
|  | A | B | C |
| A consumer visits an Internet site to get more information about tires. |  |  | ✓ |
| A man feels a bicycle will make his daughter happy. | ✓ |  |  |
| A customer buys groceries at the store. |  | ✓ |  |
| An investor studies the market for art before buying a painting. |  |  | ✓ |
| A woman orders a sandwich and a drink at a fast-food restaurant. |  | ✓ |  |

**8.**

|  | Value-expressive function | Ego-defensive function |
|---|:---:|:---:|
| May involve a product that protects a consumer from some threat |  | ✓ |
| May involve a product that consumers believe will make them more popular | ✓ |  |
| May involve a product that consumers believe will make people dislike them | ✓ |  |
| May involve a product that is harmful to the consumer who buys it |  | ✓ |

## Listening Review Test

| Answer | Explanation |
|---|---|
| **1.** B | Scott tells Professor Calhoun, "I've decided, uh, I'm going to drop your biochemistry class." |
| **2.** D | Scott says that Professor Delaney has advised him to drop one class. Professor Calhoun says, "With all due respect to Doctor Delaney, I couldn't agree with him less." This means that she respects Professor Delaney but completely disagrees with his advice. |
| **3.** A | Professor Calhoun agrees that the unit on atomic structure, etc., was difficult, but she says, ". . . here's the good news! That's as hard as it gets! It's all downhill from there!" She means that the rest of the course will be easier. |
| **4.** D | Professor Calhoun suggests that Scott get tutoring (private instruction) from her teaching assistant, Peter Kim. |
| **5.** C | Professor Calhoun encourages Scott to stay in the class. She tells him that she thinks he can pass the class if he gets a little help. She says, "You're going to do just fine!" |
| **6.** A | Stanley asks Martha why she has come to the library, and she tells him that she has been "using the *Encyclopedia of Art,* looking up some terms for my art history class." |
| **7.** C | Stanley has lost some index cards with his research notes written on them. |

| **8.** B | In a surprised tone of voice, Martha asks Stanley, "You really like to get a jump on things, don't you?" *To get a jump on things* means "to get an early start." |
| **9.** C | Stanley says, "The, uh, book stacks . . . that's what they call the main part of the library, where most of the books are shelved." |
| **10.** A | Stanley thinks that his note cards are probably in the periodicals room (where journals and magazines are kept), and he says, "Let me run up to the periodicals room and check." After he finds his notes, he and Martha will probably go to a coffee shop on Williams Street. |
| **11.** B, C, E | Choice B is correct because the professor says one sign of writing readiness is "making random marks on the page, sometimes accompanied by drawings." Choice C is also correct. The professor says, "Another sign of writing readiness . . . they ask adults to help them write something by guiding their hands." Choice E is correct because the professor says, "Some kids produce symbols that look more like printing, but with *invented letters.*" Choice A is NOT correct. The professor suggests that children build up their hand muscles by using scissors and modeling clay, but this is not given as a sign of writing readiness. Choice D is not correct because this is a sign of the symbolic stage, not of writing readiness. |
| **12.** C | According to the professor, "Many experts divide the process into more stages." |
| **13.** B, A, D, C | The professor says, "In this system, the first stage is the symbolic stage." Later she says, "The next stage of writing is called the phonemic stage." Then she says, "After this comes the transitional stage." Finally she says, "Okay, the fourth stage is called the conventional stage." |
| **14.** B | The professor says, "It's easier for kids to learn to write in, say, Finnish, or Spanish, which are more or less phonetic languages." |
| **15.** C | Choice A would likely be produced by a child in the writing readiness phase. Choice B includes only the most dominant sounds but does not involve separate words. This was probably written by a child at the phonemic stage. Choice D involves only some minor spelling mistakes and represents a child at the conventional stage. Choice C, the best answer, is a transition between phonemic and conventional. It involves separate words, and the writer makes an effort to record all the sounds in the words. |
| **16.** B, C | The professor emphasizes two points about teaching writing skills: that "writing activities should be *fun*" and that "communication should be the main focus for writing." |
| **17.** D | This lecture provides a basic description of double stars. |
| **18.** C | According to the professor, "Most astronomers think about a quarter of all stars are binary stars." She also says that "some astronomers estimate as many as 75% of all stars will turn out to be binary stars." |
| **19.** A | A *comes* is the dimmer star in a double star. It is the Latin word for *companion.* (The brighter star is called the *primary.*) |
| **20.** C | Mizar-Alcor is a "double-double star," according to the professor, because both Mizar and Alcor are binary stars. |

**21.** B — The professor compares a double star having stars of contrasting colors to "two jewels of different colors lying on a piece of black velvet."

**22.** C, B, A — Albireo is given as an example of a double star in which the two stars appear to be of two different colors. Algol is given as an example of an eclipsing binary, in which one star sometimes blocks the light from the other star. The professor says that Mizar-Alcor is "one of those optical pairs I was talking about."

**23.** C — The professor says that the method he uses to classify SBUs is called the BCG method because it was developed by the *Boston Consulting Group*. It is also called the "Boston Box" and the "Growth-Share Matrix." It is NOT called the General Electric/Shell method, which is another system for analyzing a product portfolio.

**24.** C — The professor says that "SBU #3's shoes aren't selling all that well. This SBU is called a *problem child.*"

**25.** D — The professor implies that the term *cash cow* is used because this type of SBU provides "a dependable flow of 'milk' " (meaning *profit*) for a company.

**26.** B — A marketing manager would be most pleased by a move from a "dog" to a "cash cow" because a dog is both low-growth and low-market-share whereas a cash cow is low-growth but high-market-share, and a cash cow brings in substantial profits.

**27.**

| | Yes | No |
|---|---|---|
| Increase market share in an SBU and turn a cash cow into a star | ✓ | |
| Reduce investment in an SBU and collect short-term profits | ✓ | |
| Buy a well-performing SBU from another company, creating a new star | | ✓ |
| Sell a poorly performing SBU and get rid of a dog | ✓ | |
| Raise prices on an SBU's product and change a problem child to a cash cow | | ✓ |

The first choice should be marked **Yes.** This is the strategy Langfield-Smith calls **building.** The second choice should also be marked **Yes.** This is the strategy Langfield-Smith calls **harvesting.** The professor doesn't list buying a star as one of Langfield-Smith's strategies, so you should mark the third choice **No.** The fourth choice, which Langfield-Smith calls **divesting,** should be marked **Yes.** However, the professor does not give raising prices on an SBU as one of Langfield-Smith's strategies, so the last choice should be marked **No.**

**28.** A — He says that, "In my opinion, though, dogs may have a place in a portfolio."

**29.** B, C — We know that humans became aware of the humpback whale song in 1968, so choice A is not correct, and we know that Roger Payne discovered that humpbacks sang, so choice D is not correct. The professor says, "We still aren't exactly sure how they produce the sounds," so B is a good choice. Choice C is also a good choice. A student says, "I'd like to know what these songs mean" and the professor responds, "Well, you're not the only one who would like to know that!" There are some theories, but apparently no one definitely knows the meaning of the whales' songs.

**30.**

| | Low-frequency sound | High-frequency sound |
|---|---|---|
| Travels a long distance | ✓ | |
| Probably carries a lot of information | | ✓ |
| Has a simple structure | ✓ | |
| Is generally considered the "song" of the humpback whale | | ✓ |

The low-frequency sounds can be heard from at least 100 kilometers away, so you should check **low-frequency** for the first choice. The high-frequency sounds "seem to contain a lot of information," so you should check **high-frequency** for the second choice. The low-frequency sound has "a relatively simple structure," so you should check **low-frequency** for the third choice. The high-frequency sounds are "what we generally think of when we think of humpbacks' songs," so you should check **high-frequency** for the fourth choice.

**31.** C, D, A, B — The professor says that "The most basic unit of humpback music is a single sound, or **element.**" Elements are arranged into patterns called **phrases,** consisting of three or four elements. A collection of phrases is called a **theme.** There are seven or eight themes in a **song.**

**32.** C — The professor says that a song lasts from ten to twenty minutes.

**33.** D — The professor says that the whales generally only sing during their winter breeding season, which is spent in warm waters, and that they sing more at night than during the day.

**34.** B — The professor indicates that no one knows for sure what the songs of the whales mean. Therefore, she says that the student's theory (that whale songs are a form of oral history) might be correct.

## Listening Tutorial: Note Taking

### Note-taking Exercise 1
(Answers will vary. Any understandable abbreviation is a good answer.)
1. bus orgs
2. sole prop   s. prop   s p'shp
3. pt'ship ptner'shp
4. corp
5. lmtd lia co, l.l.c.
6. advant.
7. corp tx
8. s. agnt
9. respon'ty   respon   resp
10. leg docs lgl docus
11. dist. leg. ent.
12. artif pers.
13. st'hlders   stkhldrs
14. prof prft
15. invstmnts   invests
16. dble tx'tion
17. exec

18. brd of drctrs    brd of direcs    bd. dirs b.o.d.
19. pop
20. hyb

## Note-taking Exercise 2

1. business organizations
2. sole proprietorship
3. partnership
4. corporation
5. limited liability company
6. advantage
7. corporate tax
8. sole agent
9. responsibility
10. legal documents
11. distinct legal entities
12. artificial persons
13. stockholders
14. profit
15. investments
16. double taxation
17. executive
18. board of directors
19. popular
20. hybrid

## Note-taking Exercise 3

(Answers will vary. Any understandable notes are good answers.)

1. Topic: most comm forms of bus structs (bus orgs)
2. 1st : sole p'ship most comm & simplest
3. Not much diff sole p'ship & pt'shp excpt pt'shp owned by > 1 pers
4. Some pt'ships: silent parts who inv $ in co but not invlv'd w/ mg'ment decis.
5. Corps are <u>distinc lgl ent'ies</u> artif. pers
6. Most shr'holders don't attnd, give votes top corp offcrs = voting by proxy
7. Howev, d-to-d ops of corp perf'd by exec offcrs + corp br'cracy
8. BTW, CEO often chrmn of brd + top exec offcr
9. LLC = hyb org combines best of pt'shp + best of corp

## Note-taking Exercise 4

(Answers will vary. It is not necessary to reconstruct the sentences word for word.)

1. Today we're going to talk about the most common forms of business structures, the most common forms of business organizations.
2. So first, let's discuss the sole proprietorship . . . did you know it's the most common form of business organization? Also the simplest.
3. Basically, there's not much difference between a sole proprietorship and a partnership except that a partnership is owned by more than one person.
4. In some partnerships, there are *silent partners,* partners who invest money in the company but have nothing to do with management decisions.
5. Corporations are (this is an important concept) distinct legal entities. They're even called "artificial persons."
6. Most shareholders don't bother to attend, and often give their votes, assign their votes, to the top corporate officers. This is called *voting by proxy.*
7. The day-to-day operations of the corporation are performed by the executive officers and by the corporate bureaucracy.
8. By the way, the CEO is often the chairman of the board as well as being the top executive officer.
9. An L.L.C., as it's called, is a hybrid organization that combines some of the best features of a partnership and those of a corporation.

## Note-taking Exercise 5

(Yes/No answers will vary.)
**Sample Notes**
Topic: most comm forms of bus structs (bus orgs)
    In past, 3 forms:
        1. S. p'ship
        2. pt'ship
        3. corp.
Now,  4. lmtd lia co.
1. S. P'ship
   most common & simplest
    1 owner: boss
      start up @ "moment of decision" to start business
        (Pl Samuelson's example of tthpaste)
      Advantage: Txed @ pers inc. rate (< corp rate)
2. Pt'sthip
    pt'shp ≈ S. p'ship excpt pt'shp owned by > 1 pers
    Tx advant of pt'ship = that of s. p'ship
    Liability: Ea part. can be "sole agnt" for pt'ship
      (e.g. prob of 2 partners both buyng "widgets")
    1 prtnr liab not only for self but for all prtnrs
    Usu, parts. share mgmt but . . . Some pt'ships: silent
      prtnrs who inv $ in co but not invlv'd w/ mg'ment
3. <u>Corp</u>
  Most complex     most expensive (artic of
    incorp'tion) but most big co's corps
  Limited liability: Corps: <u>distinc lgl ent'ies</u> artif. pers
    Corp does bus under its own name owners
    (st'holders) can only lose invest, not pers prop
  Txation: Corps have to pay txs & so do stckhldrs on
    div'dends: dble txation
  Structure: 3 el'mts
    1. <u>stckhldrs</u>: ultim. contrl mtgs. 1ce a yr.
      BUT usu. only biggest stckhldrs
      Most stckhldrs don't attnd, give votes top corp
      offcrs = voting by proxy
    2. <u>Brd of drctrs</u> elec. by stckhldrs makes maj decis
      appt CEO sets policy
    3. Howev, D-to-d ops of corp done by perf'd by exec
      offcrs + corp br'cracy
      BTW, CEO often chrmn of brd + top exec offcr
    4. <u>LLC</u> incre'ly pop for smaller bus.
      LLC = hyb org combines best of pt'shp + best
      of corp elim's dble txation

## Note-taking Exercise 6

1. T
2. Limited liability company
3. F
4. there is no separate tax on the sole proprietorship (or it is taxed at personal income rates, which are lower)
5. the owner is liable for all the company's debts
6. a partnership is owned by more than one person
7. F
8. F
9. T
10. "artificial persons"
11. T
12. F
13. F
14. T
15. partnership    corporation

# Practice Listening Test 1

(The TOEFL iBT does not use the letters A, B, C, and D for the multiple-choice items. However, in these answer keys, *A* corresponds to the first answer choice, *B* to the second, *C* to the third, and *D* to the fourth.)

## Listening

| Answer | Explanation |
|---|---|
| **1.** B | Ted tells the professor, "I'm working on the campus newspaper and . . . and I need to get over there right after class for a meeting . . ." |
| **2.** A | Ted's intonation when he says, "I don't know what to say" indicates that he is surprised that Professor Jacobs is asking him to take part in the reading. "I don't know what to say" might indicate confusion (choice D) but Ted is not upset; he is happy and flattered (pleased) to be asked. |
| **3.** A | Ted says, "I'd really like to read the first two or three chapters of this novel I've been working on . . ." |
| **4.** B | Ted thought that Professor Jacobs didn't like his poem *Northern Lights* because the professor didn't say much about it when Ted read it in class. However, the Professor says that he "quite liked it," but he *"wanted to hear what the other students in class thought of it."* Therefore, we can infer that choice B is correct; the professor sometimes doesn't express his feelings about his students' work in class. |
| **5.** C | Professor Jacobs says, "Drop by my office sometime this week and we'll figure out which poems you should read." |
| **6.** A | Dana tells Ms. Fong, "I really have no money for living expenses, so, uh, that's why I'm hoping to land a part-time job . . ." |
| **7.** D | Ms. Fong explains that there are two types of work-study jobs, needs-based and merit-based, and that needs-based positions "are the ones funded by the government." Therefore, merit-based positions must not receive government funding. |
| **8.** D | When Ms. Fong mentions the tour-guide job, Dana says "Really? Wow, that sounds fabulous." She does *not* want a job in a cafeteria (A) and Ms. Fong does not suggest that she work either as a receptionist (B) or as a lab technician (C). |
| **9.** C | Ms. Fong says, "The first step is to fill out the financial aid forms I mentioned." |
| **10.** A | Ms. Fong tells Dana not to give up on the position, which means to not stop trying to get the job. She says "we really encourage job-sharing—two students working one position." |
| **11.** B, A, C | The professor says that the Inuit of Northern Alaska, where driftwood (wood brought to the shore by waves) was plentiful, built winter houses of wood. In North Central Canada and on Greenland, the Inuit built the snow houses that are called igloos in English. In Labrador in northeastern Canada, the Inuit built winter houses made of stone and earth supported by whalebones. |
| **12.** B | This information about the isolation of the Inuit of Greenland is not directly relevant to the topic of the lecture (igloos). It is additional information about these people that the professor finds interesting. |
| **13.** A | Since the Inuit word *igloo* means *house*, it could be used to refer to a summer house or any other kind of house. |

**14.**

|  | Yes | No |
|---|:---:|:---:|
| Build a framework to support the igloo from inside |  | ✓ |
| Cut blocks of hardened snow with a knife | ✓ |  |
| Dig an entrance tunnel | ✓ |  |
| Stand on top of the igloo in order to compress the snow and make it stronger |  | ✓ |
| Melt snow on the interior surface of the igloo with lamps and then let the water re-freeze. | ✓ |  |

An igloo is the only type of traditional dome-shaped house built *without* interior support, so the first phrase should be marked **No**. The professor says that Inuit "used knives made of bone or ivory to cut wind-packed snow into blocks," so the second phrase should be marked **Yes**. The third phrase should be marked **Yes** because, according to the professor, "the entrance tunnel to the igloo was dug out so that it was lower than the igloo floor." The professor claims that an igloo was strong enough to support the weight of a man standing on top of it, but this would not have been part of the normal construction process; therefore, the fourth phrase should be marked **No**. The Inuit used a lamp to melt a little of the interior of the igloo and then let the water refreeze, forming a layer of ice. This made the igloo stronger. The fifth phrase should therefore be marked **Yes.**

| | |
|---|---|
| **15.** B, E | According to the professor, the Inuit "held dances and wrestling matches and their famous singing competitions in these larger igloos," so answers A, C, and D are all true. There was *no* mention in the lecture that larger igloos were used as multi-family houses (although the lecture does say that five or more families lived in igloos built in clusters, in several small igloos built close together). There is no mention of using igloos for storage. |
| **16.** D | The professor says that in the 1950's, the Inuit began living in permanent housing and "only used igloos when they went on overnight hunting trips." |
| **17.** D | Professor Fuller says that Albert Einstein said faster-than-light travel was impossible, and then she says, "Who am I to argue with Einstein?" This expression means that she agrees with Einstein. |
| **18.** A | Professor Fuller says, "Then you fire intense bursts of laser beams at the sails." |
| **19.** C | According to Professor Fuller, what is required to travel to the stars is "some revolutionary drive system that requires little or no fuel." |
| **20.** C, D, A, B | The speculation stage involves dreaming up ideas for a new technology; the science stage involves testing these ideas with experiments; the technology stage involves building the technology; and the application stage involves putting the technology to use. |
| **21.** A, D | According to Professor Fuller, most of the "extra-solar" planets discovered so far are gas giants similar to Jupiter, and a few of them are small planets very close to their stars. |
| **22.** B | When she says "I don't think I'd pack my bags and head for the spaceport any time soon," she is joking since there are no passenger spaceports now, |

but what she really means is that flight to other stars will not occur in the near future.

**23. A, C**    The professor says that when Photorealism began "in the sixties and seventies, art was dominated by Minimalism and Conceptual Art, which were very *non*-representational types of art, very abstract . . ."

**24. B**    According to the professor, Audrey Flack "worked with an airbrush and she used acrylic paints," so choices A and D *are* given in the lecture. The professor also says that Audrey Flack "made a slide from the photo and projected the picture onto her canvas" so choice C is mentioned in the lecture. There is no mention that Flack used a computer.

**25. A, B**    She quotes two Photorealist painters (Chuck Close and Richard Estes) talking about the subjects of their paintings, and she gives specific examples of the subjects of some Photorealist paintings (for example, a gas station, an elderly man waiting at a bus stop, and an old, closed-down drive-in movie. (A drive-in movie is an outdoor movie theater where people watched the movie from their cars. This kind of movie theater was especially popular in the U.S. in the 1950's and 1960's.)

**26. C**    The professor says that Estes painted urban scenes reflected in large plate-glass windows. Only choice C qualifies as an urban scene reflected in glass.

**27. D**    The professor describes one of Hanson's sculptures as being so lifelike that people would try to ask the statue questions. She emphasizes the extreme realism of his works.

**28.**

|  | Yes | No |
|---|---|---|
| They feature three-dimensional optical illusions. |  | ✓ |
| Their subjects are ordinary people and scenes. | ✓ |  |
| They are often painted in bright colors. | ✓ |  |
| They may be either representational or non-representational. |  | ✓ |
| They show great attention to detail. | ✓ |  |

The professor mentions a school of art from the eighteenth century called *trompe l'oeil* that has some similarities to Photorealism. However, *trompe l'oeil* paintings feature optical illusions, such as figures that seem to be three-dimensional, while Photorealism was not concerned with optical illusions. Therefore, the first sentence should be marked **No.** The professor says that Photorealists "always painted ordinary, everyday, banal (boring) subjects," so the second sentence should be marked **Yes.** The professor also mentions that "most Photorealist paintings tend to be bright and colorful," so the third sentence should be marked **Yes.** All Photorealist works were representational, unlike the non-representational works of Minimalists and Conceptual Artists, so the fourth sentence should be marked **No.** The professor says that Photorealists "portrayed their subjects down to the smallest detail, and so their paintings look like photographs," and so the fifth sentence should be marked **Yes.**

**29. B, C**    The professor says that "By far the most damage is done to vehicles and . . . farmers' crops."

**30. C**    There is no mention in the article that dancing was ever used to prevent hail. In fourteenth-century Europe, church bells, pots and pans, and cannons were used. Cannons continued to be used in wine-producing areas through the nineteenth century, and in the Soviet Union in the 1950's, cannons shooting silver iodide into the air were used to try to reduce the size of hailstones. Cannons, therefore, have been used most recently.

**31. B**    A student asked the professor if people are often hurt by hailstones. When the professor says "Hmmm, well, it doesn't . . . it doesn't really seem like it to me," he really means that he doesn't think people are often injured, but he is not absolutely sure.

**32. B**    The professor says a hailstone "looks . . . like an onion cut in half—lots of layers." He is therefore comparing the internal structure of a hailstone to that of an onion.

**33. A**    One student says, "The hailstorm I was caught in was in April, maybe early May, so I'd guess spring," and the professor agrees that the student has guessed correctly.

**34.**

|  | Yes | No |
|---|---|---|
| Hailstones become so heavy that they fall to the ground. | ✓ |  |
| Water droplets are lifted into the cold region of a thundercloud and freeze. | ✓ |  |
| Tornado clouds circulate ice crystals inside of thunderclouds. |  | ✓ |
| Droplets are lifted into the cloud again and again, adding more ice. | ✓ |  |
| A mass of fast-moving warm air hits a slower-moving mass of cold air. |  | ✓ |

The professor says that, as the final step of hail formation, "the hailstone gets so heavy that the updrafts can't lift it anymore, so it drops out of the cloud and . . . bingo, you've got hail!" Therefore, you should mark the first sentence **Yes.** You should also mark the second sentence **Yes.** The professor says, "One of these updrafts picks up the droplet and lifts it high into the cloud, where the air is cold, and it freezes." Although hail is sometimes associated with tornadoes, tornado winds are not involved in the formation of hailstones, so you should mark the third sentence **No.** According to the professor, the process of being lifted back into the cold part of the clouds by updrafts "happens again and again. With each trip above and below the freezing level, the hailstone adds another layer of ice." Therefore, the fourth sentence should be marked **Yes.** There is no mention in the lecture that hail is formed by the collision of a fast-moving warm front and a slow-moving cold front, so the fifth sentence should be marked **No.**

# Practice Listening Test 2

## Listening

| Answer | Explanation |
|---|---|
| **1.** C | Janet tells Allen, "I'm running for re-election for the seat on the Student Council that belongs to the School of Business. But you can't vote for me, because you're in the School of Engineering." |
| **2.** C | Students vote for a representative from their own school, for president, and for vice-president (a total of three). |
| **3.** A, D | It's clear that Janet is currently a member of the Student Council because she says that she is running "for re-election." She also says "I'm thinking that next year, I'll try to get elected president." |
| **4.** A | Janet says, "...the most important thing is—the Council gets to decide how to spend your money. Fifteen dollars from each student's fees goes into the Student Council's general fund." |
| **5.** B | The idiom *don't push your luck* means "you've been lucky so far—don't try to get anything else." In other words, Allen means, "You're lucky to get me to agree to vote tomorrow—don't try to get me to go to the debate tonight too." |
| **6.** D | Alison asks Tony to be part of a "focus group." A focus group helps companies determine whether to market a product or not, or which version of a product to market. This would therefore most likely be a topic in a marketing class. |
| **7.** A | Alison tells Tony, "...when you come in the classroom tomorrow, Professor Marquez will give you a little card that tells you your vital information: your age, your occupation, how much education you have, that sort of thing...and that's the role you play when you're pretending to be in this focus group." |
| **8.** C | According to Alison, an experiential focus group helps decide which of several versions of a product to market. In Hollywood, focus groups help film companies decide which version of a movie to release, so Hollywood focus groups must be experiential focus groups. |
| **9.** D | According to Alison, "Professor Marquez says that...that the chemistry, the, uh, interaction between the moderator and the focus group is key in making sure a focus group goes well." Professor Marquez will probably concentrate on this interaction during the classroom activity. |
| **10.** B | Tony says that he is free the following day but does not definitely agree to be part of the activity until he learns that the flavor of ice cream that he will be testing the next day will be mint chocolate chip. Then he enthusiastically says, "That settles it... I'm in" meaning that now he is definitely willing to take part. He must enjoy this flavor of ice cream. |
| **11.** C | The lecturer says, "After a while, Stowe and her husband moved back to New England, to Brunswick, Maine. He encouraged her to write a book that showed the evils of slavery. So, Stowe wrote *Uncle Tom's Cabin*..." |
| **12.** C, A, D, B | *Uncle Tom's Cabin* was first published as a newspaper serial (in other words, a small part was published every day) in the *National Era* newspaper in 1851. The next year, in 1852, it was published as a book and became very popular. According to the lecture, plays based on the books ("Tom Shows") appeared "soon after the book was |

published." The movie came much later, in 1927.

| | |
|---|---|
| **13.** B | Charles Dickens is given as an example of a great writer of that age who also wrote about some characters in a sentimental way. The professor gives the character of Little Nell in the book *The Old Curiosity Shop* as an example. |
| **14.** B, D | According to the professor, this scene was part of George Aiken's play but did not appear in the book. It was also a part of the 1927 movie, which may be why "this scene sticks in people's minds" (is remembered). |

**15.**

| | Yes | No |
|---|:---:|:---:|
| It is not strong enough in its criticism of slavery. | ✓ | |
| It treats its characters too sentimentally. | ✓ | |
| It is not based on the author's firsthand experiences. | ✓ | |
| It is difficult for modern readers to understand. | | ✓ |
| It is far too long and repetitive. | | ✓ |

The first choice should be checked **Yes.** The professor says, "...some Northern Abolitionists thought that it didn't go far enough, that it painted too soft a picture of slavery." The second choice should also be checked **Yes.** According to the professor, "Another criticism is that Stowe's treatment of her characters is overly sentimental, overly emotional." The third choice should be checked **Yes** as well. According to the professor, "that's one of the criticisms that Southerners directed at her—that she had no firsthand knowledge of slavery, of life in the South, because she'd never spent time there." The fourth and the fifth choices should be checked **No.** The professor does not mention these criticisms in her lecture.

| | |
|---|---|
| **16.** D | The professor advises the students to read *Uncle Tom's Cabin* "cover to cover"—in other words, to read every page. (She is talking about reading the novel, not their textbook, choice B, which contains only short selections from the novel.) |
| **17.** D, B, C, A | According to the professor, all glaciers start with *ordinary snow.* When ordinary snow melts and refreezes several times, it becomes *névé,* a compressed form of snow. If *névé* lasts for a year, it becomes even more compressed and forms a compact form of ice called *firn.* Firn, buried under more and more snow and ice, finally becomes *glacial ice.* |
| **18.** C, D | According to the lecture, continental glaciers are today found only in Greenland and Antarctica. |
| **19.** B, C | A glacier may follow a V-shaped creek path down a mountainside, but the rocks that it picks up on the way "round out the bottom of the valley, and the V-shaped stream bed becomes U-shaped." Therefore, choice A is *not* correct and choice C *is* correct. Also, according to the lecture, "because they are rigid, glaciers don't take sharp corners very well, so their downhill paths are generally gonna be a series of gentle curves." Therefore, choice B *is* correct and choice D is not. |
| **20.** A | Choice D, continental glacier, is not correct. The lecturer tells us that a continental glacier is much larger than a valley glacier. Valley glaciers |

flow together to form piedmont glaciers, so piedmont glaciers must be bigger than valley glaciers. However, tributary glaciers flow into valley glaciers, and therefore, must be the smallest type of glacier.

**21.**

|  | Valley Glaciers | Continental Glaciers |
|---|---|---|
| Today cover about 10% of the world's land surface. |  | ✓ |
| Flow together to form piedmont glaciers. | ✓ |  |
| As they recede, seem to flow uphill. | ✓ |  |
| About 11,000 years ago, covered 30% of the world's land surface. |  | ✓ |
| As they grow, seem to flow outwards in all directions. |  | ✓ |

Choice A is a characteristic of continental glaciers. The professor says that the two continental glaciers in existence today, in Greenland and Antarctica, cover 10% of the earth's land surface. Valley glaciers flow together to form piedmont glaciers, so choice B is a characteristic of valley glaciers. So is choice C; the professor says that "When they recede, valley glaciers seem to be moving uphill . . . What's really happening is that they are melting faster than they are adding new materials." Choice D is a characteristic of continental glaciers. During the last Ice Age, around 11,000 years ago, continental glaciers covered much of the northern hemisphere and about 30% of the land surface of the earth. Choice D is also a characteristic of continental glaciers. The professor says "a continental glacier moves out in all directions from the glacier's central point."

**22.** A    The danger mentioned by the professor is that global warming may cause glaciers to melt and that this will cause the level of oceans to rise.

**23.** C    This passage mainly deals with the four stages of the business cycle.

**24.** B    The professor says that these terms are the ones most commonly used these days, implying that, in the past, other terms were more common.

**25.**

|  | Yes | No |
|---|---|---|
| They vary in length from cycle to cycle. | ✓ |  |
| They are measured from the peak of economic activity to the trough, the lowest point of economic activity. |  | ✓ |
| They vary in intensity from cycle to cycle. | ✓ |  |
| They have involved deeper recessions in recent years because of globalization. |  | ✓ |
| They are sometimes called *fluctuations* because they are irregular. | ✓ |  |

The first choice should be checked **Yes.** The professor says "no business cycle is exactly the same. They vary in length, for example." The second choice is not a valid choice. Cycles are measured from peak to peak, according to the professor, not from peak to trough. Check **No.** Choice C, however, should be checked **Yes** because, when a student asks the professor about this, he says, "You're right, they do vary in intensity." You should check **No** for the fourth choice. Some economists in the 1990's thought that globalization prevented downturns in business in the U.S.—which turned out to be false—but there is no indication in the lecture that globalization makes recessions worse. The last choice is also mentioned in the lecture. The professor says, "In fact, they are so irregular in length that some economists prefer to talk about business *fluctuations* rather than a business cycle." Check the last choice **Yes.**

**26.** A, B    One depression occurred in the 1870's and one, the Great Depression, occurred during the 1930's.

**27.** D    According to the professor, "What they usually do is, the government . . . the Central Bank, really . . . manipulates the money supply."

**28.** A    The professor says, "Today, though, it's no longer considered a valid theory. Still, you have to admit, it's an interesting one."

**29.** A    The professor says that most people think of science fiction as a contemporary type of film but in fact, some of the earliest films were science fiction films. She gives as an example George Méliès's film *A Voyage to the Moon.*

**30.** D    According to the lecture, the 1926 film *Metropolis* ". . . was set a hundred years in the future, in the year 2026."

**31.** C    The professor says that the movie *Them!* was about giant ants that had been affected by radiation from nuclear weapon tests. She says that there were many other movies about "big bugs" (insects) that had been radiated.

**32.** A, C    The professor tells the class that her favorite movie, *Forbidden Planet,* is "based on William Shakespeare's play *The Tempest.* It also makes use of ideas from the theories of the famous psychologist Sigmund Freud."

**33.** B    What the professor finds interesting about *ET* is that, unlike most movies about visitors from space, this one features a friendly, smart, likeable alien.

**34.** B    The professor says, "Then, uh, unfortunately, we just have time for a few quick scenes from my favorite, *Forbidden Planet.* " She is sorry that they won't have time to watch more of the movie *Forbidden Planet.*